STEVE COX

As the Sparks Fly Upwards

To
Peter
Happy Reading
Steve Cox

 Frith

First published by Frith Publishing 2021

First edition

ISBN: 978-1-8383448-0-1

Cover art by Aisling Locke

This book was professionally typeset on Reedsy.
Find out more at reedsy.com

In memory of Brenda Welch

Sign up to Steve's email list to get access to exclusive content, including maps of the main places mentioned in the story, and advanced news of the forthcoming adventures of Tom Tyler.

www.stevecox.co.uk

Glossary

A glossary of some words that may be unfamiliar

Bailiff - Superintendent of a lord's estate with responsibility for land and buildings. At times when local courts were in session, the bailiff was an official appointed by a sheriff and had authority to protect the court and carry out its decisions.

Bandolier - A leather belt hung across the body from a shoulder. Small containers of wood or metal containing measured amounts of gunpowder for a single shot of a musket were attached to the belt.

Brockle - Verb 'to break', in the Dorset dialect.

Captain - A military officer commanding a company. The rank is higher than a lieutenant and lower than a major.

Cassock - A close-fitting ankle-length garment, usually black, worn by Anglican ministers.

Chirurgeon - (Pronounced kai-rur-jon.) An archaic name for a surgeon or doctor.

Chuff - A stupid or churlish (meaning of low birth and value, a peasant) person.

Coif - A woman's lace cap, designed to keep the hair under control and out of sight.

Colonel - A military officer commanding a regiment. The rank is higher than a major and lower than a general.

Corporal - A low-ranking officer. Higher than a private sentinel, but lower than a sergeant. In this period officers were not separated into commissioned and non-commissioned categories.

Court of Assize - A session, or sitting, of a court of justice. It originally signified the method of trial by jury. During the early modern period, the term was applied to certain court sessions held periodically in the counties of England.

Dewbit - Breakfast in the Dorset dialect.

Dimpsey - West Country dialect word for dusk, gloaming, early twilight.

Ensign - A military officer usually given the task of carrying the regiment flag (the colour). The rank is higher than a sergeant and lower than a lieutenant.

Feodary - An officer of the Court of Wards.

Gaol - Old spelling for jail. Same pronunciation.

Glacis - A slope in front of a defensive wall that allows the defenders to fire upon an approaching enemy.

Goodwife - A respectful term for a woman if no other is known or more appropriate.

Journeyman - A skilled worker in a trade or craft who has successfully completed an official apprenticeship but is usually employed by a master craftsman.

Ketch - A small boat with two masts, a main mast in the middle of the boat and a rear (mizzen) mast positioned in front of the steering gear.

Lieutenant - A military officer. The rank is higher than an ensign and lower than a captain.

Lych gate - Entrance to a grave yard or church yard where a coffin can be rested. The gate usually has a roof.

Malignants - A Parliamentary term of abuse referring to the Royalists.

Match cord - A thin rope of tallow and pitch that acts like a wick and can remain lit, burning slowly. Soldiers had to take long lengths of match cord with them to ensure they had enough of it to last through a battle.

Mortar - A type of cannon that fired stones, metal balls or spherical metal cases filled with lead balls and pieces of metal. The mortar fired the ball at a high trajectory so that it dropped out of the sky onto an enemy.

Musket - An early form of firearm, approximately 4 feet long and fired by touching a lighted wick (the match cord) to a tray of fine gunpowder that ignites. The gunpowder from the tray is connected to coarser gunpowder at the bottom of the barrel, with a lead ball packed down onto it. The expansion of the ignited gunpowder provides the power to expel the ball out of the barrel.

New-style calendar - In the 1640s, the year in England began on 25 March. This is the old-style presentation of the date. England and its colonies did not shift to the new-style, designation until 1752 when the Gregorian calendar replaced the old, Julian calendar. (The change in Scotland occurred in 1600.) This change was necessary to correct progressive errors in the Julian calendar. It took more than 300 years for all countries to make this change, beginning with France, Italy, Poland, Portugal and Spain in 1582. However, the dates in the book are recorded in a way that makes the most sense to us. That is, using the new-style, and I begin 1644 on 1 January, not 25 March.

Quarter Sessions - Local courts held by a justice of the peace every three months.

Roundheads - A term of abuse by Royalists, referring to Parliamentarian supporters.

Saker - A small cannon. It was still heavy, though.

Scold's bridle - A metal frame fitted over someone's head (usually a woman) with a bar that pushes into the mouth and prevents speech. The bridle would be locked into position and the victim stood in a prominent place or was paraded around town for a specific number of hours.

Sergeant - A low-ranking officer. Higher than a corporal, but lower than an ensign or lieutenant.

Sherris sack - A fortified white wine imported to England from Jerez in Spain, which we now call sherry.

Snapsack - A soldier's pack. It was a tube of material stitched together with drawstrings and could be slung over the shoulder.

Petronnel - A long-barrelled pistol.

Vagrant - A person without a settled home or regular work who wanders from place to place and lives by begging.

Yawl - A small ship's boat, used for sailing round the ship to carry out repairs or to ferry people (the captain mostly) from ship to shore and back. A yawl has two masts, a main mast in the middle of the boat and a rear (mizzen) mast positioned to the rear of the steering gear.

Man is born to trouble, as the sparks fly upwards.

Book of Job 5:7

Chapter 1

February 1644 (according to the new-style calendar)

Tom clenched his fists. The coffin swelled out of focus as his eyes moistened, so he squeezed them shut. Spades rasped, scooping up soil and stones, to cast, with a hollow whoosh onto the wooden lid, masking the vicar's words; 'dust to dust, ashes to ashes.' The sound changed to a softer thud and the trench filled, becoming a mound. He brushed the dampness from his cheeks and let another breath escape and hang for a moment, ghost-like above the grave. Eighteen months of war they had endured, with no end in sight. But Frederik Tyler, master baker, would endure no more. His time was over.

A hand gripped Tom's shoulder. 'He was a good man, your father. He'll be missed,' said a voice in his right ear. 'The bakery's yours now, Tom. Take care of it.'

The man moved away before Tom could respond and joined the few mourners now trudging away from the grave. He watched them pass through the lych gate. The track beyond led to Cinnamon Lane and the bakery; his home, his job, his world.

The shrieks of gulls mocked him as he exhaled into the

cold winter air and ground his teeth. Tom blinked. He would never touch his father's hand or hear his voice again.

As Tom walked through the lych gate Simon, his colleague, met him.

'There's a bailiff at the bakery. He's Merrick's man, and his thugs threw me out.'

A salty mist swirled through the cobbled streets as Tom hurried to Cinnamon Lane. He raced around the corner and saw a pile of belongings growing as bedding, tools and equipment were tossed out of the front door by two men. Others were fastening slabs of wood across the lower windows. A big-bellied man in a servant's uniform stepped out of the doorway. He looked over at Tom and tossed a model boat onto the pile.

Tom roared and charged across the courtyard. The man watched him approach, then slid to the side and brought his wooden cane crashing down on the boy's head as he flew past, into the doorway. Tom turned and reached for the neck of the man who kept slashing at arm, hand or head with that heavy cane. Other men appeared in the courtyard. Tom stepped back and tried to speak, but no sound came.

'There,' sneered his opponent. 'Good dog. I take it you are Thomas Tyler?'

Tom could only nod.

'Well, see you do nothing rash, boy. I'm the bailiff of Sir Balthazar Merrick who no longer needs a bakery. You're ordered to leave. D'you hear?'

Shaking his bruised head, Tom looked around. Close by was a brass bedwarmer with a wooden handle half a yard long. He staggered towards it. Grasping the handle, he sprang at the man destroying his home. The metal pan caught the bailiff on the side of the head and his right ear split open. Tom lifted the pan to bring it down on his enemy's head. The blow never fell. Rough hands lifted him and threw him to one side. More hands held him fast against the cobbles and a welter of boots crashed into his body, groin and face.

'Tom. Tom! Can you hear me? It's me. Maria.'

Tom caught the words as a drowning man catches a rope. Holding on, he dragged himself up from sour darkness. He was propped against a wall opposite the bakery.

Maria was bathing his face with a damp rag. 'The bailiff's kicked us out too. The bastard.'

Tom groaned. Breathing hurt, and his head felt as though he'd been scraped right along the sea wall. But he had to listen. He was supposed to be in charge now, and his first act was to get beaten senseless and allow them all to become jobless and homeless. He rolled over onto bruised ribs and vomited.

Maria helped Tom over to where her husband, Simon, had loaded their belongings onto a single-axle cart. Together, they pulled the cart to the Dolphin.

Inside the alehouse, a small stone building near the quay, they huddled under the stairs. It was full of fishermen, and their fishy tang hung heavy in the room. Newcomers were hailed as they came through the oak door. Tom sensed uncertainty at the edges of everything people said.

'Hast tha' news?' was the usual greeting in uncertain times. Some spoke of the weather, some of the land and some of the

3

sea. A few brought news of the war; that General Waller had captured Arundel, or that the royalists had raided Wimborne again.

The little group sat drinking strong ale, nudged this way then that by traffic to and from the serving-hatch. No one said much. Despair settled on them, numb and silent as snow. Tom nodded at the old-timers sipping beer at the other end of the room. These merchants and craftsmen, including Jed Barker, the town crier, were the Master Baker's fellows, doing their duty by attending the wake, but they were dour company. Each one drifted over to show respect to Tom as the dead man's son, and to offer sympathy for falling foul of the bailiff.

'Don't fret, Tom. There's always opportunities for bright lads what can read n' write. The war won't last forever,' said one.

'Ar, but while 'war storms over us, who knows what'll 'appen next. Keep yer head down, lad, an' speak to the mayor,' said another.

Tom didn't know what to say, had no strength and no way to reach out to these old men. He nodded and they wandered back to their seats. Tom's head sagged. 'They're not bothered with me.'

'What d'you mean?'

'Nothing, Simon. I'm rambling. When I close my eyes all I see is that poxy bailiff burning in hell.'

Maria leant over and touched his arm. 'Aye, Tom. That fire. There was nothing you could do. Master Frederik took it hard. The spark from the oven, flour in the air. 'Twas the smoke killed your mother. It was God's will. You mustn't blame yourself.'

4

'What's that got to do with anything? That was five years ago.' Tom glared at Maria.

'I know what you mean, Tom,' cut in Simon. 'It's all the bailiff deserves. Men like that have no respect for folks.' He put an arm on the youngster's shoulder.

'I only mean… we could see a change in you, and your father after that.' Maria's voice tailed off.

'Well, I'd blow the whole bakery to hell if I thought the bailiff was inside.' Tom looked at the sad faces around him. 'How about we get drunk, eh? I need something to soften my head. It's being pounded between hammer and anvil.'

'You look like you've had enough, Tom,' Maria said.

'Don't fuss the boy.' Simon poured from a jug and handed Tom a cup of rum. 'Drink this. It'll soften the hammer.'

'I'll drink to that,' said Tom. 'But I still have to look after you two. I'm your employer now.' Tom saw his friends, who had shared most hours of most days with him, look at each other, but he couldn't decipher their expressions.

'Don't worry about us, Tom.' Simon held his shoulders and studied his face. 'We're going to Wimborne. We can all find work there, I'm sure of it.'

'You what?' blustered Tom. 'You can't. We've got to get the bakery back. The bailiff said Merrick wants the shop back. But we can explain that it's still a working bakery.'

Simon pursed his lips. 'This is no time to argue, Tom. Listen to me. You've not yet finished your apprenticeship, and I'm just a journeyman. We need to put ourselves under another master.'

'But the bakery is my family business. I'm the son of the master baker. And I have finished my apprenticeship. You've said yourself, I've nothing left to learn.'

5

Simon scoffed. 'You've done well, Tom, but there's more to running a business than getting up early and baking a decent loaf. You're hardly eighteen and I'll not be ordered about by a boy with bum fluff on his jaw.'

'This gets us nowhere,' Maria broke in. 'The bailiff has the shop all locked and guarded. How can we change that?' Her voice sounded shrill against the rising bustle and chatter of the inn. 'I've spoken to Bess and she'll take us in until we can leave town.'

'Leave Poole? What the bloody hell d'you mean?' bellowed Tom. 'This is my town. I've lost a father, a job, and a home, and now you say I've to leave my town? I won't do it.'

He staggered upright and hit his head against an oak beam. Pain scorched a path through his bones and blood pulsed under his scalp, dancing bright patterns under his eyelids.

'If you won't come, I'll see Merrick alone.' Tom imagined himself a hero, influencing others to join him in righting an injustice. The surrounding hubbub subsided as his voice grew strained.

'That bloody Merrick needs to be told what's what. That's what.' His raised voice got the attention of the other drinkers, but the words had no effect. No one in the alehouse moved.

Tom blundered forwards. 'Well, I know where he lives and I'm gonna tell 'im straight.' Pulling on the ash handle, he opened the door. 'It's a red door he lives at,' he said, and stepped into the night. The cold air closed around him, and he gasped. The Dolphin's stone wall felt icy. He clung to it as the world spun. Tom's head and innards both clamoured for attention before they calmed down and he was able to make out the dark shapes of the houses on either side of the street. The inn door opened.

'Go away!' bellowed Tom.

The door slammed shut again, and Tom moved off, away from the quay, towards the wealthier merchants' houses.

It was late. A breeze stirred the damp mist, sweeping it into corners, and the winter air ran in and out of his clothes. Despite this, Tom sweated. His body struggling with the strong liquor. He swayed and staggered up the narrow street, bumping into carts and walls and slipping in night soil, thoughts rattling round his skull.

A single light in the distance guided him to the junction of Bayter Lane with the High Street, and then Tom was searching for a red door.

'How the hell d'you tell a red door in the dark?' he mumbled as he fell over a water cask. The barrel thumped onto the uneven ground, then rolled and rocked its way over the cobbles until it bumped into a door. A faint light showed through the upstairs window of this building.

'What's going on?'

Tom recognised Sir Balthazar Merrick's voice.

'S'me, Merrick, you ugly runt.' Tom launched himself across the street, watching the first-floor window and the flickering light.

'What? Who are you, man?'

'I'm the man whose life you've wrecked. I'm the man whose house you've stolen. I'm Tom Tyler, you bastard. And if you think an eight-foot wall can keep me out: well, it won't,' Tom bellowed, and jumped up to grab the windowsill above his head.

His fingers closed around the wooden window surround and held on. The wood was old and pitted, but it was strong enough to provide some purchase to pull himself up. Merrick recoiled from the window, then reappeared, bringing a heavy candlestick holder down on Tom's fingers. He dropped like a sack of turnips and yelped.

'Grist! Phippard! To me, to me!' Merrick shouted into the house, while Tom hugged the fingers on his right hand.

Other doors and windows now opened, and more candles flickered as disturbed sleepers watched the scene.

'Get out here, Merrick, you coward! Act like a man. Give me my bakery. Give me my bakery!'

Merrick's door flew open and two figures rushed out, the first tripping over the barrel still lying against the door post. A third shape passed through the opening and disappeared towards the quay.

Tom backed off from the house into the messy centre of the street. He was rapidly sobering up and his body ached all over. He didn't know if the men closing in on him were armed, but he waited until the closest shape was only a few feet away and then he launched himself like a cannonball at the man's chest.

The force knocked them both to the ground, with Tom clawing at his face. Tom's back was pummelled by something heavy, and he was dragged off his prey and squeezed against a wall.

He couldn't move and could hardly breathe, fixed in position by a heavy stick angled across his neck, holding his head against a doorpost. The man he had attacked rolled over and staggered to his knees, swearing. The other man called back over his shoulder. 'Phippard! Tell Sir Balthazar we've got him. Well, Thomas, did you not understand what I said at the bakery?' The man laughed.

Voices drew near, as a group formed at the bailiff's side.

'Evening, Mr Grist. What've you caught for me tonight?'

Tom recognised the measured tones of Ned Porter, the turnkey of Poole; the man responsible for keeping order in the town.

Grist tenderly touched a bandage covering his right ear. 'This whelp don't understand the world. He used to live at the bakery in Cinnamon Lane, Mr Porter. Kindly do your duty and keep his ignorant face out of Sir Balthazar's business.'

The wooden rod was removed from the front of his neck, and Tom was hauled to his feet and pushed down the street.

'But you've got to listen to me, Ned. Merrick has no right to –' Tom got no further. Something hit his right cheek with such force that he pitched over onto the ground again.

'Shut up, Thomas, and be a good dog. I hope the wretch don't ruin more of your night's sleep, Mr Porter. I've seen his sort before; soft of body and soft in the head. Such scum have no place in this town.'

'Don't worry, Mr Grist. I'll keep him out of your way.'

Tom heard the words yet missed their meaning. But he could feel the cold stones of the gaol floor as he landed on them, and he could taste the thick, salty odour leaching from the surrounding fish boxes. His mind wrestled to hold back the stench, then gave up the struggle, and it seeped into turbulent dreams of death and loss.

Chapter 2

Fish. Dead fish. Fish ancient and fish newly salted. The putrid odour radiated from the cold, hard walls, from the coarse stone floor and from the wooden boxes stacked around the dim basement room and penetrated Tom's mind; the fish stink, hangover and bruises combining to wake him to a day brimful of misery. He sat up and peered around. There was a narrow grating just below the timber ceiling, letting in daylight in dusty beams that hurt his eyes. He turned away from the light to the gentle shade of the stone steps that led down from a solid door and remembered where he was.

This was Poole gaol, beneath the Guildhall, where the town's worthies met to plan the future of their little world. The fish was from boats, unloaded recently, and needed a secure lock-up. The building was the largest in Fish Street, a hundred yards from the quay.

Tom huddled in the darkest corner, away from the grating, the light and the noise of daily life in a seaport. He remembered the previous day and groaned.

What were Simon and Maria doing? On the road to Wimborne? He imagined them pushing their cart up the hill outside the town. That cart was worth much more than the meagre belongings piled onto it. His father had bought it to help Simon and Tom sell loaves in nearby villages.

Sometime later, Tom's thoughts refocused. The hill in his imagination was now empty. Simon and Maria had passed over the ridge. Scraping, then creaking, caught Tom's attention. The door opened to admit two men, one being Ned Porter and the other a stranger, thickset, with long arms that stuck out from dirty beige sleeves. His face was masked by the gloom and a wide-brimmed hat.

The men stopped when they reached Tom, and the stranger knelt down. Taking off his hat, he scanned the room as though looking for somewhere to lay it, then kept it in his hands. 'How old are you, lad?' he asked in a weary, nasal tone.

'Who are you?' Tom said, shifting to sit upright.

The man turned his head towards the light shining in through the grating and spat. 'Christ, I've had enough of sullen yokels. Listen, lad. It's a civil question and if you want to keep your tongue for arguing with your mates, you'd best recognise authority when you meet it.'

There was a pause. The man just stared, and Tom took in more details about him. His hair was long, pale and bedraggled, and the top of his scalp was nearly bald. The broad nose was pock-marked and red, and his eyes were tiny pricks of light in the dim room.

Tom shook himself. The stranger still gazed at him with those penetrating eyes.

Tom cleared his throat. 'I'm eighteen.'

'Good. We got there in the end. Now, listen to me, Tyler. D'you want to stay in this sea-rat's nest or breathe sweet, fresh air again?' There was another pause. 'I'll take that as a yes, shall I? You see, Tyler, you can walk out of this place with me now. I need youngsters like you and you need to get away from here for a while, so I think this is your lucky day.' The man smiled and showed Tom half a set of uneven yellow teeth.

Tom gasped. 'You're an army recruiter!'

'Dead right I am. And just now, I'm your best chance of keeping body and soul together. Come with me and you'll see the country, get paid for your trouble and make a bunch of new friends.'

'And if I don't come?'

Tom heard the soft reply, but read his future in the hard face in front of him.

'If I leave now, you'll rot here like these fish. Your best bet is to join old Sergeant Smith and get some distance between you and Poole, quick as you can.'

'This is my home. I'm a baker here.'

'You've got no home, no trade and no friends in this place, boy.'

Tom blinked away a sudden moistness in his eyes. He looked again at the passionless face watching him and tried to think. Should I stay? Try to reclaim the bakery? Could I make my fortune with the fishermen? Is the army my best chance of vengeance and freedom? Effort. Too much. He sniffed once more at the claggy fish stench and made his choice. 'Where are we going?'

'All you need to know is that we're aiming for the town gate.' The sergeant straightened up and nodded to Ned. They hoisted Tom to his feet, guiding him up the stairs and out of the cellar.

It took Tom and Sergeant Smith an hour to reach the gate.

12

It wasn't a long way. The streets weren't even that busy, but the sergeant had business dealings down every alley and many townsfolk approached him, asking for the latest news. Tom's body was stiff, his hand throbbed and his head ached. Each stop extended the torture, when all he wanted to do was collapse in a heap, but at least they meant he could lean against a building while waiting. Various folk nodded to Tom as they passed. But no one asked him if he had news of the war, or about his battered appearance, or his link to the rough soldier. The seagull shrieks now poured scorn on him.

As the winter air settled on his skin, Tom's mind responded. The throbbing ache remained, but his thinking became clearer, and he trembled. I'm leaving the only place I know, with a soldier I've only just met, for a life I can hardly imagine. Tom recoiled, but there was no return. By the time they reached the gate, Tom was living each moment like a wraith tottering on the knife-edge of chance. How could he ever be anything more?

At the gate they found a group of men waiting, surrounded by a dozen soldiers. The men looked to be vagrants or labourers. One or two of this small band looked around, but most huddled together, heads bowed.

In the centre of this miserable throng sat one man. His hunched shoulders and arms showed ridge and furrow muscles like branches on a hornbeam tree. His arms rested on his knees, but his stubby fingers flexed, as though throttling someone. The face of the man focused menace, through hazel eyes below a scalp covered by a dark grey shadow of short hair. An obvious outlaw, thought Tom.

The sergeant sauntered up to the soldiers and watched as

they prodded their charges to their feet. It was the middle of the winter day now, and the town bustle was increasing as shopkeepers scurried about their business.

On one corner a preacher stood and called out. 'Friends, look about you. Time passes and the world sinks into sin. The only hope we have is to throw ourselves on God's mercy. There is much grace in trusting Jesus, but no peace in choosing the world.'

The preacher was a tall, thin man, his austerity made drab by poverty. Beside him was a young woman with the same upright posture, straight nose and long neck. The woman's eyes sparkled and her lips moved quietly as she surveyed the crowd. Tom's gaze held hers for an instant, then her attention shifted to an eddy of movement working its way through the throng as the town crier manoeuvred himself onto the low wall in front of the town gate.

'O yez. O yez. People of Poole. The Town Corporation declares the bakery in Cinnamon Lane to be the rightful possession of the Honourable Sir Balthazar Merrick. Furthermore...' Jed Barker paused and glanced at Tom. '... Thomas Tyler is today cast out from this community and declared vagrant. Any belongings left in the bakery are forfeit to Sir Balthazar, to dispose of as he sees fit.'

Tom listened to the words but didn't respond. Can they do that? Yesterday I had a home, a trade, a community. Now? Nothing.

His mind gave up the struggle to understand, and he slipped into numbness.

He joined the recruits and stumbled out of his town, trudging along the Wimborne road. He was a beast being driven to market by a shepherd whose only concern was the price he would get when they were all fleeced and slaughtered.

They left the road to Wimborne and took a path leading west. After three hours of barren heath, swampy inlets and scrubby woods, they arrived at a camp swarming with dark figures, just as the night reached out to cover the land. They smelt the fires before they saw the camp – a familiar, friendly smoke. The camp, though, lacked welcome. The newcomers huddled at the entrance to the field with orders to fend for themselves, but not to leave it. Tom and the others wandered from campfire to campfire, searching for anyone who would let them join their group. No one obliged, but they managed to get a stick from a fire to start their own. They had a miserable, muted fire, not hot enough to cook on or to warm their bones. The evening wore on and the temperature dropped. There was nothing for it but to bed down for the night.

Everyone else was doing the same, but quicker. Soon every space round the fires was taken; the rest of the men blundered around looking for the driest or warmest corners. Some settled beneath a hedge, some lay like spokes, radiating from the base of a beech tree, using the low branches as a roof. The unlucky ones huddled together on the exposed slope to shiver and groan away the night.

Tom found an open patch of land against a stone water trough at the top of the field. Men lay all around, but at one end of the trough the cow pats were thick. He scooped up the cloying mess, flung it into a hedge, then slumped into the

15

space released, one question hammering in his head. Why had this happened?

Tom dreamed and saw his bakery, with the bailiff standing outside. The bailiff turned and walked away. The bakery was locked and empty, but as Tom watched, it broke into pieces that were carried away by a succession of men. The building was loaded onto the two-wheel cart and Tom was watching from the town gate as it trundled up the hill towards Wimborne. Yearning and loss filled him. He turned to left and right and saw, beside him, his father and mother. His mother's features were indistinct, but he knew it was her. The figures glided towards the quay and he couldn't get their attention.

Before the grey light of dawn penetrated the heavy, low clouds, the field of bodies was stirred by a group of soldiers, shouting, pushing and goading the new soldiers back to the waking world. Two hundred men rose like crones. The morning mist was streaming away to the northeast before life returned to frozen limbs and minds could absorb the details of another day. The sergeants and soldiers herded the recruits into the middle of the field. Tom welcomed the new morning with a determination to see that his bakery was not carried away, out of his reach.

Having been rushed, pushed and bludgeoned into position – nothing happened. The sergeants prowled up and down the rows of men for some time, then congregated at the front.

After discussion and further delay one officer, wearing tall leather boots, a blue jacket and blue feather in a wide-brimmed hat, moved forward. 'Men of Dorset,' he began.

'I'm from Salisbury,' shouted someone from the back.

'I be from Winchester,' called another.

'Well, my home is Chiddingfold. And I wish I'd never left.'

Heads turned towards this last speaker.

'Where's that, then?' enquired a voice from somewhere near the middle of the group.

'Silence!' roared the man in boots.

'Surridge,' replied the Chiddingfold man. 'There's work to do on the farm. I should'na left.'

'Quiet, the lot of you. You're in Parliament's army now and we do not tolerate insubordination. Even by ignorant farm boys from Chidford. Is that clear?'

The grumbling subsided as the officer stared at each section of the men in front, as though daring anyone to speak up and give him a chance to show them what he meant.

He started his oration again. 'Men – and I use that term loosely – you're here to learn how to fight for Parliament. Sir Lewis Fezzard has a job for you. Your homes and country are threatened by marauders and killers brought against Dorset, and we intend to throw them back where they belong.'

The man paused and sent a hard stare through all three lines of men – was he expecting a rousing cheer? Nothing.

'Your training starts now. You've much to learn if you're to become effective fighters. Before long you'll be able to rout the Royalists and string them up in the wind. Or you'll have died trying.'

The officer had been strutting in front of his audience, and he now looked back to the knot of sergeants. One shook his head and the man in boots continued.

'Sir Lewis Fezzard is your colonel and he will be here

17

himself to make sure you understand your new position.' With that he turned around and marched off to a small square tent pitched in a corner of the field. The tent was less than two yards wide, but it swallowed the man from view.

Nothing else happened for a long time.

Tom and his comrades looked about them. The field in which they stood was on a gentle slope down to a restless stream. Golden-yellow reeds fringed the water's edge and every few yards pale willow shoots or the purple buds of alder marked the stream bank. The field was clearly a pasture, with stone walls and a hawthorn hedge forming the other boundaries. The only signs that cattle had been there were the cowpats. In the centre of the pasture were two large trees. The wooden gate into the field lay discarded against the wall by the tent.

Tom had been as far as Wareham before; it was a day's walk from Poole, but this place wasn't familiar. Also, he'd never heard of Sir Lewis Fezzard. Was he a Dorset man or an outsider? Many men had passed through Poole since the fighting broke out. Those with men at their backs were usually from London or Hampshire; people who didn't know Dorset ways and who didn't care so long as they furthered their own careers.

The sergeants reappeared in front of the men. They started bawling at the recruits and moving through the lines of men, assessing their shapes and faces.

Each man was told to move to one side or other of the field. The taller, nobler-looking men were herded together beside a pile of pikes, helmets and breastplates, while the smaller, scruffier recruits were pushed in the opposite direction. Tom felt disorder around him. The lines of men had dissolved into large groups. The sergeants were working to reorganise the mass. Tom stepped backwards towards the crowd edge, closer to the field wall. This was his chance. He backed off further. No one was watching. He looked along the boundary, both ways, his heart pulsing excitement and dread into his throat.

Now! He leapt the wall and ran fifty yards into a small copse. Broken branches lay on the ground, but he jumped over some and crashed through others. In a minute or so he approached the far edge of the trees.

Four miles, six miles to Poole? If he could get back there, he could work out a plan for getting the bakery back. Tom willed his heart to settle. He stepped forward to the wood edge and noted his next goal, a hill above the road. Two fields separated him from the ridge of the hill.

He broke free of the woodland undergrowth and was in the field. Suddenly he was grabbed from right and left and brought to the ground, two soldiers on top of him.

A third shouted, 'We've got one, Sergeant.'

They rolled onto his back and Sergeant Smith appeared over him. 'Tyler. You disappoint me. Your military career has scarce begun, and you try to slink back home. But you've no home to go to. Don't you understand that, boy?'

'Get him up. Take him to the stockade.'

The wooden stockade was on a hump, ten yards from the main opening into the camp field. It was a small structure, five yards square, of eight-foot-tall wooden poles fixed together with horizontal rails on the outside at four feet, and bases planted into the ground. The tops weren't sharpened. There was no need, as there were four guards on duty, each with a cudgel. Inside the man-fold there was no shelter, and the ground was brown and muddy. Grass clumps struggled to survive the compressed stamping of frustrated men.

Tom was thrust into this enclosure and the gate locked behind him. There was only one other man in there; the angry outlaw who had been at Poole town gate. He lounged against the middle of one side of the wooden wall. Tom ignored him, moving along the opposite wall, and slid down to rest on his haunches.

'I wouldn't do that if I were you.'

'Do what?'

'Sit over there. The wind leaps the wall here and lands right where you are. But maybe you like that sort of buffeting.' The man shrugged.

Tom could feel the truth of this. His hair was in constant rufflement and the air was cold. He got up and walked to a corner of the outlaw's wall.

'What d'you do?' said the outlaw.

'I got caught. What d'you think?'

The man spat. 'If you don't want to talk, that's fine. It's just we may be here for some time, so might as well share stories of our world and how we're gonna change it.' He shrugged again.

Tom considered. He didn't feel like talking. He wanted, needed, to fix his world. But how could he do that? What good could come from conversing with a criminal?

'You're the boy we picked up in Poole, right? Tom Tyler?' The man turned and rested his right shoulder on the wall as he looked at Tom.

20

'That's me. And that's where I'm headed.'

'You're headed nowhere, boy,' the man sneered.

'You're wrong. I've got to get back, quick. If I don't, my bakery will be gone.'

'So why did you agree to leave? Or are you a law-breaker, sent out of town to teach you a lesson?'

Tom considered this. 'It's true I agreed to come, but I was unjustly locked up. I'm no criminal. I wasn't given a choice. Now I see it was wrong to throw me out. If I can get back, I can sort things out.'

'Is your father rich, then?'

'My father's dead.'

'Mother?'

Tom shook his head.

'Well, your clothes answer my question well enough. You're an apprentice from a small town. Good shoes but no one to darn your stockings and no servant to hold your bags. Forget vengeance, lad. What you need is a way to survive in this war, this winter. That, and a barrel of luck.'

'Easy to say when you're an outlaw,' replied Tom.

The man laughed. 'D'you want to know something? Two months ago I was riding high in Southwark.'

'Never heard of it,' said Tom.

'Well now, it's a mighty place, Southwark. We get all the best people there. They come from London, just across the river.'

'What's your trade then?' Tom moved around to ease the coldness in his feet.

'Call me Effra. Wrestling's my game. I put down as many as five opponents in a night sometimes. And I earned a tidy sum doing errands for the Earl of Stamford. Good money

21

for an urchin like me. Mind you, that was a while ago.'

'So what happened?' Tom was stamping his feet as he listened.

'My home was attacked and I had to clear off, sharpish.'

'London's a long way from Dorset. Are there no safe places between them?'

'I was with a friend. We reached Winchester, and he died. Then Sergeant Smith picked me up.'

'You volunteered, or were forced?'

'It was the best offer available,' said Effra in a tired voice.

'Then why were you under guard at Poole?'

'Because the soldiers fear me, that's all.'

The short winter day dragged. Grey cloud allowed through only a flat, unchanging light. The coldness eased slightly as morning shifted to afternoon. Tom and Effra walked around and worked their muscles by jumping and stretching to keep warm.

'Will you help me get back to Poole?' asked Tom.

'Why should I?'

'Because you know more about such things than I do.'

'How did you work that out? I'm stuck in this stockade, same as you, remember?'

'Why are you in here, Effra?'

'I'm not sure. Soon as the sergeants heard their colonel was on the way, I got bundled in here.'

'But when we get out, will you help me?'

'What you need, boy, is something to take your mind off vengeance.'

Chapter 3

A group of horses crested a ridge beyond the stream and the recruits heard the jingle of cavalry equipment, then splashing water, as the horsemen crossed the ford and followed the track towards the field.

Fifty cavalrymen filed into the field and faced the novice soldiers. Last of all came a small man on a large white horse that stamped and snorted as the rider brought it to a standstill. Tom and Effra watched this through the gaps in the wooden palisade.

'Good morning, men. I am Sir Lewis Fezzard, your colonel. You are fortunate to join my regiment and will do as I command. I expect each of you to learn pike or musket. Any lack of concentration will be severely punished. You must become soldiers quickly, and pretending to be an imbecile is not a way back to your former lives, I assure you.' Sir Lewis's thin mouth twitched. 'This war between King and Parliament is on a knife-edge everywhere. In Dorset we face invasion by the King's army. He brings Cornish, Frenchmen and Irish against us.' The Colonel leaned forward, 'And there are others within our county that work against Parliament. When you are soldiers, there will be no lack of enemies to fight.

'You will be soldiers, not cowardly scum. You will learn how I expect you to behave, fight and die. And you will obey me in all things. Captain Green!' He summoned the man in boots, ordered the training to begin without delay, then dismounted and walked towards the stockade.

Tom and Effra stepped back from the gate. A moment later it was unlocked and two burly soldiers stepped into the pound. Tom and Effra now stood at one end of the stockade, watching Colonel Fezzard enter, moving with purpose to occupy its centre.

'Well. I can see which one of you is a fighter. Are you Effra Bayly, from London?' said the colonel.

'I am, sir,' replied Effra, standing to his full five-foot-seven inches height and facing his colonel, head deferentially dipped.

'Then who is this?' Sir Lewis pointed to Tom.

'My apprentice, sir. He's a vital part of my occupation.'

Colonel Fezzard looked at Tom with even more disgust than he directed at Effra. Tom tried not to react, although he felt he was sliding into something dark and dangerous.

Fezzard turned and nodded to three men who had entered the stockade. Large, wide men. Leather-garbed. Scowling. They stood to one side and Fezzard turned back to face Effra with a crooked smile and light in his eyes.

'I've heard of you, Bayly. You're a shrewd man, to be sure. But I'm shrewd also. Anyone can wander round the land claiming to be a Fighter of St George. I want you to show me your skill.'

He waved a hand to usher one of the leather men forward. The man in the centre approached Effra. His body was his weapon. He flexed his arms and reached forwards, gauging distance, his hands weaving a pattern in the air.

Effra stood still as the man closed in. Tom watched, aghast. It seemed Effra had refused this challenge. He stood, loose-limbed, head bowed, feet apart, right foot ahead of the left. His fingers twitched.

Leatherman slowed as he came within reach. He drew back his right arm, then threw out his left arm, jabbing at Effra. It looked to Tom that he wanted Effra to flinch and respond so he could then swing a punch with his right arm. Tom had seen this move in the boxing matches at county fairs. Usually these fights would proceed with both boxers testing each other, before one found a weakness in the other. Tom expected Effra to lift his arms to defend himself. Instead, Effra reacted to the jab by grabbing the outstretched fist in his right hand, stepping forwards with his left foot, thrusting his left arm round the outside of his opponent's arm and gripping the front of his neck. In a fluid movement the London man then twisted backwards to wrench Leatherman off balance and drop him onto his knee. He hammered the exposed throat with a fist and Leatherman rolled back towards Colonel Fezzard, gasping for air and disabled by a dislocated back.

Tom was stunned by the speed and ferocity of the attack.

Fezzard waved forward another lackey. One stepped forward, reaching down to his belt to draw a cudgel off a sling.

Effra backed off and shrugged with open hands. 'You want me to do a job, or d'you just want me to fight each of your boys until one gets a lucky strike in? That won't do you any good. Sir.'

The colonel paused, then waved the cudgel man back to

his place.

'I concede, you're worth more to me whole than broken. You've shown your mettle. Now it remains to see if you're smart enough to recognise the opportunity I offer you.'

'What opportunity is that, sir?'

'I need a good man, right now. There are some jobs that need your particular skills. If you serve me well, there's no need for you to worry that you'll ever be in the middle of a battle. What d'you say?'

'As ever, sir, the devil is in the detail. I know I have valuable skills. I hope you realise how scarce they are.'

'When I speak to you, Bayly, I expect respect, not insolence. Is that clear?'

'I know my worth, sir. And I know there's no man this side of Paris with my particular virtues.' At this, Effra spread his arms sideways, palms forwards.

'Whatever abilities you have does not change the fact that you are a hired labourer – and you do *not* speak to me as your equal. Is that clear?' Fezzard's voice rose an octave. 'Now, given that you are in my employ, there is a delicate matter you must attend to immediately.'

An hour later Tom and Effra left camp, heading north. This time Tom was not deserting, but providing essential support to Effra's mission for the colonel. Effra had gone with the colonel to be given more information, while Tom remained in the stockade. When he got back, he threw Tom an extra tunic and a snapsack, and they were on their way.

'I don't know what's going on,' whined Tom. 'One minute

I'm locked up for desertion, the next I'm released into the countryside with a wrestler. From London.' He glared at Effra.

'I told you I did lots of jobs for the Earl. Errands, so to speak. And some of them were, aah, a bit delicate.' Effra was smiling. 'Anyway, I need you with me.' He winked at Tom. 'And I promised we wouldn't run away.'

They headed north in silence for a while.

'Why would you do that? The only thing you know about me is that I want to desert, and yet you drag me along with you. D'you think I'll not run?'

'I can see how it is, lad. You need action to take your mind from Poole. I can give you that. Sir Lewis wants me to lighten a strong-room by reclaiming (as he calls it) some items that a neighbour borrowed and forgot to return. I said, "Surely, but I need Tom with me."'

'Why say that? And why me?' asked Tom.

'I need someone. You're the smartest chuff I've met round here. The job, I can do alone. But it's always wise to have someone watching your back. I've dealt with these sort before.' Effra headed off to the side of the road, towards a small hill a hundred yards away, clothed with gorse on its sides but with heather and birch on top. 'Now, look sharp. There's a crossroads up ahead. We're to meet one of Sir Lewis's men. He'll show us where to go.'

Tom followed. The hilltop was a few dozen feet above the level of the road, enough to give it an unrestricted view south and north. Tom looked over the heathy ground below them to the south, and the road they'd just been on. In the opposite direction, a few hundred yards to the north, the road was blotted out by trees. Another road was visible at the edges of the wood, that cut through it, presumably forming a dark cross-roads at its centre. He looked back at Effra, who was surveying the ground.

Stupid man, thought Tom. Why look at his feet when he could see anyone approaching the hill by scanning the distance? 'What are you doing?' he asked.

'Checking,' Effra said. After a few minutes he came back to where Tom sat on a bare rock. 'Right. We're on our own for the present.'

'What are you talking about? Of course we're alone. Why leave the road? I thought you said we were to meet someone at the crossroads?'

'Stop whining, boy. Would you prefer to be playing soldiers with them other chuffs, then?' Effra jutted his chin out and smoothed his pate with his right hand. 'You're a sullen partner, but I'll cut you some slack as you're only a boy.'

'I'm a man. A baker. I've finished my apprenticeship, so don't treat me like a child.'

'All right. In that case, let's call this Lesson One in your next apprenticeship – staying alive. We're headed to a place someone else has chosen, to meet someone we don't know, to be taken to an unknown location. I don't like bein' unprepared, and I'd rather know as much about the meeting place as I can. And if I was whoever we're meeting, I'd have a lookout up here. But there's no sign this place has been used recently. So, either there's a better place up ahead or there's no watch being kept for us.'

The boy gazed blankly at Effra, then took a hunk of bread and cheese from his bag.

'Where would you go next?' asked Effra.

Tom reined in his frustrations. He sighed and looked out

over the woods to the north. After a few moments, he turned back to Effra. 'I'd skirt the rim of the wood there, walk down the east road. Our man is probably expecting us to come from the south.'

'Good thinking, boy. But we'll skirt further and approach from the north, by road or through the woods if the ground ain't too cut up. Don't do what's expected. It's a habit what's kept me alive these past years.'

He headed off the hill and took a wide curve, over heathland, around the woods. They reached the east-west road, then followed the edge of the wood northwards.

'This'll do us,' said Effra, as they approached a low bank heading into the wood. 'Let's follow this rise and see where it leads.'

The short day was ebbing away and darkness began to pool within the wood, but they made rapid progress over the dead undergrowth and bare ground. The only sound they made was an occasional swish past a dormant bramble, or a damp crunch as they stepped on dead branches in soft ground. Soon they could see the crossroads.

Three men waited there. Two stood together, away from a taller figure. He was muffled against the winter air by a long dark coat with a high collar that nearly overtopped his head. At his feet lay a large, grey lump that became more doglike as they stepped forwards.

The moment the huge dog's ears flicked, and he rose to face them, Effra stepped into the open and strode forward. The dog growled, and the man turned to face the two soldiers looming out of the gloom. 'You're late,' barked the man.

'I'm pleased to meet you, too,' responded Effra.

The two men showed each other a sign that they were

29

on the business of Sir Lewis, and the man nodded and then marched along the western road out of the wood, followed by his dog, then the henchmen. Tom and Effra were obviously meant to follow, so they did.

No one spoke for a while. The road wasn't difficult to follow, and Tom watched the dog loping along at the side of the tall man like a trained wolf. The dog gazed back at Tom with a predator's eyes. After long enough for Tom's knees to feel achy, at the dark end of dusk, they stopped in sight of a group of hovels.

The guide spoke. 'Your goal is Clenston House, a mile beyond this village.'

'So, what do you know of Clenston House?' Effra kept his voice light. They were both speaking softly, so that words dropped from their lips onto the ground in front rather than carrying out into the night where other ears might collect them.

'The stone house itself is unremarkable, except it stands in such a small village. A square building, many windows. Three floors high and a slate roof, with chimneys on each corner. The front door faces east and is double. There's a high porch with stone columns supporting it. The strong-room is on the middle floor, at the front. It's locked, but not guarded. Inside, there's a chest in the corner with no keyhole or opening device. Only Mr Rodgers knows how to get into it. Round the back, the servants work in the scullery and kitchen. Their quarters are about twenty yards from the house. There's a farm up the hill to the rear.'

'What's around the house?' asked Effra.

'Fruit trees to the south, open ground at the rear and planted gardens on the north side. The front of the house is set back from the road through the village. Don't worry.'

'Ah, I'm not worried. I just like to know what I'm getting into.' Tom heard the light-hearted tone of Effra's voice and imagined him winking at the taciturn guide.

They walked through the village and out into the heathland beyond. There were no lights, and the overcast sky blocked out the stars and moon. Sometime later they became aware of a house on their left, then another on the right. Dogs began barking, and the wolf with them growled in reply They hurried on towards a faint glinting light.

'Keep going. We're nearly there,' the guide hissed.

The road became a crossroads and they could see figures looming up towards them from a slope to their west.

'Quick, straight across here.' The guide led them onto a lane beside more houses. There were many dogs barking now. The village seemed to be coming to life, with two groups of humans arriving at the same time. The soldiers and their guides kept going, not wanting to meet the other group but thankful for the noisy distraction provided by the village curs.

They were beyond the village centre now, climbing a gentle slope. The guide took a path to the right, and they descended again towards more houses, sensed as dark lumps in front. Another path to the left appeared, which they turned onto, walking away from the black shapes. The guide stopped at a large tree, dog beside him, his henchmen a few steps to the side.

'The house is up ahead by those lights. You can't miss it. This is what we'll do; the front door is loosely bolted, with a retainer stationed in the front hall at night. We draw him out first, then find the strong-room.'

31

Tom imagined what would happen to the night guard, as the guide continued.

Effra cut across the instructions. 'I've done this before. You've told me where the strong-room is. All I need from you is to keep the escape route open and warn me of danger.'

'Those aren't my instructions.'

'Your instructions are to enable me to get the items Sir Lewis wants. That's all. I know how to get 'em, so don't get in my way, and keep that escape route clear.'

'I've no idea who you are, man. I've been Sir Lewis's man for years, and you don't tinker with his orders. No. We'll do it my way.'

'Well, I have the advantage of you then. I'm not afeared of him. He knows my special skills, and he's given me this job. Presumably that's 'cos none of you chuffs can do it. Now, we can do this my way, or you can just bugger off back to camp to tell him you've left me to do it on my own.' Effra gazed up into the face of the tall guide.

Silence stretched out between the men. Tom counted five heartbeats, each one louder than the last. He was holding his breath.

With a grunt, the tall man sighed and nodded. 'All right. Let's get this done quick. What's your plan?'

Chapter 4

As night bled the land of any warmth, the group headed away from the village.

Tom glanced around, his throat constricted. He had a sudden brotherly feeling for all the small animals hunted and killed by men and their dogs. The small sounds reaching them indicated only the village routine shifting from day to night, but Tom could not fit them together with the routine of Poole that he knew; the closing down of the baking ovens, the cleaning of the bakery and the sweeping of the floor, together with calls and scrapes from outside, where other shopkeepers and tradesmen were similarly preparing for evening. This was different; the small noises clamoured ominous warnings that their mission was discovered.

'Keep up.' Effra's quiet voice focused his attention.

They picked their way between old fruit trees, ducking under stiff, bare branches and swishing through long grass. Tom's legs felt leaden, belonging to a different body. He was pushing against a strong tide. He wouldn't have been able to move forward without Effra's confident presence slicing through, opening a path for him to follow.

Despite Effra's apparent nonchalance, he moved cautiously and quietly. The five men and one dog approached the house from the south, moving to their left to skirt around a long, single-storey building, the servants' quarters. Voices from it crackled into the night, and they could see twinkles of light escaping through window shutters.

They crossed a track leading uphill from the building – the road to the farm, Tom assumed – then angled back towards their target. This area was more open than the orchard. Effra stepped deliberately between large barrels and stacks of firewood, using their bulk and shadows to cloak him. By not looking at the lights, they could see enough to find their way across the bare ground.

An old wooden hut loomed out of the darkness. It had a single opening facing the house. Tom stared in and waited for his eyes to adjust to the gloom. It was a woodstore, quarter full, the rest of the space full of cobwebs and the musty wood smell of mushrooms and tramps. Both he and the hound tested the strong odour with their noses.

'Don't go in,' whispered Effra.

They sat down beside the hut, studying the building.

'Why not use the hut to hide in? If we are to hide now,' Tom said.

'There's only one way in and out. If someone comes for wood we can't slide out of sight. Sitting here, outside, I can see the house, the space in front of us, and I can keep an eye on the ground behind too. We use the shadow of the hut but it doesn't stop us clearing off if we need to.'

Effra turned away from Tom and whispered, 'Two of you men, go round the front. Watch the door. If anyone runs out – stop 'em calling out. I don't expect trouble, but we must cover the main exits. You...' Effra faced the tall man. '... Stay here with the dog. Tom and I will be back soon.'

But Effra didn't head towards the house immediately. He settled down to watch, and Tom watched Effra. What a strange man. He seemed completely in control of this situation. Tom peered into every deep shadow around them, checking there was no one near, spying on them. The effort was exhausting. Everything inside Tom scratched and bit, wanting him to leap up and run. But run to where? Effra was his anchor, his only fixed point; his way out, his link with safety. And Effra was here. Tom took some slow, deep breaths and his anxiety ebbed, allowing him to think more clearly. How did he come to be skulking beside a woodstore, as part of a criminal gang, about to break into the home of a gentleman? He realised the greatest hazard he faced was his own ignorance. He had to remain alert if he wanted to get out of this.

'How're you doing?' Effra sent a soft question over his shoulder.

'I'm doing fine,' Tom was pleased with the even tone of his reply.

The dog and his master sat easily, watching and waiting with them. They seemed so similar, Tom wondered if they were brothers. But was the man really a dog, or the dog a bewitched man? No. Tom yanked back on the chain tethering his imagination.

The noises of the countryside and the buildings surrounded him, and then the servants' noises faded, leaving the night to the earth and sky. No one came near. The darkness deepened, engulfing the big house. Tom's thoughts meandered. I'm a speck in this cold, empty blackness. Alone. More alone than I ever was in Cinnamon Lane. It was never as quiet as this. Night never pressed as thick before, never

35

so complete. The sky is a massive tunnel, a cave. Those stars look like chinks of light in a rock roof.

Effra nudged Tom and gestured to the dogman. 'We go now. Stay here and watch.' Effra faced Tom. 'Follow me.'

Tom gulped. 'You want me to come with you?'

'Don't argue, boy. Just stay low and quiet. Do what I tell you, right?'

'But...'

As Tom spoke, Effra moved, rushing silently over the ground in a crouch. The darkness swallowed him up. Tom glanced across at the man and dog, and saw the pinpricks of their eyes regarding him. He forced his leg muscles into movement and raced after Effra.

He headed for the darkest corner of the large building. Effra grabbed him as he came close. 'Stay by me and don't make a sound.' He moved to a corner where the building jutted out from its main, rectangular bulk. Then he vanished.

Tom blinked and inched into the deeper black. As he reached the corner he saw that where the house jutted out there was an in-turned section, scarcely a yard wide. This, Effra was using as a chute to clamber up to the roof edge, over twenty feet above ground. Tom followed, pressing on both sides of the chute with his arms, lifting his body and wedging his legs on either side to allow his arms to reach higher and get more purchase. Soon he was close to the parapet, where Effra grabbed his belt and slowly, quietly, hauled Tom over its edge.

'What now?' breathed Tom.

'Just follow.' Effra headed along the parapet to a point halfway to the end of the roof. He glanced over the edge, nodded, then looked back to Tom, who was tottering towards him. 'Here. See that window below? It's open. That's where we're going.' He lifted a coil of thin rope from his snapsack and carefully slid it down the wall. The rope end was lashed to a hooked piece of wood about an inch thick and a foot long, like the top of a walking stick. This, Effra fixed against the top inner edge of the parapet and tensioned it with his weight. In a moment he had sunk out of Tom's sight and landed on the windowsill.

In two more moments he signalled for Tom to follow, and soon they both stood in a dark corridor in an unknown house, in the middle of a winter night. Before they moved off, Effra took hold of the rope and twitched it, releasing the blunt hook from the stone parapet. He caught the hook silently as it dropped past him and coiled up the rope.

The two men paused for a moment, facing into the dark corridor. The outside darkness seemed thinner, lighter and safer, as Tom peered into the velvety black menace. The velvet soon drew back as his eyes adjusted, and Tom made out a long, narrow passage. He imagined bedrooms opening on the inner side. The air smelled of stale bodies, sweetened by old lavender and years of woodsmoke absorbed by the timber and plaster of walls and ceilings. It was warmer than outside.

Effra stalked along the corridor towards the centre of the house. Tom followed. He went slowly, wincing at every creak from the wooden floor.

Effra waited for him at the top of a flight of stairs. 'Step lightly, Tom. Use your toes and feel for firmness. We mustn't make a sound.'

Tom nodded and tried to slow his pounding heart.

The landing circled the flight of stairs that descended to the first floor. The second floor, where they were, was above the strong-room. They crept down the stairs, Tom's mind once again recoiling from every creak and sigh as his feet pressed on the dry boards. Effra moved stealthily to a thick wooden door above the front entrance to the house. Tom joined him and felt metal bars strengthening the old wood. Effra paid no attention to the door beyond finding the keyhole. Tom sensed his crouched, tense body and heard a light scraping before Effra stood up and gently opened the way into the strong-room.

'There's no one here. Wait by the door.'

Tom closed the door and looked at the room. He sensed Effra moving silently around it. Another image rose in Tom's mind of demons or night-creatures creeping around a house, but he kept telling himself that the indistinct shape was Effra. He listened at the door for any sound of movement from the household. Every moment stretched his nerves tighter. A need was growing in him to be outside, away from that place, safe. With the things Effra searched for or not... it didn't matter.

Tom strained his senses to reach the servants' quarters. Might one of them hear something, or return to the house for some reason? Effra made faint scrabbling noises in the room as he searched for the chest. Tom heard creaks from the corridor and focused his senses. Nothing. The silence dragged out. There. Another creak, and another. Tom reached out into the room to warn Effra, but he was too far away and Tom dared not speak. He listened. A long silence, then a creak. Was that someone creeping along the passage? Tom's throat felt tight. He flexed his cheeks to release some spittle into his mouth, then swallowed deliberately. A bead of dampness slid down his forehead. He squeezed open the door to hear better. Another creak. His eyes were now accustomed to the dark and he could make out some bulky features out there. But none of these moved. Each creak seemed to come from a different direction.

Then Effra was beside him. 'Close the door, Tom.'

'Why? Are you finished? Let's get out of here.'

'No, Tom. I've got the documents, but I need you to read them for me.'

'Sure, I'll do it on the way back.'

'No. You must do it now.'

'What? Why here? We've got to get out, Effra. It's dangerous to stay here any longer.'

'Calm yourself, Tom. No one knows we're here and we'll have to give the dogman the papers as soon as we're clear. This is where you must read them. Now.'

Tom giggled. 'And how do I do that, in the pitch black?'

'Come on, boy. I thought you had a stronger stomach than this. Concentrate. And help me figure out what we're getting into.'

Tom breathed slowly, fighting the urge to race down the steps and burst out of the front door. He knew he'd be able to run all the way to Poole. But this man exuded calmness. Tom wanted to earn his respect. He swallowed once more and nodded. 'How, then?'

'No magic. We light a taper. You sit at that table and read, and tell me what it is we're stealing.'

'We'll be noticed, surely?'

'No. You close the door and we keep those curtains drawn over the windows.' Effra placed a sheaf of papers in Tom's hand and guided him to the table. He took out his tinder box and soon had an ember that lit a rushlight.

The light was poor and flickered weakly, but Tom could make out the meaning of most of the papers. There seemed to be two main documents. One was a narrative of how a certain Sir John Rodgers of Clenston House had taken witness statements from local men, testifying that Colonel Fezzard had sold them timber, land and livestock at the market rate over the past ten years. The second was a list of men who were accused by Sir John Rodgers of colluding with Fezzard in various enterprises, including smuggling, fraud and coercion of others.

'Read the names,' commanded Effra.

Tom read a list of names. Hubert Standley, Sir Thomas Barnes, Mary Hoddard, Duke Franklin... some more... Henry Hart JP... some more... John Declark, Colonel John Bidlecomb, Postumus Peck, Josias Tizard, Jellen Basten and Sir Richard Croston.

Effra took both documents and extinguished the rushlight. 'That's a long list.'

The men stood together in the blackness, waiting for their eyes to adjust, and then they left the room. Tom focused his whole being on stepping cautiously across the wooden boards and along the corridor, pausing at each creak, fighting all the way a wild urge to run. He just wanted it to be over.

Effra fixed his wooden hook on the first floor windowsill and Tom climbed down first. He was outside the house, his breathing still rapid and shallow. Effra was now beside him, with the hook and rope coiled and packed. They paused, straining to hear any noise or movement. Tom noticed moonlight silver-edging the shadows, sharpening the contrast with the darkness, but the soft, formless night sounds gave him no clues about surrounding danger. Rather, they promised black sanctuary. They ran back to the woodstore.

The man nodded, and the dog growled. Tom and Effra skirted the edge of the garden to the north of the house and collected the men watching the front door. A few minutes later they were through the village and walking along a heath path.

Tom looked at the sky. The stars were fading, their brightness usurped by the moon and prowling clouds. He sensed his sweat cooling, and cold prickled his skin. A crowd of details crashed into his consciousness.

'That stick is too short for a walking stick,' he joked with Effra, who had picked up a stout, straight branch of about two feet long.

Tom held his hands up before his face. Even in the dark he could see they were trembling. But this wasn't fear. This was excitement, victory, survival. He couldn't stop trembling and shivering. It's a good thing, he thought, that we're moving fast, or else I'd have to run in circles just to use up all this energy. Instead, he moved alongside Effra. This man seemed to come to life in tight corners. Maybe a good friend to have in a scrape. But maybe you don't want friends that lead you into scrapes in the first place. Ahead, the dogman and the hound had stopped. The other two men were coming along behind. As Tom and Effra drew close, Dogman stepped in front of Effra.

'When I say, Tom, you jump off this track. Got me?' Effra whispered.

'What?'

'I'll take those papers now,' Dogman said.

'No, you won't. I've just risked my life for Sir Lewis and I don't want no one but me getting the credit.'

'I don't think you understand the situation, thick head. You might be a good lock-pick, but now's the time for you to hand over what you took.' He held out his hand. The dog growled.

'If you won't give us the papers, we'll cut them off you, if you know what I mean.'

Tom had no weapon. Effra had no weapon. Tom didn't know what weapons the other men had. The dog had teeth. What was he to do? Effra took the decision away from him.

A cloud passed across the moon and plunged the group into night-shade. Effra reacted first. He thumped Dogman in the throat with his stick, then jumped at the other two men. They were ready for him, but rather than cannoning into them he swerved his upper body, then crouched, lifted one man by his thighs and threw him behind him, onto the onrushing dog. The second man swung a hefty swipe at Effra, and Tom smelt blood. But Effra didn't slow. He grabbed the knife arm as it flashed past and twisted it, bringing his other arm round to connect with the elbow. Tom heard the sharp click of ligaments as the man shrieked.

Now Effra had only the dog to beat. He had dropped his stick, but now he needed it. Tom broke through his frozen stance. He reached down for the wooden branch, even as Effra was dealing with the knife man. As the dog charged, he threw it to his accomplice. Effra caught it, but the dog was on him, snapping and thrusting his jaws at his neck. Effra twisted free, but he was on the ground. Never the right place to deal with a dog. The dog rushed him again, then flew backwards.

Tom grabbed hold of a hind leg and yanked him back, enough for Effra to regain his feet. This time, as the dog jumped up, blows crashed, quick and fierce, on his snout. The dog recoiled, but the man stepped forward and the blows kept landing on the dog's head. It growled and slunk back to its master, who was sitting on the ground holding his throat.

'Don't try anything like that again, and keep that fucking dog under control,' Effra barked. 'Tom, get the knives off 'em.'

The group resumed the march, Effra and Tom now at the rear.

'You're pretty good at this sort of thing, aren't you?' Tom said.

Effra turned his head slightly, but Tom could see no details of his face, and the man said nothing.

As they walked, Tom's excitement ebbed. His worry about the burglary grew and his joy in the achievement cooled. He voiced his thoughts when the men in front were far enough away. 'So we're common thieves now, are we?' Tom's voice quavered.

'Not with me, you're not,' retorted Effra, nursing a gashed forearm. 'Nothing common about my little jaunts. And this one's on behalf of the Parliamentary Army, no less.'

'Really? Don't you think this is all about the greed of Sir Lewis, rather than the war?'

'Course it is, lad,' Effra snapped between gritted teeth. 'But what are we s'posed to do? I feel safer doing this sort of thing than marching up and down hills, learning how to die in a straight line. Give me this life anytime. If my commanding officer needs to make use of my particular skills, that gives me a value that can keep me alive.'

'But I'm no thief. I've never broken into someone's house before,' continued Tom in an animated whisper. 'I've been evicted from my home, thrown out of my town, kicked into an army of strangers, and now I've stolen from a Dorset gentleman.'

'Whoa, lad. I take your point,' Effra replied. 'But there's no going back. You either sink or swim. It's a brutal world, Tom, and you need to toughen up. Quick. You can stay as cannon fodder or you can make yourself worth more. Learn the skills to stay alive – and you'll be able to keep others alive. And that's worth working at, don't you think?'

Tom had no answers. He walked on through the night and tried to understand this new world. He was getting used to Effra's way of working. He waited before he acted. He watched before he moved, and he sought to understand his surroundings before showing himself. And when he did act, he did it ruthlessly.

It was still dark when they came in sight of the camp. Their escort of three men and a dog stopped at the guards by the field gate. Tom and Effra passed into the camp.

'Not much of a home, is it?' Effra said.

Chapter 5

The two men sat down on a stone bench in the pre-dawn darkness. Captain Green had sent them immediately down the road to a nearby church that had been commandeered by the colonel, and they now waited in the porch for a corporal to return.

Tiredness dragged at Tom's body. But he knew he needed to be fully alert to meet his colonel. Effra looked relaxed as he rested his head against the impassive wall and let his eyelids droop. Only the controlled, regular breathing hinted to Tom of his alert state.

The corporal bustled back into the porch and nodded for them to enter. Within the church, equipment was piled on pews on both sides of the central aisle. Tom noted a tower of cooking pots and, next to it, a box of short, stiff swords, each one with a simple, hemispherical hand guard protruding from a cheap leather scabbard with a tin tip. At the far end a curtain had been hung across the church to separate the chancel, where the communion table was fixed and the vicar stood during services. The wooden pulpit was near the left-hand wall and a rustle of the curtain here caught their attention. Sir Lewis appeared, wearing a blue and gold silk dressing gown that glistened in the fluttering light of the candles flanking the aisle. The colonel ascended the three steps to the pulpit thoughtfully, and faced his burglars with a fierce gaze.

'Well? Explain yourselves.'

Effra stepped forward, 'Sir. We're here to report a successful operation last night.' He said no more and returned the malevolent gaze of his colonel.

Tom felt the silence lengthen and hang menacingly between them.

'Don't play with me. Just give me the papers.'

Effra reached into his bag and held out the package rolled up into a narrow tube approximately two feet long. Sir Lewis scampered down from the pulpit, strode up to Effra and snatched them from him.

He pulled off the ribbon and scanned the contents. 'Is this all?'

'We did what we were told, sir. We met your man, and he took us to the house where, after great difficulties, we freed your letters.'

Sir Lewis's eyes narrowed and his nose seemed to grow more pointed. 'You've done well, Bayly. Resourceful fellow.'

'We've done you a great service, honourably delivered,' Effra whispered, but his voice cut through the cold air like a stiletto knife.

'Honour? You're just a common thief. I could have you strung up from this beam tomorrow, don't forget that.'

Effra's thin lips tightened, 'I don't forget that, sir, but I can be a great asset to you. No one is better than me at untangling problems or discovering secrets. And my guess is that Tom and I could be of more service to you alive than dead.'

'I know who you are, Bayly. You can't hide in this bleak

countryside. Men of quality will always know what you are. So don't beard me. You're a tool, an instrument to be wielded by your betters. Never forget that.' Fezzard paused and looked around at the dank church walls, then back at Effra.

'So, all you want is more work. Is that it?' The colonel wandered back to the curtain. Without turning round he parted the cloth and passed beyond the veil, sending back his dismissal. 'I'll call you when I need you.'

Tom and Effra looked at each other and waited, but when nothing further happened, they turned and left.

On the way back to the camp, Tom confronted Effra. 'Who are you, Effra? The colonel seems to know a lot about you.'

Effra slowed down on the narrow track back to camp. 'There's a whole pack of men looking for me just now. I can't tell all, Tom. Just trust me. And if I can trust you, we can serve each other and perhaps stay alive. Our best defence now is to be useful to the old goat so's he won't kill us outright. But watch yourself, Tom. You can never trust a gentleman. They tread us down, squeeze us for their own ends, then throw us away when we're broken.'

Tom thought back to Sir Balthazar Merrick. 'Then I'm done for. And you've just volunteered me to a gentleman to carry out more crimes and who knows what. How can we possibly get out of this twisted mess?'

'Who knows?' Effra shrugged. 'Things have a way of unravelling that always amazes me.'

Tom and Effra rejoined the recruits as they were kicked and shouted awake. They were bundled into a corporalship of twenty-three men, with a trained soldier as its corporal. There were four musketeer corporalships, each lined up in six ranks of four men. These groups were then drilled up and down the field next to the camp, as though they were marching into a battle. Once in position, the front rank presented wooden sticks, dummy muskets, to a pretend enemy and shouted 'bang', before turning to the right and filing down the right-hand side of the group to form a new rear rank, while each new front rank went through the same motions.

There was one break for breakfast in mid-morning, but it was dark when they blundered back into the camp, smelt the woodsmoke and saw dozens of cooking fires from the pikemen. The men lined up facing the stream. The sergeant dismissed them and they dissolved into small groups to beg or steal a light from the other fires.

Tom and Effra joined three musketeers who were already blowing on a mat of wood shavings surrounding a smouldering stick.

'Mind if we join you?' said Effra. 'It looks like our best bet is to help each other stay alive, and that includes dinner time.'

'So, what do you bring to the party?'

At this, Effra drew a rabbit from his tunic. 'I've got the meat. I bet you're the turnips, so let's sit down and try to warm up.'

'Very funny,' said one.

'That's the best offer we've had today,' another replied.

At that moment, the group heard a commotion further off.

'Here you go, lads. Nice juicy coneys to cook. Just add vegetables and you've got a tasty stew.' The sergeant stood behind a waggon guarded by two soldiers and tossed three dead rabbits towards each fire within reach. He looked at the wrestler and the others huddled around the fire. 'Got something to eat already, have you?'

'Not us, sergeant. Why d'you think that?'

'Huh, just. Nothing. Here, don't eat them all at once, boys.' And off he went.

The five men settled around the fire, two of them still fussing to get the flames well alight, while their mate sat back, puffing on a long thin pipe, and skinned the animals. Tom and Effra stretched out on the damp ground and got to know their comrades.

The men tending the fire were brothers from Wimborne, Samuel and Gideon, and the rabbit skinner was Ifor.

With the rabbits skinned and gutted, they were skewered onto hawthorn sticks and placed onto a makeshift spit over the fire. Ifor didn't discard all the innards; he produced a pewter pot half full of water, slid the heads, hearts, livers and kidneys in, and placed it in the fire to warm up into a rich gravy.

Before the pot was hot, the sergeants did another tour of the camp, passing out a small loaf to each recruit to mop up the fat, blood or gravy of the meal.

It took a while for the warmth of the fire and the effect of the meal to loosen the men's tongues and share something of their stories.

Ifor Scovell was a wiry Welshman with receding grey-flecked hair, but his home was in Blandford and he wandered the countryside selling pots and pans. He was nearly forty, he said. 'One direction is as good as another, and so I accepted the sergeant's kind offer to walk for a while in company with some like-minded lads.'

Samuel and Gideon Palmer laughed. Samuel was

smoother, taller and leaner than his brother. Gideon was stocky, with a freckled and pockmarked face.

'Our father is a wool merchant in Wimborne, and life has become less comfortable of late.' Samuel grinned lopsidedly.

'Our friends know us as lively, good fellows,' his brother cut in. 'But not everyone appreciates us.'

They spoke about Samuel's adventures with the squire's daughter, and the decision to be elsewhere for a while.

'We're not worried, though. We'll be able to slip back in a month or two,' said Samuel.

Effra laughed. 'If the army's finished with you.'

Effra shared that he worked for an earl in London. He didn't mention what he and Tom had been doing. Ifor noticed his wounded arm and bathed it, applying some herbs he had in his snapsack.

'And you, Tom. Who are you?' asked Gideon.

'I'm from Poole. I was apprenticed to my father, a master baker. His only child.'

'That's unusual. Most lads are apprenticed to other families,' said Effra.

'True, but our small business needed me. My mother died five years ago, and I learnt the ways of a baker early. My father never considered leasing me out to another baker.' Tom gazed into the fire. 'My apprenticeship is finished now. My father's dead, the bakery repossessed, and I was left with one option: to follow Sergeant Smith here.'

As the evening drew on, men wandered out into the nearby coppice to collect more fuel for the fires. There was a low murmur from the groups of men, but no one stayed up late. There was no strong drink or even beer to be had, only water from the stream. Everyone was cold and tired. The fire helped the men to relax, softening their muscles and minds as they curled up like dogs in front of the flames, gradually creeping forward as the fires faded into glowing embers through the night.

Tom slept badly again. Effra's words ate into him. Stay alive or get slaughtered. Follow orders or learn the skills to stay alive – and become useful to the powerful. Tom mulled over these ideas. What do I have that I can offer anyone? Displaced, dispossessed, deserted by those who know me. Can I get any lower?

And yet... Effra is part of that jetsam of life. And he's got a whole range of new skills I've never seen. Intriguing, impressive skills. And Effra chose me as an accomplice. Does that mean I have something that's helpful to Effra? That's unlikely, if a complete town can reject me.

I'm healthier than most. But a strong body is useful only as far as it can knock down an enemy or stand in a pike block. That's not much of a hope for keeping body and soul together. It's better than being weak and sick, though. My body's my only weapon and resource, but how can I use that to show everyone I'm not worthless? I need something extra. Effra has cunning, clearly. Can I use my brains as a weapon of self-preservation?

But this reasoning was leading him towards being a criminal. That was obviously what Effra was. Could Tom emulate Effra? Did he want to? Stealing was a mortal sin. And what about killing? If he was to stay alive, it was likely that he would have to send someone to Hell, or Heaven, to save his own skin. Would that damn his soul?

Tom woke up cold and stiff. Ifor had already stirred the fire around the pewter pot, and they all dipped bread into the warm stock for breakfast. The men weren't left to themselves for long and Tom, with his new comrades, was soon on parade, being drilled in the movements he'd learned the day before. Together with the pikemen, the new unit was marched across the field with pikes in a central block and musketeers on each flank.

The evening fire was again a welcome sight, and more rabbits were distributed with bread to form the meal.

'If we stay here any longer, we'll clear the area of coneys for good,' grunted Gideon as he caught an animal flung toward him.

'Think of all those rabbits' feet, though,' said Samuel. 'We'll be the luckiest soldiers in the army.'

'So, Ifor, do you know any stories? What about telling us a Welsh saga to pass the time?'

Ifor's eyes lit up at Effra's request. 'Ah, you want a tale? I haven't sat and yarned for ages.'

Everyone settled down to enjoy the story – there was nothing else to do, anyway.

'There was a man living in Wales during Catholic Mary's reign. He was scarce more than a boy, really. But he was poor. And he couldn't feed himself or his widowed mother. Times were hard and all the cattle, all the crops, all the wool and all the trades were controlled by Englishmen, who fleeced the Welsh, lined their own pockets and sent the wealth back to England, to the Queen.'

Ifor stopped, puffed on his pipe, and waited for the reaction from his English audience. The English hearers straight away called back, laughing and justifying their nation.

'Anyway…' Ifor raised his voice to regain control of the situation. 'The lad's name was Twm Sion Cati and he was a stout Protestant, so he prayed about what he should do. Next day he went to the market to buy a pitcher for his old mother. When he got home, he filled it with water and carried it in to his mam. But the jug leaked. There was a hole in it, see. Twm was mortified, but being a direct sort of lad, back he went to speak to the crockermonger.

"'Hey,' he said, "you sold me a pot with a hole in it, man." But the tradesman wouldn't listen. He had better things to do than argue with a starving boy. Well, Twm wasn't standing for that. Oh, no. He upended the jug right over the man's head.

"'Have a good look, why don't you? And tell me, can you see any light in there?"

Well, of course he could, and he had to replace the pitcher with a new one. And Twm tested it before taking it home. On the way, a friend joined him. "Well done, Twm. You gave that old cheat what he deserves and I've a gift for you to say thank you." And he put a brand new pot in his arms.

"'When you put the man inside his pitcher, I swiped two pots. I've got the best one, but this one is for you."

'So, Twm thought about this and decided he had a better chance of keeping body and soul together by thieving than by working, and from then on he grew in cunning and trickery and his mother never starved.'

The fire, the food and the enjoyment of a shared tale relaxed Tom, and he sank into sleep, wrapped in his tunic. He edged forward through the night to follow the warmth of the cooling embers, as dreams broke in on his peace.

He was back at Poole. The wind plucked at his hat and brought water to his eyes. The minister had finished the burial service and was walking back to the church. Walking beside him was Tom's father. How could Tom fail to recognise those shoulders?

'Father!' he called. There was no reply. Tom followed. He ran, he called. But he got no closer, neither did he get a response.

The minister and the master baker turned a corner, and Tom was left standing in a street. No one stopped to acknowledge him. He was outside their lives, not part of their world. A shudder rippled through his whole body.

Grey dawn arrived, and with it the corporals and sergeants bawled and kicked the recruits awake. Tom shivered and stood with the others, but darkness returned as heavy, low clouds rolled overhead and released a torrent of icy rain on men, animals, plants and land.

The rain helped to get the men upright. In summer the trees give some protection, but in winter water sweeps straight through the crowns. Within minutes the fires were doused, the men were drenched and there was no prospect of anything but to stand and endure. The storm lasted half an hour, but it felt to Tom and the others that it went on for hours. There's no difference between drenched and double-drenched, so after a while the men stopped crouching and simply stood, waiting for the downpour to pass. When it did, the sergeants reappeared from their small tent. Tom saw them survey the sight, then confer for a few minutes before approaching the men.

'Well then, my lovelies,' shouted Sergeant Smith. 'Let's get you in your ranks.' He drew himself up to his full height. 'Corporals! Get your men in order. Two minutes to parade.'

Men don't move smartly when wet, but it didn't take long for the corporals and soldiers to beat the recruits into something like an orderly group.

Another day of drill; learning how to wheel from front to side, to change a column into a line, trudging up hill and down again. Slipping in soft ground and catching muddy clods on clothes and body. The only relief from this labour was when, approaching the top of a hill, everyone heard a thundering through the earth and feared an attack from cavalry over the ridge.

The whole company scattered before a stampeding herd of cattle. Relief caused the men to collapse in laughter, releasing their tension. Everyone knew that the next time it was likely to be a real enemy chasing them.

A week they spent drilling and marching. Then arctic cold screeched down from the north, coating everything in deep snow. Training gave way to survival. Without tents or huts, each night was an agony of cold, of keeping the fires going and huddling together for warmth beneath the nearest cover, be that log, wall or hovel. Only the officers got the hovels. Men were found dead in the morning, frozen to the ground. Those that lived inhabited a cold, white world without space for much thought other than food and warmth.

The blizzard blew itself out after three days. In that time it had reshaped the landscape. Roads were hidden beneath wide meadows of snow, hedges became frozen walls, and the soldiers' presence showed as a dirty streak across this desolate, pitiless land. They had to move. So they went south, into the fortified town of Wareham, to join the existing garrison.

Chapter 6

No houses were allotted to them, so they cut wood, borrowed timber, cropped dead grass and filched bricks to build a camp of huts in the northern corner of the town, close to St Martin's Church. Firewood was fetched from the woods nearby, on the boggy ground stretching eastwards towards Poole Harbour. The afternoon was damp and blustery and it took time to get the campfires going and dinner sizzling on wooden spits over them.

Night fell early, the wind gusty but without snow. The men huddled beside the earth and timber town wall and chatted to take their minds off the cold.

'Wooing? They think wooing is like fishing with a pole and line? They may be right.' Samuel stretched out on the damp straw and put his hands behind his head. He was listening to a loud conversation at the next campfire, his mouth curling as his eyes seemed to look into his past. 'It's closer to fishing with a net. Lasses let you know their interest.'

'Aye, but you must know how to speak to them, or to get them to mind you, surely, Samuel,' said Tom.

'Rightly, 'tis a gift, maybe. It don't come hard, but I see it's not natural for some.'

'Well, what is it, then? What's your secret for getting under a maid's frock?' Effra said.

Samuel winked and smiled but said nothing.

'I can tell you what he's got that others don't,' said Gideon. 'His secret weapon is his voice.'

'You never told us you can sing,' said Tom.

'You never asked. And where in this stinking camp is there a fiddler to sing with, or a maid to flatter?'

'Well, at least show us this awesome weapon. Give us a tune.'

At that, Samuel broke across the conversation with a clear, powerful voice, rich in tone and skilful in timing.

'A poor beggar's daughter did dwell on a green,

Whose goodness and beauty might well grace a queen,

A right bonny lass and full dainty was she,

And many did call her pretty Bessie.'

'So, that's it then, is it, Samuel? Hold a maid's eye and sing prettily till she falls at your feet?'

'Don't forget Samuel's pretty face, Tom,' added Gideon.

'Rubbish!' Samuel laughed. 'There's girls for every kind of man, so I've found, and you have too, Gideon. But I suppose I please most that I meet.'

'Something's missing,' said Effra. 'Is it just the pleasing of the eye and the ear?'

'Just smile, look interested, make the girl feel warm towards you. It's not hard. The songs I sing soften the female heart.'

'Samuel has a way with soft words that makes girls melt,' chipped in Gideon again. 'We can both persuade an innkeeper to give us another drink, but my brother is a master at breaking down a woman's defences. If I didn't know better, I'd say it was magic.'

'We love drinking at an inn with a woman keeper. Some-times we'll drink all night for a penny!'

'But now you're driven out from your home. How will you manage?' asked Ifor.

'Not driven out! We left to see the world. We won't be gone long. Our neighbours have short memories, and this war will soon take their minds off our misfortunes.'

'That's soft, Gideon. Those misfortunes weren't ours. Like men sleeping under a weak wall, we suffer when the wall falls, but we didn't make the wall, or push it over. Others did that.'

'But we're the ones with the bruises, brother.'

'Doesn't sound like you were sleeping under that wall,' Effra commented.

Both brothers became sullen and there was no more conversation that night.

Another sorry morning broke upon a group of men still wet and unconfident as soldiers. But each dawn brings hope, and the men's spirits lifted as their stomachs got to grips with what was left from supper.

The camp looked from a distance like a town of pigsties, small structures huddled together with a sea of mud between. These huts were built onto wooden frames interlaced with hazel and willow stems, onto which turves and soil were added, making the surface weatherproof, somewhat. Most were large enough for half a dozen men, but size varied according to need. Outside each group of huts was a campfire and the usual paraphernalia of cooking and eating.

Tom's education included instruction from Effra, who, they learned, was willing to pass on his skills with knife, quarterstaff and cudgel to his comrades, taking care to do this away from the eyes of the officers. Tom marvelled at the breadth and depth of his knowledge of weapons.

'So, how come you know all this stuff, Effra?' Gideon quizzed him as they settled around another fire.

'I was brought up to it,' Effra said, as his head eased back to allow him to look straight up into the sky. 'I've been lucky. My ma couldn't tame me, but while on the streets I got into fights and one day when I'd just been beaten by a bigger boy, a gentleman came by and offered food and training so I could flatten any of the other boys.'

'What did he want in return?' Samuel winked knowingly.

'And how old were you then?' said Tom.

'So it was a kind of apprenticeship?' added Ifor.

'I was only a yard high, so I was pretty young. He took me to a stable at the edge of Wandsworth. There were other boys there and we learnt together, all the hand weapons, but not muskets or petronels. I gave no thought to money; a full belly was all I needed. They let me take food home to my ma, so the arrangement suited us all.'

'How long were you there?' Gideon said.

'All my childhood, until I was big enough and strong enough to be set loose on other fighters. I loved it. I didn't always win, but I made money for my patron and enjoyed the thrill. I once saw a play at the Globe Theatre. It was very like one of our fights.'

'So, you were play-acting at fighting? I thought you were serious?' Samuel's smile had slipped into his usual sneer.

Effra laughed. 'There's a fine line between entertaining an audience and saving your own skin. I wasn't a fancy performer but I got the job done, and most of the crowd respected that.'

Sir Lewis seemed to respect Effra too. Just as the muske-teers were about to resume drilling after a midday break, Effra was called out of the ranks and ordered to report to the colonel.

'Tom. We've another delicate task for Sir Lewis,' Effra said to Tom when he got back. 'Grab your hat and sword.'

They collected their horses from the horse lines and care-fully walked them out of Wareham. On the icy, windswept heath to the northeast of the town, they mounted up.

'But where are we going?' said Tom, trying to stay on the horse's back.

'Wimborne,' Effra shouted back against the east wind.

The horses were not cavalry mounts, but draught animals borrowed from a waggon. Brown and sturdy, short and slow. At least they took some of the exertion out of the journey, but to unaccustomed riders it just relocated the effort, making muscles ache that had never been subjected to such treatment. They travelled above the snow-caked paths, but they didn't get to Wimborne much faster than if they'd walked.

They left the animals in a field by a house scarcely larger than their hut. A man stood beside the hovel. When Effra nodded to him, he nodded back stiffly, watching them with large, dark eyes.

Walking into the town, Tom hoped no one would recognise him from his previous visits to Wimborne, selling bread.

Effra glanced around as he stepped down the edge of the narrow street, avoiding the usual muck and rubbish, and across empty plots between houses. Tom could see from his posture and movement that cares were dropping from his shoulders. Effra came to life when on a mission. But the task he and Tom and were on was an unpleasant one.

They strolled into the centre of town and headed for the King's Head. The tavern was a long, low building, with whitewashed walls and dense, mossy thatch. It seemed to be the most popular house on the street, judging by the number of men, women and children streaming in and out. Effra made straight for the front door. Passing from the early evening gloom into the flickering candlelight of the drinking place, the two soldiers pushed past labourers and merchants, looking for a vantage point from where they could watch.

'Get a couple of beers, Tom,' Effra said, settling himself on a bench by a draughty, green-tinted window.

Chapter 7

A winter dusk, light fading, heavy dark clouds threatening
more snow. The inn in Wimborne was busy, as usual. There
were men perched or slumped in most of the corners, eking
out a pot of weak beer or sharing jokes with neighbours.
There were as many women as men coming in and out, but
the women were mainly collecting jugs of beer and they took
these away with them. Children, too, were milling about. To
Tom the inn looked as though it had once been an ordinary
house, but now most of the ground floor was a single, long
room, with wooden pillars strategically replacing internal
walls. A strong oak table in the far corner held a collection of
pewter and pottery tankards and wooden plates. Beside this
was a door, through which the landlady frequently passed,
bringing food, drink and tobacco or more rushlights for her
customers.

Effra and Tom slouched by a window where they could
see the main door and look across the high street. They were
waiting for someone in particular, and their beers were only
half drunk when he appeared. A merchant, judging by his
well-made tunic and hose. A frugal one, if the understated
brown colour and lack of lace was anything to go by. He
was a large man, unruly dark hair on head and jaw hinting

at a life lived outside, and broad shoulders indicating he had once earned his dinner through manual work.

Effra immediately approached him, smiling. His direct approach caught the man's attention. 'Master Jenkins? Are you Robert Jenkins?' Effra spoke at a normal volume, but this was only just audible against the growing hubbub in the inn.

'That's me. Who wants to know?'

'My name isn't important, but my message is. It comes from Sir Lewis Fezzard. Shall we share a beer and chat about it?' Effra was still smiling.

Jenkin's face suggested feverish mental activity before he nodded and followed the soldier back to the window seat. He sat opposite Effra and Tom and leaned towards them so they could hear his next words.

'You tell your master I've nothing to say to him. I emptied my chest to help him defend Dorset, but that means he'll have to wait till next year for any more. I can't raise money until I sell my cows and crops. They're not ready yet.'

'It's very public-spirited of you to help defend the country. But what Sir Lewis needs now is the rent on your properties for the last two years. This war doesn't change your contract with him and you now owe £43.'

Effra and Jenkins looked directly into each other's eyes. Tom caught only a dark twinkle in Jenkins's face in the weak light but he knew the look on Effra's face: a stern, not-to-be-denied glare.

Jenkins seemed to notice this, too. His gaze flickered then fell. He looked at his feet and said, 'I haven't got the money. You'll just have to wait.'

'I don't think you mean that, Master Jenkins. You see, I

know you've got men outside this inn to protect you, but that just shows your failure to see things right.' Effra spoke slowly and clearly, but softly enough that only Jenkins and Tom could hear. 'We've been sent by Sir Lewis, all nice and polite, like, because nobody wants any trouble about this. Two years is really a hell of a long time to forget to pay the rent. I know if I did that, my landlord would be spitting musket balls.'

'But I haven't got the money,' hissed Jenkins in exasperation.

'You do have the money, Jenkins! And do you know how I know that?' Effra paused only momentarily, then carried on. 'Because if you don't have the money, next week you won't have a farmhouse or barns. You won't have ploughs to scrape the earth or crops to grow. You won't have cows, pigs, children or wife to sell. You have given Sir Lewis a right pain in his arse about this, and if he doesn't get his rightful due he has four hundred trained soldiers that know exactly how to waste a farmer's land.'

Tom heard Effra's even tones and saw the effect of the words on Jenkins's face.

'But we both know there's no need for any of that, don't we?' This time Effra did wait for a response from Jenkins. It took a while in coming, but after a pause his shaggy head twitched.

Effra nodded back. 'Now, we're going to stick to you like your winter shirt until you hand over the full amount owed. Then my associate here will give you a note for the money to show this is all proper and legal, and you can then get on with whatever farmers do in winter.' He smiled and rose from his seat. 'So, where to, Master Jenkins? Take us by the shortest route to your money and this nightmare will be over.'

'It's in Shaftesbury,' Jenkins spat through gritted teeth. He didn't stand; instead he leaned back on the chair and set his back against a timber pillar.

'Don't mess me about, Jenkins. If your money isn't in Wimborne then let's go and see someone here who can lend you some.'

Resistance was still in the farmer. Effra sat back down. 'All right. We'll try a different line for a minute. I know you have a house in Wimborne. It's not your main house, but you use it a lot, and you're here every market day and Sunday. Is that right?'

'I have men outside, right now.' Jenkins's eyes were blazing and his whole posture threatening. 'I can kill you both, throw your bodies in the river and plead ignorance to Sir Lewis. It may not get me out of debt but God's bones, it'll hurt you.'

Tom was worried. They were twelve miles from their comrades, facing a belligerent local man with men at his back.

Effra, though, was unmoved. 'Jenkins. I don't want to see you suffer over this, ah, misunderstanding, but although you may do us some mischief I'd wager Tom and I are a match for any number of yokels you could throw at us. And, by the time you could call them over I can put out both your eyes and break your jaw.' Effra smiled evilly. 'I won't kill you. No. That would make collecting the rent so much harder, but my mischief, Jenkins, is far more likely than yours. Now, you have ten seconds to make up your mind. Just take us to the money and we can all go home.'

Jenkins paused for nine of those seconds, then blurted out,

'You win.'

'Then let's be on our way. Tom, you go out first.'

Tom headed for the door. Passing through, he noticed two bored men leaning on the house opposite the inn. When Effra and Jenkins came out these men straightened up and stepped across to them. Jenkins shook his head as they approached.

Jenkins took Effra down the high street and then they ducked down a narrow alley. The two men followed their master and Tom followed them. At the end of the alley Jenkins and Effra entered a low door in a wall with no windows at ground floor level. Before the two men disappeared Jenkins shouted for his men to wait outside and Effra gave the same order to Tom.

After less than a minute Tom saw a glow appear on the first floor, where there was a narrow balcony and shuttered window. Another minute, some scraping and banging, and then Effra called down for Tom to come up. Tom burst through the door and raced up a short flight of stairs. In the upper room Effra and Jenkins were looking at a pile of coins on a flimsy table.

'Count it, Tom. Make sure it's all there and give Master Jenkins a receipt. Then we can be on our way.'

Jenkins watched them with a petulant face as they descended the stairs back to the alley. The two soldiers walked briskly back to the main street.

'Don't look back and don't walk too fast,' Effra whispered.

Once in the street they raced to the next alley, and Effra cast his eye over the nearest houses in it before peeking back round the corner. 'Check there's a way out down there.'

Tom could see a narrow path with two-storey houses

either side. There were no balconies or overhanging rooms above their heads. At the end of the alley was a sharp turn to the left. Tom ran to this and found it opened out into a courtyard of damp ground, badly paved, with butcher's shops along one side, animal paddocks on another. He raced back to his friend.

Effra was watching Jenkins and his men talking at the edge of the street. One man turned stiffly and walked towards them.

'Let's go, quick.'

They ran to the corner and reached it in time to look back and see the dark shape of the man pass the alley.

'Back to the horses, I think. That's job done.'

'I can't go yet,' said Tom. 'I must go and see my friends Simon and Maria.'

'Don't be daft. It's dangerous to spend more time here than we have to. We've got what we came for. Let's go!'

Tom turned on Effra, 'I said I must speak to my friends. If you won't come you can leave me. I'll see you back at camp.'

Effra stood for a moment regarding his comrade. 'You've a lot to learn, young Tyler. Do you know where they live?'

'It's at the other end of the town. I asked the alewife when I got the beers.'

Effra shook his head.

'So. Lead on, Tom. Time is precious.'

They took a circuitous route, avoiding the high street, but Wimborne wasn't large and they soon arrived at a barn-like building by a water mill. Tom knocked at a dark door.

The door jerked open by a foot and a face peeked through.

'Maria? Is that you? It's Tom.'

The door slammed and Tom heard shouts from inside,

then steps on a stone floor. The door opened again.

Maria and Simon stood on the threshold together. They looked at Tom, suspicion on their faces.

'It is me, you know.'

'We know.'

Simon looked at Maria and she shrugged in reply.

'We have to be careful, Tom,' Simon said. 'There's been a lot of soldiers around here. We don't know who to trust.'

'Well you can trust me. You should know that.'

'Of course,' said Maria. 'Come in, Tom, you're welcome here.'

'And I'm with a friend. Effra Bayly,' added Tom, as Effra stepped into the faint light escaping from the building.

That was a difficult moment, but Maria and Simon held on to their hospitality as they eyed the tough, stocky soldier.

'I get that reaction a lot,' said Effra as he followed Tom inside.

Sitting at a low table in front of a small fire, Tom was able to ask the questions he'd been rehearsing for the past month. What had happened to the bakery? Had all his belongings really been confiscated? And did everyone in Poole think he was an undesirable vagrant?'

Simon filled in the missing pieces of information. The bakery was no longer a bakery, but it wasn't yet anything else. Merrick had it boarded up, guarded by a watchman.

Simon and Maria had left Poole the day after Tom, but they visited every market day to sell bread and pies. There was general sympathy for Tom, according to Maria. No one was in a position to say or do anything, though, and Simon and Maria had a few of Tom's belongings.

And then there was the final question. What should he do

68

now?

'You look pretty much like a soldier now, so stay in the army. At least you get fed and paid,' said Simon.

Tom laughed. 'You think I look well fed? We're treated little better than a pack of stray dogs. When there's bread or meat there's scarce enough to go round, and when there isn't we just steal from each other or from the local people.'

'What alternatives do you have, Tom?' Simon's voice had an edge to it.

'I thought I could join you and Maria, here in Wimborne, and we could go back to Poole. We've worked together almost our whole lives!'

'That's not going to happen, son,' Effra chipped in. 'Your life in Poole is over and whatever chances you get from now on, there's no going back.'

Simon and Maria nodded. Tom looked into the fire.

'Would you like some supper? We have some bread and there's a bit of dripping to spread on it.' Maria moved to a corner of the room.

'We'd best be on… ouch.' Tom stopped and rubbed his shin.

'We'd very much appreciate a quick bite, if it's not too much trouble.' Effra corrected Tom's reply and gave Maria a friendly smile.

It was a morose meal. Tom said nothing, Effra had nothing in common with the bakers and they were obviously waiting for their guests to leave. So they did.

They were soon back at the horses. Effra approached the hovel beside them with suspicion and care, but when he was sure there was no one waiting in ambush they collected their transport. Effra tossed a copper coin to the old man, his face

69

black and featureless but his posture recognisable from their arrival, and they trotted away from the town.

Outside the town, Tom turned on Effra. 'You think you know someone, but you don't, until you're in need. Then they let you down.'

Tom seethed in frustration and anger. He could not return to Poole, to the bakery or to his old life and friends. That knot of fantasy could no longer be sustained in his imagination. But betrayal? It left him floundering. Thoughts, sensations, new truths lodged in his mind. He was cast out, utterly. Nowhere to go – except back to a camp of brutal thugs. He was becoming one of them; men already expert at thieving and lying and now learning the martial virtues of killing and dying. He swung a leg as though kicking a pebble, forgetting he was on a horse, and his foot thudded into the side of the animal's head. It snorted and lumbered quickly off the side of the road. Tom fought clumsily to regain control of the beast and moved back alongside Effra.

'They seemed like good people,' Effra said soothingly.

'And what would you know about it?' said Tom.

'I can tell good from bad. It ain't that hard.'

'Well, I thought they were friends. I know it's difficult, but we pretty much grew up together.'

'You're on a different road to them, Tom. You can't expect them to take you in. You're no longer a boy, or a stray puppy. You're a rough soldier, and if you'd stayed with them it would've got them in a pile of shit and you in a worse hole. They did all they could; they shared their supper. That's no mean hospitality these days.'

The night became colder, more vindictive. A harsh sleet arrowed out of the darkness and stung Tom's face. He pulled his Monmouth cap low over his eyes and hunched back into his cloak. The rain found his skin anyway. Drops of water formed on his cheeks and quickly banded together into rivulets drawn down to his chin and mouth.

It was some time before Tom realised the stream of water trickling over his lips was salty. 'Can you teach me, Effra? To fight, to survive?'

'I can show you some stuff. I've already started that, haven't I? But learning always depends on the learner. How much do you want to learn, boy?'

They handed the horses back to the waggoner on watch at the horse lines.

'Stack the saddles in the equipment tent, rub the horses down and give them a feed from the fodder over there,' the watchman said, all the while gazing into the embers of his fire.

'We only used the bloody things for a few hours. We don't want to adopt them!' Effra mumbled.

When they'd finished they found Captain Green and gave him Jenkins's rent.

Before morning something hard collided with Tom's foot. He swayed along, through the night, bouncing as the horse picked its way down a lane. His foot twitched away from another blow. The dream evaporated and Tom awoke on a couple of boards in a makeshift hut. Someone was kicking him. Cold and dark surrounded him and the smallest movement ached. He peered up from the floor at the roof. Hot breath made him wince.

71

'Up, boy. Get up!' Effra's face was an inch from Tom's, and his voice, though only a whisper, blasted sleep away.

Outside, a faint light from a crescent moon, visible behind racing clouds, reflected from packed snow. The two men faced each other, shivering.

'You still want to learn to survive?' Effra asked.

Tom didn't know what he wanted at this hour, but he knew he had to say yes.

'Then let's start. There's no easy time or way. It hurts. You stay alive when you tell the world you won't die. Remember that. If you won't kick Fate in the balls and tumble him back to hell, you will die.' Effra seemed very sure about this.

For an hour Effra began to open Tom's mind to his world of survival. How to stand in front of a potential enemy, how to think and to see, to focus but to remain aware of surroundings. It was a morsel only. A start. And Tom learnt quickly.

'Remember. In a street fight, always assume there's a weapon; a knife is to be felt, not seen. And if there's a weapon, fight dirty. Don't play to the crowd if your life is at stake. And Tom, don't fight unless you have to.'

Tom stood still, watching the eastern sky lighten. He must remember these rules.

'Enough, Tom. We'll go over it again, many times. Now we go back to our military life. Soldiering and surviving aren't the same thing.' Effra ducked back into the hut and kicked his comrades awake.

Another day in Wareham camp had begun.

The whole regiment was now a force of four hundred and fifty men, half of which was at the start of its training. The order of the day, and of the next month, followed a clear programme, beginning with familiarity with orders, familiarity with weapons and familiarity with each other. As military competence grew, reliance on each other grew also. Tom and his comrades were each issued a four-foot long match-lock musket, three feet of match-cord, a gunpowder flask, a bandolier with a dozen small boxes for charges of gunpowder and a small leather bag for lead shot.

Large parts of each day were filled with drill, marching down roads, over fields. They each had to know what to do in every circumstance, so that the unit would move as a single entity. An organism with only one brain: that of the officer giving the commands.

And after learning how to move and march they had to learn how to fire their muskets. The musketeers were taught thirty-four movements to carry, load and fire the weapon.

And after learning how to march and how to use a weapon they had to learn to fight. A different skill altogether, but one closely reliant on those military habits being drilled into their minds and bodies. As their proficiency increased the manoeuvres became more aggressive, designed to accustom the whole unit to approach an enemy so as to allow pikes to thrust and muskets to 'give fire' at a target. The fighting aspect of the training was the most difficult to practise; they could enact sham battles but these didn't fully provide the experience they needed. Nothing Tom had ever done could prepare him for the shock of standing in a field watching an enemy advance with the intention to inflict pain and death.

The arrival of a long caterpillar of waggons helped the men

look and feel like soldiers. The waggons contained clothing and equipment. Each man was issued with boots, a woollen hat and a grey coat with long sleeves, a narrow collar and a single line of white ribbons down each front edge, a cheaper option than buttons. They put them on over their existing clothes, as extra layers against the cold.

The size of the coats varied but the average was a bit larger than many of the scrawny conscripts. Some men had sour faces and looked like small rats in big sacks; others resembled stiff dolls bursting out of shrunken clothes. It took over an hour for the larger men and the larger coats to come together and for the smaller men to find better-fitting ones. A similar scene followed the issuing of the pull-up boots. These were left in a pile on the ground and each man rummaged through it until he found two of a size similar to his feet. There was no distinction between left and right foot.

Chapter 8

Early April 1644

Three hours they marched, battling into the teeth of a westerly gale, surrounded by wind that snatched up their noise and left them approaching their enemy in a deafness filled with roaring. They halted on the slope of a low ridge, huddled together, heads bent into the wind, shoulders hunched against its force.

Tom watched as riders galloped up to the commanders, reporting and gesticulating even before they'd dismounted. It took only a few minutes for the officers to fan out from the knot of commanders and to summon their sergeants, and still less time for the sergeants to stride along the column of musketeers and pikemen and begin the manoeuvre to get everyone off the hill and onto a wedge of low-lying land between two northern hills, with a small river wriggling around a large manor house. The wind eased. It had failed to whisk away the mist that clung to the river and the intersecting streams below them. Tom looked down on a grey land, wreathed in white, with the roofs and chimneys of the building jutting upwards through the river's sweat, as though gasping for air.

Pikemen stood in a dense block in the middle of the line, with musketeers on each side.

'Stand fast, men,' shouted Sergeant Smith into the wind.

The men stood and watched a small group of horsemen descend the ridge and squelch across a misty field to a highway cutting through the landscape from east to west. The scouts turned right and cantered along the road westwards, towards the house, into the mist. After a few minutes one rider reappeared out of the fog and waved his plumed hat in the air. The group had secured the bridge over the river.

The regiment surged down to the road. The stretched-out column of men broke into three separate pieces as each musketeer company and the pikemen performed their own manoeuvres to prepare to march downhill. Tom's company was behind the pikes and the trudge across the field was slow-going after over three hundred men had already taken that route, but they made it to the narrow, potholed road and hurried to catch up their comrades.

The regiment drew up in front of a ten-foot high stone wall with a fine-wrought iron gate, weaving a pattern between two miniature tower gateposts. As Tom formed up, facing the wall, Colonel Fezzard's emissary rode up to the gate and demanded the surrender of the house and lands of Athelhampton.

'First section, about turn,' ordered Sergeant Smith, and Tom realised he was meant to march out of the formation.

'You men. Follow me.' The sergeant strode further down the road, followed by Tom and his companions.

They marched west, to a bridge over the River Piddle, then further on, through a muddy dip and along a gentle curve to a smaller stone bridge spanning another stream. The parapet was two-foot high, enough to stop a cart wobbling over the edge but easy enough for a man to jump clear, if a cart trundled across too quickly. On the far side of the bridge, as Tom peered across it, the road seemed just as poor. The track twisted to the left and hid behind a clump of scrubby trees after a hundred yards, but the mist and poor light prevented anything more being seen.

'The colonel doesn't want you getting in harm's way today, so your job is simple. Stay here, and if the enemy tries to get across the bridge, stall them, tell us, and fall back to the regiment.'

Simple rules that even a ploughboy should be able to follow, Tom thought. Sergeant Smith also must have thought them sufficient, as he said nothing more but stalked off towards the interesting part of the day. But the command left many things unsure.

'So, who's in charge?' whispered Effra.

Tom looked around at the faces in front of him.

Effra was the obvious choice, though he was distracted and edgy. Ifor had already put his snapsack on the corner of the bridge wall and sat watching his comrades while filling his narrow pipe. He always dealt with things in an unhurried way, but he was no leader. Samuel and Gideon were arguing as usual. Samuel's braying, sardonic laugh hung in the air along with the mist, and his brother's frustration bellowed out. Those two never let others into their private world.

Tom shrugged. 'We could take it in turns to be corporal?'

'That's settled then,' said Effra, slumping onto the bridge parapet with Ifor. 'You be corporal this year, Tom, and we'll see who's still alive after Christmas and decide who's next.'

The other men grunted appreciation and Tom looked

round, trying to think of a retort. Nothing came to mind, so he shrugged and stood in the centre of the small group.

'If that's what you want, fine. But if I'm corporal, that means what I say goes. And my first order is for you, Samuel and Gideon, to go over the bridge and stand at the bend in the road. This mist will lift soon and you'll be able to see what's coming easier from there. As soon as you see someone approaching, tell us. I'll come over to see for myself. The rest of us need to work out our positions in case we get a visit from the enemy. Ifor, you stay here. Effra, you come with me; let's look up and down this side of the river so we know the lie of the land.'

It sounded reasonable. It didn't seem too irksome and no one objected to the orders. Samuel and Gideon just looked at each other, then ambled over the bridge. Ifor carried on trying to get his pipe to light.

'Hey, Samuel,' called Ifor. 'It's your turn to tell a story. We've no warm fire to sit by, but why should that stop us?'

'I'll give you a song, shall I? My voice won't carry to you unless I raise it. How's this?'

Samuel was standing near the bend in the road, on the far side of the bridge. His baritone voice easily muscled its way through the mist to his comrades, while Gideon stood near, one eye on the highway ahead.

'When I survey the world around
The wondrous things that do abound
The ships that on the sea do swim,
To keep out foes that none come in,
Well, let them say what they can,
'Twas for one end the use of man,
I wish him joy where'er he dwell,

That first found out the leather bottle.'

Tom realised he was smiling as he looked at Effra. Effra scowled back.

'What's wrong?' asked the new, unofficial corporal.

'Nothing.'

'That's the angriest nothing I've ever seen.' Tom said.

Effra stepped close to Tom and whispered, 'I can't stay here much longer. I must be gone. Soon.'

'Effra, you can't just wander off in the middle of a war?'

'That news you read to us about the battle at Cheriton...'

'Good news for us, and Cheriton's only forty miles away, so they say,' Tom butted in.

'Good news for Parliament, but it'll bring war this way. It's made me think. It's time I headed back.'

'Your Lord Stretford?'

Effra face softened. 'Earl Stamford. No. Bigger issues rest on this, lad.'

'But what about the colonel?' Tom's lips felt suddenly dry, and he licked them repeatedly while shifting the weight of his musket in his arms. He strode over to Ifor, then looked over his shoulders to where Samuel was still singing. He stepped close to Effra. 'What will I do if you disappear?'

'There's no easy way to say this, lad.'

'You can't, Effra. You mustn't.' Tom's voice was rising, and he heard the note of panic in it.

Effra ushered Tom to the opposite side of the bridge from their comrades. 'You're a good man, Tom.'

'Don't butter me.' Tom snatched his elbow from Effra's grasp.

Both men looked across at Ifor. He wasn't taking notice of their talk, but Tom kept his voice low. 'Why do you want to clear off? I don't understand.'

'You're not meant to understand me, boy,' Effra growled. 'Stop thinkin' I'm your mother.'

'So. You're going back to wrestling and thieving? Is that better than what we're doing now?'

'I'm trying to tell you that bein' in this army is wearin' me too thin. That's all. There's stuff I should be doing elsewhere, things are closing in on my and I'm bloody sure I'm going, before I get my head blown off.'

'But… you can't leave without me, Effra. I don't think I'd survive.'

'You're tougher than you think, Tom. Don't forget it.' Effra guided his friend onto the road back to Athelhampton.

'Well…' Tom's mind was spinning. 'Tell me before you go. I'll come, too. We can slip away to Poole and, and…'

'And nothing, boy. Have you still not scraped that place off your boots?' He put his face close to Tom's. 'They've wiped you off their arse.'

'So, where are you going?' retorted Tom. 'Or will you keep running further from London and your tame duke?' He pushed the older man away and scanned the bridge. 'Well, we've avoided getting blown up today. And that's down to your other, unofficial skills, Effra.'

'Aye. It must mean the colonel has another of his "little jobs" for us. So, let's be thankful for that. But I have to tell you, Tom, I'm looking for a way out. And I'll be going alone.'

The mist dissolved over the next hour, and then they heard shouting and the crackle of muskets. After another hour, they thought they could pick out a slight brightening of the sky toward Athelhampton House.

By midday, they knew they were watching it burn down.

Effra and Tom stood in the main hall of Athelhampton House, looking at the damaged oak panels on the wall, with Tom willing the heat from the fire behind Captain Green to reach him. But the large walnut-topped table and the captain's broad back in front of the hearth blocked it. He eyed the satchel on the table. Not much of the rest of the house remained.

The room was cold, despite the fire and many candles. Tom could see the effects of heat and burning on the walls, the furniture, the ceiling. The smell of the charred timbers was still strong. Tom looked at a scorch mark on the wall behind Captain Green and felt that blaze from five years ago.

Heat, smoke, confusion. 'Mother, are you there?' Tom's eyes stream as he peers into the storeroom. No movement. Where is everyone? Try the main room. Maybe she's there. The memory skips, lightning speed, to the courtyard. Tom watches neighbours pull down the thatch with hooks on long poles and throw buckets of seawater over the walls of the bakery as the whole building writhes and shrivels in the fire. Father emerges from the smoke carrying a limp figure. Mother. Maria hurries to help and they carry her into Jed Barker's house. Another skip, and Tom peeks into the room. Mother lies on a mattress. 'Thank God we found her. She was in the storeroom, by the sacks of grain.' Tom stares ahead, 'In the storeroom?'

'We have another job for you, wrestler,' the captain said.

Effra said nothing. Tom anchored his mind back in the present.

'There's some tidying up for you to do before we leave Athelhampton, and Sir Lewis needs it done quick and sharp. This satchel holds everything you need.' The officer reached out and tossed the bag to Effra.

He looked inside. 'Parchment, candle and a packet. What's this?'

'That's your orders, soldier.'

The captain smiled coldly. 'You must break into Dorchester and go to the northern part, to the house of a Mister John Churchill, to his strong-room and to a strong-box behind the fireplace. You must on no account be seen or caught. Do you understand?'

'But Dorchester's held by Royalists,' Tom said.

'Retrieve some documents, leave that packet in their place, and then rejoin the regiment. We're moving to Upwey, south of Dorchester, in the morning, and so we expect you to meet us there. Take who you want, within reason. And Bayly...' The captain pointed an unloaded pistol at Effra's face. 'Don't get any funny ideas. If you don't come back, it won't take long to catch up with you. You wouldn't want anyone in London to know you're here, would you?'

Effra and Tom were dismissed and left the ruined house.

'What did he mean about reporting you to London?' Tom frowned as he looked at the contents of the bag.

'We've got to get moving straight away.' Effra walked with a tension that Tom could feel. He was crouching slightly, as though expecting someone to jump out on him every step of the way. 'This is going to use up a year's worth of luck,' the fighter said. 'That, and more.'

'You haven't answered me,' Tom insisted.

'We'll take Ifor, Sam and Gideon. We can trust them. More men means more risk as well as more might.' Effra puzzled out the details and Tom watched, a twisting, burning unease in his chest.

They picked their way through the cluttered grounds back to their campfire.

'Check the parchment. That's where Fezzard's secret lies,' Effra said.

The two men moved further away from some soldiers and sat behind the massive bole of an oak tree to look at the rolled-up scroll. They used a tinderbox to strike a spark to light the candle so Tom could read.

'I'm not doing any more till you explain what's going on. The officers know something about you, and that is putting all of us in harm's way.'

'All right,' began Effra. 'They know I'm hiding from some very nasty gentlemen who want me dead.'

'The Duke of Stamford?'

'No, the earl always treated me well and he never knew me except as a wrestler. But there's others that won't stop till our fighting order has been ground to dust. All of us that remain are being hunted.'

Tom sat, absorbing this information. 'If that's true, you're not safe anywhere near the regiment.'

'You're right, but nor am I safe out in this roiling mess of a country. With so many military patrols it's tricky keeping out of sight.' Effra straightened his back and shoulders. 'Seems now's a good time to test their threat.'

'I'll come with you,' blurted Tom.

'I've told you, I'm going alone. You baulk at the danger here? I'm heading into deeper waters, Tom. We're both better off apart, I reckon.'

'My life here exists because you've helped me. I know I'm still a novice at this killing game, but I can come with you and watch your back.'

83

Effra reached over and gripped Tom's shoulders. 'I tell you what. I won't run before we do this jaunt, and I'll give you warning. I can't do more than that, lad. Now then, tell me what we are about tonight.'

Tom looked into the satchel and drew out a paper with instructions identifying a house in Dorchester. It explained how to find a room hidden behind a fireplace and described a batch of papers to be 'retrieved' from the room.

'What do you make of it all, Tom?'

'Just that our job is to liberate information that helps Sir Lewis. But they've given us no idea what that information is. Then there's a further instruction to place this packet of papers inside the safe.'

Effra nodded. 'Right. That's clear then. Clear as my mum's stew, but why give us written instructions? They know I can't read.'

Tom smiled. 'They know I can.'

At the fire, Ifor sat beside a rack of plucked and gutted partridges. Samuel and Gideon were arguing over some coins they'd scavenged during the afternoon, but they all gathered around Tom and Effra when they appeared.

'Finish the grub. There's work to do tonight. And I need you three to help Tom and me.' Effra, as usual, took command of this expedition for the colonel. Tom was still trying to puzzle out the what and the why of their task.

'So, what's brewing, man?' said Ifor to Effra.

'We need a team to carry out a particular job for Sir Lewis.'

'So this time we go together?' asked the Welshman.

'But what's in it for us?' said Samuel, craning forwards.

'We're going to Dorchester. We have a package to collect. It won't take long, but it could get tricky if we run into any

Royalists.'

'Ha. You expect we might *not* run into them?' Gideon challenged.

'We have a secret weapon, boys,' said Tom. 'Don't forget that. Effra has spent a lifetime doing things like this. He'll see we're all right.' He looked across to Effra.

'And we don't have much of a bargaining position,' added Effra. 'We're not promised a reward or anything like that. We're soldiers and what we've learned is that we're not safe anywhere there's an army. In fact, I reckon we're safer out on our own than herded together with the knuckleheads we've got round here.'

'Good point, Effra,' said Samuel.

Ifor disagreed. 'What we know is usually safer than what we don't know. These be risky times and we're safer in a big group like the regiment than drifting about on our own.'

'Well, Tom and me ain't got a choice, but you can stay here, if you want a boring night.' Effra looked intently at each of his comrades.

'When do we leave?' they all said.

'We're off as soon as we can finish the food and check our equipment,' said Tom.

'But the birds ain't done,' called Samuel.

'Well, bring them anyway. We may need them later,' Tom replied.

In ten minutes the five men were striding through the camp. Hailing the guard, Tom explained they were on an errand for Captain Green.

'Not so fast, Tyler.' A voice came back from the opposite side of the guards' fire. A stocky figure stepped forward from the gloom. It was Sergeant Smith. 'I'm coming with you.'

Tom's heart sank, but he kept his voice light. 'We'd be pleased to have you, Sergeant. But we've got a lot of ground to cover tonight and, begging your pardon, I doubt you'll be able to keep up.'

'Damn your insolent mouth. I didn't ask your permission. I told you how it's going to be. I can keep up with you lot. You forget I was marching round Europe before you were thought of. And, for a start, you can leave your muskets and grey coats here. You won't need them tonight.' He threw an old tunic to each man to wear as a replacement.

Effra patted Tom's shoulder and whispered, 'Don't worry. We'll give him the slip later.'

That small word 'we' sounded agonisingly comforting to Tom.

Chapter 9

The night was dark and icy, with just enough starlight to show them the way, though not enough cloud to warm the air. They met no one on the track leading out of Athelhampton, back over the bridge they had guarded. The ground rose and fell as they crested small hills and passed over barren heathland. The darkness got thicker when the lane cut into a hill and bank and a hedgerow towered above them.

After an hour the track met a larger track that disappeared to west and northeast: the main road between Blandford and Dorchester. They took the road to the west; they were only a few miles from the town now. They'd met no one, but the closer they got to Dorchester the greater the risk of meeting Royalist soldiers.

After another half mile, they heard jangling ahead. Quickly they scurried up a steep bank and through a hedge. Crouching down, they waited for the source of the noise to pass. Tom guessed ten or twelve men passed by, then more. The rattling and their speed and bulk indicated they were foot soldiers. Maybe there were twenty or thirty of them. They waited a full minute more, then the Parliament men climbed back down onto the road, only to be sent scurrying back by more noises ahead. This time a group of horsemen trotted

87

past.

Looking across the field where they crouched, Tom could see faint twinkles in the darkness towards the west.

'That must be Dorchester,' whispered Sergeant Smith into his ear. 'Let's head straight for it. We can't keep dodging patrols on the road.'

They skirted two wide, dark fields before approaching the town over a low, open hill. As they descended its far side the ground got boggy. Soon they reached a small river, blocking further forward movement. They crouched down to assess their next move.

'Well, we either wade across or find a bridge,' Tom whispered. 'We could go straight across. The rush of the water will mask our wading.'

'No, I ain't doing that unless it's the only way,' said Effra. 'I ain't tiptoeing through someone's house dripping wet. And we've got to get back, remember.'

'Let's try a bridge first,' said the sergeant. 'We're north of the road. My guess is the closest bridge is to the south, to our left. We'll try that.' He moved decisively through the group and headed south.

Progress was slow, with much peering into the gloom to find the driest route. Later, Gideon, in front, paused and waited for the others to bunch up. Ahead was a bridge. By the light of the moon they saw three guards stamping their feet on the frosted stone road to keep warm.

'What do we do now?' said Tom.

'We wait,' said Effra.

They spread out along the edge of the river, between multi-stemmed alder trees, eyes fixed on the bridge ahead and the highway leading up to Dorchester, which was only a couple of hundred yards away on the other side.

Tom, Effra and Sergeant Smith studied their surroundings together. The nearest squat, defensive walls were silhouetted in the darkness by lights from within the town. The road led from the bridge up to the east gate, where there was another bridge. From there, the wall reached southwards from the gate and turned west after about four hundred yards. To the north of the gate the fortifications were a black smudge, parallel with the river. Between the bridge and the town was a disorderly collection of houses, with the squat outline of a church at the centre. They waited and watched.

'Bayly, have you got the instructions about Mister Churchill's house clear in your head?' the sergeant whispered.

Effra nodded.

'And you, Tyler? Do you remember what the paper said?'

'Yes, Sergeant.'

'Then give me the instructions. We don't want them poxy words getting found by anyone in Dorchester, do we?' The sergeant took the paper from Tom, tore it in pieces, then buried them in the bottom of a puddle.

After half an hour, three men sauntered down the road towards the bridge. There was a bit of chatter between the two groups, then three pairs of boots scrunched back over the cobbles, leaving the fresher men on duty.

Still the sergeant waited, assessing the vigilance of the guards. They were initially alert, but then settled down on the stones of the bridge parapet. To start with, the men spread out along the bridge, calling across to each other. Soon, though, they drew closer together and sat facing away from Effra and Tom.

'Are you ready for this, Tom?' asked Effra. 'You know what we must do?'

Tom swallowed and nodded. He remembered a fight with a comrade in Wareham. It had been a silly tiff, rather than a serious fight. 'Couldn't we just knock them out?' he asked, but he knew the answer.

'Rouse yourself, lad. You can't do this without fire in your belly and fever in your head,' hissed Effra. 'Stoke up your anger. And take your cue from the sergeant and me.' Effra nodded curtly and left Tom to figure out how to rouse himself.

Tom looked down at his upturned hand. It was dull black in the dark, but he felt beads of cold moisture forming in his palm. He clenched his hand tight and thought about Merrick, about losing the bakery. The bullying bailiff. He remembered all the shame and indignities from his life, all the injustices and stupidities, and threw them on a fire in his belly, feeding it and coaxing heat and flame into being. He recalled all those who had ignored or wronged him, and infused their memory with venom. He threw these on the fire, making it flare up. He knew in this land, in this war, he had no place if he couldn't fight for his life and his comrades. Then he pictured Effra and their conversation by the bridge, adding impotent frustration and naked fear to the fire. Finally, Tom added himself to the fire, full of self-loathing that he couldn't do such a simple thing as finding his mother in a storeroom when the bakery was on fire. His resolve was hardening now, and Tom gripped his knife in a sweaty hand. Effra nodded to him to follow.

Effra, Tom and Sergeant Smith slithered towards their target. They paused at each movement of their prey, but it soon became clear their presence wasn't registering with the guards.

They came close to the bridge and the stone structure loomed above them, casting a deep moon shadow like a cloak. But darkness wouldn't cover their movement once they were on it.

'Follow me,' Smith whispered, and he launched himself forward.

The three men marched onto the bridge, as though (hoped Tom) they were returning soldiers from the garrison.

The guards' reaction to this sudden appearance suggested they were expecting comrades and not enemies. The distance was short, and they were sleepy, so they didn't stop the strange men striding up to them, and they didn't see the long knives until it was too late.

Tom roared between gritted teeth, as he engaged a young man with a kind face and trusting eyes. The guard had no time to lift his musket before Tom's body smashed into his and they fell to the ground. Tom's knife was ready. He shut his eyes as he jabbed the blade at the body of the man, who squirmed and lashed out with his arms. But Tom was too close to be hit, with one forearm pinning his opponent's neck. He stabbed quickly, again and again. The tunic resisted the strikes, but the blade soon found its way through to the belly. The guard exhaled and Tom's hand was suddenly slick with blood. He twisted the knife, turned the tip upwards, and thrust and thrust into heart or lung.

'Shush, lad.' Effra's hand was on his shoulder. 'Enough. The man's dead and you're shouting loud enough to bring him back. Shush.'

Tom stood and trembled. His mind was numb. He stood

immobile while the dead guards were stashed under the bridge and the group met up on its far side. He looked at his hands. They trembled, and his tunic and breeches felt wet and sticky. His feet were blocks of ice. Around him, a dark puddle glistened. He pointed at it.

Effra swore. He and Gideon fetched the tunics from the sentries and they all mopped up as much of the blood as they could. The rest would have to seep away through the cobbles and dirt.

They paused to get their breaths and their bearings, then they set out towards a group of houses, round a church and over another short footbridge, before they could approach the town walls. The timber palisade, six feet high, was set in an earth bank from four to twelve feet high. They followed the dark outline, moving left to a corner of the walls. Sergeant Smith stopped and the others caught up.

Gideon peeked round the corner, while Effra assessed the height of the timber palisade. About six feet just there, on a four-foot high mound.

'Hey, Sergeant. There's another gate and another group of guards twenty yards round the wall,' Gideon hissed.

'Forget that. We're going over the top here,' said Smith.

Effra braced himself against the wall and hoisted up Samuel, who planted his feet on the ledge formed at the top of the mound, then reached up, grabbed the palisade top and pulled himself onto its edge, balancing with his stomach. Turning and reaching down, Samuel hauled Tom up and the two of them helped up Gideon, Ifor, Sergeant Smith and Effra.

The activity of grabbing his mates' arms and shoulders helped to settle Tom. He was still shaking from his action at the bridge, but as he jumped down inside the town, he felt better.

They jumped down to ground level to avoid any prying eyes. All except Effra, who moved back to the corner and, crouching on the fire-step, looked around to get his bearings. It seemed the gate guards were the only sentries nearby. Three soldiers were posted outside the gates, while two gate wardens hovered around the gate itself. Effra jumped down and rejoined his comrades. They were crouching behind a shed at the bottom of a garden. It felt as if they were in a vegetable patch rather than inside a defended town.

They loped along a beaten soil track, past mounds of earth and unidentified dark, agricultural shapes to a street, then turned right, heading for the centre of the town.

Mr Churchill's house was in the northern half of the settlement. Near the town centre there was more activity around them. The men slipped back into shadows and corners to avoid attention.

'This is stupid,' said Sergeant Smith. 'Us tiptoeing around is more like to arouse suspicion than if we step right down the middle of the street.'

'That's a good idea,' said Effra.

So they stepped out into the street and sauntered along, stepping over the filth yet to be collected by the night-soil men. They kept their eyes open and, when they reached a main junction, Effra turned to the left without hesitation.

'Halt! Who's there?' Two soldiers stepped out from the shadows to their left.

'At last. Someone with authority.' Sergeant Smith pushed to the front and slapped the first soldier on the shoulder. 'We're looking for a drink, comrade. Can you help us?'

The soldiers looked at each other before the first said, 'What's the password?'

'Well now, young sir. We've only arrived in Dorchester today and we've been sleeping off our journey, so the password is bound to be different now. And besides, no one mentioned it when we came in at the gate.'

'And which gate would that be?' The soldier wasn't being deflected.

'It was the one near the bridge. We've been scouting the land to the east of here. Towards Blandford. But let's not talk of the war. Tell us, friend. Where do poor, thirsty soldiers go for refreshment in Dorchester? It's not one of those towns that's outlawed drinking, is it?'

'And you,' the second soldier said, pointing at Tom. 'Why's tha' breeches sopping wet?'

Gideon answered for his comrade. 'The daft chuff fell in the midden.' He slapped Tom round the ears.

The others laughed and Tom squirmed, just as he would have done if it were true.

The two guards turned away to consider what to do. Sergeant Smith stayed close to them. Tom caught the gist of their conversation.

'Orders are to report any suspicious movements to the captain. You know that,' hissed the first soldier. 'But our guard duty's over. If we take this lot to the castle, we'll have to guard them till everything's checked. We'll be lucky if we get four hours' sleep before tomorrow's duties.'

'And look at us,' the sergeant added. 'We're no Roundheads. All we're looking for is a drink, same as you.'

The first soldier scowled and hesitated before saying, 'You're not tricked out like Colonel Talbot's men, but then neither are half the other soldiers here.'

'Aye. Them uniform coats don't last long. We all look like scarecrows.' Smith laughed.

The soldier laughed too, and nodded to his mate.

'Well, comrades. Seeing as we're looking for the same relaxation let's find it together. Come with us and you can buy us a gallon of scrumpy.' The second soldier winked at Smith and the others.

They waited a moment while the guards reported back to their officer to finish their duty, then returned and led them down a side alley, going south, away from Mr Churchill's house. Soon they were beckoned into an alehouse.

Effra pulled Tom to one side. 'This is where I leave you for a while. Keep them talking, Tom. I'll be back soon and then we'll bugger off fast.'

Tom gave him an intense look.

'Don't worry, lad.'

'You're off, Bayly?' Sergeant Smith butted in. 'Just bring back something that proves where you've been. Got it?'

'Yes, Sergeant,' Effra said, before dodging out of sight.

The soldier ushered them into the makeshift inn and didn't comment that he now had only five new friends.

Tom looked around as he settled onto a wooden trestle bench in a corner of a small room that already contained seven men, all on the short journey from merry-drunk to maudlin-drunk. The two soldiers had relieved Sergeant Smith of three pence and disappeared into another room. Tom whispered to his comrades where Effra had gone. Soon the soldiers reappeared, bearing a flagon and beakers.

'So you lot were asleep this afternoon, were you?' asked the second soldier.

'Why? What happened?' Tom answered carefully.

'There was a right to-do in the town square. One of them Puritan preachers was shouting at everyone.'

'What's so unusual about that? There's hundreds of preachers in Dorset,' piped up Samuel.

'Ah, but this one has a sister, a shrew. As loud and frightful as her brother. They made such a fuss, telling everyone that to make war was against God and that his judgement was coming.'

The other soldiers laughed.

'Aye, they didn't find many converts amongst us. The captain came up and pulled them away from the townsfolk. They nearly started a riot.'

'We enjoyed the townsfolk giving someone else a hard time for a change,' added someone.

'Aye, they're still here, somewhere,' someone else said.

Tom kept an eye on how much cider was being consumed, but all the team knew the stakes and just sipped at the drinks. Time inched past as they listened to one story after another from the surrounding soldiers. They kept fairly quiet and weren't challenged to add to the conversation. Only Sergeant Smith was able to hold his own with the banter. But the soldiers were getting rowdy, and Tom noted the games and challenges were getting more boisterous.

In a lull in the conversation one soldier belched loudly, then announced, 'Well, let's drink a toast to the success of our great venture tomorrow.'

Tom's mind had wandered but he leaned forward to hear the soldier more clearly.

'Good health and a straight aim to the musketeers and the gunners about to blow out the brains of Sir Lewis's regiment.'

A roar of approval met this proclamation. Tom and Sergeant Smith looked at each other.

'Is that what we've been scouting the road for?' Smith spoke softly to the soldier as they clinked glasses. 'The buggers never tell us anything.'

'Aye, it's the same with us,' was the reply. 'But did you notice how empty the town is? That's because every man jack of us is turning out for the ambush.'

Tom and Sergeant Smith gleaned that the ambush of their comrades was to be at Woodsford, some miles down the River Frome from Dorchester. It sounded like a large-scale operation, with men from Prince Maurice's army combining with garrison men from Dorchester and Weymouth to trap the Roundheads between a hill and the river.

Tom declined a challenge to join three soldiers racing to finish a quart of ale, but there were more men in the room now, jostling and shouting. The mood was getting tetchy and elbows felt sharper.

An empty quart tankard slammed onto the table and a man howled, nursing bruised knuckles before launching his good hand into the face of a surprised drinker. In ten seconds the room was a roiling, seething mass of flailing arms and bobbing heads, with men falling on each other and the furniture. Sergeant Smith called his men to him and they fought their way outside.

'Which way now?' called Ifor.

'Over here,' came a call from the opposite side of the street.

As soldiers spilled out of the alehouse, Effra collected his comrades and they headed back to the town wall. 'Job done, lads. Let's get out of here,' Effra called over his shoulder as he placed something in Sergeant Smith's hand and headed down a muddy street.

They paused near the wall to watch the nearby gate.

'Effra! Stop a minute. The Royalists are out to ambush the regiment.' Tom's news broke in on Effra's concentration. He became still for a moment.

'Twists and turns. You never know what's coming, do you?' he mused. 'But what we need now is to get out of the town, and there's nothing for it but to jump back the way we came.'

By the last house before the bridge they could see three relief sentries sauntering down to relieve their comrades. They crouched down in the moon shadow of the house and watched. The fresh guards reached their post and looked about them. They called out to their mates, then stamped their feet while they waited for this anomaly to resolve itself.

No one answered their call.

'Come on,' said the sergeant, and he stepped from the shadows onto the main path to the bridge. The guards watched them approach. Cold sweat erupted on Tom's arms and shoulders as the group strode right up close to the three men.

'What's happening here?' asked the sergeant.

'We, ah... We're not sure. Who are you?' one guard said.

'Don't worry about that now. Where are the sentries you're relieving?' The Sergeant's tone impressed Tom and had the same effect on the guards.

'We don't know, sir. We can't find them.'

'Well, if we see them down the road we'll tell them you're looking for them.' The group passed the guards and headed for the far end of the bridge.

'Right,' the guard replied. 'I guess you're trying to catch up the rest of your regiment before the ambush.'

Tom stopped and turned. 'That's right,' he said. 'How far ahead of us are they?'

A frown crossed the soldier's face. 'What regiment are you with, then?'

Tom didn't want to get into another tussle. 'We're headed for Blandford and I can't say more.'

'Most of the others headed through Fordington, to the south of the river.' The soldier sounded more agitated.

Tom turned to face him more squarely and, at the same time, slipped his right hand behind his back to grasp his long knife, sheathed at the back of his belt. He squeezed the handle to stop the tremors of his fingers rippling up to his shoulder.

He cleared his throat and tried to make his voice sound deep and wise. 'That's as may be, but we've got to think of what comes after the battle, soldier.'

The guard nodded slowly. 'Well, good luck. And, if you see the other guards tell them their balls are going to be roasted when Colonel Talbot catches up with them.'

Tom forced a laugh. 'I wouldn't be in their shoes for all the beer in Dorset,' he replied, then turned to catch up with his comrades, aware that his legs were shaking.

Chapter 10

The moon set, and above the small knot of men hurrying carefully along the track, clouds gathered, blocking starlight. Tall trees, like suspicious black trolls, banished all light beneath them. The group paused by a fork in the road, then turned down the smaller of two tracks, taking them away from the highway and the trees.

'We've got to get back to the regiment, quick as we can,' said the sergeant.

'I take it they aren't headed for Upwey, then?' Tom asked.

'We didn't want you peabrains to know our next target.' The older man shrugged. 'You might've got caught or sold out to the King's men.'

'So where're our lot headed?' asked Ifor.

'The plan is to raid Woodsford Castle. It's a manor house south of Athelhampton, owned by Royalists.' The sergeant's words were low but urgent. 'We heard of a meeting of Royalist sympathisers there, and we wanted to catch them on the hop while helping ourselves to the Strangways family silver. It seems we've been sold a poisoned pullet by our informer.'

'What next, then?' asked Effra.

'We must get to Woodsford before the regiment. Warn

them.'

'But it's nearly dawn now. We'll be travelling in daylight soon,' chipped in Ifor.

'The roads are our most direct route.' The sergeant was thinking aloud and his features were becoming visible in the pre-dawn greyness. Tom was close enough to smell dirty leather and desperation on him.

'That's madness,' hissed Samuel. 'How can we walk through an ambush?'

'Well, we don't have a better plan, so get used to it and stop mewling!' The sergeant stomped off down a lane between two fields.

The others followed, as he set a fast pace along narrow empty lanes. They strode along, and often disturbed foxes or pheasants, badgers or rabbits.

Tom's mind wandered as they stomped through puddles and along the edges of cart ruts. Was this a chance for him to steal back to Poole? Could he, even now, return and set up a bakery in Cinnamon Lane? Was it worth it? He had friends with him, especially Effra. But Effra was likely to disappear sometime soon, and he didn't want to be left facing a battle with only a pair of bitter twins and an old tinker to watch his back. Then he remembered that, as of this night, he was also a killer. A murderer, but in a war. In a righteous cause, surely? Tom wasn't sure where right and wrong lay in this fight. King or Parliament? It just depended which recruiting sergeant got you first.

Effra caught up with Sergeant Smith and called for a rest. The clouds above them were a lighter grey. 'We need to know where we are,' he said.

'Well, it's clear where the river is.' Ifor nodded to their

right at a ribbon of mist that looked as though the sky had split open and a strip of cloud had dropped to the ground.

They headed straight for it, over grass fields, scattering sheep in all directions. The mist silently embraced them and gave Tom a feeling of protection from prying eyes while also robbing him of his vision. Sounds reached them in their isolation; sheep or birds, and flowing water, but there was no sense of distance. The edge of the river swamped the banks, so following the edge was clear yet wet and boggy. Dawn was growing now, but the mist hung on.

They turned left and followed the watercourse eastwards for a while. Then Tom heard banging and shouting from the opposite bank. The group stopped among trees near a road heading over the river directly towards the noise. They each feared the loss of the mist but needed it to lift to see what was going on.

'Can you see anything over there, Tom?'

'Give me a minute, Sergeant. I can see something. This mist is swirling, but... Aah, I see them now.'

A gap in the mist opened and a throng of soldiers appeared, fussing around a dozen light barges. Two were already on the water and the rest were being readied for use.

'We must be getting close' said Effra. He and Tom were peering across the river, through a flush of early alder leaves. The soldiers on the other side showed no sign that they knew they were being watched.

Smith kept them moving, 'We don't know how far away our lads are. Come on.'

Samuel called back to the sergeant, 'Nor do we know how many enemy stand in our way, or where they are.'

The road was empty. The mist closed around them again,

and they reached the far side and descended to the stream edge.

'We must stay ahead of those boats. They'd easy spot us if they get close.' The sergeant was wheezing but setting a fast pace along the sheep track by the river.

On they went, stumbling at sudden swampy dips and struggling through scattered willow clumps. The dark grey mist showed a silvery edge that gradually flared to yellow. The riverbank veered to their right, and they followed it towards the light. Distant shouting reached their ears. They shambled on, then two loud bangs shook the air. Tom looked up as the mist shredded and melted away. They stood beside a clump of tall, sinuous willows, some stems leaning into the river and some over the field. The leaves were bursting from pale buds on buff twigs, and there were enough shoots near the ground to provide some cover.

The comrades stood and looked across a junction where their river met a larger one and turned east. Beyond the river, some ten yards wide, was a meadow, then a crescent of low hills and, between these and the river, a large, oblong, grey building by a road that ran parallel to the watercourse. They could pick out men in grey tunics marching towards the building. and then they saw more soldiers, in orange coats, standing by the building, barring passage.

On the centre of the crescent hill a detachment was hurrying around the steep scarp towards the building.

'That must be Woodsford Castle,' the sergeant said.

'That's our men outflanking the castle, then?' said Gideon.

'Not really a castle, just a gentleman's house,' said Samuel.

'But we're outnumbered. And attacking? We need something more to drive out those defenders,' said the sergeant.

'And they've got cannons,' added Ifor.

'Come on,' said Tom. 'Let's find a way across the river. We can help.'

Sergeant Smith grabbed his arm and pulled him back. 'Don't be hasty, Tom. We're too far away.' He sounded tired. 'The most we can do is watch, and pray there aren't any more Royalists hidden in the castle.'

'What's that?' Samuel pointed at the hill.

The detachment had stopped moving towards the castle and faced about. Behind them could be seen other men. The detachment saw them as enemy by their reaction. A hundred or so soldiers rapidly turned sideways, and the sharp report of their volley was seconded by a line of white puffs that clung to them.

The volley didn't seem to have stopped the enemy, and suddenly the detachment swelled and broke into random groups as Royalists crashed into them. Tom couldn't see where all these had come from, but the effect was catastrophic on the Parliamentarians. They were pushed helter-skelter towards the sharp hill edge.

One after another, men tumbled down the scarp. The first to go had slipped or been pushed, but quickly others saw what happened and followed their comrades. More and more men dropped off the hilltop. Their adversaries stopped at the edge.

Near the river, the chief part of the Roundhead regiment approached the castle. The cannons boomed again. The soldiers marched faster as they got nearer the defenders and their peril grew.

Effra looked to the rear of the regiment, where a road curved round the slope of a smaller hill onto level ground by the river. A column of cavalry trotted into view.

'If that lot are Royalists, we're mincemeat.'

Tom noticed tiny beads of sweat forming on Effra's forehead, and there was a strange intensity in his gaze.

It didn't take long to recognise that the horsemen were aiming their steeds at the Parliamentarians. Maybe the Roundheads sensed the cavalry. Certainly their speed increased, and they threw themselves at the men defending the castle. A volley from the Royalists staggered the regiment, but it recovered its momentum and fell on its enemies. Tom could tell that the fighting was savage. Individual conflicts were difficult to make out, but the heaving mass of soldiers told of the desperate struggle.

The issue was finely poised for some time, then the Roundheads drew back in disorder.

'Look behind you, look behind you,' Samuel was hopping from foot to foot and shouting.

But the men of his regiment responded sluggishly to their danger. Perhaps they heard the thundering hooves, or they may have felt the shudder of the ground beneath. Suddenly the awful truth stung them into action. But reactions varied. Knots of men crowded together, and Tom could see pikemen forming squares, with musketeers pressing up against their bodies to give greater weight to the pikes that were now facing the danger. But not enough men still carried their pikes following the attack. Most pikemen and many musketeers had scattered before the horsemen arrived, heading for the hills and the river, and some even ran back towards the cannons and the enemy infantry.

The enemy infantry held their ground and seemed content to watch the cavalry at play. The fifty or so horsemen gained momentum as they approached the Roundheads, crashing into the foot soldiers, scattering them like beads, leaving the occasional knot of prickly pikes. Most of the horses swerved around these hedgehogs and chased the men running away. Some charged straight at the pikes and, unable to manoeuvre because of their fellows, impaled horse or rider on the sixteen-foot poles. The pikes staggered back, but mostly held firm. The cavalry quickly sought easier prey. There was no musket play to harry the horsemen. The musketeers hidden among the pikemen had presumably not had time to reload after the attack.

From the hill, the remnants of the detachment met those fleeing the cavalry. Comrades running from the enemy on the ridge bumped into those escaping the Royalists near the river, all heading from one danger into a worse one. Utter chaos.

The Royalists were disciplined, Tom noted. The men on the hill pushed their enemy down the slope and the soldiers by the castle pressed forward, collecting prisoners and squeezing resistance from their opponents. All the while, the cavalry milled around, hacking at heads and bodies with swords that had been sharp only an hour ago, but were now blunt, chipped and blood-soaked.

There was no longer a regiment for Tom and his comrades to rejoin. What was left of the proud Roundhead formation was being pushed towards the river. Some men had reached the river and were looking to throw themselves in. But now barges and rafts arrived to shut this escape route. The comrades crouched down, watching the annihilation in disbelief. How could it be? Why hadn't the officers recognised it was an ambush? And what were they to do next?

For perhaps two more minutes they watched, mute, open-mouthed, gaze hollow.

Then Sergeant Smith broke the spell. 'Come on, lads. We can't stay here. They'll sweep both riverbanks to catch runners, and we need to be long gone.'

He tracked back the way they'd come. The others followed, crouching and dodging, chasing the mist to use its protection as its remaining shreds evaporated before them. Tom's skin prickled as he rushed.

Once round a bend they felt able to ease the pace. Tom's empty belly growled as hunger and fear sapped his strength. The day was well underway now, and he'd only eaten a pie at the inn since the midday before. He stumbled, feeling giddy. Samuel and Ifor looked similarly distant as they kept pace, but Smith, Effra and Gideon hiked with purpose. Effra seemed more composed now they were moving away from the battle. As they rounded the next bend, they heard voices and immediately dropped behind some tall reeds.

Gideon crept forward, and the others nursed hunger, tiredness and jangling nerves for ten minutes until he returned.

'There's one of those rafts up ahead. It's run aground. Looks like there's some casualties and everyone's running round shouting at each other.'

'How many?' demanded Smith.

'Nine upright, three lying on the bank and four in the boat.'

'Can we get at all of them?' asked Effra.

'Or tiptoe round them?' Ifor raised his eyebrows wearily.

Sergeant Smith removed his hat, bowed his head and smoothed what was left of his hair with a greasy hand. 'There are no easy roads. We need to go through these men. And then take their boat upstream past their reserves.' He looked up and smiled his wickedest smile.

Samuel giggled nervously. 'How many more times do we have to do this?'

'As many as it takes,' the sergeant replied.

Chapter 11

Effra, Tom and Smith circled into the field and crawled on elbows and knees to within twenty yards of the boat. They watched and listened. Through snatches of argument, they heard there'd been an accident and their officer had been injured by a pistol discharge. The corporal and the officer's servant had argued about what to do next, and the barge then capsized or crashed into the bank.

Corporal and servant continued their frank exchange of views at the riverside. Each man stood his ground and hissed in growing volume at the other. The soldiers either watched this performance or distanced themselves from the whole fiasco.

Sergeant Smith watched, then he looked at Tom and Effra. 'Come on.'

The three men jumped up and ran at the boat shouting.

Ifor, Sam and Gideon heard the shout and saw their comrades charge. They moved into position.

There were no musket shots before Tom and Smith hit the corporal and servant. Neither had time to defend themselves, and they collapsed beneath a cut and thrust of their assailants' short swords.

Effra raced past and engaged two men at the edge of the

bank. They were unarmed but alert now, and backed off from Effra's sword slashes.

Then Gideon and the others slew two guards. Their muskets were aimed at Effra and Tom, but there was no lighted match to fire the guns. Facing the wrong way, they didn't see the attack from behind.

Smith and Tom joined Effra, facing four. Two of the injured men leapt up and joined the last guard facing Gideon's team, while the third injured man bolted into the field.

On the boat two soldiers reached for the oars while another clumsily tried to get past the injured one to pull up the painter.

Slash, thrust, punch. The defenders were dripping wet and the riverbank was slick and bloody. Desperation energised men suddenly fighting for their lives. After the first shout there was no noise, except grunts or yowls of pain.

The attackers had the advantage of weapons and more stable footing. Two defenders slipped, then slid away from the fight. One soldier gripped Smith and they tumbled together down the bank.

A tough-looking man wielded a musket like a club and kept Tom at bay. Effra spotted the barge pulling out into the current. He ran down to the water's edge. The men in the boat were pulling at the oars, but the soldier in the bow couldn't free it from the spike which held them at the river's edge. Effra threw his sword at him. He flinched and overbalanced. The barge swayed out into the river, then swung towards the bank as Effra slipped under the water.

The musket clubber lost his footing and Tom barrelled down the bank to stab the man in his left side. He collapsed into the water, then slithered out, clutching his wound. Tom grabbed the boat-rope to bring the vessel back to the shore. The oarsmen crowded forward, but Gideon and Samuel appeared beside him. They, too, wielded muskets as clubs.

Tom could see the fight go out of the boatmen even as they rushed forwards. The odds were against them now. The boat grounded on the bank, causing him to jump sideways to avoid it. Then it pitched violently and all three boatmen cascaded to their left and bounced off the gunwale into the river.

Effra released the side of the barge and grabbed a throat. He held on, teeth clenched and mouth a determined slit, while the other two men, floundering for their feet, shouted their surrender. He held tight as the struggles of the drowning man subsided. Then he looked up. Tom, Samuel and Gideon had done their part.

It was all over in minutes. Manic activity and violence made every moment take an age to live through and used up severe reserves of energy, from men who were already tired and hungry.

Tom's world spun as he struggled up the bank. 'Are we all here? Where's the sergeant?'

Gideon and Samuel were wading out of the water and unable to answer, but Ifor's voice cut through the swash.

'Over here! The sergeant's hurt.'

Tom eased a jacket beneath the sergeant's head as he lay in the boat's bow. The older man groaned and tensed his body but didn't open his eyes. Tom glanced down at the wound, a sword thrust beneath the ribs. Blood was leaking through the cloths wrapped around it, and the man's face was pale. The wispy grey hairs on his head faded into the grey cast of his pate.

Looking around, Tom took in the sodden timber boards of the longboat. They only had four oars for the eight rowlocks. There was now no equipment in the boat. All the kit and supplies had been lost, except a taffeta standard that was muddied and wet, and a pikeman's helmet that Gideon picked up from the ground.

'I'm good enough for a pikeman. I'll have this,' he said.

There were four Royalist bodies laid out on the riverbank, and most of their remaining comrades were wounded. Some, it seemed, had run off. Tom caught an inquisitive glance from Effra.

'He's got a deep wound. We daren't move him. We must use the boat.' Tom said.

Effra looked up and down the river. 'Right. There's only one way we can go; upriver, and hope to get the sergeant to a healer.'

'Right.' Tom nodded, then spoke to Ifor. 'Help me see to the sergeant while Effra steers. Samuel and Gideon, you take the oars.'

'What about them?' Gideon nodded towards the wounded Royalists.

Tom looked around. Leaving an enemy behind could put them in danger, but he couldn't stomach any more killing. 'We're miles from anywhere. They can't easily give us away. They're wounded so they can't move fast. That gives us time to get away.'

Gideon looked at Effra, who strode over to Tom and put

his hand on his shoulder. 'There's enough killing gone on already. It's a risk, leaving them here, but I'll have no part in killing men what've already surrendered.'

Tom gulped. His mouth and throat were dry. He closed his eyes and summoned spittle to moisten them. After a moment, he was able to order the men to load everything into the boat. That they were already doing this wasn't the point. They were acting under his authority now.

Effra walked over to a clump of willows. He called Tom over. 'We ain't finished here yet, lad. We need to know what we'll find upstream, and the only ones what know it are those Royalists. You and I must speak to them to find out what they know.'

'How?' Tom asked. 'We daren't stay here much longer.'

Effra looked over at the Royalists. The officer wasn't badly injured. He was a young man with long fair hair and narrow shoulders. The others weren't doing any voluntary moving any time soon. 'We must separate him from the men. We don't want them talking together and possibly giving us a false story that'll send us to their fellows.' Effra strolled over to the officer and invited him to join him and Tom among the willows.

The man looked suspicious, but he came, hoisting himself up while clutching an injured shoulder.

Among the trees, dappled light shone through the fresh, silvery leaves and played on the wet clothes of the men.

Effra began the interrogation. 'We need information, sir. And we need to borrow your boat.'

'I don't parley with rebels,' was the reply. 'And it seems to me you've taken the boat without a by-your-leave anyway. You'll get no information from me.'

113

Effra's face hardened, but before he could respond Tom spoke. 'We understand your situation, friend.'

'You're no friend of mine.'

'I sympathise with your predicament. How did you come by your injury?'

'Those God-damned idiots hit a log just as I was loading my pistol. It fell onto the deck, discharged and the ball hit my shoulder. We were heading downstream to...' Here the officer trailed off and his eyes flicked between his two interrogators.

'We know what's happened downstream,' said Effra. 'What we now need from you, sir, is some idea of what we face if we row back upstream. What can you tell us? What regiment are you with? Who is your commander and where are you based?'

The officer's face showed distaste for the conversation.

Effra added some pressure. 'It seems to me, my lad, that your day hasn't got off to a good start. But when all is said and done, I always think it's more important how things finish. Now, I can see you're in pain. Do you want a quick route to making it stop?' Effra paused as the ambiguity of the statement sank into Tom and the officer.

'I'm ready to die for my king, rebel.'

'What my friend means is that your day can improve from here, but only if you tell us truthfully what you know,' Tom said. 'It seems a very low value you put on your life, to throw it away for a few paltry comments. We don't want your death. We just need to know something of the road ahead.'

The officer considered this.

In a few minutes of conversation, Tom and Effra had all they needed. They checked by questioning the other

Royalists, but met the typical surly attitude of labourers.

'They're ignorant oxen, the lot of 'em. And the officer's information's not trustworthy,' said Samuel. 'They'd sooner lie than help us.'

'You're right, and we can't rely on it, but we can test it as we go.'

'And we saw the launching place as we passed it earlier,' said Ifor.

Tom nodded. 'What we've been told about pickets on the river at least keeps us aware that we're likely to come across them somewhere.' He shrugged. 'It's not much, but its something.'

It didn't take long for the rebels to be ready for the boat-trip upstream. They loaded the standard, the pikeman's helmet, four bandoliers and four muskets into the boat, then waved goodbye to their enemies and launched out into the centre of the river. As the prow of the boat entered the main current, it swung downstream, and Sam and Gideon's thrashing and paddling did nothing to change that. They flowed with it.

Pulling on the oars, they finally got the boat back to the bank, thirty yards from the Royalists, where the slower current enabled them to point it upstream once again and inch westwards, keeping close to the north bank. They ignored the scornful comments from their enemies and rowed past them with quiet dignity.

It was a big boat in a small river. The water level was high but this, while widening the channel, drowned the banks on either side, which meant the boat either bumped along, scraping over submerged vegetation, or had to be moved away from the water's edge into the main current. Here, the river was deeper, but the current pulled more strongly. With an inexpert crew, progress was slow.

At the next village sentries hailed them. They just waved back and said the day had gone well and the rebel regiment was destroyed. The guards smiled and nodded and asked no more questions.

They came to a bridge, where they were challenged by an officer. Tom explained they'd been sent upstream to find more men to reinforce another attack on the enemy. Would the officer volunteer his squad to add to the strength of the attack?

The officer considered for a moment, then declined, saying his orders were to watch the bridge. Tom commiserated and asked what troops they were likely to meet ahead.

'There's Captain Robert's company a mile or so upstream. I'm sure they'll be pleased to assist.'

'Thank you, sir. That's very helpful. Good day.'

After rounding the next bend, the river widened where a tributary joined it. They ditched the boat on the southwest bank and headed across a meadow towards higher land.

'Well done, lad. That information was timely. We don't want to meet a company of anybody's just now. And that barge depot must be somewhere near here, too.' Effra chuckled as he took his turn carrying the sergeant on his back.

'There's a house over there,' said Ifor. 'We can get a blanket to carry him in, perhaps?'

The low, thatched cottage was deserted. An animal pen, fenced with wattle panels, was to the left and two chickens pecked irritably in front of the ramshackle door. Tom approached the front with Effra, while Samuel and Gideon went round the back and Ifor stayed at the edge of the road with Sergeant Smith. Effra found a pile of stout hazel sticks. Working quickly, he chose the longest and thickest pair as carrying poles, then lashed shorter poles to them to brace the frame, but they could find no blanket or other clothing to use to support the sergeant in the frame. They tried the flag they'd taken from the Royalists, but the material wasn't strong enough. There was nothing for it; Tom and Gideon removed their tunics and these were laced round the poles as a cradle on which Smith could travel.

Effra brought the makeshift stretcher back to Ifor and Smith.

'He's in a bad way,' said Ifor.

'Never mind. We daren't tarry here. Let's go,' said Tom.

'Where can we go that will allow the sergeant to rest, Tom? He needs attention.'

'Ifor's right,' said Gideon. 'We've shelter here and there's no one around. We could rest up awhile before we push on. I'm done in.'

The prospect of rest filled everyone's mind and there was no will to keep moving. They rested in the lee of the hut, beneath an overhanging section of thatch. They huddled together against the fresh April air, taking turns to stand guard.

Tom closed his eyes, but his mind was racing. He was free of the regiment, but the Royalist ambushers were between him and Poole.

'Stay alert, Tom,' Effra whispered. 'We need sharp wits to stay alive.'

The afternoon approached dusk, and the wind freshened as the temperature dropped. Half-rested, but aware of more activity down by the river, they roused themselves and tested out ways to carry the stretcher; on shoulders, at waist height, with Samuel, the tallest, or with Effra, the shortest.

'The sergeant's asking for you two,' Ifor said to Tom and Effra.

They stood over the sergeant. His pallid skin had shrunk on his face and his eyes stood out, brightly urgent. 'Effra. You've got the packet you took from Mister Churchill's house?' They had to lean close to catch his words.

'Aye. I took that before we put you in the boat.'

'Well, give it back. It must get back to the colonel.'

'If it's that important, I'm the best one to have it. You couldn't stop a mouse stealing it, sergeant. I'll give it you when you're stronger.' Effra turned away.

'Which way, Tom?' asked Ifor, as he and Samuel settled the sergeant on the stretcher.

'West. To that hill.' Tom wondered what was in the packet now tucked inside Effra's tunic. 'We can follow the path to the field, then strike straight across and up onto the wooded ridge. We'll rest there.'

They struggled on. The groans of the sergeant faded into the background as they picked their way across broken ground and watched for approaching patrols.

For the last section they were trudging uphill, through early grass and constant mud. Samuel took the rear end of the stretcher, as his height fitted with the shorter Ifor on the slope. By this time the frame was supported on their shoulders, but weariness and a sharp, salty wind was slowing them down. There was no barrier between the field and the wood, just a thick layer of last year's bracken, prickly brambles and other stringy weeds, survivors of the winter. They pushed through this vegetation and the challenge changed from stepping over ploughed farmland to crossing soft woodland soil, crisscrossed with a cat's cradle of small woody stems and fallen branches. Large trees swayed in the stiffening breeze and between them younger trees grew skywards, aiming to be as big as their mothers. Hazel and hawthorn grew at the edge; oak and ash formed the main wood.

'Keep going, lads. We'll rest at the top. I want to see what's on this hill before we go to ground.' Tom spoke in snatched breaths, while pushing himself forward through the undergrowth. No one argued.

Before the crest of the ridge, the wood stopped. The trees seemed hesitant to grow closer to the wind and the sea, trunks and branches crouching lower behind the hill top and leaving a grassy area just before the ridge. The other side of the hill couldn't be seen, but Tom and Effra walked onto the ridge and saw more grass sloping gently down towards the south.

'Not such a bleeding fortress as we'd hoped.' Effra gazed around.

'The wood is safe so long as no one knows we're here. But if they did it'd be a trap and we'd be easily swept up by any patrol that knows its business.' Tom turned and noticed the others waving for them to return.

At the edge of the trees, below the ridge, they were shielded from the wind but could still hear it shaking branches above them. Samuel, Gideon and Ifor stood looking down at the sergeant.

'He's dead,' said Gideon. 'We carry him all this way and the bugger dies on us.'

Tom trudged over to the sergeant.

119

'What d'you expect?' said Samuel. 'He never did us a favour when he was alive. Why would that change when he dies?'

Smith had gone, leaving behind flesh and bones in the shape of a man. The body was still and shrunken, no longer energised from within. The last dead face Tom had looked into was that of his father. He placed his hand on the sergeant's shoulder.

'He was a hard man all right,' added Ifor. 'But no harsher than the other sergeants.'

'Well, that's the funeral preach over then,' Effra said. 'Let's get him buried and we can toast him at the next inn.'

'Bury him? How'd we do that? No, our sergeant will have to wait here to be plucked apart by the crows.' Gideon spoke truth, but it brought no comfort, just a sense of desolation.

No one spoke for a while, each man rummaging through his own thoughts – some of the sergeant, some of the exertions of the day and some about the unknown future.

'Well…' Effra broke the troubled silence, speaking over the windblown trees. 'We can't do much else today. We'll have to stay here overnight. And that means sentries.'

Everyone groaned, but again there was no alternative. At that moment they heard a further groan, from the edge of the wood. Tom heard it first; a moaning, an indistinct noise that could be speech but that sounded eerie and disembodied, on a windswept hill in a late winter dusk beside a dead man.

'Is that the sergeant haunting us?' said Samuel.

'Aye, what else could it be? There's no one else within miles of us,' Gideon retorted.

'Well, we'd best investigate. I'll go and see what it is. Maybe it's a calf we could cook?' Tom said.

'We've not eaten since yesterday, but is it wise to have a

fire tonight?' Ifor grimaced.

'I don't care,' said Gideon. 'If it's meat, let's kill it and eat. A fire won't be seen in this hollow.'

'We can't cook a ghost, especially if it's Sergeant Smith,' Effra said.

'Just watch my back. I'm going over to check it out.' Tom's voice was strained.

He approached the edge of the wood, from where the noise continued to emanate. The others stood, spread out in an arc, looking for signs of movement anywhere in the woodland. They all drew their long knives.

Chapter 12

Five live men, and one dead one, on a hill. There were no enemies within five miles, but fear of the unknown gripped the men that breathed. Far from home, alone, anyone can be prey to the dark ambitions of the faerie folk.

As Tom reached the trees, he saw a figure caught in a hollow edged with holly and filled with dead, rotting branches. The figure groaned again as Tom pushed through the undergrowth to get a better look.

It was a woman. As his eyes became accustomed to the dim light, Tom could see a young maid in a white apron over a blue bodice and blue petticoat. A plain linen coif covered half her hair. She lay floundering among the broken sticks and stems with her arms pinioned behind her and a scarf wrapped round her mouth.

Tom stepped forward cautiously and pulled the dead wood away from the woman. He pulled her to open ground and looked at her bonds. The rope was too tight round her wrists and elbows for him to use his knife, but he unpicked one knot then another, then used his blade to release the maid. She sagged to the floor, pulled the gag from her mouth and howled as blood ran back into her arms.

Effra had reached Tom and the two men helped the woman

out of the wood.

'Well, this is a hell of a day!' Gideon whistled. 'Am I imagining it or did we just find a woman in a woodpile on a hill, while we're running away from a Royalist army carrying a dead man with us?'

The woman hugged her arms then swung them around to improve the blood circulation as she stretched her legs, walking around the level, grassed area.

Tom could see that they were all gawping at her. 'Ifor and Effra, you two head for the trees and bring back some wood to burn.' He nodded to them as they trudged away. 'Samuel and Gideon, find us some food. You might be able to catch something before it gets proper dark.'

Gideon reached into his tunic and brought out two dead, bedraggled chickens. Samuel copied his brother, bringing out two half-cooked partridges, equally crushed.

'We've got four birds for dinner. Job done.' Samuel said. Both men grinned.

'That hovel we stopped at?' Tom laughed.

'And from our fire at Athelhampton.'

'Well done. Now go down the hill and get some water. And bring back as much bracken as you can carry.' With that, Tom turned and faced the woman.

She was still pacing around the open ground, head angled down, but eyes watching the men. A narrow woman, tall and thin, with a long neck and auburn hair shaken loose from her coif.

Tom nodded to her. 'I understand your predicament, goodwife, but would you help me prepare the fire?'

'Please give me a moment to collect myself.'

'Of course.' Tom paused and looked sideways at the young

123

woman as he scanned the hill, noting she was wearing start-up boots, the same as the soldiers. She must be a couple of years older than me, he thought. Then he turned to watch the backs of Effra and Ifor as they passed into the darkening shade of the wood, and at the tops of the trees as they danced in the sharp wind.

'I'll collect some kindling then,' he said, 'Just rest. I'll be back shortly.'

'Are you fleeing a battle or are you deserters?'

'We're for Parliament, in Sir Lewis Fezzard's regiment,' said Tom. 'There was a battle at dawn, at Woodsford. We're not deserters. We're just, ah... displaced.'

Tom got the fire going with his tinderbox and, when the others returned with water and wood they settled down to relax.

'Now then, madam,' Samuel said, leaning back on a grey slab of stone with his long legs stretched out and one arm over a grassy tussock. 'We've accepted you into our fellowship, but we know nothing about you. Tell us something of your story? And what we should call you?'

There was a slight pause, and the men gazed at the young woman.

'Bathsua suits most occasions, I find.'

'Well then, Bathsua it shall be,' said Samuel. 'And I'm very glad to meet you. Now, tell us how you come to be on this hill. Does your husband know where you are?'

Bathsua squatted down in front of the group and spoke clearly and simply with her eyes focused on the grass at her feet. 'I will tell you the truth and trust to your common decency. I have no husband. My brother Quintus and I were in Dorchester to preach the gospel. That town is in a ferment these past months, and he wanted to be a voice of calm and grace for the townsfolk. But the turmoil there goes beyond what a few words can settle. We preached for a couple of days. Then, this morning, the constable arrested Quintus and threw him in gaol.' She lifted her eyes to meet those of her hearers.

'I argued. I shouted and I hammered the heads of the men dragging my brother away. It had no effect. So I stood on a cattle trough and preached myself, carrying on Quintus's commission. It could have only one outcome. They arrested me, too.

'That weren't the first time, so we was told,' said Gideon.

'Pardon? How do you know that?' enquired Bathsua.

'We heard it yesterday, in a Dorchester alehouse,' said Samuel, sniggering.

Bathsua looked thoughtful, then continued. 'They didn't want to keep me in prison, so they led me out to the courtyard and told me to hold my tongue, and go back to Wareham. I said I could never stay silent when my Saviour wanted me to share his love with everyone. This caused a stir. One man hit me in the face, but his neighbours turned on him for hitting a woman. I could tell they intended to turn me out of the town.' Bathsua's eyes blazed as she looked at each soldier.

'They grabbed me and fastened my arms together while someone called for the scold's bridle.' Bathsua snorted. 'They couldn't find it. Instead, they bound my brother's scarf around my mouth to stop me preaching. Then they jeered, kicked and pushed me out of town. The constable took me to the bridge at Fordington, then left me.

'I walked for some time, but when I heard someone coming, I was ashamed and hid. Then I headed out over the fields to the wood, hoping to find a way to free myself before returning to free my brother. But I fell into a hollow and couldn't find a way out. I'm grateful to you for rescuing me.'

Bathsua still looked down. The surrounding men shuffled their feet until Ifor broke the spell.

'Well, I'm glad we've been of assistance.'

There was a general murmur of assent, then an awkward silence.

'I have a question for you.' The woman's gaze was now direct. 'Are we cooking honest meat or stolen?'

There was a pause. 'We found an abandoned hut with a few chickens. Our need was greater than theirs,' said Samuel.

'Well, ask your conscience if you acted aright. The owner of the hut was most likely out in the field, or at market in Dorchester. You had no right to steal, however hungry you were.'

'We'll eat the meat, anyway. I trust you'd rather not join us for supper, then?' Effra said.

The woman nodded and Effra shrugged. The partridges were broiled on sticks over the fire, with the plucked and gutted chickens dropped into the Royalist helmet, where they stewed with bones and skin. Knives were used to pick apart the cooked meat or stab the floating pieces in the makeshift pot.

As they ate Tom, broached the subject that he'd been struggling with all day. 'So, which way do we run?'

'Our homes are in the east. That's our best bet,' Gideon said.

'That suits me,' said Tom.

'Grown men can't run back to their beds and their mums like they did when they were kids,' said Effra.

'You have only two choices: Poole or Lyme,' Bathsua cut in.

'Why do you say that?' Tom asked.

'Because I've seen the Royalists descend from Sherborne and occupy Dorchester, Weymouth and Melcombe. Poole and Lyme are the only garrisons for Parliament left in the whole of Dorset.'

'And Wareham,' said Gideon.

'You think Wareham still has a garrison? I thought that was your regiment. Who's left to keep out the army that ambushed you?' Bathsua's comments made the men thoughtful.

Samuel cleared his throat and said in a low voice, 'There is a third option. We could join the Royalists. They've got the country well in hand now. Poole is a small town, and isolated. It can't stand long against an army. And Lyme is smaller still, I think.'

'But we're for Parliament!' said Tom.

'Don't be daft, Tom,' said Gideon. 'I'm not fighting for a cause, but for my mates and my dinner.'

'But we're fighting the Irish, French and Cornish. The king is using foreigners to crush free-born Englishmen.' Tom looked round.

Each face around the fire confirmed Gideon's words. 'Gideon's right. This fight isn't our cause. We're the weapons of others, fighting a war we don't understand, for the benefit of our betters, not for us.' Effra sounded bitter.

Tom felt small. A few moments ago he had been directing this group, bringing them to the hill, telling them to fetch wood or water. Now he felt like a child. Of course, their experience in the regiment was as Roundhead soldiers, but their commander was a rogue. The other officers were schemers, and the old soldiers' only concern was their own comfort.

'Maybe an honourable surrender is possible. They're unlikely to kill us as prisoners, surely?' Ifor spoke into the pause.

Tom recalled Captain Sydenham's execution of prisoners in Poole.

At this, Effra stirred. 'One thing I've learned in my life is that you don't trust yourself to another. Men are weak and can be bought or scared into changing their minds, their coats and their morals. I won't surrender my body and leave some stranger to decide my fate. Not while I can make my own choices.' Effra glared at the surrounding faces. 'D'you think we'll be treated well as deserters from a beaten army? If Parliament is losing, the Royalists will be happy to mop up any resistance, beat and pillage any prisoners and scorn any turncoats. That don't sound comfortable to me.'

This brought murmured agreement.

'Well, if we're not going to desert, let's just bugger off home,' Ifor said.

'Won't work,' said Gideon. 'Effra's right, we can't slink back home while the country's stirred like a wasps' nest.'

'Aye. Best to stay together. At least we can watch out for each other,' said Samuel.

Tom tore a clump of grass strands at his feet. 'But which way? Poole still stands and is closer than Lyme, and over ground we know.'

'But the whole countryside is crawling with malignants,' said Ifor.

'So is the route west,' said Tom. 'If we can get round those

Royalists at Woodsford, maybe we could make it.' He twisted the grass stems into string with his fingers.

'But if we go west, we move away from our known enemies,' said Effra.

'Lyme is certainly served by a vigorous garrison. And it's been recently bolstered by Colonel Blake arriving from Bristol,' chipped in Bathsua.

'Aye, but Bristol fell. So he's as much a fugitive as us,' Ifor said.

'Well, the patrols they send out seem heartened by his arrival with 500 fighters.'

'Why do you want to go west, Bathsua?' asked Gideon. 'You seem to know a lot about the Lyme patrols.'

'The Royalist soldiers will no doubt pillage the cottage Quintus and I own in Wareham. I can only choose between following the soldiers to my home to sift through their leavings or to rouse my cousins and free my brother. They live in Charmouth, near Lyme. So, what would you choose in my place?'

'That's an understandable goal, Bathsua. But our homes are in east Dorset, except Effra there, from London, and we're almost out of our country already. Further west we don't know the land or the people, and the King's men are everywhere.' Gideon spoke, and Tom nodded vigorously in agreement.

'Ordinary Dorset folk are not so easily cowed. I'm sure there's many still favourable to Parliament,' the woman said.

'Aye, but how do we tell them apart at a distance? We can't afford to get it wrong,' Samuel said.

'We daren't travel openly,' Tom said. 'It would be good to meet a Lyme patrol, but most soldiers using the road will be Royalists.' He felt queasy. Had they undercooked the chicken? An image of him playing outside the bakery formed and seemed to call to him. With the loss of the regiment, there was only one safe place in Tom's world – Poole. His old yearning for home welled up inside.

'And whoever meets us, friend or foe, will probably shoot first and talk to our ghosts later,' Ifor joked.

'I've been to my cousins' many times. I can guide you,' Bathsua said.

Tom shook his head clear of his reverie. 'Bathsua, what's the land to the west like?'

'I've travelled from Dorchester to Charmouth in one day before. But more often it's a two-day journey, broken at Bridport. The road is passable, with few villages, but there are steep hills in the way. Not many woods, but small sunken paths, biting into the hill, with gorse and scrub to either side.'

'It might work,' said Effra. 'There's risk, whichever road we take.'

'So we're not going east. We go west. To Bridport. And Lyme.' The statements were almost questions. Tom looked at the faces around the fire and pushed back his disappointment. Every step he took seemed to take him away from the world he knew, grew up with. Now he was headed towards the other end of Dorset.

Chapter 13

The night was bitter, despite the small fire. Yet Tom tossed and sweated. He was playing in the street again. A toy boat of wood with a straight stick stuck in its centre and a rag for a sail sailed over the cobbles, round a corner and into a yard where he docked it by a stone, imagining tiny sailors unloading bales of wool and fish. Suddenly, a cold ache sighed into the scene, like a north wind, and the sailors melted. Tom had to get home. He was in Cinnamon Lane. His father stood outside the bakery, sharpening a knife. Tom called, but he didn't hear. He turned and entered the bakery. The door shut, leaving Tom freezing and unable to call out.

When the party of cast-offs awoke, they were all soaking wet from the dew. Tom groaned and rolled nearer to the fire. Effra was already upright beside him, and he poked the younger man with his boot. 'Up you get, Tom. We need to be on the move. The cows and sheep all know it's morning – listen.'

Tom sat up and could hear a crowd of noises: bleats from sheep and lower-pitched rumbles from bullocks or cows. The field below the wood must be full of animals. 'What about the package?' Tom whispered.

Effra winked. 'Hidden in my coat. You can read it for us

when the woman's not around.'

Bathsua sat in her sodden bodice and skirt. She didn't seem to know what to do for a moment, but then with a shrug she rose.

Ifor passed a piece of meat to her, which she sheepishly accepted. He then tossed lumps to his comrades. 'Take this, lads. We won't get anything else to eat till we find something to take or beg.'

'I don't want to be held responsible for turning you into a thief,' Bathsua replied tartly.

Ifor laughed. 'Who and what we are isn't down to you, young goodwife.'

Samuel and Gideon were up, and it took only a few moments to gather their belongings.

'Which way, Corporal?' said Samuel.

'Bridport is west, so we must head away from the rising sun.'

'That's easy, then. We'll just wait for this grey blanket covering heaven to clear. Is that right?'

They all laughed, except Tom. He felt his cheeks flush, but before he could respond, Bathsua spoke.

'I know Dorchester is that way, to the north.' She pointed through the woods. 'That's the way I struggled here yesterday. So we must walk in this direction.' She pointed west, adjusted the coif on her head, stepped over a cowpat and marched purposefully across the northern slope of the hill.

The men looked at one another, then across to the shrunken body of Sergeant Smith.

Samuel caught up with her first. 'He's not a real corporal, you know. We elected him corporal among ourselves when we were on guard duty a while ago.'

'Well,' said Bathsua, 'it certainly looks like he's your leader, Samuel.'

From the hill where they'd slept, they descended into a shallow valley and climbed the next hill. There was nothing to be seen but grass and sheep. They set a fast pace to loosen up their joints and encourage the drying and warming process. The second hill became a long ridge and the little group trudged across its top. By mid-morning they were walking along the edge of a scarp above sloping fields of grass or bare earth and copses of trees. Tiny hamlets could be seen from their vantage point. Beyond this agricultural landscape, a few miles away, was the sea, a glistening grey surface, restless under a blank sky.

To the north rolled one grassy hill after another, as far as they could see.

'How far to Bridport?' Tom said as he stood beside Bathsua, surveying the horizon.

'I'm not sure. I've never walked this way. I've always travelled the road before.'

'I want to avoid the road. I don't want to meet a cavalry detachment while we amble along,' Tom said.

The woman nodded, and he watched her with a sideways glance. She was tall, maybe an inch taller than him, slender with a straight back and long neck. Her nose was angular above a prominent chin and a thin mouth. Her auburn hair was mostly beneath her white lace coif, but wisps floated this way and that where the journey had dislodged them. As he looked, he recognised her as the woman with the preacher at Poole when Ned Barker announced his exile.

'I think I've seen you in Poole. Last January.'

'Oh? I was there with my brother. He was preaching. Were

you listening to him?'

'No. I was being kicked out of town by the town crier.'

'I remember that.' The woman creased her forehead. 'You looked a sorry bunch to go for soldiers.'

'Well, we've survived up to now,' said Tom with a small grin.

A little while later, Bathsua spoke again. 'I'd say we're nearly halfway to Bridport.'

Tom nodded and Effra looked around at the maid. 'We may be there by mid-afternoon, then.' He stomped forward, leaving Tom and Bathsua walking side by side.

The others dropped out of sight below a ridge of the hill, and Tom felt it was pleasant walking through the Dorset countryside with a young maid. He was a soldier, a man. He had grown up and was no longer the boy who had left Poole.

What the woman thought, he had no idea.

The idyllic walk didn't last long. Over the next ridge they saw the others of their group huddled in the lee of a fold of land. Ifor called to them and they were soon squatting down, out of the sharp early-April wind.

'I thought we could do with a rest,' said Effra. 'Seeing as we're doing well, it seemed this was as good a spot as we're likely to come across. Here's the last of our food, and our beer bottles have a little water left.'

They shared what water they had.

'Small beer. Very small beer,' said Ifor, describing the mix of water and remnants of beer in the leather containers.

'Right then. Seems to me we'd best be on the move.' Effra looked at the sky as he stood up, then trudged off westwards.

They came across the road an hour later. It was a brown snake of a thing, passing between two hills. There was no one in sight.

'Do we follow the highway, or stay clear of it?' Gideon said.

'We daren't use it when we can't see what's over each ridge. I'd rather be on the hills.' Tom spoke, then waited for the others to chip in.

'If we cross here and follow the hills we'll get to Bridport,' Bathsua explained.

'Right, let's do that. We'd better keep right away from the road, or at least far enough away so we don't get any nasty surprises.' Effra was already walking up the closest hill.

The grass tips were growing, and the ground was firm at its surface, despite the winter that had just passed. They tried to walk parallel to the highway, but soon gave up tracking it and just walked west.

Over hills, down long slopes, across shallow valleys and up the next grassy mound they walked as the afternoon stretched on. The clouds thinned and lightened, and a weak sun added a faint golden tinge to everything. They dropped down the shoulder of another hill, into cool shadow, aiming for the road that approached a town nestling along a river, on a narrow undulating plain. Bridport. Hills rose on the further side of the town: tussocky, stony dumplings in front of larger brothers that formed a long ridge running northwards from the sea. They met the road, then headed down a side track towards the river on their right, not meeting anyone on the way.

Half a mile further on, the track widened and gouged a stony way to the edge of the river. The water rushed over the ford, cold and urgent.

'How deep?' said Ifor.

135

'Go and check, Samuel.'

'Check it yourself, Tom. I'll follow you if it's shallow.'

Tom's cheeks reddened and Effra stood and leaned on his musket like a walking stick. Tom looked around. All the men were looking at the river, not at him. He dared not look at Bathsua. He stepped forward into the swirling water. The depth increased as he inched out into the main current. The farther bank was only a dozen yards away, but the channel in the centre was nearly up to his crotch. The current, though, wasn't very strong. He waded back to his friends.

'It's fine. Just go across in pairs to assist your balance.'

Before he'd finished, Gideon and Samuel were already crossing. Effra and Ifor followed. Tom looked about him. Bathsua was facing towards the road.

Tom approached her. 'Can I assist you, Goodwife Bathsua?'

He didn't wait for a reply, but scooped the woman into his arms and turned to the ford.

'What? What are you doing?' the woman hissed.

'I'm helping you stay dry.' Tom stepped forward into the cold water.

'But I'm quite capable of crossing myself. Put me down.'

The others were near the opposite bank, watching over their shoulders with smirks on their faces. Tom couldn't go back now.

'Please don't worry. I'll keep you safe.'

'I've just told you I don't want you to carry me. Don't you understand?'

Tom was wading out into the centre now, but Bathsua's wriggling was an added factor to deal with, as well as the current and the uneven riverbed.

'We're nearly there. Please calm down. This way you stay dry.'

In the deepest channel he had only three steps to take to reach calmer, shallower water. At that moment a branch swung round the river bend and swirled across the centre channel. It was a fairly small branch, but Tom didn't want to collide with it. He stepped forward to avoid it, but his foot slipped and he jerked forward. Bathsua let out a brief shriek, and he corrected his balance by straightening up. This brought his centre of gravity past his hips, further than he intended and, having avoided slipping on top of the woman, he pulled her down onto him as he fell back.

He tried to keep his head above the water, but Bathsua stepped on his chest and pressed him down to the bottom. When Tom resurfaced she was climbing out of the river and his comrades were doubled up with laughter.

A few yards from the ford was a cottage. From this, a woman emerged. 'Goodness. What a commotion. We don't usually have such an eventful fording.' She handed a blanket to Bathsua. 'Here, my dear. Come and dry yourself. Let's get you away from these coarse men and their prying eyes.'

'That was priceless, Tom. Whatever possessed you to pick the maid up?'

'Couldn't you see she's a spitfire?'

'There's a right way and a wrong way to woo, and that was definitely not the right way.'

'Shut up! I wasn't wooing. I was trying to show her some respect.'

The men laughed. Tom stomped off into the bushes opposite the cottage. He emerged once he'd drained the river from his clothes and put them back on. He rejoined his comrades sitting outside the thatched hovel.

'So, what next?' said Ifor.

'We bypass Bridport and keep walking, I suppose,' said Tom.

'It's good we're off the main road, but Royalist patrols might use this ford as well as us,' Effra said.

Bathsua emerged from the cottage and a faint light, from rushlights, could be seen behind her. 'I've spoken with Goodwife Cole here. We can stay the night and be on our way at first light.'

Effra spoke up before any discussion could start. 'That's good, Bathsua. There's no need for us to blunder around in the dark. And it'll give Tom's clothes time to dry properly.'

'But how do we know the woman won't betray us to the Royalists?' said Tom.

'Come in and talk to her yourselves. Make your own minds up about that,' Bathsua said.

They all followed Bathsua back into the room that made up the ground floor of the cottage. It was hardly more than a small barn, with a raised sleeping area at one end, near to a solidly built chimney, with a bright fire burning at its base.

'Bathsua's told me about your journey and your aim.' The cottager spoke.

'What? She's told you we're going to Lyme?' said Samuel hotly.

'No, Samuel. I told her we're going to Charmouth, to my family. You've just told her you're aiming for Lyme!'

'No matter. It was obvious, anyway. What other safe place is there, if you're not for the King?' The woman busied herself poking the fire and lighting more rushlights. 'Tsk, I can see you're soldiers and you're not marching like you have a warrant for your patrolling. My guess is that you're for Parliament, fleeing from Dorchester, or somewhere suchlike.'

The men shuffled uneasily.

'Don't worry. Jessie and me are no friends of the King. Captain Leary and Lieutenant Morris command the outpost at Chideock House, and Sergeant Snook and their men visit us regularly. We try to stay out of the way, but they use the ford most days.'

'Do you expect them to come through today?' Tom asked.

'They've been and gone already. Don't worry. If they stick to their routine, they won't be back until tomorrow afternoon.'

'Is there a routine they follow, then? Can you tell us anything else?' Effra said.

'I know there are forty of the thieves, plus a new gang from Sherborne. They sit in their square house, at Chideock, with their detachment at Symondsbury, and come out looking for the patrols from Lyme. They often head for Beaminster when they hear of any enemy up that way. Then they join others at the old oak, on the road to Melplash. That's mostly the horsemen do that. The foot soldiers and their sergeant just terrorise the likes of us. Requisitioning, they call it, but really it's stealing from us that's got little to live on and less to spare.'

The woman's husband, Jessie, came back soon after and while the two were busying about the cottage and Bathsua was keeping herself to herself, Tom called his comrades together. There was still enough light to see by, but it was fading.

'Effra, show me the papers. Let's find out what secrets the

colonel is trusting us with.'

'Here,' said Effra, handing over the packet.

Tom sat on a log and opened the papers, while Effra continued, 'It was a grand house they were in. I wondered if I'd know the right papers to swipe. The strong-box was a big block of a thing. Good job I've met them sort before.'

'What's the secret to getting into a strong-box, Effra?' asked Gideon.

'They're usually big, solid cabinets. The lid is the way in, but there's a whole fancy mechanism hidden inside it. When you know the principle of that mechanism you can easy tickle it open.'

The first paper in Tom's hand was a large page of closely written text. The first lines showed it was the last will and testament of a high-ranking gentleman. Sir Miles Fleetwood was Receiver General of the Court of Wards and Liveries and the subsequent paragraphs went into detail about his urgent desire to confess his sins and receive forgiveness before he met his maker.

'I once saw a box unloaded from a waggon. It was strong alright. No keyhole or way in at all, that I could see,' said Ifor.

'You're right,' replied Effra. 'They're made with the keyhole hidden. You have to find it before you can get at the mechanism.'

The next paper was a letter of authority to Mr William Churchill from a Sir Rowland Wandesford making him a 'Feodary' (a word unfamiliar to Tom) in a case of the Court of Wards. There were long, legal sentences that seemed not to relate to any part of the life of an informal corporal wandering through the countryside, or to his strange, former colonel.

'Well, tell us then, Effra. How did you get into the box?' said Samuel.

'As usual, I found it easier to go round the back. I took advantage of the cook arguing with a man-servant in the scullery. I was in to the main-room before anyone saw me. There was no sign of any gentleman at home, so I waited for me eyes to adjust to the gloom before I sought out the box.'

'Where do the gentry usually keep such things?'

'Where would you put your valuables, Samuel?' Effra replied.

'For our sort, the customary places are under the doorpost and up the chimney, Effra. But you don't expect me to tell you where to look in my house, do you?'

'Right. And big men are just little men puffed up. So I went to the side of the fireplace and found a door that led to a basement. Cold and damp it were, but no one would stay down there for long. It's only to keep things out of the way. You see, Samuel, you'n me don't have much to protect or fuss over, so any treasure we keep well away from busybodies and we leave it alone. Our betters have more treasure and loads of papers about it, and they like to sit and look at it. So they keep it hidden, but within easy reach. And what they can get at, so can I.' Effra winked.

The third document intrigued Tom. It was a list of costs and remuneration; accounts going back ten years, for a Sir Lewis Fezzard.

'What've you found?' asked Effra.

'I'm still trying to make it out,' replied Tom. 'It's a set of accounts for Fezzard. They are addressed to the Court and they detail major transactions over the last ten years.'

'And do they tally with what those witnesses said in them other papers we took?'

'Difficult to say,' said Tom. 'The light's bad, so I can only make out some parts. It seems, though, that Fezzard is trying to persuade the Court officer that he got very little benefit from the sales. I can't see more.' He passed the papers back to Effra.

'And what of the other papers, Tom?' asked Gideon.

'Legal matters. A will, a commission for Mr Churchill. They must mean something, bundled together with Fezzard's accounts, but I haven't figured it out.'

'We need a nice quiet place on our own, in the day, to look properly,' said Effra.

'One day after the war, maybe,' quipped Ifor.

They all walked back into the cottage. The dark was spreading, and bringing cold with it.

Chapter 14

The cottage was warm with eight adults, three goats, a pig and a cow in it. Outside, the night cold bit the thatch and crisped the mud. Any water not flowing froze.

At first light Effra roused Tom, then the others. They thanked their hosts and, having been given directions again on how to bypass Bridport and Chideock by skirting inland, they headed down the track.

Some time later they crossed another stream by a rickety timber bridge and began to climb out of the valley. The going was easy, though a distant sun behind them struggled to break the cold grip on the land as they followed the winding track around the rear of the hummocky hills. Rising all the time, they met a dirt road crossing their path.

'Left or right?' said Gideon.

'We've got to get onto those big hills directly ahead of us. Which way does the road go next?' Tom was thinking aloud.

'We should be past Symondsbury by now,' Bathsua joined in.

'We turn right.' Tom was definite, and they all plodded up over a slight rise.

They felt the hooves through their boots a fraction before their ears confirmed the news. Horsemen. Moments later, a squad of cavalry trotted over the ridge.

'Scatter! Go west.' Tom had no more time to shout instructions.

Fear and panic filled every mind. They raced along the hedgerow, looking for a way into and across the ploughed field.

The cavalrymen spotted the group fleeing, and were galvanised into action by the hunters instinct.

Each of the fugitives dived through the thinnest part of the hedge they could find, then hurtled downwards, heading for a stream at the field's further end. The horsemen were not far behind. There was confusion and delay as each horse jumped up and through the hedge at a narrow gap. It wasn't long, though, before groups of horsemen were ranging over the field in pursuit of their quarry.

Effra, Tom, Gideon and Bathsua reached the stream ahead of their pursuers. They ran in among a narrow group of willows and alder and launched themselves into the water, wading quickly out on the other side and up the slope of a small hill.

Samuel and Ifor had taken a different route across the field and found themselves in a wider, boggier part of the stream. Behind them, half a dozen cavalry hallooed.

Ifor reached the far side of the watercourse and hauled himself out beside a gnarled tree trunk. Samuel was frantically wading further downstream, and the attention of the pursuers was fixed on him. Ifor didn't wait. He followed a sheep-run, which wriggled its way through a thick patch of gorse, around the hill. Hearing shouts behind, he crouched down, but carried on heading away from his enemies.

On the opposite side of the hill the gorse luxuriated

and spread over the whole slope, but animals had been rummaging through it. Tom and Gideon were in another small wood in a fold of the gorsed slope, with Effra and Bathsua nearby. They spotted Ifor's wriggling form and called to him.

When Ifor joined them, Tom asked after Samuel.

'Don't know, for sure. He was wading downstream with the Royalists after him... last I saw. They must have caught him.'

Gideon hammered his fist on an ash trunk.

'Nothing we can do here. Let's go.' Tom nodded, and they followed another sheep-path up the next slope.

The land seemed to be one continuous collection of hills, slopes, valleys and streams. Fear gave them energy, but after two hills they paused to look back. There was no pursuit.

Was this ground unsuitable for horses? Had the gorse turned them back? Tom wondered.

'I think I can see them in the distance.' Bathsua was near the top of the hill where they'd stopped. 'There's a flurry of colours down there. It looks like they're headed towards that village.' She pointed with her slim right arm.

They looked ahead and saw, in the middle distance, in another hollow between hills, a church spire with a large house near it and a grey smudge that suggested other buildings. One striking hill looked steep and high, close to the right of this village. It had a clump of vegetation tufting its top.

'Why'd they give up? They nearly had us all,' Gideon said.

'They may have bigger fish to fry. Perhaps we surprised them in the middle of some other enterprise.' Bathsua's suggestion made sense.

'But what do we do?' Gideon sounded desperate. 'They've got Samuel.'

'We mustn't do anything rash,' put in Effra quickly. 'Maybe we can get closer to the village and look for a chance to spring him, but that's a risky business.'

'Just the kind of business you're supposed to be good at.' Gideon stared at Effra.

Tom was studying the horizon while listening to the debate. 'Look. That steep hill might show us what's happening down there. From there we might get an idea of what to do.'

'They'll have an outpost on the hill, surely.' Ifor was unconvinced.

'Well, we'll have to deal with them if we find them,' Tom said.

They all nodded, though their nods betrayed more desperation than confidence.

Tom headed for the steep hill, but Effra pushed his way to the front. 'Not straight, Tom. You come at this sort of problem careful and slow like.'

'Like what?' Tom didn't stop, but slowed so Effra could come alongside as they emerged from a wood that reached halfway up yet another dumpling of a hill.

'Those larger, longer hills a mile away stretch right down past the steep hill, towards the sea. Let's get up there and work our way towards our target. Remember, Ifor may be right about the outpost, so we need to sneak up without being seen.'

The others heard this and agreed. Tom nodded, and they changed tack, headed west instead of south and aimed for a ridge that was backlit by afternoon sunlight. Soon they were climbing the ridge. The track stayed to the east of the wide hilltop, so they stayed with it, avoiding the top of the ridge in case they were seen silhouetted against the sky.

The path seemed to lower itself into the body of the hill, worn down over generations and centuries into a 'hollow way'. Ferns grew on the banks to either side, and small trees joined branches to form a leafy archway through which they now marched. It gave nowhere to run if the next bend revealed an enemy patrol, but it hid them from distant views.

The steep hill was easily identified and the sunken track brought them near to it. Between them was a deep, dry valley and a shoulder of land connecting to the lower slopes of the target hill. Trees and shrubs grew in clumps around the hill, and they had no view of the village beyond.

They stopped in the track and watched the summit of the steep hill for some time.

'I can't see any sign of an outpost,' announced Effra eventually. 'Let's go in two groups. That way, if one is spotted, the others can get away.'

Effra and Tom went ahead. Ifor, Gideon and Bathsua were told to follow once they'd seen their friends at the summit, but Gideon refused to wait and stayed with them. Bathsua watched, then trudged along behind. Ifor raised his arms in surrender then followed her. They strode down among occasional sheep, to the saddle connection to the steep hill, which they ascended on the side away from the village. Bracken and brambles were on the lower slope on their flank of the hill, and it took time to pick a way through and step over them. The grassier top half ended in a patch of dense, wind-blasted bushes with a few trees poking twisted heads above the shrub level.

The spinney was too dense and prickly to crawl into. The

men sat in front, with the vegetation at their back, trusting to the fading light and the distance from the village to thwart any watching eyes.

Ifor and Bathsua soon joined them, and the five sat with their backs to the thorns. This also gave them protection from the biting southwest wind.

As they sat, they looked down into a village with a square-built structure and small courtyards between outbuildings connected by arched gateways. A church was beside this building, separated from it by a path passing northwards out of the settlement. Cottages were on the opposite side of a road that formed a crossroads with the path beyond the church and building. Tom noted that this highway must be the one their pursuers had used. The road headed away from the church, eastwards towards Bridport. A second road, by the large house, led southeast over a wooded col.

There was a small stockade in front of the church. It looked like a town pound. Usually these held only the occasional sheep or cow, but they could hold stray dogs or enemy soldiers. One man guarded a closed gate, while two others stood, backs against the stockade, facing into the setting sun.

'Effra! There they are. In the stockade by the church. Do you see them?'

'I see him, Tom,' Gideon exclaimed. 'I recognise his frame. That's Samuel. So how do we get him out?'

'Hold your horses, Gideon. We can't just knock on the door and ask if Sam can come out to play. And we can't mount much of a raid to break him out.' Effra's face was creased in concentration. He was speaking as he thought.

'This must be Symondsbury,' broke in Bathsua. 'I've never been here before, but I know of it from walking the road between Bridport and Charmouth. That road at the south end of the village meets the main highway over there.' She pointed towards the sea.

As everyone looked in this direction, they could make out where the long ridge of hills dipped before it reached the coast. It made sense that a road would crest the ridge there, and then descend to Chideock.

'Don't rush me, friends.' Effra watched Samuel as he spoke. 'That's how mistakes happen. I remember, there was once a master thief in London. He was uncatchable. For years he filched jewels and fine clothes, wine and coin. No one could stop him. Then, one day, his wife told him the mayor was coming to dinner, and they had no wine to offer him. He told her to buy some, but she wanted better fare than from the market. So our master thief had to break into a nobleman's cellar close to Parliament. "And the mayor arrives in an hour," shouted his wife. What did he do? He improvised – which can be a good thing. But under time pressure you have to take risks – the more the pressure, the greater the risks. And our man was in a tight corner.

'Now,' Effra continued, 'the thief knew how to break into the nobleman's cellar. He knew where the wine was. Easy, you might think. But as he entered the cellar, he knew he'd made a mistake. The wine was gone, replaced by barrels and men with firelocks and nervous fingers. The thief never got the chance to talk his way out of the difficulty before he was shot dead, by Catholics guarding gunpowder to blow up the king. It was the wrong time to take such risks. He went from a bad situation into a worse one.'

'Could happen to anybody,' said Gideon.

'Did you know this man?' said Bathsua.

149

'I know his type,' replied Effra mysteriously.

'I take your point, Effra,' said Tom. 'But we can't avoid risk and we'll have to go down there. Sooner, rather than later.'

Just then, Ifor called their attention back to the village. A small group of horsemen had formed outside the church. The men in the stockade were brought out, and the group moved along the road.

'They're headed south,' Gideon breathed.

'That's towards the main highway.' said Tom. 'They must be headed for Bridport or Chideock.'

'Chideock, surely,' spoke Bathsua. 'If they were going to Bridport, they'd've taken the road beyond the church. No. They're coming west.'

'Then that's fine.' Tom stood up, his silhouette still obscured by the thorns behind him. He watched for a minute longer, then turned to the others. 'Come on! Let's go. We've got to move fast.'

Skylight was shifting to starlight. Tom skidded down the slope with Gideon beside him.

'I don't know what your plan is, Tom,' Gideon said in snatched breaths as they ran back to the sunken road. 'But I'm with you. Anything to get my brother back.'

Chapter 15

'Move!' barked Tom.

The five figures ran down the grassy hill. Sloping, damp, uneven ground. Slipping, falling, ankles twisting, tumbling, head over heels, rushing to get down to the road fast. The highway snaked over the ridge and descended towards the little town of Chideock. The five slithered onto its muddy track. Above them, just beyond a bend, was the Royalist detachment, approaching with their prisoners. They would be in sight at any moment.

Out of breath and dishevelled, they paused to collect themselves. They adjusted clothes and accoutrements to look more like a detachment of soldiers. Daylight was fading, but the moon tinged clouds with silver and would soon be shining on them.

Tom, scanning his comrades, whispered, 'Follow me. Keep your mouths shut and your eyes open,' then turned and marched up the road, towards the enemy. Within a minute the horsemen came into view, their outline barely visible in the growing gloom.

'Halt! Who's there?' a horseman hailed the group.

'We're from Chideock House, with a message for Lieutenant Morris.'

'The devil you are"' sounded a voice from the rear of the men. A horse pushed its way to the front and a thickset figure bent down from the saddle.

'What's this, soldier? A message, you say?'

'Aye, sir. Captain Leary sends his compliments and asks if you received the earlier message, as he's not heard from you.' Tom struggled to keep his voice level and soldierly. Inside, his heart juddered.

'What earlier message? What's going on, man?'

'The rebels are moving against Beaminster tonight and you're to meet the captain at the rendezvous, the old oak, as soon as possible.' Tom spoke the lie with as much urgency and conviction as he could, trusting that the lieutenant would interpret it as commitment to the Royalist cause.

'Damn. We'll have to hurry these two then. Corporal Timms! Bring the prisoners forward. You must rush them to the house, then return and catch me up as best you can.'

'That's not necessary, sir. We can escort any prisoners you have.' Tom smiled and lifted his arms to show it was a reasonable offer.

The lieutenant grunted and sat pensively upright in the saddle. Tom held his breath.

'Right. You take them. And see you report to me tomorrow. They're your responsibility and I'll rip out your tongue if anything goes wrong.'

'I'll take good care of them, sir.' Tom spoke over the hubbub of the horsemen turning their steeds round and shoving four men towards their new guards.

'What's this?' Ifor sounded uncertain. 'Four prisoners, sir?'

'No, you idiot. Two rebels and two servants returning to the House. What's that to you?'

'Just precautions, sir.' Tom stepped in front of Ifor as he elbowed him in the ribs to shut him up. Now they had two more problems.

Effra, Gideon and Ifor took up station on either side of the two manacled men brought forward by a trooper, ready to march down the hill. The horsemen then trotted back up to the crest of the ridge, but the lieutenant stood watching the foot soldiers.

'You, man! What's your name? I want to be able to find you again in the morning.'

'Smith, sir' answered Tom. 'Corporal Smith.'

'Well, Corporal, I suppose we'd best exchange passwords, just to make sure we're following protocol.'

Tom gulped and his mind spun. 'I wasn't given a password, sir. Sergeant Snook gave me the message in a hurry and he must've forgotten.' A lame excuse.

The lieutenant stiffened and cursed. 'God's bones, man! Does that sergeant never do things soldierly? And you new men need to learn our ways. How're we going to win this damn war when you can't follow simple instructions? You've even brought a woman on patrol!' He turned his horse in disgust and trotted back up the hill after his men.

Tom stood rigid, still.

'You should breath now, Tom.' It was Bathsua.

He inhaled like a diver coming up for air, noisily and joyously. He was scared, his life hanging by the thread of a barefaced lie. But the ruse had worked, for the moment.

'Let's catch the others.'

Bathsua hissed back, 'What do we do about the servants? They could betray us.'

Part of Tom registered that she had said 'we' and 'us', and

153

he felt pleased that the woman saw herself as part of their group, but he said, 'Not if we handle things carefully.'

He slowed his walk to give himself more thinking time. Bathsua kept pace with him. Tom spoke his thoughts, 'If we're to knock them on the head we must do it now, before we reach Chideock. We daren't go far; our disguise won't fool anyone in the town.'

'I believe you're a fair man, Tom Tyler, and if we're going to act, it'd better be straight away. But I'll have no part of any murder,' Bathsua said.

'Let's get this over with,' said Tom, hurrying to catch his fellows.

At his call to halt, the soldiers ahead turned with dark faces; they knew action was needed. Samuel, hands free of his rope fetters, grinned. His fellow prisoner and the two servants shuffled and drew together.

'We have a problem, friends.' Tom addressed those he didn't know. 'We aren't going to Chideock House and we must either take you with us or prevent you stopping our journey. What should we do?'

The older of the two men stepped forward. He was of medium height, with a bowed posture, his head forward of the books held in his right arm. 'Sir, my colleague and I are mere servants. He a gardener and I tutor to Captain Leary's children. Do you intend to murder us?'

'We don't wish you ill, but we're in danger ourselves and want to be well away from here.'

'I see your predicament, but maybe there's a solution that allows us all to stay alive.' The man forced a smile, yellow-stained teeth glinting and reflecting the weak moonlight.

'What's your plan, then? Be quick, man,' Tom said.

'You could take us with you. Once beyond Chideock we can be left by the road while you scuttle away wherever you choose. You can blindfold us. By this you will be doing us a favour, keeping our body and soul connected, and we will do you the service of not watching where you go and not causing you to commit a mortal sin by killing innocent men. I give you my word, we won't attempt to escape while passing through Chideock, nor will we raise the alarm before we get back to the House.'

'Don't trust him,' said Gideon. 'Our necks are at risk and we've got to get through a rat's nest, so let's not take chances. Don't worry, Tom. Samuel and I can do this. We'll walk them into the bushes there and catch you up in a minute.' Gideon and Samuel grabbed the tutor and gardener, ready to push them to the side of the road.

'No. That's not how we'll do it,' retorted Tom. 'You, Mister Tutor. Tell us. Is there a path round the town that gets us safe to the other side?'

'You could wander over the hills, but unless you understand this country, you're likely to come to grief, either by injury or arriving where you don't want to be. No, your best course is straight down this road.'

'He's lying,' spat Samuel.

'Samuel, what do you know of these men? Are they Royalists, d'you think?' Tom said.

'They joined us as we met the road from Bridport. The tutor there, he knows the lieutenant and asked to walk with us.'

'I do know Lieutenant Morris, but not well,' said the tutor. 'My sympathies in this war are for anyone who can bring it to an end. Ordinary folk hate this strife. We have lives to get back to. I don't want any trouble, either from Parliament or King.'

'You are saying,' said Gideon, 'that for a quiet life, if asked, you would tell where we've gone.'

The tutor dropped his books and wrung his hands. 'I don't think you are ruthless rascals. I believe you are good men, in a tight spot, that's all. Don't stain your lives with my blood.' The tutor turned and implored Bathsua, 'Mistress, can you vouch for the humanity of these men? It's painful to talk of one's own murder in this way.'

'I believe they are honourable, sir. I've only travelled with them a short time, but they've not hurt me. In fact they rescued me.' She looked pointedly at each soldier as she said this, as if infusing the group with her own values.

'All right, master teacher. You've made your point.' Effra stepped into the conversation. 'We aren't murderers, but we are desperate and we won't tolerate betrayal.'

'Aye,' Tom said. 'You've given us your word that you won't betray us tonight. We hold you to that.' Tom looked at Effra, then Bathsua, then at the others. They all waited for his next words. He paused. 'We must trust your words, but we'll also be walking very close to each of you, with a long knife rubbing cosily against your backs. I promise, if you're fair with us, we'll leave you hale and safe as soon as we can.'

Tom nodded to the tutor, then at Effra, then he looked back up the hill. They'd been talking for too long. At any moment the lieutenant might reappear. He set off downhill, heading away from one enemy, towards another.

The others followed quietly, but the pace was brisk. The group marched down into the centre of the little town, past small, thatched cottages and rougher huts and hovels.

Beyond a wooden bridge the road turned right, where a track led up a hill, and led inland past more buildings, stone ones. The moon was out now and in the distance Tom could see a three-storeyed building, with torches marking the entrance to a small courtyard and lights glimmering from windows.

'There's the home of the Royalist garrison,' said the tutor. 'There are no guards by this corner. They're all around that house.'

'And this track?' asked Tom.

'It takes you up to the ridge where you meet the main road at Morcombelake. You can head west from there. It's a rough road, but adequate for your needs, I'm sure.'

'Let's go, then' whispered Effra.

They strode up the track quickly. The ground was muddier than the road, and the steepening slope meant that speed was sacrificed for grip. Their pace slowed, as though an invisible force was holding them back until they could be discovered. Tom sweated until they were out of sight of the last house. The gradient eased and they sensed the top of the ridge. He stalked forward, setting the pace. Now, as they followed the track round the shoulder of land, Bathsua pointed to a dirt path heading uphill on their left.

'I think I've climbed this hill before from the other side. There's another track coming up soon. We can take that and get off this road. I think it leads to a friend of my cousin's. We should be safe there,' she whispered.

Tom nodded and called the group to a halt. 'We've come far enough. Let's say goodbye to our friends and continue without them.'

Effra and Gideon sheathed their swords, which had been pressing against the tutor and the gardener.

'Now, Mr Tutor. I'm relying on your honour to walk back down to Chideock House and not raise any alarm until you reach it. Do I have the word of yourself and Mr Gardener?'

'You do, sir,' said the tutor, with the gardener nodding. 'I can't say we've enjoyed our little walk, but I've had worse journeys. When you get to Lyme, please give Hugo Prescott's compliments to the Reverend Bush. He and I are old colleagues and a little falling out between the King and Parliament is no reason to spoil a friendship.'

Tom answered, 'I'll do my best to pass on your message,' before his mind wondered how the tutor he knew their destination. 'Now go. Step slowly and we'll watch you out of sight before we move on.'

'Yes, clear off, the pair of you,' added Samuel.

'What about me?' Samuel's fellow prisoner was free of his bonds and uncertain which way to go. 'I know where you're headed. Can I join you? I've fired a musket once or twice. I can fight with you against the Irish. I never did like those papist bullies.'

Tom looked at Samuel, who nodded his assent. 'He was pleasant enough company in the pound.'

'You can come, then. But tell me, does everyone know where we're going?'

The man shrugged. 'The Royalist tide is high just now. You're going the wrong way if you want to reach Poole.'

Tom laughed bleakly to himself. Even up to a few days ago, his aim had been to find a way back to his hometown. Now here he was, heading the other way into unknown country. Heading into the unknown, with their destination an open secret. If the servants shared that information, a patrol from Chideock could be after them within a few hours. Should they have kept the tutor and the gardener with them longer? Tom's nerves were shredding. He needed rest. Watching as the servants faded to shadows and disappeared into the night, he sweated.

The little group stood by the path leading up the hill, then turned. Up they went, further along the road, until Bathsua found the second path. This they followed into the deep shade of the hill, beyond the reach of moonbeams or prying eyes. Moving became impossible in the blackness. They groped their way into the cover of a wood stretching over a dark ridge. There was no light, and each of them felt their way inch by inch over the wet ground. The slippery strap-like leaves underfoot smelt of ramsons. The garlicky smell engulfed the party as they pushed through the herbs. Eventually they congregated around a clump of trees with thorny understorey. They were invisible in the night, but Tom had no idea if their resting place was sufficiently secluded or would be exposed come daylight.

Everyone was exhausted; they slept.

The grey light of morning grew and Tom opened his eyes. He looked up into a patchwork of small branches. The leaves emerging from the buds were fresh and green, with beads of moisture at their tips. The tattered leaf edges looked as though a faerie tailor had snipped them all with his scissors. Tom knew some tailors in Poole. He imagined these men as elves, spending every night prancing and snipping innocent leaves.

He rose carefully from his bed of well-rotted thorns, leaves and crushed ramsons. The garlic scent was slight, now his nose was accustomed to it. He stood on the crest of a small mound, with hawthorn trees growing in a thicket around its edge, larger oaks filling the sky above and beyond them. Branches had partially protected them from a shower during the night, and their sleeping site was less damp than the ground beyond the trees, outside the wood.

The open ground fell away in front of him towards the west. Grassy fields with short hedges stretched from the edge of the wood, down the hill, then off to the west, following the coast. The fields to the south rose again, narrowing to a tip, like a triangular hill at the edge of the sea.

The sky was grey and the light was lifeless. As Tom gazed at the view and wondered how far it was to Lyme, he saw Bathsua sitting at the woodland edge, hugging her knees. He approached her and cleared his throat. 'Good morning, Bathsua.'

'Oh! Good day, Tom. You startled me.'

'Is it far to your kin in Charmouth?'

'D'you see that long ridge across the valley? At the far end is Charmouth, where my cousins live.'

'And how much further is Lyme?'

'It's the next town west from Charmouth. It's not far.' Bathsua was speaking to Tom, but she kept looking west.

As the silence between them lengthened, he felt uncertain and the memories of the ford at Bridport resurfaced. 'Bathsua, I feel I should apologise for what happened yesterday.'

'So much happened yesterday. Ah! At the ford, you mean.' The woman kept her back towards him.

'I was just trying to help you across the river.' The words sounded inadequate to Tom.

'You mean, you wanted to impress your comrades with your courtesy. But I made it clear that I needed no help from boys. I can look after myself.'

Tom heard the angry edge in the words. 'I don't want another argument. I only hoped we might speak without hostility. There's so much in life that leads to regret.' He squirmed inside at his lame words.

'Life is indeed full of regret. I can't hold on to a slight from a boy. But you need to learn to control your anger or you'll become a restless man, Tom.'

'I wasn't angry at you. It was just frustration.'

'I didn't mean the ford. You have anger gnawing at your bones all the time. You must let it go.'

'It's frustration, I tell you, not anger. Can't you see that? As I try to do one thing, circumstances push me towards another.'

'Listen to yourself. You talk of one thing but show another.' Bathsua stood and turned round to look at the target of her tongue.

'I... I...' Tom's gaze slipped off this hard woman and landed on the bracken at her feet. 'We'd better all get moving. We, ah... we'll be caught in the open if a party from Chideock spies us.'

'Tom!' called Effra. 'Our newest recruit has gone.'

Chapter 16

Tom walked back into the wood. As he reached the mound, Effra nodded at an empty hollow in the ground. 'He must have tiptoed away earlier.'

'Good riddance, then,' Samuel chipped in from his place beneath a hawthorn bush.

'But you vouched for him last night?' Tom said.

'I spoke from what I knew. This morning I know more and I see we're better off without him.'

'But we're more vulnerable. He could betray us.'

'That's true,' said Effra. 'Let's hope he just sneaks home and stays well clear of nasty troopers.'

'Let's get going,' Tom said. 'And Samuel, keep watch at our rear. See that we don't leave too easy a trail, and listen out for pursuit.'

'Aye, aye, Captain,' said Samuel as he rolled over and lay down again.

'Leave him,' whispered Effra to Tom, who gazed daggers at his back.

There wasn't much to arrange before they could get on the move. Preparations consisted of easing their tired frames from horizontal to vertical, brushing leaves, twigs, thorns and soil from clothing and stepping off the mound (only

Gideon and Tom still had muskets).

The journey down the hill towards the west began over sheep pasture and through withy gates between hawthorn and blackthorn hedges. The path across the bottom of the narrow valley soon turned into a climb up the long ridge Bathsua had pointed out. The ridge top was an empty sheeprun pitted with muddy puddles. They could be easily spotted by anyone for several hundred yards in either direction. But there was no one in sight, so they hurried across this exposed ground and dropped into the more wooded, northern flank of the hill.

Bathsua walked just ahead of Tom; she knew the way better than any of them. He watched her supple body bend and bob back to an upright posture as it pushed through thickets, with her long neck holding an inquisitive head that was forever checking their direction and looking for familiar features.

He barely spoke to the woman. Clearly she had a low opinion of him, but his role as corporal meant that he had to keep some authority, which meant he had to stay close to her as she led them to Charmouth. And he was drawn to her youthful energy and decisiveness. Although they seemed to clash over every action or word, he wanted her involvement in each decision taken, each problem discussed.

Today, though, was the last time Bathsua would journey with them. She was intent on rescuing her brother, and then they would be on God's business of converting everyone in Dorset to their particular brand of Christianity.

He was musing on this and watching her bottom rise and fall when she stopped. 'There, Tom. That's the way to Whitchurch,' she whispered.

The dirt track snaked along the bottom of the hill at the

edge of narrow meadowland beside a gushing river.

'That's the River Char.' Bathsua spoke again. 'If we turn left and follow the track we'll be in Charmouth in an hour.'

The others had caught up now.

'The wood doesn't follow the road. It's just grass, both sides,' Gideon said.

'You're right. There's nothing to be gained by staying in it. We might as well use the solid path and get to Charmouth quick as we can,' Tom decided.

'This wind is rising. I reckon we're in for a dousing soon,' said Ifor. 'So the quicker the better.'

An hour later, soaked by a cold-edged April shower, they reached a huddle of cottages beside a stone bridge over the river. Here, sheltering from the icy wind that had temporarily run out of rain, Bathsua advised them to wait while she checked all was well.

'No,' said Tom. 'There's no sign of soldiers or horses in sight. Let's get to your cousins quickly, so we can dry out and rest.'

Bathsua shrugged, then walked over the bridge. She greeted a group of women returning from washing clothes in the river, but soon they were all huddled outside a cottage door in the middle of a line of homes along the only street in the village. Bathsua walked round the back. A minute later the door opened, and she and another woman with the same long neck, oval face and sharp nose welcomed the men into a warm, dry space. Behind the woman, two younger maids jostled to embrace their cousin.

Despite the facial similarities that proclaimed kinship, the older woman was stouter than Bathsua. Cousin Tabitha had a no-nonsense air and a way of setting the men at ease.

Cousins Elizabeth and Daisy shared the family likeness too.

'Cousin Bathsua vouches for ye, so 'tis good enough for us. We're simple folk, but we know the love of Jesus and we share what we have.'

'My cousin Micah has been sent for. He can tell us how safe it is between here and Lyme,' Bathsua said to Samuel, who was standing beside her.

While they waited for Micah they all shared a couple of blankets that were provided to dry their bodies. Later, two men appeared at the door. One was a large man; large round head with lots of grey hair to his collar, muscly shoulders, barrel-shaped body and thick, sturdy legs. He wore a leather jerkin and woollen hose. The second man was younger, about Tom's age. He was a more slender version of the large man, wearing a loose-sleeved brown jacket over a coarse whitish shirt. Both were soaking wet despite their wide-brimmed hats, which had at least stopped the rain that hadn't come at them sideways.

'Ho. Welcome, cousin Bathsua. What news d'you bring?' said Micah. 'And what scrapes have you been getting into now?' He bounded over to Bathsua and hugged her, with no worry about the others watching. The younger man followed, and the three shared an embrace.

Bathsua then introduced the soldiers to Micah and his son, Nathan.

'Are ye for King or Parliament?' He nodded at their reply. 'So, you'll be heading for Lyme, I guess. You know there's a Royalist army coming this way?'

The large man went over to the open hearth and kicked the embers from last night's fire. 'Well. The men of Chideock ride past often, but they can't stand before the Lyme garrison, either in numbers or quality.'

'We've not seen scouts or raiders from Chideock for three days.' Nathan joined in the conversation. 'I can guide you there along the small paths, away from the coast road that's crumbling into the sea. I know where the best ambush places are. You won't bump into an enemy with me.'

'Thank you, Nathan,' said Tom.

'You can't go yet. We've still got a half dozen sheep lost on the hills. I know your mind, Nathan, and I'll not have you slacking off to play war while there's family work to be done.'

'We can help you find your animals,' said Gideon. 'Samuel and me did farm work around Wimborne.'

So that was arranged. Gideon, Samuel and Tom (the youngest members of the group) accompanied Micah and Nathan, while Effra and Ifor stayed and rested. They had, they said, no skill or inclination for farm work and were exhausted by the journey.

Tom spent the rest of the day climbing hills and looking into valleys. They found the sheep and returned to Charmouth before the early spring evening turned dark. Only then did Bathsua have the chance to talk to her cousin about Quintus. The soldiers were not party to the discussion; it was family only, but Tom imagined Bathsua would press for all her kin to travel to Dorchester to help release her brother. When the family came back into the main room Tom could tell, from the way she held her shoulders and her tight, frustrated steps, that Bathsua had been thwarted.

166

'You're welcome to stay the night, my friends,' Micah pronounced. 'Early tomorrow Nathan will guide you over the hill to the mighty citadel of Lyme. There, I'm sure, you'll turn back the tide of Royalist tyranny. But I shan't go with you. There's proper work here, caring for my family, so I'll leave all this marching and killing to you.'

Behind Micah, Tabitha jostled and found a way through with a stack of wooden bowls in which were servings of a brown stew. Bathsua had an armful of dark rye bread. The food nourished the stomachs and hearts of the wanderers, who hadn't eaten a proper meal since the ford beside Bridport. The stew contained peas, turnips and at least one chicken.

'Micah. It's not the fattened calf, but I think you've killed the fattened chicken for us,' Effra said between slurps.

'You're most welcome, friends. I be in your debt for looking after cousin Bathsua.'

'I can get myself here without help, Micah. I don't need an escort of rough soldiers.'

'Well said, Bathsua!' cried Samuel.

'Well, as I understand your recent adventures, you were very blessed to fall in with this company. I hope you're suitably grateful to these men.'

Bathsua reddened, but had an answer. 'The tide rises and falls. They helped me, I freely acknowledge. And I, in turn, aided their journey, leading them to Bridport and Charmouth and even to this grand house and glorious feast.' The red cheeks now animated her face with the glow of competition.

The friendly warmth of the family and the fire in the hearth, as usual, relaxed their bodies and loosened their tongues. Evening was spent discussing the war, the weather and the livestock, and telling stories.

At evening's end the family climbed the stairs into the upstairs room, while Tom and the others settled down around the fire.

'So, what are we going to do with the papers?' said Gideon. 'Let's hand them over to an officer when we get to Lyme, then we'll be clear of Sir Lewis for good.'

'We can't do that straight off,' said Tom. 'On our first jaunt Effra and I read a list of Fezzard's accomplices. It was quite a list. What if some of them are at Lyme?'

'I can't remember all the names, Tom, but you're right. If we show our hand too quick we could be in more trouble.' Effra looked at the roof for a few seconds. 'There was a justice of the peace, a woman and a sack full of other names. I'm too tired to recall them.'

'If we keep the papers, we must hide them before we get there. They're sure to check our kit when we arrive,' joined in Samuel.

'Let's stop on the way, tomorrow. I'll read the papers again, in daylight, and we can decide either to ditch them or keep them close.

'Now, we'll each take an hour's guarding. Each sentry is to patrol the cowshed and garden and the outside of the cottage. Call me if anything happens.'

'Right you are, sir,' quipped Effra.

Tom gave Effra a dark look, then went out the front door to do the first check. Everything seemed peaceful. He looked at dark, ragged clouds sliding over the sky. His life seemed on a course of its own. He felt no power to control events, as though he rode one of those clouds, rushing to nowhere, shredding to nothing as it does so.

'Corporal Tyler? Where are you?' Tabitha bustled through the cottage, heading for the front door with her arms full. Beyond the door, on the muddy surface of the main street, the small band of soldiers were stamping their feet and checking their equipment in the thin morning light.

'Here you are. A bottle of beer, a hunk of bread and a haggis for each of you. That'll keep your spirits up on the journey.'

'We are forever in your debt, beautiful lady.' Samuel bowed.

'Get on with you.' Tabitha's laugh was high-strung and forced, Tom thought.

Micah appeared and stood before Tom and Effra. 'My son Nathan is coming with you. He'll show you the way and join the garrison with you. I ask you, as my guests, to look out for him. I know he has to make his own way and show that he's a man. But we all need friends by our side.'

Tom could see the emotion in Micah's face, but he had no words of comfort for this big man.

Effra spoke. 'Thank you for your great hospitality.' It's not every home is open to wandering soldiers in these times. Your Nathan is a fine young man. We'll keep him close and see he doesn't face danger alone. You have our word.' With that, he shook his host's hand.

Tom checked their equipment again; they only had two of the Royalist muskets left, with about six feet of match for each one, plus one shot, little wadding and no gunpowder. This didn't bother Tom much. They would presumably get new kit once they arrived at Lyme.

The young corporal wondered what Lyme was like. Would they be welcomed? Would the Royalists already be there? Micah suggested Prince Maurice's army hadn't yet reached this part of Dorset from Exeter. The Dorset cavaliers were small detachments, like Chideock and Dorchester, waiting for the victorious King's army to roll eastwards in a triumphal march on London. Surely the entire country was rising to set King Charles back on his throne.

They were all ready to go. Samuel and Gideon cheered as Nathan appeared, carrying a satchel twice the size of their snapsacks and with his mother hanging on his left shoulder whispering parting words.

'Right, all here? Let's go,' said Tom.

'Wait!' Tabitha called.

Then Bathsua came round the side of the cottage. She had on a borrowed petticoat and shift and had a bundle slung over her shoulder, beneath a large sage-coloured frieze cloak, lined in blue. Her coif was hidden under a wide-brimmed hat.

She took her place at the front of the group, beside Nathan. Looking behind her, she met Tom's eyes with a glittering intensity. 'Is a maid not allowed an adventure?' she said.

Chapter 17

Within an hour a water-laden mist blew in from the sea as Nathan led them to higher ground further inland. The mist ebbed back to the coast, but their clothes stayed wet. After another hour of picking their way over sheep pasture and through forgotten spinneys, the clouds parted to reveal an April sun. The cold air was bright, but teeth-chatteringly cold. They kept moving.

Effra seemed lost in thought. Tom came alongside him. 'There's no way we can stop and read those papers. And anyway, I thought you might be off back to London by now.'

Effra nodded. 'It's on my mind, for sure. But we've got to be sure we can wriggle free of the colonel. Now's not a good time to be wandering alone between towns.' His foot slid off a damp stone and he reached out and grabbed Tom's shoulder for support. 'Those names you read to me on our first job. I've been wracking my brains to remember them. There was a Standley, a Barnes, the JP was a Hart. The rest is a jumble, except that I recall the names Declark, Bidlecomb and Croston. But that's a poor haul from a long list.'

'Why would any of them be in Lyme? We're nowhere near Dorchester.'

'Because these landed men have family and business

connections all over the place. We don't know the risks yet, Tom. Until we do, our best course is to keep our secrets hid.'

'Do you think they'll search us when we arrive?'

'Let's see how things look when we get there.'

The little group stepped down a crumbling cliff path and approached a tiny town nestling at the bottom of a valley, perched on the sea's edge. Descending, they could see hundreds of figures moving about within the settlement. Moving closer, they noticed that most attention was being paid to the outer boundary. This boundary was nothing like the town walls of Poole or Dorchester. It was just a discontinuous trench in front of buildings linked by timber palisade or masonry. Tom watched holes being punched through the outer walls of houses, presumably to allow muskets to fire through. Here and there, soil and turves were stacked up against the walls.

Within this meagre line of fortification were three squat platforms, redoubts hunched behind earth banks. Each had a handful of cannons scattered over the level space; they reminded Tom of the jacks used in the children's game, tossed onto a table and lying randomly. The defensive walls looked too weak to stop an army. What danger were they heading into?

The group reached the bottom of the cliff and, joining a well-worn track, approached the nearest redoubt. Here they were challenged by sentries, posted a stone's throw ahead of a timber gate marking where the narrow road became a town street. A fourth platform, or fort, was being built between the gate and the sea, with a stout timber linking wall.

'You're right welcome if you can fight,' said a lean soldier, one foot lifted onto a boulder, his head cocked to one side. 'But don't bother if you're looking for a peaceful place to settle.'

'We're here to stand beside you.' Tom nodded to the soldier, who grunted.

'We'll soon find out the truth of that. Come on, then. Before you can join our work, you must meet Captain Pyne. He'll know what to do with you.'

The sentry called to the gate and four men appeared with staffs at the ready. They approached in a loose, unmilitary way, but looked alert and confident.

The newcomers were taken into the centre of the town to The Mermaid Inn, where they were ordered to lay out their snapsacks and weapons to be inspected. Effra helped Bathsua unsling her bundle and everything was laid out in a small room. Two corporals searched each soldier, then poked and prodded their belongings. After a few minutes, each was called individually to give an account of their presence in Lyme.

Tom was the last to be interviewed, except for Bathsua. He left her sitting alone on a wooden bench. The others had not returned.

In the main room of the inn Tom was presented to a tall officer of lean build, a short-cropped sandy beard and hair, and piercing blue eyes. His clothes were the same as any fisherman would wear, but he was clearly accustomed to command.

'So, you are the corporal?' The man raised an eyebrow.

'Unofficial corporal, sir. We've travelled from Woodsford. It's taken us a week, cross country.'

173

'As the crow flies, or as the rabbit runs, eh? Your men tell me you're their leader. I need to know what your plans are. Your regiment is far away and you're travelling away from them.'

'True, sir. Our regiment was beaten up at Woodsford, and when we saw them being herded together by the Royalists like sheep, we decided to head in the opposite direction.'

'What happened to Colonel Fezzard?'

Tom paused and glanced around the room. It looked like a pub in Poole. The men in attendance looked active and purposeful. 'We didn't see him in the fight.'

'And you?' The officer sat down beside a small table pushed against the slight bay of a window. He watched Tom with penetrating eyes. 'You haven't explained why you're here. Am I to believe you were so panicked at seeing your regiment attacked that you scarce paused for breath till you reached us? What made you come all this way, Tom?'

Tom swallowed. Now was not the time to explain about the burglary, but he had to come up with a plausible answer. 'We were on detached duty, sir,' he began hesitantly. 'We'd been sent to Dorchester and were heading back to the regiment, but we got there too late. The whole regiment was captured in the ambush. We turned round and retraced our steps, stealing a boat to head upstream. Our sergeant was wounded, and he died before the end of the day.'

'What was the detached duty?'

'We were commanded by our captain to visit Dorchester on an errand for the colonel.' Tom's eyes strayed to the wall behind his interrogator, and his answer seemed slow and vague to himself. Yet the officer didn't delve deeper.

'Who did you meet between Dorchester and here?'

Tom could see no alternative but to relate all that had happened to them since Dorchester. The officer was interested in the numbers of Royalists at Symondsbury and Chideock, and he laughed at Tom's ruse to rescue Samuel. When Tom had finished his story the man stayed silent, gazing out of the window.

'So your leader died, you gained a woman, rescued a comrade, picked up two recruits and lost one. That'll do for now. I can see there's a deeper story there somewhere, but it can wait for another time.'

The officer opened the door and shouted. 'Parks, take this corporal and his comrades over to Fort Gaitch. Tell Colonel Blake he has some more volunteers.' He looked into Tom's eyes, 'Welcome to Lyme, my bold corporal. My name is Captain Pyne. I hope you live to sing of our exploits. You may have heard that the King has sent his nephew Prince Maurice with an army to subdue us. You arrive at an interesting time.'

'Yes, sir. All Dorset has heard of you.'

Captain Pyne smiled. 'I know.'

The bright morning was fading as the group, including Bathsua, was led across town. The view of the town from above had been lit by the sun, showing them a place full of warm reds, soft blues and pale yellows, speckled with colourful figures. Now, walking through the narrow streets, clouds cut off the sunshine and shadows stretched grey hands over all the activity around them. This gave a more sombre feeling to their meeting with the men standing on the platform named Fort Gaitch.

175

The interview with Colonel Blake was brief. As newcomers, they were to relax for now, but to be prepared for sentry duty overnight.

'And what is my role in your army, Colonel?' asked Bathsua.

The colonel smiled at her. 'We can't offer all the bustle of a market town just now, Goodwife. But we're glad you've joined us. There are many ways you can help our struggle. The women of Lyme are fearsome creatures and you won't lack opportunities to contribute, I'm sure.'

Tom saw Bathsua's face flush pink, but then she looked down at her clothes and nodded. The rest of the afternoon was spent watching the work on the town wall and familiarising themselves with their new surroundings.

By dusk they'd learnt there were about two thousand civilians in the town, plus around a thousand fighters. The governor was Colonel Ceeley, but the defence was really organised by Colonel Blake, a stocky Somerset squire. He came to Lyme from the defence of Bristol and many regarded him as a talisman, a fellow countryman for whom they would march into hell. Indeed, some of them thought hell was already on the march to meet them.

There was news of General Waller's army. After the battle of Cheriton, Winchester had surrendered, but the Roundheads had come no further west. No help was coming from that direction.

The first evening was a strange, quiet time. Effra seemed edgy, Samuel and Gideon were sullen and withdrawn, and only Ifor seemed unaffected. He whistled tunelessly as he set the cooking fire outside a house which was now part of the town wall and already contained a dozen soldiers. He looked relaxed as he roasted fish, then quietly puffed on his pipe. Nathan fretted while helping with the supper, restless to continue his exploration of the town. Tom tried to speak to Bathsua about their conversation outside Chideock. But she was evasive and soon wrapped herself in her blanket.

Effra wasn't finished, though. He roused himself and said, 'If no one's going to tell a story, it'll have to be me. Listen up, everyone.'

All eyes swivelled round to watch and listen.

'A tailor lived in the north country. But he didn't live well, he struggled. The stitches that held his garments together didn't work on his life. Things got so bad he decided to sell his soul to the devil.

'He thought: If I can't earn enough to live well, I can at least have a bit of comfort and pleasure in this world, and who knows what might happen in the next? Not me.

'He wrote a letter to the devil offering him his soul in fifteen years' time. He put the letter under his pillow and went to sleep. Next morning the letter was gone, the bargain was struck and a shiny shilling was left in its place.

'The tailor smiled, thinking he'd be cold and hungry no more. He'd dine on the best food and drink the best wine. But oh no, that's not what happened. Over time his shears got blunt, his needle broke, his cloth split, and his customers forgot to pay.

'I should've kept my soul, thought he sadly.

'These misfortunes meant he forgot his bargain and the measly shilling he'd had by it. There he was, a long while later, sitting on the floor repairing a tunic, when there was a loud knock at the door and in came a tall, dark stranger. The tailor showed the man all his fine cloths and garments, but he took no interest. Then, as he brought out his best green broadcloth, he glanced at the stranger's feet, cloven, and he recognised him. At that moment the devil grabbed him by the neck.' Effra grabbed his own neck, dramatically.

'"Time's up, old man. Pay me what you owe." And he dragged him out the house.

'"Can't you give me even one wish before you drag me to hell?" he cried, all along the road. He complained he'd not benefited at all from the bargain, so it weren't really no bargain at all. "Just one wish," he shouted.

'Well, the devil knew he'd not done anything more than leave a shilling for the silly chuff. "All right. You can have one wish," he said. "And be quick about it."

'The tailor lifted himself out of the puddle where he'd been dropped and thought fast. This was his last chance. What should he wish for? As he paused he saw a black horse grazing in a field. Quick as you like, he spoke up. "I wish you'd jump on that horse and ride straight back to hell and never scare poor tailors no more!"

'Well, what d'you think? Off gallops the horse, the devil on his back, and he's not been seen round those parts from that day to this.

'The tailor watched all this with wide eyes. He prayed to God, said thank you for his wit and promised he'd never complain again about his life. But folks soon heard about his brush with the evil one and they'd come to meet the tailor, buy him a drink and listen to his story. Many people visited his shop and bought his wares.

'It weren't long before the tailor found he was spending more time talking than tailoring, so he hired some apprentices to do his work, married a wealthy widow with an alehouse and sat in the snug talking for the rest of his days.'

'Very good, Effra. And the moral is?' said Nathan.

'The moral is, young man, be careful who you let into your life. There, that's a sobering thought. Good night all.' Effra settled himself down and was asleep before any of them.

Chapter 18

Between Gaitch's Fort and Marsh's Fort, along the northern edge of the town, Tom's group was given responsibility for a short length of the defensive wall, called the Town Line. There were no enemies outside Lyme; the land in front was dark and unthreatening and they watched the regular activity around the town gates as horsemen and infantry headed out, then back, after raiding the nearby countryside.

Bathsua collected fresh bread from a bakery in the town and they washed it down with small beer brought in a large pewter jug. The group moved quietly around, unsure of what the day would bring. It wasn't long before a sergeant strode up and ordered them to report to Captain Coram at noon. Until then, they were at ease.

Tom settled back down beside the embers of the fire, placed his hat over his face and bade everyone good morning. Ifor headed over to the Mermaid to seek news of a friend and Samuel, Gideon and Nathan were off to the quay to watch supplies being ferried onto the beach from the Cobb, a stone platform a hundred yards from the beach, to the west of the town.

Tom felt relaxed for the first time in days. The morning was bright and warm, and the town bustle seemed far away, but an element of tension snaked into the quietness. He shifted his hat and saw Bathsua crouching by the fire, opposite Effra.

'You're still awake, Tom?' she said.

'Just about.'

'Well.' She continued to stir the ashes with a smouldering stick. 'I'd say now is a good time to speak about those papers from Dorchester.'

'You found them, then?' said Effra.

'Found and read.'

Tom sat up straight.

'We needed them to be safe. I gambled you'd not be searched as we were,' Effra explained.

'So you thought you could tangle me up in your schemes?'

'You read the papers?' said Tom.

'What else should I do with documents in my bags?' Bathsua fixed him with a penetrating stare.

'You see the difficulty we're in, then.'

'Rather, the way out of your predicament is clear to me.'

'And what way is that, Bathsua?' asked Effra.

'You must hand them in to the commanders here. The information affects the war in Dorset, surely?'

'No. Them's only papers relating to our colonel and his dealings with other gentry. It has nothing to do with the war.'

'What. Not even a letter promising to change sides? I'm no military strategist, but I think that's information one side wants about one of its colonels.'

Tom and Effra lurched to their feet.

'Show us. Where does it say that?'

'There's more there than we realised, Tom.'

181

Bathsua smiled. 'So you carried them all the way from Dorchester without looking carefully at the contents.'

'We had no chance to sit, look and plan. You were with us, then the men from Chideock, then Nathan.'

'Well, you have a chance now.' Bathsua went to her bundle and lifted out the packet of papers. She tossed it over to Effra, who passed them to Tom.

'Look again, Tom. What have we got?'

'They all relate to Sir Lewis Fezzard,' said Bathsua. She spoke quietly above the peaceful embers of the fire. 'The will tells of a scheme to enrich both Sir Miles Fleetwood and Fezzard, by lying about land sales. The letter of authority commissions Mr Churchill to investigate the case, and the accounts try to convince the Court of Wards that the sales brought very little benefit to Sir Lewis.'

'That says nothing of any betrayal or changing sides?'

'The last page was a letter to Prince Maurice, assuring him of his intention to do a mighty deed in Dorset for the King.'

'We can't take those papers to the leaders here.' Effra cut across Bathsua. 'We saw another paper with a list of names of Fezzard's confederates. We think some may be here, in Lyme.'

'How can they hurt you?'

'We don't know who to trust: Colonel Blake, Captain Pyne, or the rest of the officers. Fezzard may have his men anywhere.'

Bathsua considered this. 'So you want to sit tight until you know the allegiances of the officers?'

'Or we burn the papers now.' Effra took them from Tom and held them above the fire. 'We've two choices – hand them over and hope we aren't either gutted by a Fezzard thug or tried for burglary, or destroy them and nobody need ever know.'

'You can't do that when treason is being planned.'

'Forget your morality, Bathsua. This is real. It's dangerous. An enemy that knows we have this information would stop at nothing to get it back. Nobody knows, unless we tell them. So, stay silent, and we stay safe.'

'There's a third way,' said Tom. 'Why don't we hide the papers until we're sure who we can trust?'

'Because that won't stop the treason. It's the same as destroying them.'

'Why are you so inflamed about Fezzard's loyalty? And so careless of our safety?'

'I see where this may lead. You are like a tornado, sucking anyone close by into your schemes and wiles.' Bathsua stepped over the fire to retrieve the papers, but Effra stepped out of reach. 'And why should I stand by and let you put others, like Nathan, in danger? He is innocent of the world.'

'You ask us to hand over letters that could mean our death, and you wonder that we pause?' Effra was still stepping back from Bathsua's advance.

Tom spoke above the growing voices. 'I thought you were a friend, Bathsua. Our journey has led us to rely on and trust each other. But your harshness makes little sense.'

The woman stopped and looked at Tom. He saw a flush of pink sweep over her face and her eyes glinted sharply, then lost focus.

'All right, keep them,' she said. 'I need to pray about this. I won't say anything to anyone until I've sought the Lord. Then I'll tell you what I think.' She picked up her hat and walked towards the town mill.

Tom looked up at the sky. Streaky grey clouds trailing tattered edges hung below darker clouds of grey. Not much sign of the sun, but he thought it was about noon and his small squad was at Cobb Gate waiting to report to Captain Coram. The wind had barbed edges, and the men leaned against the stone wall that shielded them.

'Lousy weather,' moaned Ifor. 'We've not had three days of dry weather since last summer.'

'Summat's wrong with it, I reckon,' Samuel added.

'Don't be daft. Weather's weather. It's the same now as it's always been.'

'No, Tom,' said Ifor. 'There's summat wrong. Spring's often late. Summer's full of wind and rain. Last winter wasn't so bad, though.'

Samuel snorted, 'That winter was a mild one? I felt every pinching frost.'

'Ifor's right,' said Effra. 'I remember '28. There was no summer at all that year.'

'I've heard old folks talk about that,' Gideon said. 'I remember droughts and sun in the '30s. Our da bemoaned the weather, but me and Samuel enjoyed it.'

'Well, I'm not enjoying this.' Samuel kicked a rock towards the sea.

Nathan just gazed into the wind, at the Cobb, his eyes streaming.

A soldier wearing a sergeant's scarf over a nearly clean, faded blue jacket, and lightly muddied breeches above damp stockings marched round the wall.

'You lot. Fisher women are we? Yer s'posed to be soldiers, so stand up and look like it.' His voice rose from stentorian to storm-force in one sentence.

'Right.' The sergeant continued in a quieter tone. 'Captain Coram tells me you're to be the hub of a new unit and you've to train a group of eager lads that want to fight with us. Tyler. You're the corporal, so form your men up and march them to the church. Your new charges await. Follow me, I'm right behind you.'

Tom's squad marched up Church Street, and behind the church they found eighteen young men huddled together waiting for something. The sergeant was that something. He brought everyone to order and, in terse monosyllables, explained that Tom and his squad would turn them into soldiers. He pointed at a pile of muskets piled against the church. 'Get to it, Tyler. No time to lose,' and with that he was gone. Off to terrorise some other squad, Tom guessed.

He stepped forward. He was scarcely trained himself, with only a few months' soldiering experience, but compared to these yokels he was a seasoned warrior. That thought squared his shoulders, and he mimicked the corporals of his old regiment and barked at the boys to stand straight, listen up and obey him if they didn't want to feel his stick across their backs. That worked. Nathan joined the new men, and they were formed into two lines with Ifor, Effra and Samuel inspecting them for smartness. Tom used this time to discuss with Gideon what to do next.

'Well, what do they need to know?' Gideon asked.

'How to stay alive long enough to hurt the enemy. That'll do for starters.'

'Then we must teach them that.' Gideon nodded. 'But we can't go through everything we've learnt since January. We'll have to boil it down to the basics.'

'They'll have to take sentry duty.'

185

'And they'll need to listen for commands and make sure they respond straight away.'

Tom had been organising this information in his head into a sequence that he could use. 'Drill, so we can teach musketry as a unit, then how to attack and defend with the musket and then working as a compact unit and being ready even at night.'

'That'll do for the first day,' Gideon grinned. 'Let's rescue our charges from Effra.'

All afternoon was spent getting the new soldiers accustomed to standing still, holding a musket and pretending to pound the skulls of Royalists. The day ended with them marching back across town to lodgings in two houses near Tom's original team.

'Who's your friends?' asked Bathsua, when she came back from her own adventure.

'Our numbers have grown,' called out Samuel. 'I've been promoted to colonel and the others are all captains. These men are our bodyguard.'

'Aha. So our lives are saved. Can we go home now, or do we have to wait for the formal surrender of Prince Maurice?' The woman laughed.

'What of your day, Bathsua?' Tom asked.

She looked at him for a moment, as though unsure what to say. 'I'm to work with Lady Eleanor Drake, organising the supplies for the townsfolk. She's assigned a garret in the town for me. It will be a good place for me to pray.'

'You won't be camping with us then?' Tom said.

'I'll still come and eat with you, as often as I can.' She smiled. 'I need to keep an eye on cousin Nathan, remember.'

Three days they had of practising soldiering and fighting a shadow enemy before the real war overtook them. The time went quickly for Bathsua. No longer the assistant or outsider, in this short time she became a valuable support for the leading woman in the town. Lady Eleanor recognised her qualities, and Bathsua was forged into a tool for getting things done.

For Tom also, the time was productive. His role was clear and there was minimum interference from the officers, who were busy taking troops of cavalry out to spy on the Royalists and drive in all the local livestock to feed the garrison. Then they had to attend meetings to organise every aspect of town life.

Despite these efforts, supplies of food were low in the town. Each man received bread and cheese, or dried fish or a piece of meat when it was available, but bellies ached and eyes wandered often to the Cobb or to Gun Cliff, hoping to see barges unloading or sails on the horizon. Tom noted how his section of men often fared well with food. Someone always seemed to find something extra to bring to the pot.

One evening Bathsua noticed the thickness of the stew. 'And where did you come across venison like this, Ifor?'

'The deer must run somewhere. Sometimes it's across our path.'

'This town's no deer park, soldier. But there's a stock of deer meat hanging up in Horse Street. Is this meat from there?'

'We're not your children, mistress.'

'And what does that mean, Samuel? That your pilfering is nothing to do with me?' Her voice rose. 'We sit here, bearding a fierce enemy, with a nearly empty larder, and you tell me it's no business of mine where your food comes from?'

'You can't blame us for looking out for ourselves,' Effra joined in. 'Every man is doing the same. Look around the town, Bathsua. You'll find every campfire scrounges for extras.'

'I know nothing of what happens at other campfires, but I thought I did know you.' She looked each man in the eye. 'And what I thought was that here was a group of honest men with decent standards that could be relied on. It seems I was wrong.'

Gideon and Samuel glanced at each other with puzzled expressions. Effra wiped his face with his big right hand. 'Bathsua, girl. You've been with us for some time now. You do know us.' He spoke wearily. 'We've given you no cause to think we're better than anyone else.'

'Well, this is an opportunity for you to show me you are more than thieves and liars. You can either convince me that you will not steal any food supplies during the siege or...' Bathsua paused and her eyes searched the Town Line for inspiration. '... Or I will no longer be visiting your campfire. And if I hear of any further thieving, I will report you to Colonel Blake.'

Bathsua stared at the men and the men stared back. No one spoke. After a brief pause, she added, 'Let me know your decision tomorrow,' and stamped off, heading for her garret room.

'Blimey. That storm blew in from nowhere!' said Ifor.

'She's got a point, though,' said Tom.

'She's got a damn cheek, telling us how to live our lives,' said Samuel.

'You've got to give her some slack on that point, Samuel,' said Gideon. 'She's been telling us how we should live ever since she met us.'

'Aye, that's my cousin.' Nathan grinned.

'Well, what are we going to do – say goodbye to the maid or change our victualling tactics?' said Ifor.

'Life and chance will put things in our way,' Tom said. 'Let's just agree not to pinch supplies from the central stocks in the town. I guess she's right, we are all in this together, so if we steal from each other we cause other problems.'

'We can live with that,' Samuel and Gideon agreed, with a sly nod to each other.

Effra, Ifor and Nathan agreed.

'So you speak to the girl tomorrow, Tom,' said Effra.

'Why me? Nathan, you go and square things with your cousin.'

'No, Tom. You're the corporal. You get to do all the really shitty jobs.' Effra spoke to Tom, but he winked at Nathan as he did so.

189

Chapter 19

Tom strolled through the town on a sunny April afternoon looking for a preacher; there were twenty-five, according to Ifor. He was seeking Widow Wilson's home. He found it opposite St Michael's Church, a modest, narrow building wedged between two more comfortable residences, as if being elbowed in the ribs by both. The grey front door opened to his knock and a wiry old woman asked his purpose.

'Is Reverend Bush at home?'

'Aye, he is, but who's asking?'

'I'm Tom Tyler and I bring a message from a friend.' He was aware this sounded suspicious, but he stood still while the old woman looked him up and down through slitted eyes.

Then the eyes widened and softened. 'Ask him yerself. He's through the house, in the yard.'

Tom made his way down a hall and through an open door into a back yard containing one goat, assorted goat droppings and two wicker chairs, on one of which sat a middle-aged man. He wore a brown sleeveless tunic over a formerly white shirt, and yellow breeches showing bare legs beneath the knee. He looked stocky. His round head had a fair covering of short grey curly hair and his brawny forearms and legs had a down of the same colour. The man turned and Tom noticed a book in his hand, but his gaze was immediately drawn to the face of Obadiah Bush.

The older man smiled and crow's feet creased his temples. 'Good day, soldier. Do I know you?'

'No, sir. I mean Reverend. My name is Tom Tyler. I only recently arrived in Lyme.'

'Well, you're right welcome, son. Sit and tell me how you come to be here.' Reverend Bush reached out and dragged the second chair beside his own. 'Now. You've already seen war. I can tell that. What brings you here to me?'

Tom sat mute beside this solid figure.

'Take your time.' The man smiled and Tom felt a warmth from him that eased muscles that had been tense for days.

That audience lasted barely twenty minutes before a soldier intruded and called the minister to another duty. In that period Tom related the message from Master Prescott, and something of his own journey to Lyme.

'Thanks for your visit, Tom. I hope I will be welcome if I visit your unit. Where's your station?'

Tom told him, then the preacher left the house and strode towards Fort Newell, behind the church.

Next day, work on the town line became feverish. The Royalists were close and the defences still looked so feeble. Officers were everywhere, pointing and shouting. By mid-afternoon energies flagged and the work slowed.

Then a rider galloped through the gate of Captain Marsh's

191

fort. 'Royalists. On Uplyme Hill,' he announced.

Soon, no further announcements were needed. It seemed to Tom that the whole population was lining the walls from forts Marsh to Gaitch, to watch an army arrive.

The first to appear was a troop of cavalry, on the slopes of the hill above Marsh's Fort to the northwest of the town. The townsfolk could see the pennons fluttering and the light glinting off helmets and breastplates. These stood alone until another two troops joined them. Then a block of foot soldiers appeared. More infantry formed up across the road to Uplyme. Still more Royalists arrived, to the west of the first troop. Soon the whole ridge was bristling with more than a mile's length of colours and men.

The townsfolk and garrison watched all this as though it were a play for their entertainment. The appearance of each regiment prompted a cheer and applause from the crowd. When the dispositions were complete, the Royalist soldiers roared, the horses neighed and their muskets and pistols crackled. There was also a deeper boom, heard just before a cannonball shot over the heads of the onlookers and buried itself in a field within the town. The assembled townspeople roared back.

Tom looked around him. No one seemed overawed by this show of strength.

Then, from the assembled army, three horsemen rode forward. Two balanced carbines on their left thighs, holding the gun barrel in one hand and the reins in the other. The leather of their gloves matched their long leather boots. Shimmering breastplates covered buff coats but left crimson sleeves on display. Their faces were inscrutable beneath pot helmets with three horizontal face-protecting bars. The third man wore a plumed hat of black beaver felt. His coat was also beneath a breastplate, and his sleeves were crimson and yellow in narrow hoops. He held a trumpet in like manner to the carbines. The long brass trumpet was decorated with lace pennons in crimson, yellow and black. This group approached the gate of Marsh's Fort, watched by all the townsfolk.

Ceremoniously the group drew up ten yards from the gate, the horsemen flanking the trumpeter. He drew the instrument to his lips and began a call to announce his presence. At this, citizens in the fort began pelting him with stones. Most of these missiles missed, but the trumpeter understood the message and shortened his recital, then drew a scroll from his pocket.

'I am the messenger of His Royal Highness Prince Maurice, Count Palatine of the Rhine and nephew of His Majesty King Charles of England, Scotland and Ireland. My master bids me declare to you his intention to take and occupy this town of Lyme Regis on behalf of His Majesty, and to call all true Englishmen in the town to support his army in taking possession of the place.'

The trumpeter re-rolled the scroll and sat immobile while Colonel Ceeley, who was the governor, and Colonels Were and Blake, rode out and drew up their horses nose to nose with the Royalist mounts. All this, while the trumpeter was being treated to catcalls, more stones and other rough shows of disapproval from the townspeople. When Colonel Ceeley raised his hand, the shouts of the people subsided.

'We are honoured the Prince wishes to visit our humble town. However, we cannot agree to entertaining him when he arrives with such a large and insolent rabble.' Cheers erupted from the Town Line.

'If he would be gracious enough to send his army away, he would be very welcome to come in and speak with us. Until such time as your master shows us this courtesy, we will, be assured, resist every attempt to enter our town.'

The trumpeter paused, then nodded to the colonel. He and his escort wheeled their horses and stepped back up the road in as dignified a way as possible when being pelted with stones and other softer, smellier missiles.

As the evening wore on and the light faded, the townspeople watched their enemies spreading out. They reached west and south, towards the Cobb; they moved eastwards, down onto the narrow meadows near the Lym River. More soldiers appeared, coming down the hill on the east side of the town, extending the line across the rough track to Charmouth. An entire army, focusing its might on tiny Lyme. Could they resist such a force? Tom had no idea.

As night settled, the mood of Tom and his comrades became more solemn. The fire seemed incomplete to Tom without Bathsua. Nobody knew what to expect in the morning, and conversation was subdued.

'Ho, do you have space by the fire for some old bones?' Reverend Bush appeared out of the dark.

'Gladly, Reverend.' Tom shifted to make space, and Gideon sat up to offer roasted goat to their visitor.

'Are you prepared for tomorrow, lads?'

'Aye. We'll be ready for them Cornish and French.'

'And the Irish.'

'And the Devon men,' Gideon spat.

'They'll not find us wanting.'

'I don't doubt it,' said the reverend, looking at the soldiers round the fire. 'But are you ready to meet your maker? Our lives are fragile things at the best of times, but in war?'

'We do what we can, and we take whatever comes. There's no other way for a man to live,' said Effra.

'Ah, Effra, you speak as a man that's seen much.'

'I've seen much, and know what men are capable of.'

'Wisely spoken. Jesus once said the same. He knows what is in the core of every man's heart. He sees our fears and knows our thoughts and desires.'

'Reverend, do you then agree with the preachers that say once we yield our lives to Christ we can do whatever we want?' Nathan asked.

'There may be grains of truth in much folly. Those preachers take what Jesus says and twist it into something never intended. Christ brings us freedom, but that freedom isn't to live in a way that dishonours him or hurts ourselves or our neighbours.'

'Ha. So the freedom he brings is like the freedom of the stocks; you're free to sit there, with your head jutting through the yoke, until someone lets you out,' Samuel said.

'In my experience it's the men who insist on doing things their way that end up with their head in the stocks,' said Reverend Bush, 'or in a noose. On a night like this, men are often aware of how alone they are. Friends come close and give support, but only God can reach into your heart to fortify it. The old word "comfort" means to bring strength, and God stands ready to comfort us tonight, and tomorrow too.'

'Aye, well, I may take thought to being good tomorrow, Reverend,' said Ifor.

'He that says he'll be good tomorrow means he'll be wicked today.' Bush laughed.

Another voice, from the opposite side of the fire, joined the talk. 'It's only when God lays men on their backs that they look up to heaven.'

'We didn't see you there, sir,' said Ifor.

'No matter, soldier. I'm not here to catch you out, but to check you're ready for action tomorrow.' Colonel Blake stepped forward into the firelight.

Everyone attempted to sound confident.

'We can cope with anything the enemy can throw at us,' said Tom.

'I don't want you to cope! I want the enemy not to cope with you!'

Tom felt the colonel fixing him with his eyes, then scanning the campfire, claiming the attention of all the men around it.

'Think, men. Use your cunning and your wiles. Do the unexpected. Puzzle your adversary and he won't know what to do.'

The soldiers listened, grim-faced.

'Tomorrow, Prince Maurice will attack. We must be ready for him. Expect pain. Expect to be surprised. Make up your minds to be cleverer and more determined than him and we will prevail.' He swept all the upturned faces with one more fierce look, then he was gone, looking for another campfire, and Reverend Bush followed him.

Next morning, very early, the booming of artillery silenced the birds. The enemy had spent the night preparing a battery above Marsh's Fort. Cannonballs flew overhead and crashed into walls, roofs or ground. Little damage was done, but breakfast was forgotten as the defenders digested their first experience of a siege. The bombardment was regular; one gun fired every ten minutes, then a second gun (with a lower pitch to its boom) fired every quarter-hour. A third gun popped in between these with a higher, lighter bark. Each boom was followed by a crash somewhere in the town. The terror came from not knowing where each ball would land.

'To your stations, men,' shouted officers all around the town. No one knew from which direction the attack would come, but all knew one was coming.

Tom's squad were stationed along the northern side of the Town Line, midway between the forts of Captains Marsh and Gaitch. The morning was grey and Tom shivered as he took up his position by a small hole in the six-foot high, two-foot wide wall. This was a loophole he'd punched open himself to give a view of the land beyond. That land was open ground with grass and gorse. There were hedgerows around fifty yards away, and some larger bushes where the hedges turned from running parallel to the wall to running at it. Someone should have cut those bushes down before now.

Tom gestured for Samuel to take his place, then he toured the positions of the rest of the platoon. Every man looked sturdy and determined. Though not even half-trained and only half-dressed, these young boys believed they were a match for the Royalist army, with its French and Irish mercenaries, its Devonish and Cornish veterans and its

197

battle-hardened officers.

He was proud of these farm boys. Then he realised that most of them were older than he was. 'God. What a year,' he said to himself.

'Corporal!' a musketeer called, pointing into the field. 'They're coming.'

And they were. Hundreds of men were lining the hedgerows and creeping forward where there was cover. Tom could hear them shouting now, and he realised musket balls were buzzing past. 'Stand ready, men. Blow your match. Cock your match. That's it. Easy now. Do it like we practised. Now, present together. Wait for each other. Give FIRE.'

Small musket volleys felled the foremost of the enemy and caused others to scuttle sideways, looking for cover. More balls pinged off the Town Line or entered the houses either side of Tom. These balls were mostly swallowed up by the thick turves and stony soil packed on either side of the house walls, a necessary strengthening if the buildings were to be an effective part of the Town Line.

The morning was growing foggy and acrid. Gunpowder smoke hung along the wall, but it quickly blew away from the attackers. Tom could see that their enemies had mostly taken positions behind cover. They were now sending a deliberate rain of lead at them, but they weren't charging towards the line.

'Watch yourselves, lads. Fire towards places where you know the enemy are skulking. And fire together!' he shouted. He watched as his men carried out his orders, then he backed out of the building and found his old squad.

The cannons continued to add their heavier weight to the

fight, and Tom could feel the disorientating effect of danger and adrenaline.

'Come 'ere, lad.' Effra pulled him in to the wall. 'Now's no time for promenading.' He passed Tom his musket and nodded at his place. Ifor was nowhere to be seen.

'Where's Ifor? And Nathan? Are they wounded?'

'No. An officer ran by asking for reinforcement along the western wall. They're under pressure there, it seems.'

'They can't take my men without asking! Can they?' Tom looked to Effra, who just shrugged.

'You know Nathan. He couldn't stay still, and Ifor went to cover his back. The rest of us thought better of leaving you with your babies.'

'Man the line, men.' The call came from behind them. An officer stood with sword raised. 'They're holding their position, so don't let them think we're asleep.'

The next hour was spent in a rapid whirl of load, look for a target, fire, duck, and repeat. Every so often, buckets of musket balls were delivered by men who Tom and Effra took to be from a reserve force kept back from the fighting. Gunpowder arrived in the same manner. The ammunition bearers would lope across Sherborne Road and throw themselves against the protective walls. Men there were tasked with rationing out the powder and balls to squad members who crept out of the line to replenish their comrades' weapons. Beer and bread came forward in the same way.

'Where's that damn boy?' Tom snapped at Effra.

'You're not his father, Tom. And you've made yourself a painful stick if you're going to beat yourself up every time his excitement runs away with him.'

199

'You're right. But I promised Bathsua I'd keep an eye on him.'

'I know.' Effra sounded tetchy. 'I promised Micah that too. But we're in a battle. Keep yourself safe first. Then look after your mates close by. Even that may be beyond us.'

Tom's head drooped on his forearms as they rested on the top of the town wall.

'All right, Tom. I'll go and find Nathan and Ifor. I'll tell them they're needed here. You need to stay here and direct the battle.' Effra grinned.

Tom nodded in relief. 'Don't be long, Effra. I need you here too.' He went back to the platoon. The only way he could deal with his first battle was to assume the role of corporal. The young men listening to him never guessed the terror screaming inside him.

Chapter 20

Effra didn't return till the Royalist attack stopped. Tom had kept his platoon together, and they'd been a persistent obstacle to the enemy to their front, but he could tell they were being fixed in place so that another part of the Town Line could be attacked. During lulls he could hear a greater struggle going on to their left.

The men were stood down around seven of the clock. Samuel and Gideon headed off to the town mill to collect food and drink. Tom got the fire going while Effra, Ifor and Nathan watched him. They wouldn't talk about the day... not until the brothers returned.

As they ate, Tom learned of the fight that had gone on two hundred yards from him. Ifor told the tale.

'We walked into a fog. Men on the Town Line, south of Marsh's Fort, could just about see each other, but nothing of the enemy. Cottages outside the town were set alight. They must've been full to bursting with straw and pitch, they threw out such dark smoke for so long. They used the smoke to get close. They settled down among the rubbish and ditches near us and galled us with musket fire. We kept them there; they could neither move forward nor back, but somehow they kept being resupplied and so they kept at us.

201

We lost some men, but not so many as you'd think.'

'They lost more than us,' Nathan butted in.

Ifor paused in his story, and Tom saw that the day had worn him down.

'We've had a boring time,' Gideon said. 'After you left, Colonel Blake invited us to spend some time in the meadow below Fort Davie. Maids brought us beer and meat all through the day.'

'It was at least four times,' chipped in Samuel.

'We got a good sleep in the afternoon, though Tom did tell Effra to pop over and ask you to keep the noise down.'

'Well, if you're so fresh you can bloody well take my sentry duty,' Ifor snapped.

Nathan laughed. Then it was time for Tom to check the sentries, while the others settled down to rest weary limbs, red-rimmed eyes and jangled ears.

The night passed quietly as weary soldiers and townsfolk slept or tried to sleep. Next morning was crisp and bright, and the Royalist battery began pounding again soon after Samuel had kicked his comrades awake after his sentry duty. This time, though, Tom heard five different booms, all deep ones. That meant heavy balls, fired from heavy cannons. None came their way as they munched on rye bread and strips of dried meat, washed down with a mug of beer.

After the previous day, it was a relief not to be attacked again. The main Royalist attention shifted to the defending artillery. And its sole target was Captain Marsh's fort. Around midday a captain arrived with a group of gunners and a two-wheeled cart.

'Ho, boys, how goes it? Get yerselves over here while the enemy are busy elsewhere. There's knowledge and wisdom

I want to impart.' He motioned for the gunners to unload the cart while Tom's platoon assembled by the road.

'What baubles have you got to show us, sir?' Effra asked.

'It looks like a tinker's fair,' said Samuel. 'Hey, Ifor. Where's *your* wares? Surely you could teach these amateurs a thing or two.'

'Aye. I've no idea what those outlandish pots are for. You wouldn't get a wooden penny for those rusty things.'

'Well now. Don't be so hasty, men. These pots and shells are the future of siege warfare.' The captain cut across the banter. 'What we have here are grenadoes. These flasks and what-not contain all sorts of man-killing stuff, to blow a man apart if handled correctly.' He nodded at the gunners and they lifted up a selection of the spherical cases so all could see. Most were about the size of a pint pot. Some were metal canisters and others pottery jugs sealed at their necks. All had a short length of fuse dangling from one end.

'The grenadoes are filled with gunpowder or wildfire and the fuse is lit. Now – and this is the important bit – before the thing blows up you must throw it with all your might over the wall and into the onrushing enemy. There it will explode and stop them dead.'

'Are we going to get a load of these grenadoes to throw at the Cornish, then?' asked Gideon.

'We don't have many of them in Lyme at present. Those we do have will be stationed at strategic points and used when needed.'

'Does that include us, here?' Samuel said.

'Well, no.'

Samuel sneered, 'So what are you showing us for, sir? Are we so likely to be bored in this siege that we must learn new

203

and surprising ways of waging war, then be told we can't use them?'

'Aye, what next? Will we have to take turns firing our cannons? Do we not have men enough for these special tasks?' Gideon said.

'Don't take on now, boys. You need to know your profession, and that is soldiering. And to know it better you must understand and recognise all the ways you might blow your enemy apart, or he you.' Captain Drake paused for dramatic effect before continuing.

'As well as throwing these things at your adversaries you must know how to prevent his grenadoes exploding.' At this point, the captain showed them an empty grenado.

'When the enemy attack they may throw us grenadoes full of gunpowder or wildfire. Listen carefully. Gunpowder will explode and leave small fires that are easy to douse with water. Wildfire, however, must be quenched with milk or urine. Wet hides and pails of water and milk will be provided at regular places around the Town Line.'

The gunners showed the men more closely what the grenadoes looked like and how they worked. Then they loaded them back into the cart and trundled down the road to show the next platoon.

Gideon laughed. 'I think I'll station myself beside a pail of milk. If a grenado comes my way and it's of gunpowder, it'll blow me to kingdom come. The wildfire will just burn, but the milk will save me.'

'And you can always make cheese of it, if no grenadoes come over the wall,' added Samuel.

Bathsua joined them for their evening meal of smoked meat strips and watered-down cider. She spoke of her work organising teams of women to deal with all the business of the town, from child minding to washing to regulating small shop-holders.

'Some townsfolk expect the Royalists to blow away in a day or two, like a summer storm. They think their lives must stay the same or else the whole world will crumble to dust. Well, our world may crumble, but ignoring it won't help.'

'We've all told stories round the fire, Bathsua,' said Ifor. 'What about you? What stories can you share with us?'

Bathsua's face lit up. 'All right,' she said. 'There really is only one story worth telling.'

'No, woman!' Effra interrupted. 'We get enough sermons from the garrison preachers. We don't want to hear your gospel round the fire, too. Don't you know any fairytales?'

'Sometimes I think your plan is to bludgeon us into submission so you can present us to God like a bunch of culled seals,' Gideon remarked.

Tom kept quiet and watched Bathsua deal with this ribbing.

'Aah. Then listen to this tale. Back in the time of the Israelites, before they had a king, they were ruled by judges. One judge was Deborah, a woman. In her time the Canaanite king sent his commander Sisera to oppress the Israelites. Eventually the people cried to the Lord for help.

'Deborah, the judge, was also a prophetess, and God told her he'd heard the cries of his people. She summoned her commander, Barak, and told him to take ten thousand men to Mount Tabor, where he would defeat Sisera's chariots. But Barak's stomach turned to water. "I'll only go if you come with me," he said.

205

'"Very well," said Deborah, "I will go with you, but because you don't trust God, the honour of the victory will go to a woman."

'The Israelite army gathered on Mount Tabor. Sisera, with his mighty army of chariots, attacked them there. But Barak swept down and defeated them. Sisera's chariot broke and he fled on foot to the tent of a man called Heber.

'Jael, Heber's wife, didn't approve of her husband's friendship with Sisera. She met him by her tent and said, "Come in, my lord, do not be afraid." So he entered the tent and rested. While he slept Jael took a tent peg and a hammer and drove the peg through Sisera's temple – and he died.

'"Come and see the man you're looking for," she said to Barak, and she showed him Sisera's body. So, that day God smote the enemy of the Israelites, and used a woman to do it.' Bathsua sat with a defiant tilt to her head and a crooked smile on her lips.

'I was wrong, boys,' Gideon said. 'She's not out to bludgeon us after all. Though I'll be wary if she ever comes near me with a hammer and peg,'

No one continued the banter. All they wanted was sleep. Bathsua patted her knees and stood up, wished everyone good night and left for her garret room.

Next morning Tom and Ifor watched a column of men sally out from the gate in Marsh's Fort and race uphill. The attack caught the besiegers by surprise and drove them back. On went the attackers, up the steep slope to the new battery, and there they hacked and smashed at the cannons, to stop the besiegers throwing their balls into the town. They didn't have long, though, before a regiment of Cornish infantry swept the raiders back down the hill.

'Magnificent,' said Nathan. 'Shame we weren't involved.'

'I think there'll be fighting enough, even for you, Nathan.' Effra patted his young friend's shoulder. 'Don't be greedy.'

Next day another battery was built and more cannons hurled metal balls at Gaitch's Fort.

'We can't just sit here and watch! Can't we drive them gunners back, like they did from Marsh's Fort?' Nathan's frustration was shared by many.

Tom found it difficult to argue for caution, and by dusk there were nearly sixty men seething to get at the new battery. No officers were around to speak wisdom to them or sanction an attack, and the soldiers' mood soured. When supper – a measly portion of bread and cheese – arrived, each man's eyes strayed over the Town Line.

'I bet they're sitting down to a tasty dinner.' Samuel voiced what many thought.

'Why should they feast when we starve?' Nathan was pacing up and down, working himself into a rage.

Others were doing the same, and in a moment the sixty men rose up like a swarm of flying ants and clambered over the breastworks. There was no plan, and the wisest course was the quickest, so they trotted towards the new battery near a bridge of the Lym River, about five hundred yards from Gaitch's Fort. Their approach attracted no attention and they met no organised defence, so the attackers vaulted the soil gabions and wicker defences and landed in the battery, scaring the gunners. Soon Tom's men found themselves the masters of a wooden platform containing a battery of four cannons.

'What do we do now?' Tom said to Effra.

'Grab what we can, damage what we can't carry, then leg-it,' Gideon said.

'Sounds good to me,' said Tom, who then bawled orders to the men to search for useful tools and food, especially food. He got a squad together to defend the northern rim of the battery while others worked at disabling the guns. The rest rifled through the tents and belongings of the Royalists who had fled.

Moments passed vividly to Tom. When he saw infantry forming up in front of them, he hollered to the men, 'Time to go.'

'Look what I've found,' crowed Samuel, holding up a half-roasted shoulder of mutton. Others had found provisions and a stack of pickaxes and shovels, which were hefted onto willing shoulders as the attackers disappeared over the gabions, heading for the Town Line.

Ten minutes later, the soldiers were in their defensive positions. Tom checked that everyone was accounted for and that the booty was shared, before the smell of mutton drew him back to his campfire.

'A good day's work, I think,' Effra said.

'But what are we going to tell Bathsua?' said Tom, and they all laughed.

Songs were swelling the evening air when a group of men marched into the middle of the campfires.

'What in God's name is going on here?' Colonel Blake was livid. His rage was supported by two other officers. 'Who gave the command to raid that battery?' The colonel drew himself up to his full height and chose a raised area to stand on so he could look down, menacingly, on the soldiers.

'No one gave an actual order, sir,' piped up someone.

'We just agreed on it and did it,' added another.

'Sir. I'm the corporal that went with the men. I was the one in charge, if anyone was.' Tom stood to attention in front of the colonel. 'It's like we said, sir. We ate a meal that wouldn't fatten a pigeon and it galled us that those gunners could eat theirs, then blast away without us objecting. So we decided we would surprise them.'

'But without orders? That's mutiny, soldier.'

'Pardon me, sir?' Effra butted in. 'If I remember rightly, Colonel... You spoke to us a few days ago and said you wanted us to scare the shit out of them Royalists and make them not know what to expect. Well, that's what we did. We didn't stay put. We didn't let them get comfortable, we took the battle to them, all sudden and unexpected like. And it worked. How many men did we lose, Tom?'

'One man got his hand cut, sir.' Tom paused. 'And we brought back seventeen pickaxes and shovels. And we bashed the cannons about a bit. And we grabbed as much food as we could lay our hands on. Sir.'

The colonel's chin dropped onto his chest and he surveyed the men facing him through stern eyebrows. A grumbling arose from his belly as he considered. The men stood to attention and waited.

Then his face changed, and the grumbling became a guffaw. 'I can't condone disobeying orders, corporal. But you're right to do the unexpected. I want fighters in this town. And you are fighters, all of you. Congratulations on performing a difficult raid without losing a man.'

The colonel turned to his companions. 'What d'you think

of that, Captain Pyne? Major Langer?'

The other officers mumbled guarded praise.

'Right, take the tools down to the arsenal, then get back to your second supper. And Tom! You got away with it this time, but don't attack without orders again. Is that clear? You're supposed to scare the enemy, not your own officers.' Colonel Blake waited for Tom's reply before he and the officers sauntered towards Marsh's Fort.

Chapter 21

Life in the besieged town developed a pattern. The Royalist bombardment was sporadic but continued throughout each day. The enemy attacked all the places along the Town Line that looked vulnerable but found a determined defence at every point. The defenders learned quickly how to move about under musket fire. Captain Marsh's war ended when a sniper shot him in the head at his fort. Colonel Ceeley changed its name to West Fort after that.

Then the weather took a hand and separated the brawling armies like a butcher throwing water over two dogs. It became wet and windy, foggy and cold. Sentries struggled to keep their matchcord alight along the Town Line. In some places the sentries stood inside houses, but booths were also built to keep sentry and matchcord dry. Colonel Blake worried that this would lead to the guards huddling in the huts, so he changed the watches more frequently in bad weather.

After breakfast on Sunday, the fifth day of May, Bathsua arrived at Tom's campfire. Tom took note of her pink dress with a white apron, a darker red shawl and a plain coif controlling most of her dark hair. Her face was fresh and her hazel eyes were bright and sparkly as usual.

'Reverend Bush is preaching by the open ground at the bottom of Church Street. Are any of you going to the service there?'

'Why that one, Bathsua? There's two dozen preachers in the town. Don't you want to hear the one at St Michael's Church?' Samuel goaded.

'Because, Samuel. Reverend Bush is the man who has taken the most interest in you soldiers. He's been here when others have stayed beside a cosy hearth. He's the one who fights with you and prays for you. I thought you might be interested in what he has to say.'

'Well, I'm not coming.' Gideon, Ifor and Effra echoed Samuel's answer.

Tom thought differently. 'I like Reverend Bush. I'll come.'

So Bathsua and Tom went to church together. As they walked, she asked, 'Do you trust the officers yet, Tom?'

'What has God said in reply to your prayers? Are you to report us for burglary?'

'I believe God wants me to leave the decision in his hands. I have no liberty in my heart to take your papers to Colonel Blake. Are they well hidden?'

'Yes. We've put them out of reach of itching fingers.'

In the square below St Michael's Church and near the bridge over the Lym, there was enough room for hundreds of men to sit and listen to a preacher raised a couple of feet on a small timber platform. The service started with prayer. Lots of prayer. Prayer for victory, for mercy for the injured and bereaved, for wisdom for the Parliament in fighting the war, and for the King that he might escape his evil counsellors.

Then Reverend Bush stood up, squat and indestructible in a long, dark coat, buttoned in front, with sleeves of increasing width near the cuffs. He wore no hat over his grey, curling locks. He smiled at his congregation.

'I take my sermon today from Psalm 73. This psalm is not about God's victory over an external enemy, but of man's victory over the inner enemy.'

At one point, Reverend Bush seemed to Tom to look directly at him.

'God is good to Israel. He's good to his people. Those who belong to him are pure in heart. But we're often distracted by others, who seem to bask in God's grace and preferment.

'We must remember who we are. And what trouble we cause for ourselves. Eliphaz, Job's comforter, was right when he said, "Man is born to trouble, as the sparks fly upwards." For all our cunning, we get in trouble and need to be saved from ourselves, as much as from the things around us.

'In every man's heart is pain, hardship and want. These God uses to challenge, not to taunt us. They are lovingly used to show us our need of God's grace. Knowing this, we will see the wicked wither like grass. But our place is beside God, whatever our struggles.'

Bathsua nodded throughout the oration. Tom's attention drifted in and out. A few phrases caught in his mind, but at the end of the hour-long preach he was ready to sit and relax.

Monday's dawn arrived above the clouds, but at ground level a heavy sea fog hung over everything, as though the entire town was inside a loosely packed mattress. No one could see more than twenty feet around them. Every man was alert. Blake expected the Royalists to use the fog as cover for an attack.

'I can't hear a thing,' said Tom.

'No need to whisper, boy. We can't go through the day like we're in church. Speak up,' said Effra.

'We can hear you, rebel,' came a call from beyond the Town Line.

Effra and Tom moved to the wall to look through a loophole.

Tom said, 'We hear you too, Peeping Tom. But you've been struck blind again, I think.'

'Aye. Who can see owt in this soup?'

'So, are you about to storm us, d'you think?' Tom said, nodding to Gideon, who had just joined them.

'Ah. I might warn you of that, my friend. But how can I be sure you would repay me by holding fire till we could speak face to face?'

'Fair point,' said Effra. 'Our officers wouldn't like it if we invited you up to show you our city.'

'Well, we heartily wish this fog would lift. Living inside this cloud is miserable. My tunic's soaked, my feet are soaked, and it's only my fatherly duty to wife and children stopping me asking you to speed my arrival in heaven.'

'You're right. Fighting when tired and wet is hell. There's only one thing to do, friend,' Gideon said.

'And that is?'

'Take advantage of the fog and go home. I can tell you're a

Devonshire man. Home's not far. Your children need their dad.'

'Enough of that, rebel.' This was a different, more military voice, penetrating the thick mist. 'We're fully prepared and you won't wait long until we present your vile little town to the King, and the whole West Country is in our hands.'

'Well, if the King is to visit Lyme, this is the best weather for him,' Tom answered. 'Any other time and he'll see what a dump the place is. Not much of a prize. In fact, I don't understand why you've stopped here at all.'

'Very funny. I'll look for you when we take the town. We'll string you up with your officers. You all deserve to be hanged. What's your name, soldier? I'll add it to our list.'

'I think it's already there, friend. My name is Robert Blake,' Effra said.

The fog stayed thick and grey. The men stood at their posts hour after hour, awaiting an attack, straining their ears and shredding their nerves. Nathan and Samuel went to the mill in what seemed to be the middle of the day and brought back bread, cheese and beer. Tom made frequent tours of his twenty-four men to check that everyone was awake and alert, but also to ease his agitation with movement.

Dusk settled early over the town. Officers inspected the defences and quietly shared that there was a hot meal for them at the mill.

Tom brought his platoon together and detailed two men from each squad to stay at the line while the rest headed for the mill to have a quick meal and then return and allow their comrades a break. He detailed Samuel and Nathan from his own squad.

'Well, I'm not staying out here any longer. I need a fire and a hot meal.' Samuel stomped off, so that all Tom could see was a shape disappearing into the darkening fog.

'It's all right, Tom,' said Nathan. 'I'll stay here. I don't need anyone else. There's enough of us left here. If there's an alarm I'll let you know, otherwise you'll be back soon and I'll get my rest.' He smiled and laid his hand on Tom's shoulder.

Tom clenched his teeth in frustration, but he nodded and patted Nathan's arm.

'We'll be back in about a half hour. I'll tell Bathsua to keep you a heaped pile of whatever we get.'

'I'm hungry enough to eat the doorposts.'

Tom joined his comrades as they streamed across Sherborne Road, flowed round the sides of the houses and passed through the field leading to the stream. The bridge over the stream slowed things down, but they soon reached the mill and found trestle tables outside the building, with maids bustling around lines of seated soldiers and crowds of others waiting their turn. Each bowl served four men with stew that contained a mix of boiled meat, oatmeal and whatever vegetable leaves or turnips were available. Each man got a wooden spoon and a small hunk of rye bread, along with a beaker of beer.

Tom sought Bathsua out. She was supervising a team of women preparing the food and cleaning the platters.

'Hallo, Tom. We'll be with you soon as we can. We're trying to keep the pots simmering, but it's difficult with so many men coming at once.'

'That's fine. We'll wait our turn. I wanted to ask you to make sure Nathan doesn't miss out. He's on guard.'

'I'll do what I can.' Bathsua nodded, turning back to her job.

Tom rejoined his squad, and they waited at the trestles. The evening darkened as they stood, but eventually they were ushered forward to a table. Racks near the tables were for their unloaded muskets, but they had to keep their bandoliers on, and those with swords had to take extra care. Each man hung his matchcord around his musket, making a glowing, smoking haze around the firearms.

Tension leaked from the tired bodies of the men. Effra and Gideon were joking about something, and Ifor and Samuel were chatting to the surrounding soldiers. Tom's eyes dropped, and his mind wandered into a brighter, warmer place. It was the hills above Dorchester. The sun was clear, the air pure, and he felt content.

A trumpet call sounded through the gloom, recalling Tom from sunshine to weary, grey dusk. Then another, from a different direction. The soldiers responded at once.

Tom shook himself awake. 'To the line! Back to our places. Hurry!'

A mob bustled round the musket racks. Tom got in front of his men and diverted them up the slope to the stream.

'No time. Back up the hill. Get to your station.' Tom looked around, but couldn't tell if all his platoon were with him. They had to get back quick. There weren't enough guards to keep out a determined attack.

Tom leapt across the stream to avoid waiting for the crowd using the bridge. Most of his men followed his lead. They raced up the slope to the rear gardens on the south side of Sherborne Street, and met enemy musketeers flooding round the sides of the houses. There was no time to do more than shout fiercely and charge. There was no safety in turning and running the other way.

The enemy echoed the shout and rushed forwards, and the two groups meshed among the vegetables. Tom had his long dagger in his right hand. He punched the first attacker in the face with the dagger butt and left his collapsing body to the men behind as he swung the blade at the next man, who parried with his musket but didn't avoid Tom's left hook, which sent him sprawling. Effra was beside him now. He worked dagger and sword together and was in his element, sweeping enemies out of his way. Tom couldn't understand Effra's fear of a large battle, yet his relishing of this combat.

The defenders reached the rear of the houses and cleared the alleys leading to the road. At the road, more Royalists slammed into them and drove them back to the cabbages. There was no space, except to thrust, to parry, slash, block. Men on all sides, jostling, falling, threatening. They slipped down the hill again as the enemy's momentum surged.

They were back near the stream, pressed on three sides. Reinforcements reached them over the bridge. The fog thickened. Night settled, turning war into dark terror. The damp grass was now slick with blood. Then the crowds of Royalists shook as musket volleys slammed in from Tom's left. Another and another volley turned the tide. The enemy flinched, edging away from the defenders. The garrison musketeers stepped forward in front of Tom's men, and a block of pikemen pushed the enemy back with sharp points.

Tom halted his platoon. It had grown to fifty during the fight. Sergeants moved among the weary defenders, shaking them back into a disciplined force, then Captain Pyne was in front and leading the men along the stream towards Gaitch's Fort, where more Royalists needed subduing.

Campfires were mere embers by the time the garrison had

cleared the town of enemies. Stiffness and exhaustion set in, wounds wept and bruises bloomed. The victors of the fight hobbled around like cripples. Tom checked his men and found there were three dead, fifteen taken to the chirurgeons, and Nathan was missing.

They found Nathan's body after midnight. He lay on his back. It was difficult to tell the difference between moisture on the grass and Nathan's blood as they moved him. There was a single musket wound in his chest. Samuel and Gideon argued about letting Bathsua see him like this. Deep exhaustion filled Tom, but anguish and pain and loss churned in his mind and he could only sit in front of a fire, letting mindless flames lick damp timber into dead ash. There was no rest in inactivity, merely blankness.

At daylight the night sentries came back to the fire and found their comrades awake, but scarcely responsive to their presence. They understood.

The army chirurgeons organised the women volunteers into teams, and Bathsua worked through the night, helping with the casualties. The Royalist attack had produced far more injuries this time. Their knowledge of healing was limited, but no one in Lyme had experienced such wounds and injuries before Prince Maurice's army arrived.

At dawn Tom stood on the corner of West Street. Bathsua emerged from the Guildhall near Gun Cliff and saw him through the shredding fog. Her steps quickened towards him. Tom's face was swollen, and he limped slightly.

'What's happened? Is everyone all right?'

'It's Nathan.'

'No. Is... he bad? Take me to him.'

'Bathsua... Nathan is dead.'

219

'But you were...?' Bathsua turned away. 'Show me, Tom.'

Tom led her back to Sherborne Road, where the bodies had been laid out. They didn't speak, and Bathsua walked a pace behind him all the way.

Effra, Ifor, Gideon and Samuel stood over Nathan, watching Tom and Bathsua approach. The woman didn't look at any of their faces. She knelt down beside her cousin. She reached out to smooth his jacket and gently lifted his head into her lap. Then began a rocking, forwards and back, as the woman left behind a chill patch of deadly ground in Lyme to re-inhabit another world, another time, in which she and her cousin lived and laughed. The men retreated and watched from a distance.

At last, Bathsua rose to her feet and looked around. She spotted them, still huddled nearby, and walked over. 'I was wrong to tell my uncle Micah that you would look out for Nathan. I see you are weak men who care more for your stomachs than for your comrades. But why should I be surprised?'

'Mistress Bathsua...' began Effra.

'Don't try to justify what has happened, Effra Bayly.'

'I'm not. All I can do is tell you our hearts ache for this young man, and for you.'

'Don't presume to share my grief, soldier. Will you tell Micah and Tabitha? Will you dare to take Nathan's place in his family?' Bathsua's voice was rising.

'We know we can't do that,' Tom said.

'We would give anything to go back to last night and make different choices,' said Samuel.

'Empty words,' Bathsua said, then turned her back and walked away.

Before full daylight had chased away the last of the fog, the Royalists sounded a parley and asked for the body of Colonel Blewett, the highest-ranked officer killed so far. Colonel Blake nodded curtly from the parapet of West Fort and soon a small cart lumbered out of the gate to stand in the road that had so recently been cleared of dead soldiers.

Tom, along with many others, left his post to watch the exchange. Following the crowd, he watched out for Bathsua. When he saw her, he elbowed his way to her side.

She didn't acknowledge his presence.

'Bathsua, I want to...'

'I don't want to hear it, Tom. Please leave me alone. Otherwise I might tear your eyes out.'

From the platform inside the fort Tom watched the cart and two men, just outside the gate. A coffin, draped with a shroud, filled the well of the four-wheeled vehicle.

Within two minutes a single horseman, plus a similar cart, approached down the hill. The Royalist horseman drew up in front of the colonel.

After a silence between them lasting about ten seconds, Colonel Blake spoke. 'So, Captain. By what authority do you take charge of this man?'

'What? Sir, what do you mean?'

'Just that you ask us to yield him to you, yet you show me no authority requiring me to do so. Nor do you offer to pay for him.'

'I have no orders about haggling for Colonel Blewett.' The captain looked shaken by the suggestion.

Blake had been standing on the front of the cart, beside the carter. Now he swung round with lowered chin and patted the coffin. Then he jumped down onto the cobbles

221

and approached the captain.

Looking up at the horseman, the colonel waved forward the cart. 'Take it. We are not so poor that we can't afford to give you the body of a brave man.'

Blake's mouth was smiling, and he acknowledged the ragged cheers of the Lyme men, but Tom watched how his body moved and thought there was no grandstanding there, just dogged defiance.

The captain seemed to notice the colonel's mood, but misread it. 'Sir. This dreadful waste of life should not be. Can't we parley and agree a way to our possessing of the town and your being able to withdraw with honour?'

'Do you think our resolve wavers? We have just thrown back a major assault by your army, sir.'

'That may be, Colonel, but d'you think we won't grind you to dust? We've been stopped at the first essay. That's all.'

Blake looked at the horseman with his head cocked to the left as though he was considering his reply, or maybe he was measuring the mettle of the man.

'Here you see how weak our works are.' The colonel spread his right arm around, as if to reveal the defences behind him. 'They are not things in which we trust. So, tell your Prince that if he desires to bring his army to fight, we will pull down ten or twelve yards so you can come in, ten abreast, and we will decide this matter.' Blake's body was shaking and his voice was unsteady as he finished. No man could doubt his determination, and there was an immediate roar from the garrison and townsfolk present.

The Royalist officer had no answer to this declaration and merely nodded, then turned and walked his horse away from the town. His carters had turned round their cart and loaded the coffin, and they followed him up the hill.

Tom puffed out his cheeks as he returned to his duties. What if the Royalist had accepted Blake's offer? Would he really have broken down the wall to let the Cavaliers in? This siege was crazy. Tom sensed the stress in his comrades' bodies. How much greater was that weight on their commanders? Colonel Blake was surely going mad. As soon as he was free, he sought out Reverend Bush at his house.

'Aye. It's hard, Tom,' said the preacher. 'I've been at the burial of sixteen soldiers since breakfast. It's a terrible business. Colonel Blake feels the pressure more than most. But he's not mad. Not yet. He believes that we can win, if we act together. That's the meaning of his audacity.'

Tom nodded and looked down. Chickens scraped at the ground around his chair. 'Do you remember Nathan? He was killed when we left him on guard at suppertime.'

'Aah. Is that Bathsua's cousin?' The Reverend hung his head. 'How does she do?'

'She's withdrawn from us.'

'Yes. I see.' The Reverend's head was up again, face lifted to the sky, but eyes closed.

'I'm worried about her. Can you help?' Tom realised he had no clear idea what he wanted from the minister, apart from some magical way of removing this deep grief they all felt. And for Bathsua, he wanted a way to re-establish their friendship.

Reverend Bush gripped Tom's shoulder. 'I will go and see Bathsua. Offer what comfort I can. And I'll come and see you and your comrades.'

Chapter 22

Reverend Bush spoke to Bathsua, and he visited Tom and his comrades every day. He was often patrolling up and down the Town Line between Forts Gaitch and West, helping and encouraging each man. But Bathsua's absence from their campfire was keenly felt each evening.

Time eased the bruises and wounds. Life in the town settled to a monotonous endurance of the regular cannonade, with occasional sorties to disrupt the Royalists, or raids to thieve some weakly defended resources. Food supplies dwindled and daily rations shrank to eke them out. Gunpowder, lead shot and matchcord were used up even faster than the food.

Tom and Samuel were on Gun Cliff. They stood together, watching the work in front of them. Below them, men swarmed around a barge of equipment from the warship Mayflower. Ifor had wandered off to an alehouse. Effra and Gideon were further down the beach unloading another boat.

A yawl came alongside the jetty and an officer and a boy stepped out and marched onto dry land. The officer paused and called over Tom and Samuel. 'You two. Here. Get up to the top of St Michael's tower and ask Colonel Were to meet us in the Guildhall at once. Tell him it's urgent.'

'Aye, sir. And you are, sir?' Samuel asked.

'I am Sir Richard Bastwick from the Mayflower. Now hurry, man.'

'What's going on?' said Samuel as they hurried along Church Street.

'Whatever it is, let me speak to the officer. It's not for you to take the lead like that.'

'Don't start,' sneered Samuel. They walked on. 'What difference does it make, anyway?'

'Course it makes a difference,' said Tom as they skirted the church porch to reach the narrow entrance door at the bottom of the tower.

Samuel rushed to get to the door first, and Tom was behind him all the way up to the top of the spiral, stone staircase.

'It makes no difference, Tom,' Samuel said, over his shoulder.

The corporal seethed and bided his time. As Samuel stepped over the lip in the doorway leading to the open platform he moved closer to him and slipped his foot between Samuel's ankles, sending him sprawling to the floor. This commotion drew the attention of an officer leaning against the opposite parapet who turned as Tom stepped forwards.

'Urgent message, sir,' said Tom.

'Yes? From whom?'

'Er. Sir Richard Bustik, sir. He's just arrived on the Mayflower and needs you to attend him with other officers in the Guildhall.'

'Does he now? Whatever's up?' The officer gazed into the distance while he considered. 'Here, man. Take this.'

225

He thrust a two-foot long leather tube into Tom's hand. It was heavier than it looked. 'This is my perspective glass. I'm watching the enemy reposition their artillery. I need you to keep an eye on them. They're dismantling the guns at Colway Meadow and we need to follow where they're taking them.'

'Yes, sir.'

The officer briefly showed Tom and Samuel how to aim the tube in the direction of interest and to look through one end. He then rushed off down the stone steps, his sword clattering behind him. Tom was amazed how clear and near the device brought the Royalist works beyond Gaitch's Fort.

'So, you did that well, then,' said Samuel.

'At least I stayed on my feet.'

'But you cocked up the message, idiot.'

'Don't call me an idiot. I outrank you in this army.'

'Don't I know it. You throw your spindly weight around, every chance you get.'

Tom squared up to the taller man. 'Well, if you'd learn to obey orders, you'd be a better soldier and your mates could rely on you.'

'Don't start on that again.' Samuel pushed Tom in the chest. 'It was your decision to leave Nathan on guard. Don't dump your blame on me.'

'You bloody well know I did that 'cos you wouldn't stay with him when I told you to.' Tom pushed Samuel.

'Like that would've made a difference. What could I have done to hold back the whole fucking Royalist army?'

'I dunno, but you might've given a bright young lad a warning and...' Tom aimed his right fist at Samuel '... p'raps given him a chance of a life.'

226

Tom dodged a punch then swung his other arm. The perspective glass thudded into Samuel's right temple, then recoiled out of his hand and over the parapet. Each man threw another punch before they realised what had happened. They rushed to the barrier and looked down. There, beside a gravestone, was the broken shape of the spyglass.

'Shit. What do we do now?' said Samuel.

'Shit, shit, shit,' said Tom.

'We'd better go and collect the bits.'

They cradled the bits of leather and paper tube, with their mangled wire supports and internal lenses, and went back up the tower to await their fate.

'You're still a bloody idiot and you don't even know why,' hectored Samuel.

'What d'you mean?'

'He asked us to send Colonel Were to the Guildhall.' Samuel fixed his comrade with his gaze. 'You blurted out the message to the wrong officer.'

Tom stayed immobile for a moment, then sagged against the parapet. There was a murmur from below and the two men could hear their doom approach up the spiral staircase.

'Not a very long meeting, was it?' Samuel said.

In a few moments, a group of officers stepped onto the platform. They took in the scene before them: two soldiers, one holding the broken pieces of the most modern and expensive device for watching a distant enemy. The first to reach them were Colonels Were and Blake, followed by Sir Richard. Several others then emerged from the stairs. All remained hushed until the officer who owned the perspective glass reached them. He pushed through the small crowd and explained how they could pinpoint the enemy positions.

Tom watched the officer's face halt in mid-sentence as he spotted the offering he held. The voice choked, the cheeks flushed, and despair and anger warred with each other in his eyes.

'What in God's name happened here? I left you a bare quarter-hour ago to monitor the enemy.'

Colonel Blake stepped beside the bereaved officer and took charge of the situation. 'Explain yourself, Tyler.'

'I... we... had an argument after the officer left, sir.' Tom knew it sounded feeble. 'I hit Samuel over the head with the spyglass.'

'It bounced off my head, sir. And over the battlements there.' Samuel pointed.

Colonel Blake drew himself up to his full five-foot six inches. 'Not only is this dereliction of duty, but it's wanton destruction of weapons that we badly need to defeat the Prince. Do you know how many spyglasses we have in our garrison?' Blake jutted his chin towards Tom.

'No, sir,' replied both soldiers.

'Well, as of this morning the total number was one. You have single-handedly dealt us a blow that the Prince hasn't managed in all the weeks he's been sitting out there.'

'Sir. The responsibility for this accident rests with me. It was all my fault. I am the senior one of us.'

'That's right, Tyler. And for this you must take the brunt of the punishment.' Blake's face was impassive. 'You can't possibly replace the spyglass. Such things cost many guineas. You'll have to find some other way to recompense Lieutenant de Clare. But for now, your reckless act means that you can no longer be a corporal and you're demoted to private sentinel.'

The force of the colonel's ire drove Tom and Samuel back to the far edge of the roof. They were forgotten as the group of officers huddled on the north side of the tower and discussed their latest plans. The two comrades heard about a necessary raid. It was a dangerous one, beyond the northwest border of the county. They needed an ambush. A train of special artillery was on its way and the aim was to stop it reaching Prince Maurice's army.

Tom's chest churned. His face prickled with shame, while his body wouldn't stay still. His mind replayed, over and over, both the strike with the leather tube and the reprimand from Colonel Blake.

At a lull in the officers' talk, Tom butted in. 'Sirs? I'd like to volunteer for the raid.' Having said this, he stood to attention.

Colonel Blake looked across to him and pondered for a moment. 'Yes. I know this man. His squad has fought well so far. I think he'd be suitable for the job.' He nodded at the other officers, then looked at Tom. 'It's a dangerous job. I wouldn't punish you with this, but since you're willing, you can come.'

'Me too, sir,' Samuel blurted.

'Right you are, soldier. You're dismissed for now, but report back to the Guildhall at nightfall.'

'Tonight, sir?' asked Tom.

'Yes, tonight. Now get out.'

At the campfire, Tom called his squad together. 'Friends. I've an announcement to make.'

Effra and Ifor stopped playing a game of dice, and Gideon walked over from watching the enemy beyond the wall.

Bathsua arrived just then, too. Samuel had been quiet on the walk through the town. He now stood to one side, with a slight grin on his face.

'What's happened?' asked Ifor.

'I lost my temper with Samuel and we fought and… well, the long and the short of it is that I'm no longer your corporal.'

'You what?' they all chorused.

'Colonel Blake demoted me to plain soldier like the rest of you.'

'Samuel, tell us what happened,' demanded Bathsua.

Samuel's account drew more astonishment from them. 'And the reprimand ain't the whole of it.' he concluded. 'Tom and me have volunteered for a secret raid and we've to report to the colonel at nightfall.'

'I let you out of my sight for one poxy afternoon and this happens,' exploded Effra. 'Well, you'll not go on your raid alone. We'll all come.'

The rest seconded Effra's decision.

'But I can't ask you to do that,' said Tom.

'I know. 'Cos you're not our corporal anymore,' Gideon said.

'You know,' said Samuel, 'when we got to hitting each other we hardly realised we'd used the spyglass as a weapon. And by then it was too late.'

'I can just see the thing curling over the side of the tower.' Gideon gleefully imagined the scene. The mood was infectious and Tom lurched unevenly between mirth and shame.

'And Tom's face, when the officers came up the tower. Like a boy that's just broken his dad's pipe.' Samuel's laughs cracked his voice. 'He just stood there, offering the broken spyglass to them with that helpless look.' He couldn't go on, but collapsed onto his brother.

'Well, it seems my year's up sooner than I expected. Who's next for corporal?' Tom said.

'Not on your life.' 'Not me.' 'Keep it,' came the responses.

'I can see how this is going. You boys are meant to be the backbone of the garrison and you can't keep from fighting each other or getting in harm's way,' Bathsua teased.

'The only chance we have of staying safe is to keep our heads down and hope we don't attract the attention of our beloved officers.' Effra winked.

'We have a fellowship of sorts, we are good fellows; we fight for each other and avoid daft, noble gestures,' said Ifor.

'You mean like the one Tom and Samuel have made to try to make up for their cock-up?' joined in Gideon.

'Exactly.'

'Good luck with that,' Bathsua said. 'And what were you arguing about, anyway?'

Samuel and Tom exchanged glances.

'It was about loyalty,' said Samuel. 'About looking after each other.' His voice trailed off.

Bathsua flushed. 'You mean Nathan?'

Nobody spoke.

'Well. I've come here tonight to ask for your forgiveness. Reverend Bush has spoken to me many times about Nathan. It's wrong for me to blame you. How can I share God's grace with a heart of bitterness? So I ask if you will allow me back into your fellowship.'

'Bathsua, girl. You are our conscience, our beating heart. We've missed you, lass.' Effra spoke for them all.

The pause in the conversation stretched out until broken by Tom. 'Come on. Somebody be corporal. Please?'

'As far as I'm concerned, you're our leader, Tom,' Ifor stated. 'You may not be a corporal anymore, but we'll all follow you and no other.'

'But you can't all say that. What about Samuel?' retorted Tom.

'What d'you mean? I vote for you, Tom.'

'But what about our argument? It was that what led to our fight.'

'I dunno. You're our leader, Tom. You're still an idiot, but I don't want the job, and none of us could do better. I'm your man.'

'Well, in that case we'd better get cracking. There's not long till sunset,' Tom barked, the smoky fire moistening his eyes.

A sergeant arrived before they left. He was sent to command the platoon and he knew the rest of Tom's squad would volunteer for the raid. 'Colonel told me,' he said.

Tom looked back as they turned onto Sherborne Road, on their way to the Guildhall. Bathsua stood beside their campfire, watching them with a strange expression. Would he ever see her again?

Chapter 23

The steps of Tom, Effra and the others on the wet stone rang in their ears, and the smell of spring growth after rain leaped at them as they passed through the sentries posted around the edge of the churchyard, and joined the small group of soldiers in a room above the church porch. Colonel Blake wanted no one to know about the raid unless he told them. In the meeting he spoke quietly, even though there were three dozen men in the room.

'We've heard today that the Royalist artillery will be reinforced by a mortar.' The colonel looked at the faces around him.

'You mean Roaring Meg, sir?' someone at the back said.

'Exactly. That notorious monster is on the way here. We know that the artillery train is spending tomorrow repairing its carts, then it will cover the last stage to Axminster, probably over two days. Once they reach Axminster, it will be difficult to get at them. We expect their escort to be at least doubled for the short journey to join the Prince's army. So our best chance of stopping them lies on the road between Crewkerne and Axminster. We must hit them hard when they don't expect it, break or disable the mortar, then scurry back here as fast as we can.'

'What escort is with it, sir?' an officer asked.

'Our information is that there is a company of foot and a troop of horse. Plus gunners and men detailed to look after the mortar and ammunition, and also carters to manage the oxen.'

'Do we have a plan, sir?' someone at the back squeaked, then cleared his throat in a manly way.

'We do, but we daren't share that till we're outside the Royalist lines. No good you getting caught and giving the game away, is there?'

'And how are we going to get out of here, sir?'

'There's no moon tonight, so it's ideal for getting out to the warships and back into Charmouth by boat.'

Another officer showed everyone out of the room and directed them down to the jetty.

'Tyler! Over here,' called the officer. 'We had some reinforcements today.'

Tom and the others crowded round the major, who nodded to two men sitting on a stone bench in the courtyard. They rose and joined them.

'Captain Cooper, these men are from your regiment. I thought you'd like to see them, and they you.'

Tom looked at the captain, and Venning, his sergeant glanced at Effra, who was equally nonplussed.

'Good to see you, men. It's been some time since you left us.' The captain grinned. 'I know you have a task to attend to, so we'll meet up again when we've got settled.'

And at that, the two men sauntered towards Davey Fort.

'Who were they?' asked Ifor, looking at them as they disappeared round a corner.

'Never seen them before,' Tom said. 'What's going on?'

'And what can we do about it?' said Samuel.

'We've got to be canny, for sure,' Effra said. 'We aren't the golden boys, we're flotsam in this war, but whoever Captain Cooper is, he's an officer, and it seems he's got the clout of Colonel Fezzard behind him. That counts for something, and we'll be slapped down if we react wrongly.'

'But we've got to tell somebody that they're imposters!' Tom rejoined. 'And we know Colonel Fezzard plans to change sides. Doesn't that count for something?'

'Effra's right, Tom,' said Gideon. 'We'll have to stay low and figure out what their game is.'

'That assumes we can find that out,' said Ifor. 'That won't be easy. They know who we are. We don't know them. And presumably they mean us harm, for God's sake.'

'You men! Get in the boat. Don't dawdle,' called an officer.

Two small boats swallowed up the raiders and their commander, Captain Pyne. The sea was choppy and the journey out to the Mayflower an anxious, stomach-knotting trial. The night was dark, the sails on each boat were black, and the shore where they were to land was only a faint line glimmering in the distance. There was no way of telling whether anyone had seen their approach, or whether there would be a company of Royalists waiting to kill them.

As the boat keels ploughed into the gravel, the raiders jumped into the surf and waded ashore. The lightening of the boats allowed them to lift in the water and the skilled sailors veered off and headed back to the warship. In moments, Tom was standing on the beach, soaking from the chest down and unable to see more than a few yards in front of him.

'This way,' someone hissed, and Tom joined a group of dark shadows queuing to receive equipment and moving away from the shore. They faced a steep cliff face a few dozen yards up the beach, and this delayed them until they found a steep valley with a narrow stream cutting down to the sea. The group disappeared into this crack in the coast.

'Check equipment,' was the whispered command from one raider to the next.

Tom laid his musket and equipment down against a boulder. He attached a short, two-foot long sword hanging in a scabbard to his belt on his left side and hung two flasks on straps over his shoulders, one filled with water, the other with gunpowder. He coiled a couple of yards of matchcord round one shoulder, and a bandolier with pots of gunpowder and a leather bag of lead balls on the other. The pots were wrapped in linen to silence any knocking as they swung together. He'd brought his own snapsack with a tinderbox, bread, cheese and a hunk of meat, and this hung down his back. He picked up his musket.

The raiders moved in five groups of six men, each led by a corporal or an experienced man. Upfront was Captain Pyne, plus a lieutenant and a sergeant. The groups had to stay within a few yards of each other to make sure no one got lost; the darkness of the night was deepening and the risk of straying into a bog or losing contact with the others was real.

The first section was uphill, following the small watercourse away from the beach, climbing over broken ground with thorny bushes and soft soil which sapped the strength of their legs step by step. Eventually the land flattened out and they marched over grassy fields. Then there was another climb, up to a ridge. They crossed the ridge one group at a time, before heading into scrubby gorse and thorn trees.

The way was downhill now, but still dark. Progress was slow, with many halts to retrace steps onto a more promising route that avoided blundering into the gorse or thorns. Once beyond another road at the bottom of the hill, they felt a different land beneath their feet. The ground was more level but softer, the grass sward pimpled with sedges. Soon they reached a small river, still full of winter's rain. Captain Pyne sent two men to look for convenient crossing points nearby. There were none.

They forded the river in pairs, and once again everyone was wet from groin to toes. On the other side of the river they headed for drier land and climbed steadily onto another grassy ridge. They stopped while Captain Pyne consulted with those raiders that were local men, then they went forward again, keeping to the high ground as much as they could.

Across another shallow valley, this time through corn fields, new shoots poking up between stones, then up the opposite side and past the northern end of a wood, seen outlined against the dawn sky.

'Come on, lads,' said Lieutenant Rudd. 'We keep going until we can see our destination, then we'll rest awhile.'

They pushed on, up slopes and onto ridges that rose like dull green waves in front of them. The growing morning light allowed them to see the old tracks leading from one hill to another. Tracks first used by ancient Britons, but now only by drovers' herds. The early morning cloud was a solid grey.

Another hill. They followed the top edge as it swept up to meet a taller ridge, this one with summits sticking up at either end. They kept this ridge to their right and followed a level path onto its west flank.

Beyond the ridge, Captain Pyne gathered his force together to look back. 'Take note, men. If we find ourselves separated and need to shift for ourselves, head for this place. The wood can swallow you up. We'll pause here to regroup before heading home.'

'How do we get back into Lyme, sir?' asked someone.

'Don't worry about that yet. Time enough once we've brockled the mortar.'

'And that's another good question, sir. How are we going to stop the thing being used against Lyme?' asked Effra.

'And what is a mortar? Never heard of them before, unless you mean one of those apothecary's bowls,' said Tom.

'Patience, everyone. We'll chat about that shortly.'

They were squatting down beside a quickthorn hedge on a lane. Captain Pyne stepped into the middle of the damp soil of the lane and used short lengths of thorn twigs to represent cannons. Then he moved down the track and made some piles of stones.

'You're not far wrong when you think of an apothecary mortar, Tom. A mortar is a massive bowl into which stones, metal balls or gunpowder-filled shells are put, then lobbed into a besieged town, represented by these piles.'

'You mean like those grenadoes Captain Drake showed us?'

'Yes, only bigger,' the captain replied. He pointed at the twigs on the road. 'All the guns and cannons of the Royalists fire like this.' And he showed the men a stone in his hand, a cannonball leaving a twiggy artillery piece and arcing along the lane, describing a shallow curve to show the trajectory of the ball.

'We know our earthworks can swallow many cannonballs. Although, I grant you, not all of them. The mortar fires in a different way.' He broke a twig into a short fragment and pushed it into the road surface, with the end pointing almost vertical.

'It throws the ball up into the sky and drops it onto unsuspecting people and buildings.' Here the captain walked from the mortar towards the stone piles, lifting his hand high above his head and bringing the stone crashing down on one of the piles.

'If the projectile is a shell full of balls and metal and has its fuse set rightly, it explodes just as it nears the ground and can cause terrific damage. But even worse is the effect on the defenders. These shells cause panic and surrender. We can't allow that, so we must at all costs stop this weapon being used against us.'

The captain pointed over the valley in front of them. 'There is the village of Thorncombe. It's midway between Crewkerne and Axminster, and we're banking on it being the resting place for the mortar train today. We must be in position and ready. Our job is to destroy or disable it so that it won't reach Lyme.'

Gideon looked around the assembled raiding party. 'How many men did the colonel say are in this train, captain?'

'Around a hundred and twenty, perhaps.'

'Then we'd better have a bloody good plan.' Gideon's comment met with murmured agreement.

'Ah. There you have it, Gideon. Our plan is still in the forge. I know what we have to do; I just haven't figured out the details.' The captain looked around him, into the face of each of his men. 'We either disable it in Thorncombe,

239

somehow, or we ambush the train further down the road where there's a sharp bend.'

'But I don't understand how we can damage such a solid bowl of metal.' Tom spoke up. 'Is it like a gun we can spike so that the fuse can't pass through the barrel?'

'We've brought hammer and spikes to do that. But it'll only delay the mortar a short time. I'm sure there's a blacksmith in Axminster who could redrill the hole. No, we need something more permanent.'

'Could we blow it up by putting gunpowder around it and lighting a fuse?' Gideon suggested.

'That will blow the waggon apart, but it's unlikely to be strong enough to break the mortar.'

'You said the shells it fires are full of gunpowder,' said Tom. 'Could we load a shell into the mortar and explode it without blowing it out of the barrel?'

'God's bones. I think you've got something there, Tom.' And the captain creased his brow while thinking this through.

'We'll need to get up close to the gun, sir,' said Effra.

'You're right. But we have friends in the village. We can hide until night and creep out and do the deed while everyone sleeps.'

They spent another half hour honing this plan, then the captain gave his orders. The groups would hide themselves by a hedgerow half a mile from Thorncombe. They would move closer once the Royalists had scouted out the area and set their sentries. The aim of these men was to support Captain Pyne and his group, who were to go into the village centre. Despite the risk of doing the job in Thorncombe, it was their best chance, he said.

Effra, Tom, Gideon, Ifor and Samuel weren't so sure. They had the job of accompanying the captain into the village. They had to get there well before the Royalists, who were expected to arrive around midday. It was now late morning, so the group pushed forward quickly.

'Do we walk into the village square like a bishop at a baptism, sir?' asked Effra.

'Not unless we get lost. Just follow me. And make sure no one sees you.'

241

Chapter 24

As soon as they reached the edge of the village Captain Pyne led his group off the road, along the rear fences of the yards and the vegetable patches of the houses. These had frames of strong timber crucks, and wattle and daub walls speckled with flints and rocks set in the mud plaster. The rear yards weren't long, and as the houses were set close together, each yard was narrow and bordered by wattle hurdles. These fences enabled the group to pass unobserved along the boundaries, crouching down to avoid being seen by villagers in the yards.

The captain stood upright every so often, scanning the buildings behind the nearest houses, looking for the church. Its squat tower gave them the bearing they needed. Within a few minutes they found the house nearest it, opposite the tithe barn, and let themselves in. There was no one in the room. The captain ordered Gideon and Samuel to get up onto the raised deck at the far end. This was the family's sleeping area above the hearth and was reached by sturdy wooden steps. Facing the open space between church and barn was a small window, shuttered with a hurdle, shaped to fit the opening. Gideon didn't remove the shutter, but used his knife to widen a space between the slats to make it easy to look out over the village.

'It's very quiet,' Samuel whispered loudly.

'I can hear the smithy on the other side of the barn,' Gideon said.

The uncertainty of the visitors grew, but soon the door latch clunked and a man entered. Effra, Ifor and Tom were standing inside, ready to react.

The newcomer stalled any rash act by holding his hands out in front, palms facing the soldiers. 'Whoa. Who are you? And who gave 'ee leave to use my house without asking?'

'He has a point, don't you think?' called down Gideon.

'We're here to meet James Barnes. We have a message from his kin.' The captain pushed Tom and Effra back into the room.

'That's me. Who are you?'

'I'm Thomas Pyne. We've come from Lyme. Have you been told of our coming?'

'For sure. I'm glad to meet 'ee, Captain. I know why you're here.'

'Good. No need to say more.'

'What d'you need from me, sir?'

'We need somewhere to hide until tonight. Our plan is to brockle the mortar then run away.'

'He makes it sound so easy, ay?' Samuel nudged his brother.

'Well, the Royalists are bound to camp between the church and the barn, so this house is a good vantage point,' the captain said.

'Sir! Riders,' Gideon hissed.

The thrumming of horses' hooves on the dry road grew louder, then faded and was followed by a command to halt. Tom and the others bolted up the steps to look through the

243

shutter. James pushed through the group and shifted the wattle shutter so that he and the captain could see into the open area in front of the church.

'Tom, Effra. Get downstairs. Stay by the door and find some other places to watch these horsemen.'

'There's a pantry beneath this deck,' said James. 'And a window looking towards the church there.'

'Right,' said Tom. He moved back down the steps and through another door into a small storeroom with an opening in the outer wall.

The shutter was on the floor already, so Tom could look out without drawing attention to himself. Effra moved back to the main door.

Five horsemen had dismounted and their leader was striding towards a man leaving the church. The man he confronted wore a black cassock down to his ankles and a wide-brimmed black hat. In his arms was a stack of books. This vicar looked to Tom to be in middle age, but lean and tall. The horseman stood before him and said something, but the clergyman continued his measured walk through the lych gate and away from the other horsemen. Once outside the church boundary, he replied. And he was now near enough for Tom to catch the conversation.

'I understand your needs, captain, and I'm sure you can understand mine.'

'We aren't here to negotiate, Reverend. There's a column of soldiers about to arrive and we need all available quarters for our overnight stay to ensure our mission isn't delayed.'

'I see, but you don't have any right to requisition my church. This is a house of God for this village. It's in my charge and I won't let you have it for quartering either a bunch of smelly conscripts or a troop of horsemen and their mounts.'

'Your reputation, Reverend Bragge, is that you are loyal to the King?'

The vicar turned and squared up to the officer. 'I fully support the King in this war, but that doesn't include the desecration of my church.' The vicar glared. 'There's ample space for your men in this square and the tithe barn is near empty, so that gives more room for men and beasts. I'm sure you'll find willing villagers on whom to billet the officers, so there's no reason to give you access to the church. It's the Roundheads that make a point of ransacking churches. I'm sure you wouldn't want His Majesty's soldiers to get the same reputation, would you?'

'Of course not, Reverend…'

'That's settled then. I'll keep the church locked while your soldiers are here, and you keep them away from the churchyard. Good.' The vicar turned away and left the Royalist officer dumbstruck. He quickly recovered himself and barked orders to his subordinates to find quarters for the officers while he went to inspect the barn.

James's house was an immediate target for the billeting soldiers. James replaced Effra by the door and answered the heavy knocking, while Captain Pyne and his men quickly sank behind any cover they could find.

'Welcome. What do you want, soldier?'

The Royalist ignored the greeting. 'How many live here?' He stood at the doorway, looking round at the main room and the first-floor decking.

'There's me and my wife and three young 'uns.'

'What's through there?' The soldier pointed to the door on the other side of the hearth.

'Just a small room.'

'An artillery train is arriving today. We'll use your house to billet five officers for one night, then we'll be gone. Here's a chitty for this service to the King. You can get reimbursed once we've beaten the rebels.'

'But there's not room for my family and another five men!'

'If there's no space for you, you must visit relatives. You aren't needed to provide food, so stay out the way.' The soldier slammed the door as he left.

James opened the door and watched the soldier stalk down the road. Meanwhile, Captain Pyne drew the men together.

'We can't stay here with five Royalist officers on the way.'

'We'd better shift quick. But where to?' asked Effra.

'There's one obvious place,' said Tom. He recounted the conversation he'd heard, and Captain Pyne considered the information.

'All right. We move to the church tower, quick as we can. It will give us a good vantage point, and providing the vicar keeps the Royalists out we can rest before tonight.'

James passed some food to them before they left. 'It'll be pilfered by the Royalists anyway, so I'd rather you had it.' It wasn't much, only two small loaves of bread, a loaf of cheese and a gallon of cider, but it was welcome.

They spent a short while spying out where the Royalists were before racing across the open square and diving over the flint wall, where they huddled before using a short line of yew trees to cover their approach to the church. The heavy door at the bottom of the squat, thirty-foot tall tower was barred, so they tried the vestry entrance on the north side of the church, furthest from the square. It was locked.

'Let me at it, boys,' said Effra pulling his lock-picks out of his tunic. A few moments, and they were inside.

'Keep moving. Let's get to the tower,' the captain urged.

The church appeared empty, but Tom knew the vicar would be back soon to stand guard over it. Steps led up to the tower at the west end of the building, the font occupied the centre of its base, and there were two bells encased in a timber cradle six feet below the high ceiling. Steps led around the walls up to the bell platform, where a trapdoor opened onto the top of the tower.

They climbed onto the stone floor of the roof, but kept low as the parapet was only a foot high. Settling down, they peeped over the parapet and watched the open square where they expected the Royalists to arrive.

They waited, listening and watching. The day was cloudy but dry, the wind cool but not uncomfortable. After two hours, the artillery train still had not arrived. After another hour, a group of horsemen rode into the square and the vicar scurried into his beloved building. They could hear him below, banging and scraping. Then he reappeared at the lych gate, standing guard before the horsemen. They couldn't catch his conversation with the men, but no one forced their way past him.

Effra turned to Gideon. 'Your turn with a story. What's it to be?'

'Since we're on a tower, I'd better tell a story about one,' Gideon began.

'You mean you're a tall-tale-teller on a tall tower?' said Samuel.

'Well now. There was this old man and his wife that lived by a high, stone-walled garden. Inside grew all the plants you'd want for salads, stews or physick. But no one could get in 'cept the old witch what owned it, and she hated anyone wandering round there.

'One day the wife got sick, then sicker, till the man thought of only one remedy. He scaled the stone wall and dropped into the garden. He looked round carefully before darting into the cabbage patch. Out he came with a good, green cabbage, and back to the wall he ran.

'Climbing the inside of the wall was more difficult than he expected, and as he reached the top the witch caught him in a net.

'"Ho, ho. What have we here?" she said. And she tormented the old man, just like Samuel does to Ifor.

'Finally the old man could bear it no more and he agreed to anything the witch wanted. What she wanted, she said, was the first child born to the couple.

'I thought you said she was an old woman?' said someone.

'And she's sick,' said someone else.

'All right. Let's start again. The man creeps into the garden to get some herbs for his wife, who is pregnant.'

'That's more like it, Gideon. You can't mess around with stories. You've got to tell 'em right.'

'May I proceed? Thank you. There's a lot to get through.'

'Well, the man was so desperate he made the bargain with the witch and she let him take three cabbages back to his wife. Then he forgot all about his promise.

'So, the baby is born and the witch rides to the cottage and claims the girl child. She carries her off and names her Cabbage, after the vegetables her father pinched.'

'That ain't right, Gideon. She weren't called Cabbage, she's called Rampion.' Ifor spoke up for them all.

'All right, all right. The man scrumped rampions, not

cabbages. But the witch gave him three cabbages as well. Yes, she did.'

'Keep your voices down, men,' Captain Pyne cut in. 'There's plenty going on down there, but we mustn't give ourselves away.' He nodded to the square below, where a small party of horsemen had arrived.

'Well, the girl grows up to have gorgeous fair hair and when she's twelve, just before she's old enough to marry, the witch takes her to a far tower and locks her in the room at its top.'

'Why'd she do that, Gideon?' Tom asked.

'Because she's a bloody witch and witches are spiteful.'

'But it doesn't make any sense.'

'You think that doesn't make sense, wait for the end of the story,' Effra added.

'The witch visited Rampion every week, bringing food and drink. But as there was no door or stairs into the tower, she'd stand at the bottom of the tower and call up to the girl.

'"Rampion, Rampion let down your hair, that I can climb up and be with you there."'

'Don't you mean; "Rampion, Rampion, here I stand, let down your hair and give me a hand"?' said Tom.

'Why not, "Ho, ho, my lovely. Give me your locks. Then I'll climb up and into your frock"?'

'You're running ahead of the story, Samuel. Hold fast. Let me finish. Rampion lowered her golden hair that was strong enough for the witch to climb up into the tower.

'One day the witch turned up and called to the girl as usual. But there in the woods nearby was a prince who was hunting. He overheard the witch and hid behind a tree to watch what happened. Well, after she'd gone, he crept up and called to

Rampion, who let down her tresses, as she thought the witch had come back for something.'

'Didn't it occur to her that the witch's voice had got more manly?' said Samuel in a gruff, bass voice.

'Aah, but witches have deep voices,' Gideon answered.

'Anyway, the girl was fooled, and she let down her hair. Up went the prince and introduced himself.

'Well, as is the way of the world, the prince visited the girl often after that and together they planned her escape. Each visit he gave Rampion a piece of silk for her to weave together into a ladder. But, before the ladder was ready, the witch noticed that she was getting fat and she no longer fitted into her dress.'

'What an idiot that prince was. Why bring her a piece of silk when he could take a silk ladder and get the job done right away? I think he didn't really love the girl. Maybe he enjoyed having her whenever he wanted.'

'Shut up, Sam. The witch guessed what had happened, and she cut off Rampion's hair, then tied it to the bedstead and took her out of the tower and into the wilderness, where she left her.

'When the prince came back, he called up for the hair, as usual, and down it came. Up he climbed and what a surprise he got when, instead of his beautiful betrothed, he met her ugly gaoler. The witch laughed and pushed him backwards out the tower and he fell into a thicket, where thorns gouged out his eyes.

'He lay there a long time before he found the strength to stand up and realise he was blind. Then he stumbled off into the wood. After years of wandering, he eventually found himself in a desert place and heard a woman singing. It was

Rampion. He called, she found him and gave him a drink of water just as he was about to die of thirst. She nursed him, and behold! His eyes got better, he could see his beautiful daughter, and they lived happily ever after.'

'What happened to the witch?' called someone.

'The witch was no more. She laughed till her warts fell off when the prince fell from the tower. Then she took hold of the hair and jumped out of the window. But the hair had come loose from the bedstead and she perished as she deserved.'

The men grunted and nodded.

'Good story, Gideon,' said Effra.

All talk stopped. Each of them listened and watched the military might now arriving in the square beneath them.

Chapter 25

A troop of horsemen whirled around the square, then cantered off along the road. Foot soldiers paraded in front of the barn, then formed groups to make campfires. Carters soon filled the space with waggons. The first to arrive was pulled by three pairs of scrawny oxen, goaded by their drivers. It didn't look heavily laden. The oxen plodded their way to the edge of the church wall, where the carters busied themselves with unhitching the animals. An ammunition waggon was next. There were boxes and bags and square wooden cradles full of cannonballs. The waggon was partly covered with a canvas sheet. This large cart drew alongside the first, and the oxen were unhitched and sent into a small field to the east of the churchyard. Two more waggons followed. One with six oxen that carried the mortar frame and heavy timbers, the last had eight oxen, and in the centre of the waggon bed sat a massive metal bowl, like an oversized bell. From the tower, Tom and Effra looked down into the gaping mouth of this fearsome weapon.

Tom sipped his cider. The cool liquid calmed him and he absorbed the sights, smells and noises of the scene below, while the wings of a dozen house martins sliced through the air around the tower.

'Remember all the details you can, lads,' whispered Captain Pyne.

Tom noted the order of the waggons as they were parked by the low, stone church wall. Beyond the waggons the barn was filling with cavalrymen and horses. Beside the barn was the smithy. The blacksmith was already at work for them. At the far end of the open area he could see a small market cross set into the bare ground and timber uprights, showing where tables squatted on market days, but most of this area was empty of structures and devoid of vegetation. A road led away from the square to the right of the market cross, which was almost due south of the church tower. Along the west side of the square was a line of neat houses, with tiny rear courtyards separating each one from the large open space. The front doors of these houses opened on to another road that wound its way through the village, passing the western edge of the churchyard, heading for Chard, the next town to the northwest. The closest house in this line belonged to James.

'I never thought I'd say this, but I wish I were back in Lyme,' said Ifor. He was lying in a corner of the tower platform, cradling his snapsack, his head resting on his wide-brimmed hat.

'We're fine, Ifor. This is better than facing muskets or pikes. We can use darkness to screen us, and we can choose our targets. I feel better here than I've felt for ages.'

'Ah. That's easy for you, Effra. You're a fighter. That's your trade. I'm just an old peddler. What I've seen these past few weeks freezes my blood.' His words were bare whispers.

Tom just about caught his words, though he was right next to Effra and only a couple of feet away. Ifor looked more like a wraith than a man. His face was grey and his skin sunken. His eyes peered out, but instead of a mischievous glint there was a dead, brownish-black smudge.

Effra turned to show a worried face to Tom, then faced Ifor and patted his shoulder. 'We're with you, old man. You won't die in this place and you'll get your wish to be back in Lyme. That fight's not over yet.'

'Aye.' Ifor snorted. 'If we get through this, I can look forward to more Royalists seeking to starve me or cut me in half.'

'There's no pleasing some people,' chipped in Samuel.

As Tom looked at his mates, he remembered Captain Cooper and Sergeant Venning. Now, surely, was a good time to speak to Captain Pyne about them. 'Sir? Do you know those officers we met when we left Lyme?'

'Never seen them before,' came the reply.

'Nor us. And we were with the regiment since January.'

'What's your meaning, Tom?'

'What we mean,' Effra said, as he leaned over Tom's shoulder, 'is that we don't believe they are who they says they are.'

'And who else would they be?' The captain chuckled.

'We think they're assassins sent to kill Effra and me.' The words hung in the afternoon air between Tom and Captain Pyne.

It took the captain a few seconds before he responded. 'Are there any reasons your regiment would send assassins after you?'

'Effra and Tom did some "errands" for Colonel Fezzard, and he wants back the papers we have of his,' Samuel said, and looked round to acknowledge the nods from Gideon and Ifor.

'These "errands". I presume they involved housebreaking and theft? Or were you in the same line of business as the assassins?' The captain looked from Effra to Tom with a penetrating gaze.

''Tis true we burgled and stole for the colonel, but we didn't have any choice and we didn't kill anyone when doing it,' Effra said.

Tom thought about the sentries on the bridge at Dorchester.

'Well. Housebreaking and larceny are serious crimes. There are other issues relating to your colonel that we already know. I can't say any more now. Speak to me again when we're back in Lyme.' Captain Pyne rolled onto his stomach and looked down onto the village square. The spring dusk was approaching from the east and the sun broke through, beneath the western clouds, casting long, sharp shadows and a rich orange light.

The activity below them continued and the men on the tower watched more infantry arrive and strip nearby trees and fences as fuel for campfires. Horsemen walked tired mounts into the square and tethered them to horse lines set up between the barn and the field next to the church.

Villagers arrived at the lych gate and split into two groups. One group stationed themselves by the main entrance on the south side of the church, while the other congregated around the gate. Their job seemed to be to stop the soldiers wandering into the church.

Captain Pyne looked relaxed as he lay on timber posts that allowed him to peep over the parapet. Though he was set back from its edge, he could see all the details of the scene

255

below. Tom thanked Bathsua's God that they had such a resolute leader.

Night came and darkness dampened the noise from the camp in the square. But even a quiet camp of over a hundred men and animals isn't silent. The villagers dispersed.

Tom marked that there were two guards among the waggons and two more in the horse lines. The guards round the campfires were more difficult to pinpoint.

'Gather round and let's go over the details again.' the captain whispered.

They waited another two hours until well past midnight. They watched how the guards moved, where they paused and rested and how often they changed. The sounds from the camp had faded from men relaxing to men settling down to sleep, to quiet chats between sentries and the occasional snorts of horses.

'Time to go,' said the captain.

They lifted the trapdoor and descended into the inky well of the church. As they inched their way down the stairs and past the bells, Tom kept his fingers sliding over the cold, flinty wall to ensure he didn't slip off the steps. They reached the ground and crept into the vestry. Effra tried the outer door and, as expected, it was locked.

'This won't take a moment.'

The lock was picked, but as Effra pushed the door, it jarred.

'There's a padlock on the outside! What the…? That bloody vicar's wrapped his church in chains.' Effra turned away from the door in disgust.

Captain Pyne tried his luck and reached the same conclusion. 'Back into the church, men. Find a window we can open.'

But there was no window that yielded to their need. And they dared not break one to make an opening. They regrouped at the font.

'So, what do we do?' the captain asked.

'The only way to the outside is from the top of the tower,' said Gideon.

'Then we'll need rope to lower ourselves.'

'I know where there's rope. The bells are rung by ropes and locked in place by them too.'

'Good man, Ifor.'

They looked up to the bell platform above, aware that time was slipping away.

'Careful, now.' said Ifor. 'I know bells. We need something to stop the bell swinging when we cut the rope.'

'There's timber on the tower roof. Samuel and Tom. Go and get it.'

When Tom and Samuel returned with two eight-foot lengths of four by four posts, Ifor was in position astride the timber bell frame. He supervised the threading of both of these through the frame and wooden wheels, to wedge the bells in the open-end, upraised position.

When he was confident the bells were fixed, Ifor sawed through a rope, then handed an end to Effra.

'Coil it up. Let's get back on the tower,' the captain ordered.

There was one timber post left on the roof. They tied a rope to its middle and wedged it under the trapdoor. Effra threw the rope over the northern side of the tower and they all heard the solid thump as it landed on the ground.

After regrouping at ground level, Gideon, Samuel and Ifor headed east, to the boundary with the field, while the captain, Effra and Tom made their way stealthily towards the waggons.

At the churchyard wall they listened for the sentry. Then Effra moved along it, to a place where there was a bush. Captain Pyne and Tom followed. At the bush, Effra told Tom to raise his head slowly to look over the top. The shrub gave him cover and he could observe the guards' movements. The two sentries were sitting on the waggon traces, chatting. Looking straight at him. Tom stayed very still, watching the guards. Although they were looking his way, he was sure they couldn't see him. His head was invisible as part of a black blob of vegetation. After a little time, he carefully lowered himself and relayed this information to his comrades.

Effra soon had a plan. He inched westwards to the lych gate, then crept back along the wall until he neared the waggons. Darkness screened him, and with slow, lizard-like movements he got under the nearest waggon. There was a campfire set a little way back from the waggons, surrounded by sleeping carters, but no one was sleeping beneath the waggons. When he was in position, he hooted like an owl, and Captain Pyne and Tom stood up and climbed over the wall.

The sentries took a moment to register the two men looming out of the dark. Tom hoped they would mistake them for comrades getting back to camp after a jaunt.

The plan worked fine. Effra walked up behind the nearest sentry and slit his throat. The second sentry heard a gurgle from his mate, but before he could bring his musket round from front to rear, Effra had skewered him too. And in a moment, Captain Pyne was beside him, keeping the sentry quiet as he died.

'Stage one complete,' whispered the captain. 'Tom, get up

on the second waggon and check the ammunition. We need gunpowder, two shell halves and any lead shot you can find. Effra, you and I need to pick out one of those stone balls.'

They rummaged slowly, carefully and quietly through the stores on the ammunition cart. There were sealed barrels and leather bags containing gunpowder. There were stone balls and metal balls, but no shell cases or anything that looked like two hemispheres that could be fixed or screwed together.

'Tom. Try the next waggon.'

Effra and the captain carried a large stone ball across from the ammunition waggon to the mortar while Tom jumped down and scrambled into the farthest waggon. From here he could see that Gideon, Samuel and Ifor had quietened the sentries at the horse lines. They were standing at one end, just as though they were sentries themselves. He turned back to the lumpy darkness of the waggon and tried to pick out the details of the metal and timber lying there. There were wooden poles, sticks with different tool endings, hammers and tongs and rounded shovels. Then he found the metal half-shells. They glinted in the fragments of light from the fires, which was enough to enable him to select two cases that looked the same.

Tom reached the mortar and found the captain and Effra ready. They set one shell half on the waggon bed and placed a large leather gunpowder bag into it. Then they arranged a dozen lead shot, each about two inches in diameter, on the bag. They had packed wadding around the shell half so it didn't wobble, but they now had to screw the other half onto it.

Tom dripped sweat from his forehead onto the shell. His

259

hands were clammy and slippery as he struggled to twist the upper half into place. He grabbed a handful of wadding for extra grip, and the metal hemisphere turned and grated. It sounded like a church bell to the three men and they froze, holding their breaths. There was no movement from the carters at the campfire. The raiders slowly exhaled.

Tom wiped his hands again and twisted some more, trying to inch the metal along the screw thread smoothly and quietly. Finally, it was ready.

'Good. Now, where's the fuse?' asked the captain.

'Fuse?' whispered Effra and Tom together.

260

Chapter 26

Dark night, lit only by a dozen fires around which exhausted soldiers slept. The line of waggons along the churchyard wall seemed darker, more still than the soldiers. But inside one waggon, Tom and his comrades were frantic to get their job done and find safety.

Tom sensed panic at the edges of Captain Pyne's voice.

'Of course. There should be a narrow hole for a thin length of match to ignite the gunpowder.'

All three men examined the ball for signs of a fuse hole.

'There isn't one,' hissed Effra.

'There must be two different shell halves. Tom, find another half, this time with a little hole somewhere on it.' The captain slumped against the mortar and Effra turned to watch the campfire, while Tom sneaked back to the farthest waggon.

Tom knew where to look and he felt the smooth surfaces of the hemispheres until he found one with a kind of nipple or lump right in its centre. He retraced his steps and found Captain Pyne and Effra struggling to unscrew the shell. The surface was getting more slippery with all their sweat. Tom had brought back a rag with his shell-half and he dried the shell before taking a firm hold and twisting the screw open.

Discarding the shell-half, he reached for the replacement.

'No, stop.' The captain gripped his wrist. 'We must make sure the fuse is ready and will work. What have we got for the fuse?'

'I've got matchcord.' Tom drew a two-foot length from his pocket.

It was too thick to push through the fuse hole. They spent more time splicing open the cord to give a long, thin string that would do the job.

'What do we do about lighting it?' asked Tom.

'God's bones!' said Effra. 'Just give me the fucking fuse.' He grabbed it from Tom and climbed out of the waggon. Slowly, calmly, he walked between the prostrate carters and held the cord to a smouldering log. It took a mere five seconds for it to light, but to Tom that seemed an age. No one stirred, and Effra stepped back to the waggon.

The captain threaded the unlit end of the fuse through the hole and coiled it around the bag of gunpowder. 'No. That won't do,' he whispered. Stabbing the bag, he pushed the fuse right into the gunpowder, which spilled out, the familiar acrid smell registering in their noses and at the back of their throats.

'Keep that lighted end away,' the captain ordered.

Effra held the fuse end, which extended from the hole now by about nine inches, while Tom twisted the shell halves together. The two hemispheres smoothly interlocked this time. Captain Pyne pushed the cord in till there was barely two inches showing. He stared at the lit end for a moment, then lifted the shell and gingerly moved to the mouth of the mortar that was lying horizontally on the waggon bed. Effra had already put rags into the mortar so that the shell would bump against something soft, but pushing the shell down the mortar barrel was still a nerve-scraping operation. They wiggled and pushed a half-inch at a time, and the shell slowly moved along the throat of the bombard. They had to be careful not to knock the fuse or to extinguish it. Finally, the shell was in place. There was just over an inch of the fuse showing.

'Is that long enough?' the captain said.

'It'll encourage us to hurry,' said Effra.

Effra lifted the stone ball and slid it down beside the shell. The two balls bumped, and they held their breath.

Captain Pyne looked at the campfire and the unwary sleepers. He peered across to the horse lines.

'Get the others, Tom. We'll wait for you on the other side of the churchyard wall.'

Tom had to stop himself running past the waggons. He had to move as though he was a bored, sleepy sentry. He hissed to get Gideon's attention, and soon the four men had jumped into the churchyard and rejoined the captain and Effra.

'Let's go. Now!'

They stood and ran to the west end of the church. They didn't use the lych gate; they vaulted the wall near the yew trees. They ran across the road and between two houses, bumping into clutter but not allowing this to slow their race away from the mortar. They heard nothing but their own fleeing. They were into a rear yard. Through an open gate, into another tiny lane and past more houses. More vegetable patches, then over a wattle fence. They could feel grass under their feet, and Tom sensed a dark field around him.

'Keep going. Head for the hedge.'

They ran, Tom expecting any second that the night would crack open with a thunderous boom to herald the start of a manhunt.

They reached the hedge and struggled through. Tom flattened himself on the ground and wriggled between two hawthorn stems, not worrying about the thorns. Ifor was behind the others. His old bones were less supple, but his need lent him power and he wasn't that far back. They rested on the other side of the hedge, each man struggling to quieten his heart so he could hear any sounds of pursuit.

'Are you sure you set the fuse properly?' asked Gideon.

They waited some more. Surely it should have reached the gunpowder by now?

Tom watched the captain. His every sense was directed back towards the square. Tom felt sure he was imagining how long they had taken to run away and how quickly the fuse would have burned down.

Maybe the stone ball had crushed it, Tom thought. Maybe someone had found it and bravely removed the ball to snuff out the fuse. 'God's truth, I wouldn't do that,' he said aloud.

'What?'

'Nothing.'

'We'll have to go back.' The captain's voice sounded flat.

At that moment there was a half-muted wumpf, then a great crash; presumably the stone ball or part of the mortar had hit a wall. Horses neighed, cattle bellowed and men began shouting.

'Time to go.' Tom heard confidence back in the captain's voice.

The raiders sauntered down the road towards the new battery called Fort Royal. They looked relaxed – arrogant, even. Bold soldiers equal to anything fate, or the Royalists, could throw at them. But within the group were men who were utterly tired of conflict. Not everyone was an adventurous soul. Ifor had rallied in Thorncombe. His handling of the bell rope had brought him out of himself and he even seemed to enjoy the race away from the mortar. Well, he enjoyed having escaped.

Pre-dawn light showed them the way ahead as they approached a heavy timber gate that was the entrance to the battery of cannons and sakers that was a major threat to Lyme. Tom's thoughts reviewed the past day, while feeling the smooth, green ribbon that had just been issued to him.

The route back to Lyme had included a general leaking of excitement from the raiders. Weariness replaced warrior spirit, and they all fled headlong to the wood on the ridge. They were there well before daylight. They hadn't seen or heard any pursuit, but as they lay up at the edge of the wood, they watched bodies of horsemen canter this way, then that. No one thought to search a woodland three miles from Thorncombe, though.

So they rested. Everyone was desperate for sleep. Sentries kept a look out, but Tom and his comrades were exempted from this duty. They pushed damp, rotting leaves into little banks to deflect the wind, and entered a black world of sweat, waiting, running and explosions.

When Tom woke it was afternoon. There was quiet activity

all around him. Men huddled in small groups, sharing the last of their food and checking their muskets, knives and equipment.

'Come on, Tom. We're off soon,' said Effra.

'You looked so beautiful, we hadn't the heart to wake you.' Samuel laughed.

Tom yawned and sat up.

'If you'd not woken up, we'd have left you a note saying where we'd gone. Honest,' said Gideon.

'On your feet, soldiers. Parade in five minutes,' barked the sergeant.

Tom's only thought was to get away. He collected his equipment and followed his comrades to a scrubby hollow, where Captain Pyne addressed them.

'I saw it. The mortar is in pieces, and so are the Royalists, fussing about like ants with no queen. The waggons are now a pile of kindling. There's a hole in the church tower, too.'

There was no cheering, but the captain said 'Well done' to each man.

They retraced their steps; down hills and up others, past Celtic forts and dog-guarded farms, then across the shallow river, where this time they found a rickety wooden bridge. At the road they turned right and headed for Charmouth.

By the time they got there, the afternoon had slid into another bright evening. They walked on into the sun. Tom noticed only workmen and women in the fields, either tending crops or herding beasts. He was glad they didn't meet Micah or Tabitha.

They didn't see soldiers until they were climbing the last hill before Lyme. Then a troop of horsemen rattled past and forced them to stand off the dirt road. The sun sparkled from each of the millions of specks of dust that flew up into the air and twirled in the light breeze before settling on the Lyme soldiers. Captain Pyne shrugged, stepped back onto the road and marched on.

They soon arrived at the Royalist camp. Sergeants harangued them at the entrance and directed them, in an Irish brogue, to an officer's tent. The men waited while Captain Pyne and Lieutenant Rudd were shown into the tent. No one seemed to consider that this group might be reckless raiders from the besieged town over the hill. Their story was that they were reinforcements sent to Prince Maurice from Bridport.

'Do you remember that tent that Captain Green disappeared into, when we were waiting for our first meeting with Colonel Fezzard?' Gideon asked Effra.

'I still haven't dried out from that soaking. Those bastard officers disappeared into their tents like ferrets down a rat-run.'

'Ah. Blessed memories, aye, comrades? We know better now, I think,' said Samuel.

The captain and the lieutenant re-emerged and saluted an ornately dressed man who stood at the opening of the tent. He wore long leather boots, and a blue shirt beneath an embossed leather jerkin. His bare head showed a receding hairline but a full, well-trimmed beard.

Captain Pyne ordered his men to follow him through a maze of tents, campfires and groups of soldiers. The elevation meant they could look down on Lyme in the fading light. They were still a half-mile or so from it, but the sight gave Tom a pang. In that place were friends, comrades and a town-full of people straining every sinew to resist the grinding of this army surrounding them.

They went to another group of tents and the captain reported to another officer while his raiders stood, shivering in the evening coolness. They were given a space to camp on, with orders to be ready for anything and permission to beg, borrow or steal what they needed from the surrounding campfires. The captain quietly ordered them to stay together and not to mix with the surrounding soldiers. They were safer on their own. The only concession was that the men could beg for fuel and embers to start their own fires.

'You know the plan. Rest tonight, but keep good watch. We'll be on our way before the camp wakes. Not far to go now. Just one more appointment to keep.'

And here they were, arriving at Fort Royal, on the wrong side of the siege line, facing another test.

The gates swung open and Tom and the others walked into an area sixty yards wide by forty deep. Earth and timber ramparts surrounded the whole area, eight-foot high with a two-foot wide ledge four feet below the lip, the fire-step from where infantry could direct musket fire onto an advancing enemy. The fire-step widened to ten yards along the western face of the battery where eight cannons of varying sizes stood in pairs, aimed at Lyme. Wattle gabions, six-foot tall and filled with earth and stones, protected the gunners. These were the heart of the redoubt and all the defences protected them. A wide ramp led up to the guns.

Captain Pyne barked at and bullied an officer at the gate, suggesting that they were needed in case of an attack.

The officer was uncertain, as the captain had no orders from his commander. 'Well, we can do with extra men on the south side. The artillery bombardment starts half an hour after dawn, so the gunners are getting ready. Do you have definite intelligence of a sally?'

'No, I don't. All I know is what I've been ordered to do. And that is to report to you. I just assumed that there must be some alarm. We'll take station over on the south, then. Good day, sir.'

Captain Pyne waved his command passed the large hut on the right of the gate and the sergeant wheeled them to the left, passing a collection of huts for the gunners and garrison. They paraded by the southern fire-step.

The men were standing in three lines, facing Lieutenant Rudd. The captain was still in conversation with the officer at the gate.

Tom looked around him. The dawn light was bringing shape and colour to structures, though deep shadows remained within the fort.

'This is no place to stay,' said Ifor.

'Too right,' added Effra. 'The longer we stay, the greater the risk.'

'Stand easy, men,' ordered the sergeant. They all slumped to the ground or rested against the timber-clad earth wall.

The captain returned, and he and Lieutenant Rudd began a nonchalant circuit of the redoubt. The sergeant quietly told each small group to put their green ribbons on their right shoulders or sleeves as a recognition sign, and to scout out their surroundings.

'Check out the latrines. Find out what's in the huts. Get to know this place. But do it softly.'

269

For half an hour, as the fort woke up to a new day, the men wandered about, discovering the layout of the place. They weren't challenged. Who would expect there to be an enemy strolling around inside a defensive wall?

The light increased, and the garrison stirred, then ate its dewbit.

Tom and Effra climbed onto the fire-step and peeked over the parapet. Halfway down was a line of wooden poles driven horizontally into the earth wall. There were sentries posted every ten yards. They nodded to the nearest guard, then inched westwards towards him and the front of the battery.

'What does the Town Line look like from this angle?' whispered Tom.

The guard was on the corner. The two men greeted him and moved a few yards along the front fire-step.

'Where's this damn sortie the captain told us about?' Tom said.

'My eyes aren't as good as yours, boy. But watch that clump of furze to our front. What's going on around it?'

Tom concentrated on the land in front. There were many furze clumps. As he looked, the ground filled with movement. Tom had the sensation of watching a soil heap that turns out to be an anthill. First you see one ant, then nearby ants are noticed, then the focus pans out and you see the whole hill is heaving with ants. In front of Fort Royal there now appeared out of the weak dawn mist groups of men hurrying across the ground.

Tom checked his green ribbon was in place, then looked at Effra. 'What do we do?'

'Nothing. Let some other bugger spot them. I don't want

270

to be here.' Effra jumped down from the ledge and walked towards the rest of the platoon.

A moment later the shout came from the fire-step. 'Alarm. Enemy in front! Call the major!'

Tom and Effra hurried to join their comrades.

'Two groups. Stay by the huts. Rudd, take charge of them. Rest of you, up on the south fire-step.' The captain reinforced his orders by jabbing his arm and pointing.

'Captain!' another voice cut in. A Royalist officer got his attention and ordered the platoon to join the men on the west wall, to protect the cannons.

'Yes sir,' said the captain.

'Right. Hold fast, men.' The captain was standing looking at the men, with his back to the Royalist officer who was now approaching the gun decks. 'Tell me what he's doing, Rudd.'

'He's calling over a gunner, sir,' said Rudd.

'That'll do. As you were, men. Orders are the same as I just gave out; one half on the fire-step here, and the others stationed in front of the huts. Rudd, watch out for that officer. I don't want him sending you anywhere else. D'you understand?'

Tom, Effra and the others were climbing onto the ledge when the Royalist officer strode back to them. 'You, there!' he called to the captain. 'I said to take your men to the west wall. Don't you understand?'

'I do. And I'm deploying my men to get the best effect. There's too much congestion over there, sir. So I'm sending them onto the fire-step to support those already in place. They can shunt sideways to maximise the muskets facing the front.'

271

'Oh. Well. I see.' The officer looked over to the western side, then back at Captain Pyne.

Muskets were now being fired along the western wall and shouts came from all directions. The officer couldn't waste any more time. 'Just get on the fire-step and support the defence.'

'Yes, sir,' Captain Pyne spoke formally but grinned at his sergeant.

On the fire-step Tom and Ifor were at the end of the line, being pushed westwards towards the corner to make space for the others.

Tom stood on the wooden planking and peeped over the parapet. He could see the Lyme men spreading out and moving forwards. They were a hundred yards away, but they were firing their muskets just to make the defenders flinch.

Ifor was crouching with his head below the parapet. His face was white and he was trembling.

'You, there. Stand up. Return fire,' an officer was calling from below.

Ifor ignored him and vomited onto the step, down one side of his musket.

'Get up, old man. Are you soldier or woman?' The next defender to Ifor gave him a kick that sent him flat on his face.

Tom stepped across his comrade and planted the butt of his musket on the nose of the soldier. 'Piss off, Irish pig.'

The soldier reeled back and fell off the fire-step, as his comrade stepped forward and thrust at Tom with a long knife in his left hand.

'Stop that,' the officer said, then collapsed as Effra fired a musket ball into his chest.

Tom swerved towards the wall to avoid the knife and thrust again with his musket butt. The Irishman deflected the strike, then closed in, grabbing Tom by the neck and thrusting with his knife.

Effra raced past the man, looping the knife-wielding arm in his own and turning to grab him round the neck with his right arm. The Irishman's attack stalled and Effra twisted his body, throwing Tom's opponent off the fire-step. But there were more Irishmen to replace him, and Effra was knocked to the ground and trampled, as Irish and Dorset men contested the space above him. He curled his body and rolled off the ledge to get away. Tom grabbed Ifor and they stepped back from their attackers as their comrades behind were sucked into this brawl. The raiders parried thrusts and strikes and jabbed at the enemy.

Captain Pyne took no part in this fracas. He was watching the progress of the attacking force. The Lyme attackers approached the side of the battery, benefiting from the confusion in the defence, but they moved cautiously.

'Get a move on, you bastards,' shouted the captain, but the men halted at the rear southeast edge of the redoubt, checking there were no Royalist reinforcements about to attack them.

Captain Pyne called out to the attackers and waved his green ribbon. Then he turned and ordered Rudd to take his men and open the gates.

In a few minutes the Parliamentarians rushed into the redoubt and the fight became a series of fast-moving melees.

Tom and Ifor rolled off the fire-step to get space to stand safely, but the defenders had also lost men that way. So the fight spread inside the fort. Jabs, punches, musket blows were exchanged, and anything liftable was thrown by one side at the other.

Tom found himself in a few yards of space, then heard a familiar cry. 'Cover us! You men, guard these steps.' The captain was racing across the battery with four men. He ran up the ramp and launched himself at the gunners. His small squad followed him. Tom called Effra and a few other raiders and they prevented any defenders following to support the gunners. In a few minutes, the captain and his team came tumbling down the ramp.

'They got reinforced,' he said as he passed Tom, musket shots raining down on them from above.

A volley rang out from nearby and the defence of the guns slackened.

Tom looked about him to see that the raiders had cleared the fire-step of enemy on the south side and a squad of their comrades were already reloading their muskets after their supporting fire. The Lyme attackers were flooding in through the gates, and the western defenders, who had been trading shots with other attackers on that side, now looked behind them and scurried north, jumping from the fort, swinging past the horizontal poles and sliding down the glacis. There were pockets of resistance around some of the huts and the other cannons.

'Follow me,' ordered the captain as he sprinted back up the ramp. Half a dozen men, including Tom, obeyed. 'Get these guns spiked.'

The captain tossed a couple of tapered metal pins, sharpened at one end, to a raider, and three men clambered over the nearest cannon, looking for the fuse hole to plug.

Another group of men ran to another gun and tried to manhandle it over the edge of the platform.

Tom stood beside the captain as he surveyed the scene. Lieutenant Rudd called from the gate and warned that a large Royalist force was massing to the east.

'Lock the gates and wedge them shut,' shouted the captain.

Musket fire became more intense and Tom realised that there must also be Royalists converging on Fort Royal from other directions. Some had climbed the outside of the walls and were firing into the fort.

'Out. Out. Let's away,' the captain shouted.

Inside the battery there was just enough time for the men from Lyme to meet and recognise the raiders before, together, everyone jumped over the western wall.

'Ho. We hoped to meet you lot on this sally,' shouted one man to Effra.

'Well, we're glad to be back. Let's just get away from these poxy musket balls before we celebrate, eh?'

The men ran away from Fort Royal, but they were running towards Lyme, towards their friends. They ran with energy – merrily, even. Tom laughed as he vaulted small ditches or scraped himself through furze clumps. The tension of the last few days sloughed off his shoulders. It was over. They had broken out from the town, brockled the mortar and successfully fought their way past the besieging army.

He laughed, even when he fell headlong into a ditch, swallowing a mouthful of mud. He was still laughing through a muddy face when he reached Fort Davey.

Chapter 27

Tom and Samuel rejoined the others at a bench near the Mermaid, carrying tankards of beer.

'Things are getting bad,' Gideon said. 'The town seems somehow different.'

'Aye. Where's the spirit gone? Everyone seems flatter than our stomachs,' Ifor said.

At this point Bathsua came over in response to their hail. 'You were only gone two days, but in that time our resolve nearly faltered. We reached the end of our meat and found the remaining flour was mouldy. Gunpowder, lead for musket balls and matchcord almost ran out, there've been fights between the garrison and the sailors, and some new recruits attacked the townsfolk.'

'I can feel the unease,' said Tom.

'More of Lord Warwick's ships are arriving now, bringing meat and cheese. The colonel knows the feeling in the garrison. He's summoned everyone to a parade today in Church Street to say something about it.' Bathsua stood up. 'Now, I must attend to my duties. You just rest there, boys. I'm sure this mild weather will help you regain your strength.'

'You can't speak to us like that, Mistress. We're heroes, we

276

are! Just back from a deadly ambush. Didn't you hear?'

'I hear, Samuel. You've told me often enough, though you've only been back five minutes. But never fear. Your secret is safe with me.'

'And yours with us,' shouted Gideon. 'We'll see you later.'

'Talking of secrets, what about them assassins?' asked Ifor.

At that moment a sergeant summoned them to report to Colonel Blake about the raid. Two hours later they were huddled in the square, near where the Lym River empties into the sea. Ahead of them were hundreds of men, standing, seething, rolling and bobbing like waves. The noise ebbed and flowed too, but mostly it grew, an incoming tide. All waited for Colonel Blake to address them from a small wooden stage at the front. When the colonel arrived along with Colonel Ceeley and Captain Pyne, he lost no time in coming to his point.

'Men, there have been ugly scenes between soldiers of the garrison and it has to stop. We must respect each other and stand together. We're in a tight place and disunity only strengthens our enemies and weakens our defence. Today, I don't care if you are the sweetest saint or the foulest heathen. If you stand with me to defend this place, you're my brother and I will put up with your particular ideas and shed my blood to keep you safe. If we split into factions, we are lost.'

In the far corner, three sergeants were muttering. Blake saw it and fixed the men with his gaze. Then one of the three called out.

'Colonel, you say we must stand together, welded into one shape, otherwise we won't prevail. But the Holy Bible says to not yoke ourselves with those walking different paths, and I know as a blacksmith that mixing metals with contaminants

277

don't increase power but weakens it. The answer must be the reformation of men's hearts. Only then can the strength of the Spirit flow freely among us.'

Colonel Blake jumped down at once and pushed through the throng, his path drawing men's eyes and bodies towards his target. Tom wondered if he would punish this insolence, but he was smiling, not scowling, when he reached the sergeants.

'I know your heart. I recognise your love for your fellow men. And I agree there's nowhere more suited to holding out the word of God than right on the threshold of hell. But our first aim is to hold this place against an enemy, and if we focus on our differences, it will fatally weaken our resolve. No! Listen to me. All of you. You who believe the Bible and you who trust to dice. We must forge ourselves into a fellowship. A fellowship of suffering, struggle and endurance. We can do it. We have the beating of anything Prince Maurice may throw at us, but only together.

'Together. That's our only salvation. And when we prevail, that is the time to rejoice, to relax, to breathe again and to consider life's significance. I can't use you if you're looking down your nose at your neighbour. I need your steely resolve. Flesh is weak, it's no match for bullets and swords. Unless, that is, it's held in place by bonds of fellowship and determination. Our greatest weapon is our unity. Fight for each other, every man of us, and those rogues outside will never crush us.'

The colonel looked straight into the blacksmith sergeant's face and grasped his hand. Looking around, he pulled the sergeant with him and reached out and grabbed the arm of a sailor.

'You two are brothers. Your lives today, until who knows when, depend on each other. So embrace, give yourself to the other. None of us can survive without trusting his comrades.'

The sergeant and the sailor nodded and pledged friendship. All those near were swept up in the emotion and cheered and reached out in friendship to those about them.

The colonel looked around and laughed. He picked his way back to the wooden stage and stood beside Colonel Ceeley and Captain Pyne.

'Keep a close watch on those groups, captain. We've begun the healing, perhaps, today. But it takes time, and mishaps can easily put things into reverse. Use regular patrols inside the town to see that comrades don't fall out.'

Tom arrived back at the campfire as his comrades stared at tiny scraps of meat floating in a thin gravy in their bowls.

'This place is going downhill,' said Ifor. 'Maybe the Royalists don't need no Roaring Meg. We seem to be falling apart by ourselves.'

'Wasting away, more like,' said Effra.

'I see what the colonel is getting at, though,' added Gideon. 'We're a right bunch of tinker's pots. All from different backgrounds. It's hard to forge a united army from us. I wouldn't want to do it, anyhow.'

'But us, here, now,' said Samuel. 'We're doing the forging. We must make it work, otherwise we'll be lucky if we come out of this alive.'

'We're not doing the forging, we are the metal being roasted and bashed into shape,' Gideon said.

279

'Well, I thought the colonel was doing some forging this afternoon. He's a great talker, that man,' his brother replied.

'He's not a bad fighter either,' said Effra.

'Talking of fighters, what about them assassins?' Ifor asked.

'Yes. There's been no sign of them today,' said Samuel.

'There's only one possibility,' said Effra. 'They're here to kill Tom and me. They're Fezzard's men, doing Fezzard's bidding. I've seen set-ups like this before. They've been sent to do a job which they'll be careful about, but they won't dally. They've come for us.' He nodded at Tom.

'They won't easily find them papers.'

'But what can we do?' said Gideon.

'It's not your fight, I guess.' Tom shrugged.

'Bollocks, boy,' said Ifor. 'We know Colonel Fezzard and we've been through enough together to do without that talk. We stand by each other. We don't leave a comrade at the mercy of our enemy.'

Gideon grinned. 'I've never been able to imagine you at the mercy of anyone, Effra. But Ifor's right. We're all in danger. If someone is aiming to kill you two, they won't let us get in their way. So we'd best be ready to defend ourselves.'

'And what's the best form of defence?' Effra had his don't-mess-with-me face on. 'Take the initiative. The only way to be safe is to know where they are, what they're doing. Then they can't stand behind that door, or drop a rock on our heads.'

'What do we do then, Effra? Assassinate them?' Tom shrugged and looked round at his mates. 'What? I was only joking. We can't do that. In a besieged garrison? Where we know half the folk, and they us?'

'We've no choice, boy. It's them or us. Believe me, I've seen how such men work. There's not much time.' Effra spoke quietly.

'How long?'

'I don't know, so we must act fast.'

The group drew together, as though plotting murder required whispers. They became more watchful. They didn't trust others to be on guard; always one of the group was awake and assigned as sentry. And they sought out their quarry. Captain Cooper and Sergeant Venning were serving in Davey's Fort most of the time, but there were worrying periods when they couldn't be found. This unsettled Effra and they finalised their plan, quick as they could, to bring the nightmare game to an end. Two days went by and the only risks to their health were the Royalist bombardment and the lack of food.

Tom and Effra watched from the second storey of a house in the town wall near Gun Cliff as a flotilla of small boats bobbed around between the Cobb and the quay. The sea-swell lifted one, then another, as the waves crashed against their sides. Every few minutes the sea erupted as the Royalists sent over a cannon ball from the battery on the cliff near the Cobb.

'They're getting closer,' growled Effra. 'That last one only just missed that barge.'

Two minutes. Another boom, another 32-pound ball. It arced over the steep slope down to the narrow beach and crashed through the hull of the largest barge drawing close to the shore. The impact shattered the timbers, producing an immediate inrush of black sea and a swift fountain of sailors pitching themselves over the sides. In moments, the boat and cargo disappeared, and other boats angled in to pick up the human jetsam.

Three more minutes passed, and another iron ball was tossed over the cliff, with the requisite boom, to land on one of the rescue vessels, which also went down within seconds, casting more men into the water. Two more booms followed, but these balls hit only the sea.

'It'll be a while before there's any more.' Both Tom and Effra knew there were four cannons in the Holmbush battery, and experience taught them that each took a quarter-hour to ready for firing. A good gun crew could manage a firing rate of four, sometimes five, per hour.

'Where's our reply? Our guns should be firing.'

'There's one of ours now' said Tom, in response to a closer boom from the garrison artillery in West Fort.

The two friends watched the remaining boats bring supplies into Cobb Gate and the beach near the Cobb. Then they heard the West Fort gate open and saw a sortie charge out towards the Holmbush battery.

'Cap'n Pyne having another go, eh?' said Effra.

'We've got to stop them blasting our dinner to Kingdom come.'

'Aye. But that raiding party looks a bit light to me.'

They watched a group of thirty horsemen race ahead of an equal number of infantry. The cavalry covered the ground to the battery quickly. They couldn't gallop because of the broken ground and the steep slope, but they cantered with intent, and the small musket guard around the cannons only had time for two volleys, one at long range and another just before the horses jumped over their barricade.

Tom and Effra could see swirls of action, as horsemen cut and slashed, while defenders swung musket and pike at them. The other raiders were closing on the battery now, but some horsemen were on the ground. Enemy were drawn to them like water sucked into a drain and there was less and less room for the animals to turn or flinch away.

The foot raiders were now in among the artillery, and Tom and Effra could make out nothing. Nothing, except a strong force of Cornishmen marching down the slope to join the fight.

'Cap'n Drake! Reserves! Where's our reserves? They need support.'

'Aye, I see,' came the response from the captain, a few yards along the parapet.

More men were already pouring from West Gate.

'That's not enough, Tom.' Effra counted the extra support. There were almost fifty of them.

'What's Colonel Blake thinking?'

'That's clear,' broke in Captain Drake. 'If we send too many men, that little fight could turn into a major engagement, and that'd be to our disadvantage. We durstn't be caught out in the open.'

'Rubbish,' snarled Tom. 'Captain Pyne's in the open. We can't just leave him helpless.'

Drake snorted. 'Don't you worry, lad. He'll bring our boys back, just you see.'

All three watched the spectacle. There were still horses and men thrashing around in the battery, but fewer now. The raiding infantry were clearing out the Royalists from the levelled gun platform, while soldiers drove metal spikes into the touch holes of the cannons. The Cornish were there now, though, and Tom watched everybody falling back. In only a couple of minutes the Lyme men were again outside the battery, with the Cornish in possession of it.

'I can see Captain Pyne,' said Tom. He was watching a tall horseman gesticulate to the surrounding men.

'That's not him. That's Lieutenant Miller. Where's the captain?' Drake sounded worried.

The reinforcements from West Gate had reached the main raiding party as it withdrew, and their loaded muskets presented a disciplined line of fire to the Cornish, giving the raiders space to retire to the gate.

The enemy tried to press, but the defenders added more fire from musketeers lining the town wall, including Effra and Tom. A few minutes more and the exhausted fighters were back through the gate and collapsed at the top of West Street. Colonel Blake heaved the great door shut while pikemen slammed down the cross beams.

Captain Drake checked their positions again an hour later. 'What news, captain?' Effra asked.

'Not good, not good.' The soldier shook his head. 'Captain Pyne took a musket ball to the body and another to his thigh.'

Chapter 28

A few nights later, sailors from Lord Warwick's fleet landed to reinforce the garrison. The boats came surfing the waves out of the star-sparkled night, onto the dark shingle near Cobb Gate. Out sprang dozens of seamen dressed in baggy breeches and loose linen shirts, and a few in short, faded jackets. Some wore shoes, but most had none.

The calls of the men were subdued, and they gave an impression of weather-hardened good humour and determination. They worked as familiar teams, catching hold of the boat sides and holding them firm while comrades emptied them of supplies. Reaching back into the boats, they grabbed their personal bundles, waved goodbye to the boatmen and then rolled into town. Once off the strand, they whistled and shouted halloo to the gathered townsfolk. Many came out to welcome these night-time reinforcements – Tom and his comrades too. They stood at the side of the road near to the little bridge over the Lym.

'Are they doughty enough for you, Tom?' Effra asked.

'They look tough, for sure. Like our recruits, strong and determined, but bare men without equipment or clothing and with what training for being in a siege?'

'Ha. They're sailors. Surely they know all about being

cooped up in a small place, and if they've seen action they already know the feel of cannon and musket shot whistling by.'

'You're right, Samuel. We'll see.'

As the sailors left the beach for the cobbled streets, they met Colonel Blake. He stood at the bottom of West Street on a stone block. His hands were on his hips, his body angled forward.

'Welcome friends. We're glad to share our town and fight with you. You may have heard of our recent difficulties with our neighbour, Prince Maurice.'

At this the sailors roared and the Lyme residents laughed, too.

'Your lodgings are ready and your stations in the town wall allotted. We've had some knocks, I can tell you, and your arrival is a great encouragement to us. With your help we'll keep those Irish and Cornish dogs out until Lord Essex can get here.'

He jumped down from his perch. 'Now, who's brought their pipe and drum with them? You sailors love to jig and dance, and here's an entire town to join you.'

The sailors cheered again and one voice spoke up. 'Alas, sir, we only had room to bring ourselves today. Our instruments hang still in our places onboard ship. But we couldn't leave our voices behind, and if you've any drums, we'll give a good account of ourselves.'

More cheering and shouting, audible right up to Davey's Fort and to the enemy lines. The townsmen drummed and clapped while the sailors sang and danced. Soldiers, sailors, townsmen and women mixed and the mood of the defenders lifted.

Effra was enjoying the fairground atmosphere. As he looked across the beach, he noticed Captain Cooper and Sergeant Venning at the top of the steps leading from the jetty. 'What're they up to?' he said to Gideon.

'Why don't we do it now?' Gideon whispered.

Effra considered quickly and drew his mates close. 'Cooper and Venning are over there, heading to the church. Let's follow and look for a chance to strike.'

Just then Bathsua found them. She had been tending Captain Pyne. Tom noted a heaviness in her movements.

'The captain is dead.' She touched Tom on his shoulder and asked him to give the news to the colonel.

'Do it quick, Tom,' said Effra. 'Then meet us opposite St Michael's Church.'

Tom led Bathsua towards West Street, away from his friends.

'It does your heart good to see folk relaxing,' Blake said to Colonel Were.

Tom approached and reported his sad news, and the faces of both men dropped.

'We were expecting it.' Colonel Blake spoke to nobody in particular. 'But it's a cruel blow, still.'

'More ships and more soldiers may be got, but such a man is rare.' Colonel Were couldn't finish.

Blake nodded and allowed his head to droop for a moment. Then he drew himself up to his full height. 'Come on, Were, we must repair our faces. It won't do to be grey and gloomy. Thank you, Tom.'

Tom could see Blake and Were drawing themselves together and engaging with the scene of optimism along the quay, but the eyes of both colonels were cold and dark. And that scared him more than most of the sights he'd seen since arriving in the little town. He told Bathsua to get some sleep, but she argued that there was work to do, to prepare the body.

Tom shook her. 'You've done your share tonight. If you want to help tomorrow, then rest now. The captain's going nowhere. He'll be ready for you in the morning.'

She nodded at this and he left her, plunging through the dancing crowd to follow his comrades.

They were huddled at the south edge of the church porch when Tom joined them.

'They've just headed down Green Street,' said Effra. 'Gideon. You and Samuel cut through the alley and see if there's any activity to our left. We'll meet you at the far end. Tom, Ifor, follow me! Let's figure out what they're up to and where they're going.'

They tried to look as though they were on their way to their campfire. They walked slowly and scoured each door and window as they passed. There were no signs of their quarry. At the junction between Green and Horse Streets they waited some time for Gideon and Samuel to join them.

They could hear the revelry from Cobb Gate as it bounced its way between the houses at the lower end of Horse Street. Then three familiar claps of thunder exploded into the night. The Royalist cannons had awoken. Like an old woman banging on the floor with her stick to get the partygoers downstairs to shut up, Tom thought. Orange-hot metal whizzed overhead, fizzing like sparks in a forge. The heated lumps of iron crashed into a house on Green Street. A hubbub of voices told him the occupants were fully aware of their misfortune.

Gideon arrived and told them they'd seen Cooper and Venning in one of the small rear courtyards, talking to another man. Samuel was keeping an eye on them.

'Go back and keep watch with Samuel. If they leave the house or courtyard, find me. I'll be at the junction here. Tom, Ifor. Go down Green Street and watch. See if they head that way.'

Tom and Ifor walked back along the street to a half-alley between two houses, where they could squeeze out of sight. They watched and waited for something to happen.

It only took a few moments. They heard a deep wail coming from behind the houses. There were no further cries and no one came out into the street, but after half a minute that felt like a quarter-hour they couldn't wait any longer; they had to find out what had happened. Leaving their fissure, they ran back to the junction.

Effra wasn't there. They ran further along Horse Street, towards the dancers.

'Here!' hissed Effra from the corner of an alley.

Tom and Ifor joined Effra. He was supporting Samuel, with an arm under his left shoulder while Gideon supported his other shoulder. They laid him on the street, where there was a faint glint of light.

Effra knelt beside Gideon, who was feeling Samuel's face for signs of life.

'Help me,' Gideon said. 'We must get him inside.'

They carried Samuel to the nearest house. Their knock was quickly answered by a wench with two young boys tugging at her petticoat. She let them use the main room and brought candles, then she and her sons retreated to their sleeping room.

Effra entered the house last and ordered Tom to guard the door. Then he, Ifor and Gideon checked their fallen comrade more carefully.

He was dead. Effra recognised the mark of a stiletto. 'Well, that confirms who we're dealing with,' he said. 'Assassins. It appears our victims are about their murderous business. But are they hunting us?'

Effra thumped a table. 'Think, boys. We must get this right. If we're the targets, they'll be circling now.'

'There's no sign of them,' Tom said. He had never seen Effra so agitated.

'If Cooper and Venning aren't after us, they must be hunting Blake, or Were or Ceeley,' Tom said. 'They're the most important persons in the garrison.'

The others agreed, only half-convinced.

'I agree something doesn't add up,' said Effra. 'If I'd killed Samuel I'd've used his body for an ambush, but they just left him. It doesn't make sense.'

'Well, I don't care who they are, I'm going to hunt them.' Gideon roused himself from his anguish.

'Aye. But don't do it like an idiot. Do it like a snake. And we'll help, lad,' Effra said.

'But Cooper and Venning have already got further ahead of us,' said Tom. 'It's time Colonel Blake knew what's happening.'

They left their fallen friend and went back out onto the street.

'Hoi, you can't leave 'im 'ere. He's dead and there's only me an' my nippers. He needs to go to the church, where the other bodies lie.'

Gideon turned on the woman, his knotted neck muscles

visible in the moonlight, but Tom pushed him aside and Ifor bustled him away. Tom promised the woman that they would be back before the night ended. She began to argue, then stopped and shrugged.

'All right, soldier. See that you do. I don't want 'im 'ere when it's daylight.' And she slammed the door.

From the town guard they learned that Colonel Blake was at his lodgings in West Street. He was still dressed when they arrived. The sentries held them at the door and called over Major Davey.

Blake saw what was happening and called, 'I know those men, Davey. Bring them here.' The colonel stood by a small fire sizzling in the grate while he listened to their tale. 'Captain Pyne told us your story, but we have intelligence of our own. I don't think I or the other leaders are targets. From what I know, our Lieutenant de Clare is their man. Follow me.' He stalked out of the room, back onto West Street.

Lieutenant de Clare was lodged in a house nearby. Colonel Blake led Tom and his team to him, while sending his aide to rouse the garrison and Major Davey to quieten the revellers and get the soldiers back to their stations. The ragged Royalist cannonade continued, and some roofs caught fire when heated iron bars landed on them, but the townsfolk were accustomed to this and the fires soon had busy teams, wielding leather buckets full of water, ladders and long hooks, pulling down burning thatch or timber. Blake had a brief conversation with Captain Coram, then marched off to other duties. Tom and the others entered a house and clattered up two flights of stairs.

'In here,' ordered the captain.

The four men entered a second-floor room, of good size for Lyme. In the room one man sat at a desk, surrounded by papers. He stood as they entered.

'Lieutenant de Clare. These are your guards. I'm sure we'll have Cooper and Venning soon, but you'll be safer with these veterans alongside.' Captain Coram turned to Tom. 'And your orders are to protect the lieutenant. Guard him with your lives. Is that clear? There's a squad of men downstairs and we've got patrols scouring the streets for our man Cooper and his sergeant.'

'Yes, sir. How long will this be for?'

'Don't be impertinent. You stay here until the situation changes. Don't open the door to anyone. If you hear a knock, the password is Vanguard. The men we're hunting are dangerous, but we'll scoop them up. Just stay put until I come back.' Captain Coram nodded at the lieutenant and left.

The four men looked at the officer. He was a skinny, medium height young man with an unruly bush of fair hair standing out in all directions from the top of his head. He was beardless and wore a woollen tunic over a blue silk shirt with a three-inch wide collar. His eyes caught Tom's attention. They were pale blue and had an intensity that was obvious even at night, in a poorly lit room.

The lieutenant looked at his guardians. Tom could see his gaze taking in their details. They didn't look much like tough, no-nonsense bodyguards; he felt weak and hungry, young and out of his depth, while Ifor was often elsewhere in a dream these days, only half-registering what was happening. Gideon was reeling from the death of his brother and kept shaking his head as if to throw off the memory of the last hour. Effra was the only one who looked a match for an assassin. His feral nature was enough to deter many arguments and his stocky frame was obviously strong and tough, but even he was being ground down by the siege; his eyes were sunken and his cheekbones more prominent than before. All of them had sores and blotches keeping bruises and cuts company all over their body.

'Well, gentlemen. You must come in and introduce yourselves. My name is Osbert de Clare, soon to be Lord of Dunster.' Tom heard catches and pauses in the officer's speech.

'Don't I know you?' the lieutenant said to Tom. 'Yes. You're the clod that broke my perspective glass.'

'Yes. Tom Tyler, sir. This is Effra Carter, Ifor Scovell and Gideon Palmer.'

'Where's that other chap you were fighting on the tower?'

'He's dead,' cut in Gideon.

The five men continued to stand and watch each other, not knowing what should happen next.

'I, ah... I will replace the glass, sir,' offered Tom.

'Don't be ridiculous, man.' The lieutenant sat down on the bed. 'Well, what a day. I am glad of your assistance, gentlemen. My work here is important, but the complication with Captain Cooper stiffens my resolve. It's time we brought this matter to a conclusion.' De Clare suddenly bent over and emitted a loud groan. He got up from the bed and carefully lowered himself onto his chair by the desk and faced the wall.

'Aah. This wretched stomach.'

Tom was unsure how to react. The others were no help. 'Is there anything we can do to help, sir?' he asked after a pause.

'Claret with sugar, that's all I can drink. Just, just spread out and don't clutter the place up so much.'

At this, Ifor and Gideon moved over to the narrow bed frame and sat down. Effra went to the window to spy out the street below, while Tom remained standing behind the officer.

'Sir. Do you have any idea why you're the target of Captain Cooper?' Tom asked.

'Of course I do. He's the instrument of Colonel Fezzard. That man was given charge of my young life by the Court of Wards. I was only eight years' old.' The question seemed to distract the lieutenant from his stomach ache.

'It was like strapping a boy to a tiger. I was moved around between shabby houses, and the management of my family's lands became subject to Fezzard's vindictive greed. The only times I saw him sane were when he was poring over the accounts of the estate. Then, oh yes, he was in full command of his faculties. I escaped, after a fashion, by going up to university. But as I grew I realised how much the man was despoiling my land and impoverishing my estate. He's salted away all the money from rents and timber and land sales, and falsified the records and documents so they show, he thinks, a prudent guiding hand.'

'So you seek justice?' said Tom.

'How I have reached adulthood is a mystery, I'm sure. But now, I'm old enough to reclaim my lands and take control of my destiny. But this, Fezzard can't allow. It would deprive him of the chief part of his income. So, ever since I lodged a challenge to his wardship, he's sought to undermine me. He claims I conspired to defraud him. The gall of the man! He even tried to get me committed to Bedlam hospital. Since that hasn't worked I feel his efforts to shake me off his back have intensified.'

'Ah. The boy is now riding the tiger!' Effra exclaimed. He came away from the window and sat on the bed while Gideon moved over to it. His head slumped onto the windowsill.

'Quite so. Well, my spies tell me he wants me dead. That would simplify his life enormously,' continued de Clare.

'We know that he plans to change sides,' said Tom.

'My information suggests he's already a Royalist, in Wareham with a band of Irish. The ambush at Woodsford Castle destroyed his regiment, but many of the soldiers threw in their lot with the King.'

'I bet he was pretty persuasive.' Gideon lifted his head and was now listening, with a fixed scowl.

'Yes. Doubtless. And this change has come when representatives of the Court are travelling to Poole from London to bring him to account. I think Cooper's presence here in Lyme is primarily to remove me from Fezzard's way.'

'That fits with what we know of Fezzard, too,' said Tom.

'We believe he has reason to treat us the same as you, sir,' said Effra.

Lieutenant de Clare frowned. 'I don't see how you fellows come into this. I know you were in his regiment, but that's hardly cause for murder.'

'But sir. Effra is an expert housebreaker and he and I were used by Fezzard to rearrange items in an important house in Dorchester while we were soldiering with him.'

'Shut up, Tom,' Effra snapped.

'We must speak out, Effra. We've been played by Fezzard, and he's used others too.'

'Exactly,' said de Clare. 'You may be able to help me see into his designs. You were stealing papers, no doubt. From whom, and where?'

'Begging your pardon, sir. What Tom is referring to is a few minor reconnaissances that Colonel Fezzard sent us on. We were carrying out orders and acting in a right military way. No more than that.'

'You're wrong, Effra,' said Tom. 'This is our chance to slide out from those murky deeds. If we speak plainly, our officers will see justice is done.'

Effra pulled Tom over to the window and hissed in his ear. 'Aye. Justice. It's justice I'm afeared of, boy. Not 'cos of what I've done. Because of the Law. It ain't something to snuggle up to, like you think.'

'Don't lecture me.' Tom tore his arm from Effra's grasp.

'Ah, I see,' de Clare butted in. 'The papers in Dorchester were, I'm sure, the findings of the investigation by the Justice of the Peace, Mr Churchill. He collected all the evidence concerning Fezzard's affairs.'

'But we didn't steal everything in the box. I took only the packet with the yellow ribbon round it,' Effra exclaimed.

'The packet, presumably, contained the most recent documents that must, somehow, have connected his misdeeds together. He must have done that to disrupt the work of the justice.'

'But what of the packet Effra left in Justice Churchill's house?' Tom asked.

'Another false trail,' de Clare said. 'Fezzard must deflect attention and blame onto someone else, so he ensured there was evidence to be found. No doubt the court feodary will get a note telling him where to find some damning evidence that exonerates him and condemns Mr Churchill.'

'Well, it's a mercy to understand at last,' said Effra. 'Now, sir. We need to keep us all safe and out of the hands of Cooper and Venning. And that may be tricky.'

'There's smoke below,' said Gideon.

Chapter 29

The pottery sphere crashed against the plaster wall and the gunpowder within swirled into the air as lead pellets dropped to the floor. Before the gunpowder dissipated, a spark from the fuse caught the powder and a weak explosion propelled the pellets downwards. For a moment the nascent flames struggled to take hold, but they were nestled onto dry fabric in piles and old rushes covering the compacted earth and soon licked outwards, becoming fiercer. Another deadly flask flew in through the window and exploded, fire erupting red and hungry in a gush of blazing liquid. The whole room was ablaze and full of smoke. Fiercer, hotter, grew the fire as it devoured the contents, then the frame, and licked its way into the next space.

A shout from outside added to the news from Gideon's eyes and nose.

'Get out. The ground floor is ablaze. Wildfire! You must flee. Get on the roof. Go north, the wind is coming off the sea. You can't go that way.'

Tom was rooted to the spot, his mind suddenly back in a small bakery in Poole, listening to wood crackle and a hot wind tear at his face.

'That's a fine guarding we got from them. We're on our

own,' said Effra, looking at the thatch ceiling.

'Quick, down the passage. Go north, away from the fire,' said de Clare.

Gideon pulled open the door, then stood at the top of the stairs. The smoke was thickening, and they heard roaring flames outside and below. But Tom hadn't moved. His blood flowed like syrup, lethargy filling his limbs, his body not responding to his brain's commands.

The lower two floors crackled and hummed like an oven, and the fire thrust thick smoke at the ceiling and walls. Effra headed north from the door a few yards to a mudbrick, whitewashed wall. Ifor brought the chair and the lieutenant. Effra paused before the obstruction for a few moments, considering whether to break it down, then he stood on the chair and thrust urgently up into the thatch to break a hole in the roof. All they had with them were their short swords. Their muskets were still at the Town Line.

Tom followed. This time it would be different. He wouldn't leave. He would stay. This time he would remember where his mother was. He would find the way to the storeroom where she was working. Yes. If he could go there too, he would stay with her. She wouldn't have to leave him.

The thatch was old and wiry. Each bundle of reeds, tied together and laid on the roof ribs, was plaited together with others so that the material was tough and resistant to Effra's efforts.

'Ifor!' Effra called. 'Use your knife. Break it down. Quick!'

Gideon joined him. Effra, standing on the chair, was now in his comrades' way, but they were making progress. He stepped down off the chair, lifted it and thrust it at the flaking mud wall.

299

Tom was still drifting along the passage. Fear and panic warred with a welcome for the flames. He had another chance to do it right. The others moved back to give Effra the room he needed to use his great strength. They stumbled into Tom.

'Tom. What'ya doing, man?' shouted Gideon.

Tom started and looked at the worried face of his comrade.

'Tom. Wake up. We need you. This is no time to turn to stone.'

Effra's strength was enough. The wall crumbled. The wooden laths and the mud-and-cowpats gave strength and shape to it but couldn't hold it together against a determined attack. Tom shook himself and shuddered as he saw the fire racing up the stairs and along the passage towards them. He lurched forwards and kicked the wall beside the hole. Effra threw down what was left of the chair and all five men set to with hands and feet to widen the opening.

Before they could pass through to the next house smoke drifted in through the gap. It was already alight.

''Ware! Fire! Anyone here?' Tom shouted into the house. He was now moving feverishly.

'Keep going! The fire edge must be close,' de Clare said.

'Unless they've thrown grenadoes into all the houses,' said Gideon.

Tom's blood, so recently syrup, turned icy. 'We must check the rooms. Someone may be injured,' he shouted.

While they redoubled their efforts and pushed through to the next passage, Tom looked in every room. In the last one, at the end of a short passage, there were wisps of smoke rising all over the floor, twisting as they rose, coalescing into plumes and bouncing back from the ceiling, swirling round the bedchamber. He paused. What was that noise? There it was again. A whimper. He checked behind an iron bedstead and found a woman, groggy and half lying on top of a child about two years old.

'To me! Injured woman. Quick!' he shouted as he rolled the mother off the child.

The child coughed, but the woman was unconscious, a dark bruise on her left temple. Tom lifted her onto the bed, then slung her thin frame over his shoulders. He had just enough energy to reach down and lift the child with one hand. Ifor met him in the passage and relieved him of the woman, but Tom held on to the child.

They rushed along the wooden floor, passing smoke rising up through the boards. Flames flickered through gaps, seeking out fuel to eat. Tom looked back. The timbers in the first house were near to collapse, and the thatch crackled and spat above him. The flames weren't so near, but the smoke was getting thicker, like sitting downwind of a bonfire.

They called and coughed as they went. Warning, listening for an answer from anyone trapped, but they had to keep moving. The smoke was keeping pace with them and every delay brought the blaze closer, to eat into the timbers and hurl more deadly fumes at them.

Gideon burst into a room in the second house. He went to the window, broke open the shutters and shouted down to the crowd in the street.

One soldier hollered back. 'Keep going north. The fire's below you and in the thatch. Men are coming to fight it and throw a cordon round the houses. Get as far along as you can before trying the stairs.'

Gideon relayed this information to the others in the passage, hammering at the next end partition. He found a strong, iron-bound box with four handles on it in the room and they used this as a battering ram to crack the wall. Desperation lent them strength and endurance. Smoke stopped their lungs and stole their energy. Tom was now frantic rather than lethargic. Effra, de Clare and Gideon were through into the third house, still carrying the box. He and Ifor pushed through, carrying their human loads. Gideon again went to enquire of the crowd from a window – there was fire below them for another two houses. Firefighting teams were working to bring it under control. Cooper must have used the entire stock of wildfire grenadoes, thought Tom.

There was nothing for it. They had to keep busting through from one house to the next. At least they were now away from thatch. The roof above was of slate tiles nailed on to wooden slats.

House five stopped them dead. The wall was brick. The battered box made no impression on it. It was thrown aside. Gideon ran to another window. The soldier who had shouted up had followed their progress. He now told them to climb onto the flat roof of the brick building, from where they could descend to the street.

Effra found a short ladder that they leant against the brick wall and climbed to break open the slate roof. They pulled down slats from as close to the roof ridge as they could reach. They gave way easily. Tom was hoisted up onto the ridge. He found the slope down from the edge steeper than he liked, but he was in command of himself now. The bricks rose to five feet above the ridge. Tom crouched down and called through the hole for Gideon to come up next. He climbed out onto the roof, then lifted Tom so he could pull himself up,

302

flip over and land on a flat timber floor. There was nothing of use for getting everyone up onto the roof, so Tom had to stretch back down to help his comrades scale the wall.

The child was lifted up next, then Ifor passed the woman to Effra at the opening and he lifted her to Gideon, who struggled to arrange the limp form in a way that he could pass up for Tom to grab. Carefully, the woman was hauled over the brick wall and Tom laid her down beside the sobbing child.

Next came the lieutenant. He was handed up to Gideon. He trembled and gripped the arms reaching down to him. On the slope he stood rigid, with his face in Gideon's tunic. Effra stood on the sloping slates and forced de Clare to lift his limbs to balance and climb onto the ridge. He juddered along, every step painful to watch. But he was moving, his ashen face pressed now against the wall. His fingers inched their way up the brickwork, and the officer's body crept upwards. When he stood on the ridge, he could look over the wall into Tom's face and reach out to him. Gideon heaved, and de Clare tumbled over the ledge, onto Tom. He lay, gasping on the flat roof and was soon joined by the others.

The group rushed down the stairs inside the house and exited by the front door, crashing into a team of firefighters throwing buckets over the last house they'd passed through. The brick house was the governor's.

Out in the road, Captain Coram took Lieutenant de Clare under his protection, while the mother and her child were laid gently on the opposite side of the street. Tom looked from one to the other. The child, still sobbing, was a small boy. He was coughing, which seemed a good sign. The woman was lifeless, like his own mother when she was

303

carried from the basement.

Tom collapsed to his knees, eyes intent on the woman. His breathing was ragged, shallow and fast. Three other women knelt by her. They slapped her cheeks, they worked her arms up and down. One even took large breaths and blew them forcefully into her mouth. Then she coughed. She coughed again and turned over. Tom gulped fresh air into his lungs. Relief surged across his body. Thank God. She'll be all right now.

The surge reached his limbs. Bitter edges burned back, like waves recoiling from the Cobb, poisoning the hope brought by relief. There was no hope for his mother. Tom didn't even know this woman's name. The recoil of disappointment left him deflated. Empty.

'We've caught them, de Clare. They were in the tallest house opposite with a fowling piece trained on these roofs. Venning is dead, but Cooper is under guard in the church.'

Tom barely heard, but the others responded with relief and exhaustion. The lieutenant returned to his 'important work' and the comrades were dismissed to get some sleep. Effra helped him up from his knees and they walked back to their place at the Town Line, the excitement of the night draining away with every step.

At the campfire, Ifor kicked the embers and disturbed an orange glow. 'Shall I build up the fire for the rest of the night?'

Tom sighed. 'I've seen enough burning wood for a while. What d'you think, Gideon?'

'Gideon's not here,' Effra responded.

'He'll be at the church, for sure,' said Ifor.

'Of course,' Tom said, as they headed back to cross Sherborne Road.

They rushed between two houses and plunged into a deeper black than the brief night provided with its open sky. They ran, across the bridge, past the trestle tables outside the mill, and clattered along Horse Street towards the church. Before the end of the road, they slowed.

'Let's not rush in, Tom,' said Effra. 'If we can find him quick we won't have to alert the guard captain. We want no more trouble.'

'But where'll he be? Waiting to shoot Cooper when he comes out, or wriggling his way into his cell to skewer him?'

'His grief won't let him wait, is my guess,' Effra replied. 'So he'll not be thinking of an escape route.'

'Quick, then. We'd best get between him and his quarry.'

They raced forward to the main porch and heard a commotion inside. A torch flared within the church and the sentry at the door looked in to see what was the matter, just as Tom barged past and ran into the nave. In front of him were four men struggling. Two others were circling the writhing, shadowy mass with their matchlocks cocked.

'Stop!'

The guards turned to face this new threat.

'He's not a Royalist. He's one of us,' yelled Tom.

The guards had borne a man to the ground and two now pinioned his shoulders to the stone floor while the third stood up.

Tom approached with his hands in the air. 'He's our comrade. Your prisoner killed his brother tonight. He's not doing anything you wouldn't do.'

A great anguished cry came from the man on the ground.

'Who are you, then?' asked the standing fighter.

'I'm Tom Tyler. I'm the corporal of this man, Gideon Palmer.'

'Stand still. All of you,' the fighter shouted, as Effra and Ifor joined Tom. 'Bart. Have you got him? Are you safe?'

His man replied that Gideon was subdued and he and his mates were uninjured.

'We were guarding Lieutenant de Clare and your prisoner was trying to kill him,' Tom explained. 'We had to escape over the roof. Then we heard you'd caught the bastard. Our comrade Samuel Gideon's brother, was murdered by him earlier tonight. He's just reacting as any brother would.'

There was a pause as the guard leader absorbed this information. 'All right, Tyler. We'll step away from your man, but you take him in hand and get him out of here.'

Gideon was picked up from the floor and held tight until Tom and Effra came alongside him. They left the church and stepped back into the fading night.

'I must kill him,' sobbed Gideon. 'He killed Samuel. How can I just leave him to an unknown justice? He'll wriggle free and be allowed to smile again, to walk down a high street and to ride out into the country. I can't allow that. Samuel wouldn't want me to let it go.'

Tom sat his friend on the churchyard wall. 'Listen to me, Gideon. You can't kill that man. He's beyond your reach. If you don't realise that, you'll be dead in a week. D'you understand me? Do you think Samuel wants you dead? Well, then. Use your head.' Tom was looking directly into Gideon's eyes, while Gideon's head rolled and he looked from one side to another, writhing with mental pain.

'Gideon, you're the smart one. You rescued me in the fire. You brought me back to my senses. Can you imagine what

Samuel would say if you lost yours and followed him, just because you couldn't think? He'd laugh at you. "Brother," he'd say, "what're you doing here? Live for both of us. How could you be so stupid?"'

Gideon gulped. 'You're right. But how? Without him?' He cupped his face in his hands and wailed.

'The pain will ease,' said Ifor, stretching his hand out and gripping Gideon's shoulder. 'It will, in time.'

'And during that time, use your brains. Wake up and attend to us. You must keep yourself safe so you can keep us safe,' said Effra.

'We rely on you, Gideon. We rely on each other,' said Tom, sobbing now as much as his friend.

The sobbing eased, and Gideon allowed his friends to guide him back to the house in Horse Street. The woman was relieved to get rid of her dead guest.

Gideon hoisted Samuel over his shoulder. 'I've carried him like this before. We were young lads and the fair in Wimborne was lively and started early. He couldn't stop himself. His eyes were the size of eggs as he tried this tidbit, drank that brew or ogled that maid. By supper time he was done in and I had to carry him home.' Gideon paused and leant against a wall. Tom could see his body shuddering. After a moment, Gideon continued. 'He sang on the way, despite his head being upside down over my shoulder. He has a beautiful voice. I love his voice.'

They set Samuel down behind the church, giving him into the care of the sexton, as they'd done with other comrades. Then they walked past the mill to their place at the Town Line. Ifor settled Gideon down by the fire site. It took only a few moments, despite his anguish, for him to be asleep.

The others fidgeted, tending the fire and adjusting equipment, calming down so they could follow Gideon into the dream realm. Tom was not so lucky. He had to report to Captain Coram to explain Gideon's actions. While there he learnt that Captain Cooper had escaped from the church and was last seen vaulting over the Town Line, heading for Fort Royal.

An hour later, dawn was over them as Tom lay down beside the fire. His friends were all deep in sleep. He relaxed his weary limbs and loosened the muscles in his neck as his head rested against his snapsack. A boom broke the morning quietness. The daily bombardment had begun. Tom was asleep before the noise faded.

Chapter 30

It was as if the Royalists smelt the desperation of the defenders. New batteries appeared on the west of the town to bombard the houses and the Town Line on the east side, while batteries on that side could fire balls over the town to its western boundary. Attacks against one or another part of the line were made to test the garrison, to drain them. It seemed to Tom and others that the defence was about to collapse.

More resources and support were needed. Lord Warwick saw this when he visited them. His sailors knew it as they ferried stores onto the land. The tars were moved by the plight of the town and they sent ashore spare boots, shoes and stockings and a generous quantity of their own rations. These swelled the hearts of the people in Lyme more than their bellies, and they fought on.

Tom and Effra were talking about these things as they wandered through the town. Ahead, a knot of men blocked the street. They pushed through this throng of seamen and came to a table set in the road. Two men sat by it, each holding out his right arm over the bench, resting his elbow on it and grasping his neighbour's hand.

'I wouldn't bet against that fellow.' Tom nodded at the

309

figure sitting with his back towards them as they passed.

'He's a solid block of a man, for sure,' Effra replied.

They stopped, despite themselves, and awaited the out-come of the struggle. The solid sailor looked like a bear facing a child. His opponent was no runt, but the seaman overshadowed him. Their hands fisted together. A third man called for quiet, and as the hubbub subsided he started the contest.

The sailor's muscles quivered along his arm from shoulder to knuckles, but the limb stayed in position. His opponent's arm flexed in a similar way, but soon there was a sense of it trembling, as he tried to force the sailor into submission.

The sailor smiled. He turned his head and winked at someone. He seemed totally at ease and, after half a minute of holding his arm like a rock against a tide, he exerted his strength and bore his opponent down onto the table. There was nothing the man could do. He was beaten before his knuckles rasped on the wooden board.

The winner stood, arms in the air, reaching up from his six-and-a-half-foot frame higher into the sky, accepting the cheers from the onlookers. 'Anyone else? Who else would like to graze my knuckles?' His eyes wandered around the street and settled on Effra.

'Hey, bullet-head. You look a likely test for Moizer. Come and joust with me.' When Effra didn't respond, the giant tried again. 'Come on, man. Let's test ourselves, do you have the strength to best me? I bet you've done this before, haven't you?'

Everyone now took up the cry and pressed Effra to stay and challenge Moizer.

Effra resisted, but it was harder to wriggle free than to let himself be manoeuvred into the vacant seat.

The two men smiled at each other and settled their elbows in the centre of the table. Effra placed his feet wide apart beneath the board and grasped its edge with his left hand as he flexed his right arm. He looked at the wood, then lifted his eyes to Moizer. The sailor had a round face, rough whiskers everywhere, a bulbous nose and large blue eyes which fixed Effra with a penetrating stare.

Effra did not flinch from this inspection, and their forearms slapped together as their hands reached out to grasp one another. Tom watched the sailor feel Effra's grip, then nod.

The umpire raised his voice and the surrounding din softened. Then they were off. Moizer's arm flexed, as before, and he leant onto Effra's arm. Effra was playing the same game, taking the strain and leaning in to Moizer.

They stayed like this for some time. To Tom they seemed to be waiting for another command. There was no movement, just a tense stillness. Moizer and Effra focused on their hands, feeling the strength of each other and pressing forward for an advantage.

The onlookers acted as though they understood the workings of the antagonists' arms and heads. They shouted and hollered, urging on one or the other. The noise rose, like the rushing of a tide into a narrow creek. Effra had already surpassed Moizer's earlier opponent, and the crowd, sensing a true contest, wanted action.

But Moizer and Effra were wrapped in a tiny world bounded by the wooden table. Time beat its way forward. The tumult ebbed. Intrigue, and the wonder of witnessing a rare sight, now replaced excitement at a quick triumph.

After ten minutes, the crowd had settled down to whispered comments and frequent coughs and snorts.

Effra looked at Moizer. Moizer smiled back and winked. Effra maintained his attention and resisted another surge of power from the sailor. 'Will we stay like this all night, d'you think?'

'I've nowhere else to go, bullet-head. Does my presence gall you?'

'No.' Effra grinned. 'But you're between me and the sea and you're blocking the breeze.'

'So I have one advantage over you then. Let's see if I can make it count.' Moizer pressed again on his opponent, but to no effect.

'Well, mates? How do you fare?' The umpire entered the conversation and the crowd re-found its voice with catcalls and cheers.

'We seem to be at a stand-off,' the sailor said.

'Aye. Why don't we both relax and find another way to test ourselves?'

'I've no objection,' smiled Moizer, a tiny bead of sweat appearing by his left temple.

Each man held his opponent's gaze until the umpire spoke again.

'On my count of three, you will each release your grip and pull back from the table. Is that clear?'

Both men nodded. The umpire counted, and Effra and Moizer broke free of each other, to a cheer from the crowd. There had been nothing to see, but all present could tell that here were two expert wrestlers.

'You have a talented right arm there, bullet-head. I don't meet many can stop my hammer blow.'

'It's not a skill I test myself in much,' replied Effra.

The sailor paused, then broke into wild laughter. He slapped his opponent on the back. 'That's rare. You match my best strength, then meekly claim you have no skill yourself. What's your name, bullet-head? I need to buy you a drink.'

Tom slept badly and woke suddenly. There by the fire was Gideon, stirring the embers. It was light and the night sentries were about to be relieved.

'I heard a tale from our neighbours' campfire,' said Gideon. 'One of them dreamt he would be killed.'

'That's not unusual, in this place, is it? Can't they persuade him it's just a dream?'

'Well, that's the point. He wouldn't listen to them and hatched a plan to keep himself safe by staying at the back and avoiding going on raids.'

'Oh. I get it. He died anyway. Is that it?' said Tom.

'That's right. Despite his care, death came for him, as it will for us.' Gideon looked down again at his stick, stirring the glowing ashes.

'Well, if he comes, he comes. What can we do about it? We can only live one day at a time and make the most of it.'

'Aye,' said Gideon.

The Royalist guns announced another morning of siege, hunger and toil. Tom stood his turn at the Town Line, defended against an attack close to Gaitch's Fort and watched West Fort bear the brunt of the bombardment.

At the campfire the four friends slumped, exhausted and

313

with scant enthusiasm for the small loaf of rye bread and piece of goat's cheese that formed the day's food ration.

Bathsua joined them, but there was little talk, just a sullen acknowledgement of each other.

Then they heard a flurry of animated chatter from the campfires closer to West Fort. The commotion grew nearer as each campfire passed on the news. When it reached Tom and Bathsua the message was clear. Colonels Blake and Were were wounded. Tom thought of Captain Pyne, dying after five days of agony, following his wounds. Not a fate he wished on anyone, least of all their leader, Colonel Blake.

The immediate conversation was about the colonels and their injuries, but it soon wandered sideways to discuss how this would affect the management of the defence. This was the worst possible news. Blake was their core of resistance and well of courage. Could he be taken from them?

'What shall we do if it's true?' said Ifor.

'Course it's true. Who would start such a rumour without cause?' said Gideon.

'I've seen men argue for hours that the sea is dry and you can walk all round the world. It don't mean it's so,' said Effra.

'Those would have been drunk men, though, Effra. Am I right?' Bathsua joined in.

'Yes, but we're all drunk with hunger and tiredness here. It could be true. Colonel Blake is always in the thick of things.'

Anxiety levels grew as the evening approached. Then an officer brought an order for everyone except the sentries to parade at the bottom of Church Street, immediately. The men walked in an unmilitary group down West Street, while Bathsua disappeared towards the town mill.

Night was not quite upon them when the crowd was fully

assembled. The hubbub was subdued, and it quietened to near silence for a moment as officers mounted the stage and sat at a line of chairs. Then a cheer swelled out from the front to the back as the soldiers saw Colonels Blake and Were join the officers. Relief seeped into Tom's body. He couldn't imagine coping without the rock that was Colonel Blake. A rock, but a man of compassion and shrewdness in his dealings with men. Losing Captain Pyne was difficult to endure. The loss of Blake would be a catastrophe.

These thoughts and conversations were in men's minds as the colonel called for quiet.

Colonel Blake rose from his seat. His face was deeply lined. He walked with a limp and announced that he was wounded in the foot, while Colonel Were had taken a musket ball across the belly. 'But we are here. We are alive and we will continue to supervise the siege. Do not fear. Remember, each one of us is immortal, until God calls us to be with him.'

There were more cheers here, and the colonel had to pause. Tom was worried, though. He was too solemn. Then the speech resumed.

'The enemy tries to undermine our determination. But our assurance rests on God's word, not on what "the father of lies" says. The devil encourages us to look at ourselves, our feelings, our doubts, our experiences. Anything to cause us to take our eyes off what God has done for us.'

The colonel was warming to his theme now, and he scowled at the crowd. 'But I have more news to share with you. We have suffered other, serious injury today. Our beloved Reverend Bush has been killed.'

A hush descended on everyone. Most there knew Bush as the man who would care for their soul and their body with

315

equal energy. Bush would go out beyond the Town Line to rescue a wounded soldier, whether Royalist or Roundhead, and the men of the garrison responded to that humanity.

Tom remembered seeing the colonel with Reverend Bush on the Cobb, sharing a moment of intimate friendship, heedless of their coats flying up around them and the spray of an incoming tide playing over them. There would be no more moments like that.

'Reverend Bush was a strong-man. A champion. He served our Saviour and got strength and power from him. But now, he's been taken from us. We grieve. But the same God who gave life to our pastor can raise up others to the same task, and our duty is to receive that strength from Him. God doesn't give gifts only to one or two, but to all his people. So, rejoice that our pastor is now looking into the face of Jesus. And that God's power and wisdom is available to guide us to victory in this fight.'

Tom heard the words and turned them over in his mind. What sort of god is it that fells his staunchest advocate in a hail of lead? What god would let men rip each other apart, both sides claiming his allegiance? And yet Bush's frequent cry was of how gracious his God was to him, and one of his favourite sayings was 'If the truth of Jesus is based on lies then my faith cannot produce fruit.' His life was full of the fruit of peace and joy. Was it possible that the God of Reverend Bush could fill others with the same faith?

Bathsua often spoke in a similar vein. For her, God's grace and favour was a daily necessity. Tom pictured her serving the men with food by the mill and crouching as she delivered buckets of musket balls to the defenders at the town wall. Her life, too, had the imprint of a greater power, infilling and moulding. The process in her was beautiful to watch, beautiful and infuriating.

The colonel's speech had finished. The men wandered away in groups, muttering or silent, so different from the usual banter and animated talk. Tom turned and saw Bathsua standing at a nearby doorway. Their eyes met and in a moment they were together.

'How long can this go on?' he asked.

'There's little meat left; we're using mussels and whelks scavenged from the beach. We need more supplies.'

'And we've used huge amounts of gunpowder and match,' Tom added.

'I can't believe we'll fail at the last, after all we've been through. But what will it cost?' Bathsua's eyes were moist. The two young people clung together.

'What now?'

'There are other encouragers, I know. But none like him.'

'Why kill Pastor Bush? What does that achieve, Bathsua? Your God is either capricious or impotent. Surely he would've recognised a good man and protected him if he could?'

'I don't know, Tom.' She hung her head and slumped onto the low parapet of the bridge. 'I know my God, but I've also seen the power of men. Their lies, greed, pride and foolishness are strong enough to affect the lives of godly people.'

'So, you agree that your God can't prevent sin.'

'It seems to me that God can bring good from things meant for evil. He can weave a beautiful cloth from a filthy rag. It just takes time, and we're caught up in our todays when God is looking forward to when Jesus comes again. Then there will be no sin, no pain and no fear.'

'No, Bathsua. You can't have it both ways. Either God is good and he can protect his children, or he isn't and he can't. When I look around I see pain and death. I don't see grace and peace. I don't believe your God is here, or that he cares about what happens to us.' Tom's eyes met Bathsua's for a moment, then he turned and gazed first across the bridge to West Street, then up Church Street. Both roads were choked with soldiers returning to their campfires.

'Walk with me,' he said.

Bathsua frowned.

'Please.'

She relented and together they strolled past the church to the cliffs overlooking Lyme Bay. The day was spent and darkness had already closed around them. Yet Bathsua and Tom could sense the spume crashing up from the base of the rocks and the white edging to the waves in the bay. The moon was not yet above the eastern horizon, but stars were visible beyond the clouds unravelling overhead.

'Do you believe in dreams?' Tom blurted.

'I believe men have them,' Bathsua replied.

'But d'you think they mean anything.'

'I believe God can speak to us through dreams, yes.'

'Well, I've had a dream that keeps coming back to me. I resist it, but it won't fade. It's like a lost dog that stands at your gate and barks. It's not yours, you don't want it and you shoo it away. But it's there again the next day, or the next. Barking.'

'Tell me.' Bathsua reached out and held Tom's left hand in both of hers.

'It's my father,' he said. 'I've dreamt of him many times over the last months. At first we were in Poole. I was running along behind him, carrying packages. I could never catch him up. I kept dropping the packages and tripping over them. Each time I woke full of emptiness. Then, after the regiment was ambushed, the setting became Athelhampton House. My father was walking around, speaking to people in uniform and in normal dress. Then he was talking with Colonel Fezzard. He would never acknowledge me, never respond to my shouts. The more I tried to reach him, the quicker he slipped away. The only one who ever looked straight at me was Fezzard.'

'Why now, Tom? Why tell me this now?'

'I don't know. I feel... I feel there's a rushing in of things. I feel I'm being drowned in these events going on around me. I'm losing everything I know, everything I care about. And I can't do anything about it.'

'And then, Reverend Bush. And Samuel, too. It's hard for you, Tom.'

'I came here with nothing. We didn't even have a regiment to rejoin. And yet in this place hell has turned to... well, not heaven, but a place of belonging.' Tom turned to face the sea. 'Am I dreaming now? Is Lyme my dream? It's collapsing around me, much like the life I see in my dream.'

'You're suffering from loss,' Bathsua said gently. 'Your father, your bakery, your old life. And the things that replaced it turn out to be impermanent as well.'

'I can't bear it.'

Without noticing, they had sat down at the grassy cliff edge. She reached out and drew Tom's head down on to her shoulder. 'You aren't the only one in pain,' she said.

'Am I to lose what I've found here? Will I awake back in

Poole? Despite all the agony, I don't want that. It surpasses what I've lost.'

'No one knows what tomorrow will bring. But if you find Jesus, the pearl of great price, it's worth any worldly treasure.'

'I'm not talking of Jesus,' said Tom. He drew away from Bathsua to look at her. 'It's you. You are what I've found. And I can't bear the thought of losing you.'

Bathsua slumped back. He could see her face in the growing starlight. Was that the beginning of a smile on her lips? The light wasn't enough to notice any flash in her eyes, but she was blinking.

'Tom. Dear Tom. You don't know what you're saying. This war's crushing all of us. I am grateful that we are friends, but...'

Tom heard the words, but caught the small catches in Bathsua's breath. He knelt in front of her. 'I trust you, Bathsua. If you say I'm crushed I believe it, but I know what I feel. Speaking to you now makes it even more clear. You are the pearl I've discovered, and it's beyond agony thinking you're in danger and I could lose you. Dare I hope that you could see me in the same way?'

Bathsua sat looking at her hands. Her head was still, her shoulders trembled. 'I don't deserve your affection, Tom.'

'Stop! Bathsua. What have you been preaching to me all these days? That God wants to give us good things. Why would you recoil when he brings affection into your life? Your God can bring this good thing out of our dire straits, surely?'

The woman still didn't respond. She sat, looking at her hands, for another few seconds. Then Tom saw a deep sigh shudder through her and her face lift and reflect the first glints of moonlight.

'Tom Tyler, you're right. There is no dilemma, just my God showing me grace in providing a friend to share with.' She reached up and put her palms on Tom's shoulders. 'And I confess, you've become dearer to me than any beyond my family.'

Tom leant towards Bathsua. Her cool face framed warmer, moister lips that softened as he kissed her. He was drawn down to the grass beside the woman as their mouths joined, expressing in touch what they hadn't been able to say to each other. They sat in each other's arms, drawing strength from being together, looking up at the stars.

'I'll do everything to keep you safe. We must come through this.'

'Don't promise what you can't deliver, soldier,' was her reply. 'In God's grace, we will survive the siege. Then you can help me rescue my brother.'

Chapter 31

An early summer's morning; fresh, dewy, with a clear sky, scraps of white cloud high above the suffering town and distant grey ones on the eastern horizon, veiling a sluggardly sun. The birds had started their usual optimistic din before dawn. A few hearty fellows rose to their feet to appreciate the natural scene, while the sentries counted down the last moments of their watch. The tranquil atmosphere was marred as men rolled away from dying fires and cursed, coughed or shouted at their friends, and found within themselves the strength to face another day.

Then, while most still chewed on dried meat or rye crust, the bombardment began, replacing the birdsong with a harsh, hateful sound that delivered fear and injury into their lives. Every day it was the same.

Tom awoke and with red-rimmed eyes joined his comrades. Ifor shuffled back to the campfire from the Town Line a few yards away, his sentry duty done. He looked what he was, an old man adrift in a world he didn't choose and couldn't un-choose.

After breakfast the comrades were free until lunchtime. Gideon and Ifor just sat beside the fire, while Effra set off to visit Moizer. Tom tagged along, then peeled off to look

322

for Bathsua. He found her at the town gaol, in the Guildhall basement, talking to Gamaliel Chase. Master Chase had been expelled from his parsonage and raided on several occasions by the Lyme garrison. On one of these, the raiders seized his horses.

'When I pleaded with them to leave me one, I was mounted behind a trooper and brought here.'

'Don't worry, Master Chase,' said Bathsua. 'Lady Eleanor has suffered herself and will recognise the injustice you've received.'

'You're very kind, my dear. But I think even Lady Eleanor won't get my belongings back.'

'But freedom comes first. Then you can work to re-establish your estate.'

'If you say so, girl. I've no strength to argue with you. What about your brother? Do you know yet if he is safe?'

'No word has reached me since that day. But Tom here has promised to help me rescue Quintus. Isn't that right, Tom?'

'You know I'll do what I can.' Tom blanched at Master Chase's conditions. There was only one chair, which Bathsua had brought, and no other furniture in the gaol. He remembered his brief stay in Fish Street, in Poole, and for a moment he felt that fish stench eat into him again.

'Master Chase has heard about Reverend Bush. There's now only a dozen preachers left to us.'

'But no one wants to listen to an old man accused of Romish tendencies. I'll be pelted and stoned if I preach.'

Tom caught the glint in Bathsua's eye. 'Bathsua, promise me you won't try to preach. The men won't listen to a woman preacher.'

'You don't understand what you're asking. God has given

323

me a skill and a commission to preach, and no leeway to decide when and where to obey him.'

'But you know what will happen. We're struggling to survive and your preaching will cause rifts and dissension. Exactly what Colonel Blake fears.'

'The heat of battle is the place where men need to hear truth. The colonel said as much. With folk passing from this world to another so often, there's no ease to forget that truth and to say, "Tomorrow. Maybe tomorrow, but not today." That's the course of a coward. I am no coward.'

'No one could say you are, Bathsua. I'd rather have you standing beside me than just about anyone else when facing an enemy. But surely you recognise there's a place and a time to brave the enemy's fire, and another to think and to plan and to stay safe, knowing that an opportunity to strike will come.'

'Ooh. Your words confuse me.' Bathsua fisted hands to the sides of her head. 'I only know I belong to Christ. I must follow my conscience and not just my head.'

'I'm not asking you to compromise your faith. Only that you don't create discord. Consider the added pain and anguish you heap on those not ready to respond to your gospel. Your life proclaims the gospel every day by your care for people. You don't need to preach.'

'Hmmm. What do you think, Master Chase?'

'I'm no guide for a fearless evangelist, my dear. I'd rather curse these soldiers and pray they be roasted on their own campfires than exhort them to leave their lives of sin. Ask me again when the war's over, Bathsua.'

Bathsua nodded and turned to Tom. 'I won't promise you. But I'll prayerfully consider the matter.'

They ambled over to the cliff at the back of the church to enjoy the mild spring day. In the bright warmth, they could imagine that the world was at peace and they were happy.

For a while, they kept the Royalist barrage from their thoughts, but that time was short. The rate of fire had increased around Fort Davey, north of the church. The two young people stood up and looked around.

'Go back to the town mill,' said Tom. 'I'll see how things stand at the fort.'

'Don't you tell me what to do! I want to help as much as you. We'll go together.' And off Bathsua stamped, round the northern end of St Michael's.

Tom ran to catch her up.

At Fort Davey Tom saw a crush of men sheltering behind the Town Line, while others were within the redoubt playing a lively game of muskets with the enemy, who were pounding on the outside with soldiers and cannonballs.

'You. Tyler! Take twenty men and barricade the street down by the church,' Captain Coram called, leaning over the rear parapet. He was ten feet above Tom, but he had to shout.

Tom regarded the redoubt. It was a squat, stone building, hunched into the ground with many feet of earth piled up around it on the three outer faces. There were two storeys with fighting places from which musketeers could fire. Between these floors was another, built with massive timbers. On this platform were cannons.

Attached to the rear face was a humble cottage with a missing thatched roof, replaced with rough wood. There was only one door, at ground level, and a window at about ten feet high, just beneath the timber covering.

The fort was to the left of the main gates. Another strongpoint almost matched it to the right of the town entrance. Here, a row of alms houses had been strengthened and given an added first floor and a defensive wall behind which musketeers could fire. Both forts had an iron-studded door facing on to the street.

'Bathsua! Over here.' A high call rang out over the lower male voices. Lady Drake beckoned from the house near the alms house redoubt.

Bathsua touched Tom lightly on the arm, then disappeared into the building to help Eleanor.

Tom gathered as many men as could hear his voice and ran down the road. He chose a spot where there were buildings on both sides of the street with few doors and windows, and ordered men to bring casks, timbers, anything heavy to throw across the road to block an enemy. Others were sent to plug up any entrances in and between the houses in front of this barricade, to prevent easy access by the Royalists. Further down the street, just passing the church, he saw teams struggling to drag two light cannons – sakers. They would strengthen his makeshift defensive line. He turned and watched with satisfaction as the barrier grew thicker and heavier. He strode back towards the gate.

On arrival, he shouted up to the first floor. Captain Coram poked his head over and Tom reported.

'Good. Lieutenant Rudd is coming down. Tell him too.'

Lieutenant Rudd looked down the road as Tom pointed out his preparations. 'We need to block the sides more.'

The officer called all the men within earshot to him. There were around eighty. He split them into two groups, those with muskets and those without. Tom had left his at the campfire near Sherborne Road. The musketeers jogged down the road with the lieutenant. The others were split into smaller groups and shuffled off the street into the forts. One other group of defenders hadn't responded to the lieutenant. They were busy defending the Town Line, bolstering the timbers and thrusting through cracks with daggers and swords. A few had pikes, but they were too thick to push through the thin gaps in the timbers and too long to be manoeuvred easily. Tom saw one pike used as a strut in the middle of the gates. It was held in place by a box and the pike was jammed into the gate two thirds up its height. The pike shaft flexed and bent as the Royalists pressed on the great door. It held while Tom watched, but it looked likely to give up the struggle at any moment.

Once through the studded door Tom found himself in Fort Davey, on the ground floor, with the dusty ceiling barely six inches above his head. The noise was terrible, but he had become accustomed to the shouts, cries and grunts associated with the musket and artillery fire. The smell always surprised him, though; a thick odour of gunpowder mixed with sweat, shit and fear. He peered through a fine dust dislodged from the structural timbers and hanging in the air. This strongpoint was Lyme's 'Stay of all', the fixed point around which all the conflict swirled. The fort defended all parts of the town because of its elevated position and the battery of powerful cannons within it.

Tom climbed a timber staircase from the musketeers on the ground floor to the gun platform above. He held his hands over his ears as he watched the gunners running forwards and backwards, scurrying like worker ants around precious ant eggs. It took him time to work out the arrangement on the platform. Four of the big guns were facing outwards and firing at the enemy in front of them. Two others, the largest of the cannons, were facing towards the town and were firing balls over the heads of the defenders and at the Royalists attacking West Fort.

Each gun, it seemed, had a crew of three and after each shot one man would race to the muzzle to ram a wooden ladle, shaped to fit the gun barrel, down the entire length of the cannon. The ladle was scraped up and down to remove any powder left, then a wet sheepskin mop was plunged furiously down the barrel to extinguish any hot embers that might remain. While the mop was used, the third man in the team stood, leaning against the wall, holding a budge barrel with leather top opened to allow the first man to scoop out the black, gritty gunpowder with his ladle. The budge barrel was then sealed against sparks. The ladle was pushed along the barrel and rotated to deposit the gunpowder at the bottom. Ladle out, a wad of material was pushed into the muzzle and rammed down, while man number three carefully selected an iron ball. This was tipped into the muzzle and gently pushed down the barrel to settle against the rags. More wadding was added and rammed into place. As the rammer stepped aside, the third man crouched and sighted his weapon. When ready he took a linstock, with a lighted match set in it, and touched a paper spill full of fine gunpowder that took the spark through a hole to the gunpowder behind the ball. The explosion of the main powder charge launched the ball at the enemy at a speed too fast to watch and with a noise that rattled teeth and shattered ears.

Tom guessed this platform was something like firing a cannon in a warship; low wooden ceiling, small opening facing the enemy and too many busy men for the space. He climbed the staircase to the second floor. Here there was no ceiling, but a four-foot parapet surrounded what was the roof of the gun platform. The top step brought Tom close to groups of four to six musketeers, loading their weapons. When ready, they nodded to each other and approached the front wall, where there were other groups thrusting their muskets forward and firing together at the mass of men attacking the fort. Muskets discharged, the front group would then retreat to the rear wall to reload, leaving space for the next group.

In the front corner of this vortex of activity, Tom saw Colonel Blake looking down on the struggle below. He moved along the parapet until he could see the enemy pressing against the heavy wooden gate timbers that strained and bulged in response to this growing pressure. Some Royalists had clambered over the shoulders of their comrades and reached the top of the gate, ready to swing down into the town. But the few attackers in this advanced position hesitated to drop into the middle of their foemen without stronger support.

Tom could see the workings of Colonel Blake's mind in the tight muscles of his face. His sharp eyes darted from point to point as he looked down on the fight. His jaw seemed immovable, but his cheeks twitched rhythmically. He looked around the timber platform, then downstairs to the ground floor, where the small group of potential reinforcements for the defenders waited; a mere twenty men armed with cudgel and sword. Pikes and muskets weren't the best weapon in such a small space.

When would they be ordered to join the fight? Outside,

the struggle continued and Tom watched the colonel walk to the rear wall and look over it at the barricades erected down the street.

Cracks and groaning brought everyone's gaze back to the gate, to see it swaying under a larger group of enemy sitting or hanging from its top, like a flock of birds alighting on a weak washing line. But these wingless magpies couldn't fly; they were dropping pell-mell onto the defending soldiers.

The colonel directed groups of musketeers to aim at the magpies, but he held back the reinforcements. He shouted warning to the defenders as flurries of opponents dropped onto them. A great crack rent the air and the gate collapsed, twisting towards the heads of the defenders, who backed away from it. The attackers rushed past and over the obstructions by the gate, and they pressed forward.

This was the moment. Colonel Blake's voice rang out over the tumult. 'Give ground. Back to the barricades!' and his order was followed with enthusiasm.

Tom descended to the metal studded door at the edge of the fort, ready for the colonel's next order.

'Out, lads. Stop those bloody malignants. Now!'

The door flew open and the reinforcements raced out, while a second group mirrored the action from the opposite side of the street. The ragged charge caught the front edge of the attackers' advance off-guard and threw them back on their fellows. But they were hard pressed to keep that advantage. Cudgels swung, swords and knives jabbed, men gasped and ground their teeth as each force strove for mastery. The defenders racing down the road had reached the barricades and Tom heard from behind his right ear another command from the colonel.

'Back to the fort. Get inside. Quick!'

They lunged with their weapons to earn an arm's length of space, then rushed through the doors. They got back in quicker than they'd gone out, but they had to hold off the Royalists while their fellows passed through one or two at a time. The colonel was the last man through the door, and it slammed shut with a reassuring thud. The attackers hadn't pressed that hard, as momentum from those behind drove them along the empty street, towards the barricades. Tom sagged against his comrades and listened to the sound of boots passing and voices yelling.

'Well done, lads,' breathed Colonel Blake. 'Bar the door and let's get back up to our perch.'

They had to be quick. The Royalists were racing down the street, looking for their enemies but finding only barred doors, windows and alleyways. In front was the barricade of barrels, timber and stones. The shouting rose as the attackers approached it. The defenders' cries echoed these until, with the enemy just fifteen yards from the newly defended line, two sakers barked death. Small iron balls and lead bullets spewed from the cannon mouths and blew away the closest attackers. Musketeers added to the hail of metal and the Royalist charge withered. More musketeers stepped up to the barricade, and another volley stung the men in the road. Another group came forward to repeat the action and, within one minute, the enemy attack became a mass of squirming bodies and a mob of men seeking the quickest route to safety. That route was straight back up the street and out of town as fast as they could manage, chased by more volleys.

Tom and his band watched this but didn't intervene. The colonel's words held them in check. 'Leave them be. We've

331

done enough damage. Let's hope those retreating remember how it felt to be inside Lyme on this day.'

The defenders stood by the wide-open gate and allowed their foes to disappear up the hill. Sergeants moved among them, giving orders to fill the space left by the fallen gates. The enemy was still swarming fifty yards away. It wasn't over yet.

The colonel gave the order, the sergeants added urgency to it, and hundreds of hands and feet searched for things for a new barrier. A team went down to the barricade and returned, with more men and whatever was man-handleable. Others ransacked the adjacent houses for timber and bulky objects. They wedged the gates upright in a drunken parody of their former glory, fixed in place by all the weight that could be delivered behind them.

With the immediate danger over, Tom looked round and saw Bathsua ministering to injured soldiers. The garrison wounded were kept separate from the Royalist casualties, but she was buzzing from one group to the next. After watching for a few minutes, Tom decided this was an intentional ploy by the woman to highlight that they all needed the same care and compassion. He smiled at her and she nodded in reply, her face made stern by her task.

'Tyler! Come with me.' Captain Coram picked out a dozen more men and marched off down the street, evidently expecting Tom and the others to follow.

He looked back at Bathsua. She was busy and didn't look up.

332

Chapter 32

The detachment marched down Church Street, over the bridge to West Street, past rows of ruined houses that reminded Tom of a hag's teeth. They continued up the hill towards another battle that was raging.

They approached the burned houses beside the undamaged governor's house. Suddenly a spray of bright-hot iron surrounded them. Heated lumps of metal ricocheted from roof timbers, embedding themselves in walls and street. The man beside Tom gasped and fell. Everyone ducked behind the nearest protection.

'What?' Heart. Pumping. Thud-thud-thud-thud. Danger. Where? Everywhere. Smell of undercooked pork and shit. Was that from him?

Time stopped. Tom wiped thick drops of sweat from his forehead. Captain Coram ahead, shouting, getting men on their feet, pushing them along the street. Fizzing bits of iron and the injured man – close. Three soldiers near him. Salty water pouring from his eyes. Someone was crying. The stomach of the wounded man was on the ground. Silvery, slick guts pooled around his body, blood and ooze mixing with the dirt of the road.

Tom crouched against a brick wall. The three soldiers

roused themselves, ran to catch up the captain in the distance, right past the wounded soldier. Tom, alone, didn't move. His body fixed in a crouch, his eyes fixed on the slimy guts of the dying man. The bombardment continued, faintly. Closer, clearer, moans of the soldier. He could think, but he couldn't move. He had to move. He mustn't stay huddled against a wall like this. What would his comrades think? What would Bathsua think?

Bathsua. Her name conjured her face, and fear. He must live, get back to her. She was the only good thing to come out of this damned siege. She was worth staying alive for.

His hands shook. He listened to the moans of the dying soldier. His moans too. Same rhythm. He coughed to get control of his voice, forced himself to stop. He used the wall, lifted himself to a standing position, eyes fixed on the soldier gazing back. Flies were already buzzing around the exposed guts. His cries and movement had stopped.

His body still wouldn't move. Tom remembered the man who had dreamed he would be killed. Gideon said. Did he have something, someone, to live for? Had he died quickly, or carved open like the man there, viciously? His love of life, will to survive, had not saved him. What would be, would be. Tom knew. But he still wasn't moving. His mind was fine. He could reason and remember. It was odd; mind so detached from body.

Bathsua, again. Where was she now? Fort Davey. She would be safe? Tom thought of the maid whose hand was shot off by a cannonball as she carried a pail of water to firefighters. No guarantees. Belief in God made no difference; it hadn't for Reverend Bush.

'Move, man. Move!' Tom shouted at himself. He swung

his right arm and gripped a corner of the brick wall. He twisted his boot, concentrating on lifting his right leg. Sweat poured from his skin. A salty drip wormed its way into his eye. He was moaning again, but he focused on moving his limbs. Then a group of women emerged from a nearby house. They spotted Tom and two came over to him; others crouched by the dead soldier.

'Are you wounded?' asked one.

He clenched his jaw to stop his moans and shook his head. The woman looked at her companion and together they guided Tom, quivering, off the street, down a narrow alley to a small yard and vegetable garden. Tom had been in Lyme for over six weeks, but he'd never been here before. Relief seeped into his body through the touch of the women as they went down the alley and he realised they weren't taking him to join the children and the wounded near the town mill.

They sat him on a rickety chair by a brick wall. The younger woman disappeared into the house while the older woman crouched and looked into Tom's eyes.

'Aye. I see you, young man.' She closed her eyes for a moment and shook her head. 'I can't tell you you're safe, but we stand with you.' She drew a deep breath and patted Tom's knee to get his attention.

He forced himself to stare into her faded blue eyes.

'Look around you,' she said, gesturing. 'This is my yard. It's a haven of peace in a hurly-burly world. This is what you're fighting for. Peace. Peace in Lyme, peace in Dorset, peace in England. One day someone will sit again in this place and breathe God's clean air, and listen to the birdsong and all their cares'll be about their chickens, their children or the weather.'

Her voice had a sing-song quality. Like a lullaby. Though Tom's heart still hammered in his chest, he allowed her words to wash into him, soothing and cleansing.

'I suppose this'll happen sometime, no matter which army wins, but peace needs justice. This struggle is for our future.' The old woman looked over her shoulder. 'Ah, here's Tilly with the water.'

He took the cup in shaking hands, but the water spilt over the edges and he couldn't stop the trembling. He steadied the cup on his knee and closed his eyes. That brought a rush of more terror. No. Dear God, no!

The old woman gripped his wrist, saving the last of the water. 'You've a job to do. You've done it well till now. Don't spoil such a precious thing.'

Tom swallowed hard. She was right. He hadn't thought before of rightness and justice. It was obvious now. Clear. What choice do I have?

'Thank you,' he whispered. He sipped the water, fighting to control himself. Deep breaths. Push back the fear. Flex fingers. Trembling. Clench fist. Movement. Flex, clench. Keep moving. Do as I say, damned body!

A little later he looked up at the two women, the older and the younger. They weren't soldiers. They were innocents in this bloody mess of a war. The turmoil in his chest changed, and an urge to protect them grew. His fear ebbed. He nodded, attempted a half-smile. 'I'll be all right now.'

The women stepped back as he stood and headed, un-steadily, through a vegetable patch, towards the Town Line.

The wall here ran uphill from the small fort near the shore towards West Fort. It was ten yards beyond the vegetable gardens of the houses. Closer to West Fort, it became the rear house walls, while the fort itself straddled the gate at the top of West Street. Near Tom, the timber barricade stood eight feet tall, with a fire-step halfway up. There were groups of men stationed every few yards. One or two of the sentries saw him and waved or nodded. They pointed uphill and wished him luck. He trudged north and soon approached a section of wall that included buildings.

He was still in a slight daze and noted only that the number of defenders was increasing. Then he heard a swish and noted a grenado rocking on the ground nearby, with a fuse spluttering and protruding from it. He stopped. He knew there were two types. Which one was this? It must be a wildfire one, he thought.

He looked around for a pail of urine or milk, or even a soaked blanket, but there were none in sight. Tom had no alternative. He hitched up his breeches and fumbled with the draw strings.

At that moment Captain Drake came out of the nearest house. He took in the scene in an instant. Striding to the grenado, he picked it up and flung it back over the wall. 'It's all right, son. Put your cock away and get back to your post.'

Tom stood transfixed, then laughter rose from his belly, jostled past his lungs and shook his shoulders as it erupted from him. The sheer lunacy of the day struck him and he was left gasping. He leant on a wall until the giggles stopped. No one had witnessed this episode. Captain Drake had disappeared back indoors and the defenders on the wall had taken no notice. Tom swallowed and inhaled a deep breath, and then another. It was clear what he had to do. He was part of a larger organism, the garrison, that had to resist the enemy to the utmost. His comrades depended on him, and he had to stay strong and alert for them, and for Bathsua. He held up his open right hand. It still trembled, but it was under his command.

He made his way to the nearest houses forming the Town Line and kept going uphill. He was looking for his comrades. His place was beside them. The noise got louder as he neared West Fort. He headed for the street, through ruined and broken houses, to get a better view of what was happening. Rubble from the buildings had been shifted to thicken and raise the Town Line wherever possible. Despite this, there was still timber and masonry lying everywhere.

Groups of women milled about on corners and behind masonry. Tom thought they were cowering against the bombardment. Then he realised there were two types of groups: those organising gunpowder and match and spare muskets and relaying these to the men at the line, and others readying stores of beer, bread and cheese to fortify the defenders. Every few minutes, pairs of women darted forward from these temporary depots, bringing ammunition or victuals to the soldiers.

'God love 'em,' he whispered.

Tom recognised no one around him. He saw only the backs of men facing the enemy, or others hurrying on errands. Then he spotted a larger frame. It was Moizer. Tom made his way over to the giant sailor.

'Aah? Tom. Good to see you.'

'How's it going?'

'As well as could be expected, lad. These Cornish keep coming at us. They're getting closer and our wall is crumbling here and over there. The enemy batteries have got our measure and play around us very effectively.'

338

The sailor was part of an extended line of men strung out along what was once a collection of neat back yards and tidy houses. The remaining Town Line was being pounded by a relentless barrage from guns placed at Holmbush, to the west of Lyme, and from Fort Royal, its cannons throwing cannonballs right over the town. Previous bombardments had concentrated on West Fort or on throwing balls into the town. Today the wall was the target and the afternoon sun shone on a scene of destruction, dust and death.

'These Cornish won't wait forever. They'll be at us again soon or I'm a Dutchman,' Moizer said.

Tom looked round, searching for some officer to take charge and to explain what they had to do next.

'Don't worry. We can hold,' said Moizer. 'We sailor boys can do wonders, but we need a bit of help here. Go and get old Bullethead. He's a good man to have by your side in a scrap.'

'I've not seen them since dewbit.'

'Well, you find 'em, and tell 'em they are cordially invited to a party here. And old Moizer is standing ready to greet them, quick as you like.'

Tom could see the enemy regiments forming up behind a fold of land near Holmbush. If they were to make an assault, they would be fed into the trenches that had been excavated close to the wall. The attackers would mass in those and then rush to break into the town. Tom looked around again. Still no sign of an officer. Which direction should he go to find Effra?

He patted Moizer's muscled shoulder and picked his way across to his campfire. Effra, Gideon, Ifor and the whole of their platoon were guarding the northern wall.

'Tom! Where've ye been, lad?' said Effra.

'Here's your musket and bandolier,' said Ifor. 'You'll need to light your match.'

'What's happening beyond West Fort?' said Gideon.

'Moizer and his sailors are holding the wall, but they need us. There's another assault brewing.'

'Well, we're ready for a bit of action. We've not had more than a handful of malignants in front of us all day.'

'I'll check with the sergeant. Moizer needs reinforcements, quick.'

Tom came back fuming in a few minutes. 'The old goat won't budge. He says he's no orders to move and won't be swayed by an ex-corporal. We're stuck here till he's told by an officer.'

'Well, I'll not stand by when a comrade needs my help. Fuck the sergeant. We go where we're needed most.' Effra had that look on his face again.

'Right,' said Tom. And the four men trotted back up Sherborne Road towards West Fort.

'You look tired, lad,' Effra said.

'Aye.'

They reached Moizer at the same time as other reinforcements. A company of Colonel Ceeley's regiment joined him, with their regimental colour displayed at the centre of the defensive position. Looking out over the rubble that was once the Town Line, Tom saw the Cornish preparing to charge. The colours of their uniforms were a churning mix of greens, blues and reds. Voices rumbled as the front men waited to advance.

Tom watched this malevolent crowd. The soldiers in the trenches seethed, pushing and pulling as more joined them.

The defenders continued to send musket balls into the mass. Then the cannonballs stopped coming. The barrage had paused. That could mean only one thing.

The Royalists erupted from the trenches and rushed towards West Fort and the breach in the wall. Many headed for the fort, carrying makeshift ladders to reach the first-floor platform. Those heading for the breach needed no such aids. They ran up the rubble slope carrying upended muskets, swords and cudgels and fierce, frightened looks.

They came on. Colonel Ceeley's company levelled their muskets. Tom's team did too. A volley rang out from them, kept low and deadly. Men crumpled, but others took their place. They rushed forward, wild and angry.

There was no time to reload; the defenders reversed muskets, drew swords, tensed muscles and prepared to meet their foes. Up came the Royalists, Cornish foot that had swept all before them on battlefields from Plymouth to Bristol. These men were unruly warriors, fierce fighters. Their reputation had not been enhanced by sitting five weeks in front of a little fishing town. Tom thought they looked tough and determined. Yet Tom knew Moizer's sailors were likewise proud, rugged men. The garrison met the charge with equal ferocity and there was no more time for thought.

Later, a minute, an hour, Tom never knew, the attack ceased. He became aware of that only when Effra laid his hand on his shoulder.

'Whoa, lad. Let them go. No need to chase. They'll be back soon enough.'

Chapter 33

The defenders of the breach stood firm. Barely. Bodies lay everywhere; some moving and groaning, some silent and still. The rubble slope rising up to the wall was strewn with weapons, equipment and men. Men inched their way back to the Royalist lines, huddles of men carrying wounded comrades.

Tom looked along the ridge that used to be the wall at a line of soldiers and sailors standing, sitting, gasping for breath, cherishing each moment free from the blades of the Cornish. He looked behind him. The slope down to the street was choked with wounded, and the dead or injured being carried away. So many. When Tom focused again on the ridge, he realised how few men remained. Across at West Fort, the fighting had been just as savage, but its garrison still stood.

He put his hand down on a stone to steady his descent to a sitting position. His grip was weak, a slight tremble. But he was still at his post. Thank God for the foggy certainties of war. There had been no opportunities to turn and flee, no space to consider the best way to absent himself from the fight. Effra, Ifor and Gideon flopped down beside him.

'Any wounds?' Effra asked.

Ifor and Gideon held up bloody arms and faces, but they

could still defend themselves. Tom realised he should have been the one showing care for his comrades, but he left that to the older man while he gathered his shattered mental and physical resources.

'We're not enough. Another charge and them Cornish'll be in the town,' said Moizer, standing over the little group, shading Ifor and Gideon.

'Don't move, big man. I needed two things just now; a long drink and a piece of shade. Thanks to you, I now just need a beer.' That was Ifor's first joke for days, but Tom could see the tinker was at the edge of his endurance.

'Glad to be of help,' said Moizer, as the group noticed the rustling of the enemy lines about two hundred yards ahead. Another charge was brewing. Groups of women bustled around them, handing out cups of beer, hunks of bread and ammunition. Muskets too were brought forward, to replace those that didn't survive braining the enemy.

'We're not enough,' repeated Moizer, as they saw reinforcements marching up West Street to join them.

Another group arrived. It was the rest of Tom's platoon. The sergeant scowled as he placed the new men around Tom and Effra. Despite the reinforcements, Moizer was right.

Tom looked up. Streaks of white cloud, like fat in a bacon rasher, showed through the spectrum of blues displayed in the sky. The sun's brightness, as it slid towards the west, was reflected down through that wispy ceiling. Sweat trickled from his brow into his eyes. The afternoon bled into evening. Breathing the rancid perfume of humans, rubble and blood, he focused on the men around him. Grim determination showed on many faces, but he saw mixed messages on many others. He recognised men struggling with pain, weariness, and the expectation that these were their last moments on earth. He recognised their hearts. He felt the same.

And now the Royalists were charging towards them again. Tom's musket wasn't loaded. He rushed to pour gunpowder, tamp wadding down the barrel, spit the ball from his mouth into the muzzle. No time to ram the ball home, so he slammed the musket butt on the ground instead. This forced the ball to the bottom of the barrel. He drizzled gunpowder onto the firing pan and closed the cover, flicked off the loose powder and blew unsteadily on the glowing matchcord. He tried to swallow. Not enough spit. No matter. The enemy were here.

'Give fire!' rang out the sergeant's command.

The muskets spoke, smoke sprang from the muzzles and the garrison hurried the balls on their way with a frenzied shout, a great cry of terror and hate and resistance from men more used to tending cattle or trawling for fish than to this rugged service. But the histories of the men meeting at that rubble ridge were of no importance. All that mattered was to avoid the thrust of sword, the swing of musket or cudgel, to recover when a lunge was parried and to push the enemy back, to make them stop. To crush heads, to cut arms and bodies, to put out eyes and to knock down that press of men rushing up to kill you. It was a hellish existence.

Where the energy came from to keep at it, nobody knew. But they had to stand firm. To run would invite a slash or thrust in the back. Tom increased the speed of his musket swings; the extra momentum took the butt through one man's cheekbone and he fell, dragging the gun from Tom's fingers. Out, he dragged his sword. Just in time to deflect the head of a billhook past his chest. Swing – the sword described an arc from Tom's right, over his head and onto, then through, the Cornishman's head. He had no helmet. Tom jumped aside and twisted the sword to free it from the dead man's skull.

There were too many of them; they pushed the defenders off the ridge, back down the slope. The rubble shifted beneath the feet of the soldiers and unsteadied their stand. Tom looked to his left. The colonel's regimental colours were still flying on the ridge. They were still holding their ground. Then the colours jerked and fell. Tom gasped. Was this the end of their resistance? He beat off another attacker. When he looked again, the colour was vertical and a great voice cut through the chaos.

'To me. To me! Come on, you landlubbers. Come on, you sailor boys. We will not yield! Come on, will ye.'

Tom recognised Moizer's voice. He struggled forward, to give the sailor support. Others did the same and the ebb rearwards turned to a flow forward, as the Royalists gave ground.

Tom pushed to his left to link up with Moizer. He could see him wielding a meat cleaver in his right hand, while holding the staff with the fluttering flag in his left. Then he caught sight of Ifor. The Welshman was standing to one side of Moizer with a group of sailors. He was singing! Calling out a nasal song in a tongue Tom had never heard. As he sang he swung an axe, this way then that, cutting a figure of eight in the air. This pattern of death kept the enemy at bay, and Ifor slowly stepped forwards, pushing them back.

Gideon was there too. He still had his musket, and he was giving vicious, measured strokes with it as the enemy came within reach. The space in front of them was growing.

345

To the left of this group was Moizer, and Tom could now see Effra standing and fighting beside him with sword and buckler. Where had he got that small shield from?

Tom and two others filled the gap between Moizer and Ifor. More men brought the line up elsewhere, and the power of the enemy surge evaporated. The Cornish gave ground and slid down the rubble slope towards their trenches.

'Send 'em to hell, lads!' cried Moizer as he took the colour forward.

At that moment a musket ball crashed into the flagstaff where Moizer was holding it. The big man hardly flinched, but he looked and saw the damage. The flag rocked and broke free from the lower staff. Effra caught it before it fell and the two men laughed together.

'By Christ! My hand,' said Moizer. He looked at his shattered fist. Two fingers were missing and blood was spurting out over what remained of the flagstaff. He dropped it to the ground. 'Take the colour, Effra. I'm to the surgeon to get a bandage. Don't waste the advantage we have now, will ye?'

'I'll be here when you get back, you turnip.'

Moizer turned to go and before he'd walked two or three steps a pair of maids rushed up to help him. More came forward with water, beer and bread. Ammunition, too. Whatever was needed was hurried to the men at the line.

Then the barrage recommenced. One ball, then another, crashed around the Town Line. Many arced towards the West Fort but there were enough for the breach, too. The balls came from both directions again, from Fort Royal and the Holmbush batteries.

'Tom! To me,' called Gideon.

Tom pushed forward and helped Gideon break into Ifor's trance to slow, then stop, the deadly pendulum swings of the axe. As the axe dropped, so did Ifor. The Welshman had used the last of his energy to keep that weapon moving. Now the attackers had drawn back, his strength was drained. He collapsed into Tom's arms. The two men carried him down from the ridge. This was no place for an exhausted old man.

They left him in a house on the east side of West Street. There were many men in the house, all emptied of their power. They'd given every ounce of energy to resist the enemy. Some had paid with hand or leg, or showed where a blade had cut or a blow had crushed. Others nursed musket ball wounds. A few had been hurt by the cannonballs, but few with those wounds survived long enough to reach the house. Ifor was senseless when they struggled back to their place in the Line. More reinforcements arrived, and the defenders' numbers grew to a less frightening strength. Effra had given the colour to one of Colonel Ceeley's officers.

'Damned liability, carrying that rag. I need two hands to defend myself in a brawl like this.'

'Where'd you get the buckler?' Tom asked.

'Ha! I found it, you might say. A Royalist officer came up to the Town Line like he was some knight from the ballads. It was easy to take his sword and shield from him. He learned his lesson, but had no life left to practise his wisdom.'

'Can we carry on?'

'Have to, lad. They've not yet had their fill.'

Women in groups shared out replacement muskets; others handed out ammunition and bandoliers.

'God bless you, lasses,' said Effra.

More beer came round. Preachers appeared in the line,

347

praying and calling for strength and victory. Tom watched all this. So did the enemy. From their trenches they began a stinging musket fire. Men on the rubble ridge fell and a momentary disorder ensued. Captain Coram ordered the men to lie down behind the ridge, and most of the lead balls then flew harmlessly over their heads.

'Why didn't we do this sooner? I can serve on the Town Line *and* get some sleep now,' said Gideon.

The cannons still roared, but there was no energy spare to mind them. Either a ball crushed you to Kingdom come, or it didn't. There was nothing to be done about it.

'Up! Up!' the order came. The Royalists were back. They reached the ridge, and the defenders stood again, resisting, fighting and holding their position. Everything seemed a dream to Tom. His body worked his weapons without his conscious thought. He dodged and bobbed, mechanically but effectively. He was still alive. His friends were still at his side and the nightmare continued. It seemed quite reasonable to him that it would carry on like this forever.

Then the Royalist tide slackened. The pressure eased and their enemies were gone, as the sun set and the deeper blue of the eastern sky stretched over them towards the west.

Tom studied the Royalist trenches. There was activity and what seemed to be a reordering of the units. They could hold out for one more attack like the last one, he thought, but then the enemy would be able to stroll into the town unchallenged. The movement in the trenches continued, then waned. Tom concentrated on what he was seeing, then realised the Cornish were moving back, away from the town. He peered through the fading light until he was sure what was happening. It was over. As night approached, the battle ended. The town held on, but at what cost? There was a ragged cheer as exhausted men sank down to the rubble.

There was still no real relief. The defenders needed food, drink, rest, but the Town Line had to be manned. Guards were posted on the line and relieved every hour. The officers and sergeants walked up and down unceasingly, keeping the sentries awake and making sure the others were resting. Tom, Effra and Gideon went to check on Ifor. He was asleep, in as safe a place as Lyme afforded, so they left him and went to the town mill to get food. But though their bellies were empty they needed sleep more, so after soup and bread they stumbled back to their campfire and lay down by its cold embers.

Next morning the three men rolled away from the dead fire and stood to face another day. Muscles stiff, bellies aching and with an even greater need for sleep. Nevertheless, they had to report to West Fort to relieve those on guard.

That duty was spent watching the Town Line being repaired, the Royalists collecting their dead and the townsfolk gathering plunder while they could. The enemy showed no signs of wanting to repeat their exertions so, after an hour, the sentries were reduced. Tom, Effra and Gideon were released to look for something to eat.

They went via Ifor and Moizer. Ifor was still unconscious. The sailor was in a nearby house. He sat with his back against a wall in a small room. His face was sunken, his cheekbones exposed like rocks at low tide. His eyes were pools of agony as he see-sawed forwards and back, holding his disfigured left hand. The bandages round the fist were soaked in blood.

'Ah, comrades,' he whispered.

'We came to wish you well,' said Tom.

Effra sat down beside Moizer. 'That was a rare fight yesterday. And you played the hero,' Effra said.

'Truth to tell, Effra, I don't recall much of yesterday. I know I was waving some damn fool flag, and I know they smashed my hand, but everything else is a faint memory compared to this raking pain.'

'Well, I know if anyone can come through this, you can.' Effra gripped the shoulder of his friend, who nodded.

Effra and Moizer sat; Tom and Gideon stood. And there they stayed for a while, all the men sharing, somehow, the pain of the shattered man.

'Well, we have an appointment with a dead chicken,' said Effra. 'We'll say goodbye, but we'll return soon.'

Moizer didn't react as Effra patted him. They left.

At the town mill they found men and women bustling about, and food and drink provided. They ate quietly and slowly. No one wanted to step back into the struggle. Here, they could pretend there was no siege, no war, and no pain and death surrounding them.

Later, towards evening, Tom and Bathsua shared a few moments together sitting at the mouth of the quay, looking over Lyme Bay to the sails, where Lord Warwick's squadron of six ships was at anchor.

'I think we're about finished,' the young woman whispered.

'On the Line, yesterday, I felt the same. One more charge would have taken them right into the town,' said Tom.

'We have bread now, and ammunition. But not enough, and my heart has no more power to feed my will. We must pray, Tom.' Bathsua caught hold of his left hand in both of hers. 'Only God can save us. We need a sign from Him that he will deliver us.'

Tom was unsure. The maid was not put off. She burst out in a passionate plea to Jesus to deliver them from their enemies and to give her a sign that He had heard her prayer.

By this time, Tom was crying. He was still unsure, but his heart swelled with yearning. He wanted to bring Bathsua to safety, to prevent anyone putting her in danger. He wanted to wrap her in his arms and protect her for himself. Her vigorous praying wouldn't let him enfold her, but once she'd finished she subsided onto his shoulder.

They stayed like that. Tom heard and felt her breath as her chest rose, then fell. In spite of the privations and danger from enemies, disease and want, there was nowhere on earth he would rather be at that moment. Being in danger with Bathsua was infinitely preferable to being safe without her.

They rested on each other as the sun dipped down over the hills to the west of Lyme. Then Tom left to rejoin his comrades and take another duty on the Town Line.

The next day Tom was awoken from his place by the fire by Bathsua.

'Tom! Come! See what the Lord has done.' Bathsua's cries woke Gideon too. Effra was already up.

'Whoa, Bathsua. Slow down. What's happened?' he said.

'God has answered my prayers. He has sent a sign.'

'What sort of sign? What are you talking about, woman?' said Tom.

'Come and see for yourself,' Bathsua said with shining eyes.

Chapter 34

The sky was glassy-grey, the ruined street a muddy strip through ragged ribbons of battered walls and crushed roofs. A crowd stood where the road veered to the left to avoid plunging into Lyme Bay. Four men and a maid halted some way back from Gun Cliff and looked out over the heads of the throng at the sails from dozens of boats. Small white sails on ketches ferrying men to land, rough, brown ones on shallow-draught barges, already bringing to shore food and other necessities, and large, billowing ones as more ships manoeuvred in the deeper water, joining bare-masted vessels that had arrived before them. An entire fleet of ships had arrived off Lyme overnight.

'Thank you, Lord. Now I know all will be well. Thank you for your deliverance.'

By the afternoon the Royalist cannons thundered their anger and blasted heated iron over the Town Line, to fall among the already damaged buildings. They shot fire arrows at roofs of thatch. Some stores were lost before they could be moved from a pile outside the Mermaid and one, then two, then six, then a dozen houses blazed up in response to the relentless bombardment. Fire-fighting teams had had almost constant practice over the previous weeks, meaning

353

that men, women and children, without fuss, collected pails and beaters, ladders and hooked poles to overpower the flames. But the many fires stretched even these veterans. Houses at the top end of West Street blazed.

Tom and his comrades looked on the spectacle from the new gun platform in the West Fort. The garrison was under strict orders not to help the townsfolk. Senior officers thought the Royalists might attack, using the fires as a distraction.

'Look! There's Bathsua. She's running between the houses,' said Tom.

'Ordering people about, as usual,' said Gideon.

They watched as Bathsua brought order to a mob of men flailing around a small house which had a tiled roof but obviously had flammable materials inside. Hot iron had burst through the tiles and tall flames spewed out between the roof beams.

'They're getting close to where the wounded are,' said Effra.

At this point a sergeant nodded towards them. 'Hold your nerve, men. Those townsmen will get the wounded out. Six more legs and no brains won't speed things up. Stay at your posts.'

Effra and Gideon scowled at the sergeant.

Tom focused on Bathsua. She was pointing and directing firefighters and gathering a group around her. These she led into a house just ahead of the fire. After a minute or two the rescuers reappeared, helping or carrying wounded men. Bathsua directed the whole operation. She told her team where to take the wounded, then she and two other women raced into the next building. The fire was matching their urgency, jumping from roof to roof, dry timber to old lathe and plaster, flaring up as it touched mattress filling, and being driven up the road by a south wind.

'Bathsua. Come on, girl. Get out of there,' Tom whispered.

'That's the house where Ifor is,' Effra said.

They had somehow forgotten Ifor, in the entrancement of watching the fires. All three men instinctively moved towards the stairs down to the lower level of the fort.

The sergeant was there, barring the way. 'Don't look at me like that, Effra. You know we're to stay here.'

The men glared at each other. Tom still watched the open door of the house. It was a dark hole beneath a glittering, smoky cloud, and he could see no movement. Then there was a flicker within the doorway. Was that the fire taking hold where Ifor and the other wounded were? Where Bathsua was?

Then she came. Bathsua emerged from the darkness and smoke. She had the unconscious Ifor slung over her shoulders, his legs dangling behind. It was as well he wasn't a giant like Moizer. Her two helpers followed, leading others. She carried Ifor across the road and laid him on the ground. The others in the rescue team had now deposited their wounded and ran back to Ifor's house to bring out the remaining wounded. This took only a few minutes, but to Tom each moment was achingly long.

He sighed with relief when he saw Bathsua, but she headed for the next burning hovel to check for anyone else injured or trapped.

'Bathsua!' He shouted at the top of his lungs. 'Stay back. Let the others finish. Stay safe.'

The woman stood stock still and looked across the fifty yards between them. Tom could see her eyes widen as she realised who had called. Her soot-blackened face had pale skin around her eyes, making them appear even wider.

She stood there, arms akimbo, glaring like an angry blackamoor, her clothes emitting thin wisps of smoke. 'Don't order me about, Tyler.'

Tom rushed to the steps, but the sergeant was still there. In his heart, he knew he was wrong to call out. He clenched his eyes shut, and when he opened them, Bathsua had gone.

Effra patted his shoulder. 'Best thing for us? Get this sentry-go done. Then check on Ifor. She'll be fine. She won't thank you for acting like her granny, though.' Effra looked up at Tom from a lowered head.

Gideon giggled.

'Yes, but...' began Tom.

'Yes, but nothing. You need to be thinking with your head, not your dick now.'

'But that's not...' Tom was defeated. He wandered to the opposite side of the fort and watched the Royalist trenches.

By the time they got off duty, the fires were mere glowing embers and the damaged houses lay pulled apart, starving the flames. Everyone acted as though quenching fires raging through a street was an ordinary thing to do.

'Let's get some grub,' said Effra.

They headed back to their campfire.

'I'll collect the rations,' volunteered Tom.

'I'll see how Ifor's doing,' said Gideon.

'Well, I'll go and look in on Moizer, then,' Effra said. 'See you back here when you've got the food, Tom.'

Tom wandered towards the town mill, thinking about Bathsua. Was she safe? Was she hurt? Would she be angry with him? Of course she would.

She wasn't round the next corner. Or at the mill. He collected rations: rye bread, nondescript smoked meat, hard cheese, two flagons of beer. Still no Bathsua. He walked back to the campfire.

There she was. Sitting beside Effra, with an exhausted-looking Ifor there, too. He'd known she'd be there. It was the logical thing to happen. He was satisfied. She looked unhurt. He was relieved. He could cope with the storm of her ire, knowing she was alive and whole.

Tom smiled. The tired talk subsided as he arrived and all eyes swivelled between him and Bathsua. Effra, Gideon and Ifor held their breaths, watching.

'I'm glad to see you, Tom,' she said guardedly.

'And I you, Bathsua. I thought you were heroic, fighting the fire and rescuing Ifor today.'

She smiled. 'I was first into Ifor's room. It's good to help a friend.'

'And it's great to have friends around, when your body lies like a wet rag and your mind is far away,' said Ifor. 'I went from nearly getting roasted to being jolted back to life in a siege. It's good to be back, I suppose.'

Tom set down the victuals and sat beside his friends. He wanted to talk, but the atmosphere was oppressive. Effra coughed and reached for the cheese. Gideon subsided into himself, and Ifor drifted in and out of engagement with his surroundings. Effra looked up at the evening sky, leaving Tom and Bathsua sitting either side of him, saying nothing but insignificant trifles about the rations.

After a couple of futile attempts at speaking freely, Tom changed tack. 'So how is Moizer, Effra?'

'He's recovering. But he's not the same man he was before

357

the fight. I can see the pain is still sapping his body.'

'Bathsua, is there nothing that will soothe his pain?' Tom asked.

'I don't have much skill in physick, but I know we used up the supplies of all the wise women long ago. There's little left of any medicinal plants or concoctions.'

'But there must be something we can get for him, isn't there? Plants are growing all around us – surely one of them can ease pain?'

'I'll speak to Mistress Gadd; she'll know what to do.'

'I'll come with you,' said Tom.

'Oh! Well...' Bathsua paused, then frowned. 'I'm not at your beck and call, Tom Tyler. You seem to think you can order me this way or that as you choose.'

Effra laid one brawny hand on Bathsua's wrist and raised his other arm into the air. 'Hold, friends. We don't mean to block your rough wooing with Tom, Bathsua, but we're thinking only of aiding our friend Moizer.'

'What wooing is that, Effra?' Bathsua had risen now and looked down at Effra with reddening cheeks as the wrestler also rose to his feet.

He still held the woman's arm, but wiped his face with the fingers of his free hand, as if in exasperation. 'Listen to me, girl. Moizer needs help. We have no medical skill and cunning. We need your help. Forget your pussy hissing at Tom and think. Please.'

Bathsua looked around at Gideon and Ifor, ignoring Tom. Her shoulders sagged as she exhaled. Taking a new breath, she adjusted her tone. 'I hear you, Effra Bayly. You're right. I'll go now to speak to Mistress Gadd. Moizer needs relief, and your friend is my friend.'

Tom watched her skirt the edge of the campfire and head off into the town. He followed her into the darkness beyond the fire glow. 'Wait for me, Bathsua,' he called.

'What? So you can order me about like a chattel?' She stepped forward without looking round.

'No.' Tom ran to catch up. He grabbed her right elbow. 'Bathsua, wait.'

She waited, silent, like a pot about to boil.

'I'm not trying to squash you. Can't you see that? I'm worried about you, and it comes out sometimes in the wrong way.'

He noted a change in her body. A little of the prickliness had gone, but her words were as sharp as ever. 'You don't know your place, Tom Tyler. When I have a responsibility, it fills my being. I don't take kindly to being buffeted, even by you.'

'I realise that.' Tom had so much more to say, but no words came. He looked at the sky, seeking inspiration.

Bathsua resumed her walk into town, and after a moment Tom followed. They strode down the remains of West Street side by side.

Mistress Gadd's house sat behind West Street and as Bathsua and Tom approached, they could hear merry conversation from many voices. Inside, they found a group of a dozen women. Bathsua spoke with the mistress and Tom followed as they stepped out into a small rear garden.

'We're on an errand for a wounded friend. His fingers were shot off during the recent fight and he needs help to ease the pain.'

'Bathsua, you know the healing women have access to all the physick plants. We don't withhold any.'

359

'Yes, but this man's pain needs something more. Is there nothing to be done? No remedy that we could collect that might help?'

'Are we talking about Moizer? I thought so. He's a big man, yet he seems smaller every time I see him.'

'Surely there's herbs we can get, or medicine we can steal from the Royalists, even?' Tom said.

'Well, I've a small stock of pasqueflower. I've been hoarding it, but I think Moizer may be a suitable subject.'

'Thank you,' said Bathsua.

'Anything else?' said Tom.

'The only other thing that might be of use is monkshood, which is a poison more than a medicine.'

'Does that grow in this area?' asked Bathsua.

'There's a patch beside the river, north of Gaitch's Fort.'

'What? We've been fighting over that bit of ground for weeks. Are the plants still there?'

'Well, they were last time I looked,' said Mistress Gadd. 'That was yesterday.'

An opportunity to help Moizer's recovery soon came, when an aggressive sally was planned to disrupt new artillery batteries.

A strong force assembled for the evening raid behind West Fort, but that didn't include Tom and his comrades. Instead they drifted down the Town Line, closer to Gaitch's Fort. Tom's heart was racing. They didn't know what to expect outside the defensive wall of the town. He remembered the last time they had tried something like this, at the urging of, among others, young Nathan. Nathan's smiling face surfaced uninvited in Tom's mind. Things had changed in the last month. The trenches were deeper, more numerous and defended by more Devonshire soldiers.

Tom shivered. This was a bad idea. He looked behind him, into Effra's grim face, still visible in the evening light. Some distance behind him was Gideon. He was facing the wall of a house and was rhythmically banging his head against the mudbrick wall.

'Gideon!' Tom hissed.

There was no answer. He and Effra retraced their steps.

'I can't get at any of them. We're fighting the Royalists. But Cooper was acting for Colonel Fezzard, who was on our side, wasn't he? I can't get at Cooper or Fezzard. What's the point of it all?'

'I know,' said Tom. 'This isn't a normal war. We're fighting friend against friend and brother against brother. It's like tearing our own body apart.'

Gideon didn't react. Tom and Effra shared a look, and Effra motioned back up the hill with his eyes. They pointed Gideon at the campfire and watched him tramp up Sherborne Road.

'If Ifor's awake, he'll look after him,' said Tom.

Then they got on with the task. The tumult of the raid going on beyond West Fort could be heard faintly, in contrast to the silence facing them outside the Town Line. They watched for an opportunity to slip over the wall unobserved.

Tom swallowed, then followed Effra to the masonry wall, eight-foot high at this point. He hoisted Effra up to the top of the wall and then dropped beyond it and staked a rope into the ground, using a metal pin. He anchored his end of the rope on the inside of the wall and used it to climb over, dropping down onto slick, dewy ground beside his friend. In front of them was a strip of land about twenty yards wide that looked as if an army had recently thundered across it. Which was true. Here and there were clumps of hardy grasses or tufts of growth from plants pushing up through the trampled undergrowth.

Light was fading. Tom and Effra paused only a moment before moving off to their right. There was no sign of movement or life from the trenches to their left, but they hurried on. At Gaitch's fort, they took stock of their situation.

Chapter 35

As the dusk drained the day of colour a mist rose silently from the nearby River Lym. Where it touched vegetation, it left tiny beads of moisture. Where it rose up from the ground it brought a darker grey to the sky, a shorter field of vision. Where the blanket of cloud engulfed soldiers, each bead on hair and heads added a fraction to their fear and bled away a tiny drop of their fortitude.

The guards in Gaitch's Fort moved sluggishly as the mist swirled around the cannons. This fort was smaller than Davey's. Though damaged, its gun platform remained unbuckled. And now the sentries counted down the time to their relief. Outside, with their backs to the blank wall of the redoubt, two men stood, listening to the grumbling conversations.

Tom and Effra looked out towards the Royalist siege line. To their right was the meandering river, blending into the mist. The riverbank vegetation in the bend was less trampled than the surrounding area and they could see clumps of high greenery, five feet high. There were also the bare stems of a dozen or more trees that had been either cut down to give a clear view from the fort or been broken during the fighting. The new growth smelled green and summery and reminded

Tom of more peaceful times in Poole.

Kneeling down, the men slowly inched their way further along the wall, closer to the river. When they reached taller weeds, they turned and headed away from Lyme. At any movement or noise they flattened themselves into the damp plants for ten or fifteen seconds, hearts hammering, every sense alert. There were no trenches close to the river, so they didn't have to cross into the Royalist lines.

It took an age to reach the tree ruins. Tom raised himself up to look across to the enemy trenches. They all looked deserted. Perhaps the soldiers had gone to support the defence against the raid. He breathed a silent prayer of thanks for this mercy.

The light was fading fast and Tom rummaged among the vegetation, trying to remember Mistress Gadd's instructions. He was looking for a plant with leaves that had many fingers and a flower stalk that stood upright to a height of around a yard, with blue flowers on it. He had his snapsack to carry the foliage. But he was unsure. The vegetation was dissolving into a dark mass. Here and there, stalks spiked upwards and some, on lumpier plants, grew rigidly in many directions. Tom and Effra struggled to distinguish plant from plant.

They couldn't take long. Their good fortune couldn't last. Tom filled his snapsack with as much green stuff as it could take, then turned to Effra and shrugged. The men retraced their steps as evening turned to night and cloaked their movements with deepening shadows.

Back at Gaitch's fort the sentries were still grumbling and Tom held his breath as they picked their way back to the start point. At the anchored rope, Tom handed his snapsack to his friend, then launched himself over the wall. He dropped inside the Town Line – right beside two pairs of feet.

Ifor reached down to raise him up, and Gideon said they'd been waiting for them. Effra threw the snapsack over the wall, and then his bulk briefly raised its shadowy height as he slipped over and down to land beside his friends.

'I'm glad that's over,' he whispered. 'Let's get this fodder delivered.'

Mistress Gadd took the snapsack from Tom and spread its contents on the table in her room. The candles cast a flickering light over the crushed stems and wilting foliage. She rummaged through it. 'A mighty haul, Tom, but there's not much here we can use.'

'I thought as much. I couldn't tell one leaf from another in the dimpsey.'

'Don't worry. This be mostly kingcups and cranesbill, but here's what we're looking for.' She held up a battered stalk. 'In this stalk is more than enough physick for Moizer. Go to bed now. Leave me to administer this to your friend.'

The sally had been partly successful; one gun was damaged, and some gunners were injured. But more men had been lost, and Captain Drake shared with Tom that they had been routed by a detachment sent to reinforce the gunners.

'And most worrying of all is that I was one of those panicked soldiers. Never have we been thrown back so suddenly. Our courage is fraying. How much more can we endure?'

Next evening, Tom was on guard duty when two deserters presented themselves at the West Fort gate. The men, a sergeant and a corporal, told a tale of Royalist desperation that the comrades were still discussing as they reached their campfire, after being relieved.

Bathsua met them with welcome bowls of pottage, bread and beer. She had brought fresh bits of timber also, and stoked up the fire.

'We had interesting news from deserters today,' Tom said, partway through his stew. 'They say the enemy despairs of storming the town and instead plans to burn us out.'

'Haven't they already tried that? And failed?' asked Bathsua.

'But now they have a new weapon,' interposed Gideon.

'Aye. They have a witch and they will, by her art, be able to burn the stone houses,' said Effra.

'And our ships will all sink,' added Ifor.

All four men stared over the fire at Bathsua.

She looked from one to another for a few seconds before bursting out laughing. 'Ha. Friends, you're making a joke?' She kept looking at them, trying to judge the news. 'What? This is true? And you, heroes of a dozen battles here in Lyme, believe them?'

There was a moment's silence before all four men spoke together, justifying their worries and pointing out the seriousness of the development.

'I don't care what wizard or witch they cozen to say what they want. This town will not fall to a whispered spell!'

'Bathsua, you don't understand these things. The world is full of powers greater than ours. We can't control the sea, the weather, the land. The witches that can do so are powerful forces.' Gideon was serious.

Bathsua sighed. 'But we have been so marvellously upheld

by God so far. For six weeks we've held back an army. All their might has not been enough to defeat us. That's because of the grace of God and the repentance of the garrison. With God on our side, we have no need to fear any witch.'

'But Bathsua, this is serious. There are godly men and women here, but many sailors and soldiers know God only as they might recognise someone on the opposite side of a fair; someone to nod to, but no more. You know God as a friend. That's beyond most of us. So we can't rely on any special grace when evil is summoned. We'd best be cautious,' said Tom.

'So what will you do? What weapons do you have against this evil power? Tell me! What will you do? You have no antidote to magic. All you know is more superstition. And yet, when a child dies, or a dog grows mangy, you point at some old woman and claim she's bewitched you.' Bathsua was on her feet, prowling around the fire. 'You men are infuriating. Strong in arm, but so weak in the head. The answer is in front of your noses, yet you choose not to see. When did Jesus ever refuse to succour those who came to him? He tamed the demons. Even the wind and the waves obeyed him. All we need do is trust in him, and the witch may go to the devil.

'I will not accept any witches' fire in this place. And If I see a stone house burning, I'll douse it with a strong prayer and a big bucket of water. And I expect all of you to do the same. Fie on you to be unmanned by such a rumour.'

She walked a few yards to the edge of Sherborne Road. Then she came back to the fire. 'Tell me this, Tom Tyler. If the deserters believed the witch could do us such damage, why did they desert?' Then she turned on her heel and stamped

367

off, heading for her garret room.

'She's done it again,' said Gideon.

Tom groaned.

A few days later a party of Royalist officers, one with his wife and maid, deserted to the garrison and told Colonel Blake, within Tom's hearing, that Lord Essex's Parliamentary army was approaching and that Prince Maurice must withdraw. Colonel Blake welcomed the news. Then he doubled the guards and put the entire garrison on alert.

Next day, lookouts at St Michael's tower saw enemy tents being dismantled. Men at Davey's Fort could see enemy guns being withdrawn.

The guns from Fort Davey and West Fort boomed out, and musketeers dodged into the trenches and hedges to test the temper of their opponents. The enemy scattered like sheep before dogs.

The musketeers were jubilant. They found little food, but the iron grip around their town was loosening.

Another day and the Royalists were gone. Mounted scouts rode out. Essex's army was nowhere in the neighbourhood, but neither was Prince Maurice's.

The garrison grew light-headed with the realisation that they had prevailed – and the continued lack of food. Admiral Warwick sent ships to Poole to bring more supplies, and patrols scoured the countryside for provisions.

The next day Tom and Bathsua strolled out of the town and walked through the Royalist lines to Colway House. Hundreds of others did the same, spreading over the valley and hillsides, picking over the flotsam and jetsam left behind by the retreating army. Everyone was on the lookout for plunder. Equipment, clothing and tools, yes, but top of everyone's list was food. Anything edible was gobbled up or squirrelled away. Officers took organised parties of soldiers to the Royalist headquarters at Colway House or elsewhere, looking for papers and maps left behind.

Tom watched men and women scurry from one pile to another. Some were laughing and joking. Many worked silently. The laughter relieved the melancholy, like glints of light in a world of grey.

But the end of the siege didn't bring a return to normal life. For Tom, freedom to walk through the enemy's camp brought no elation. Just flatness. As he looked at the surrounding faces he saw the man he killed on Fordington Bridge, Sergeant Smith, the sentry in Thorncombe, the Irishman on the fire-step of Fort Royal, and Nathan and Samuel. A heavy weariness settled on him. His nose caught a familiar scent: bread. The smell brought with it a cascade of details of his former life. Life with a family, with a purpose, with friends, joy, food and peace.

'Why did they leave so much?' Bathsua asked Tom.

'Who can say? It looks like they left in a hurry. But this stuff is scarce better than what we have.'

'Aye. They had as tough a time as us. Misery for everyone.'

Clamour from across the valley drew them to a crowd by a gun battery. Stalls were set up and blankets laid out as pitches. People brought items they'd found to an impromptu fair. This news reached others in the town, like ants telling their brothers where food is, and soon a great multitude of jostling townsfolk were milling about, bartering, chatting, picking over the spoils of victory. Beer was summoned, and musicians unpacked their instruments to accompany the occasion.

Tom, though, felt detached. There was no joy. Relief, sure, but no surging of spirits.

'It's over, Tom. We won. God be praised.' Bathsua nudged him.

'I don't think I ever allowed myself to believe we could do it.'

'Ah. But you did, Tom Tyler. No one who believes he will be defeated stays at the job like you and the others did. Your words don't give the truth of it.'

'Well, I was at the very edge of myself. Every day I wondered if I would cope.'

'Yes.' She held his arm in both of hers. 'But I knew you'd prevail. I trusted you. And now we can prepare to go to Dorchester to rescue Quintus. I'll need your strength, Tom. That place scares me, but I must go back. For my brother. People can spend years in gaol waiting for release. Think of Master Chase. He's caught up in a war and can't get free. I daren't let that happen to Quintus.'

'Moizer! How goes it?' Tom broke away from Bathsua to speak to the sailor, who was with a group of men leaning against some large wicker baskets full of earth.

'Better, Tom. I will join my shipmates with the next tide or two. We're enjoying the land and each other while we may.'

'And you? What next for you?'

'I don't know. There's no place for me aboard ship. A man with a smashed fist can't hold a rope or climb the rigging. I'll be offloaded at London. Then I'll have to see what opportunities come my way. The sea life is over for me.'

He held Tom's gaze with a steady face, but Tom understood what a challenge this would be.

The next day, there was a thanksgiving service at St Michael's Church, which overflowed with people. It was a joyful occasion. Colonel Ceeley led the proceedings, while the vicar intoned detailed prayers for continued safety and strength and victory for Parliament. Colonel Were related the story of the siege, blow by blow, naming those who had given their lives for their comrades and friends to bring them to this day of victory. Then Colonel Blake got up and thanked those who had played a special part in the defence. He spoke of Captain Pyne, of the captains and majors who had exerted every sinew to hold the garrison together. He thanked Admiral Warwick for coming to the town's aid in such practical ways. He spoke of the work of Lady Eleanor and her organisation of the women and townsfolk. He mentioned Moizer and his role in the last-ditch defence, and Lieutenant de Clare and his part in collecting information about the enemy.

At the end of it all there was a great cheer. Then three cheers for Colonel Blake, without whom, everyone knew, there would have been no victory. He, above all others, was the architect of their success.

Then there were the sermons. Not one, not two, but three mighty preaches. Each one lasted nearly an hour (the preachers had been instructed to keep them short). Bathsua drank in the spiritual wisdom, but even she was wearied by the blast of oratory, and by the end of the second sermon the spirits of most were full. The third sermon began, and

371

the people looking in through the windows drifted away to other, more pressing jobs. Those within the church leant against each other, focused on the plain plaster walls, some of their imaginations reliving scenes from the siege. Some slept. Some kept their attention riveted on the points being made by the preacher, but everyone seemed very glad when the last prayer ended. There was a heartfelt 'Amen' and another cheer rang out.

Colonel Blake addressed the soldiers of the garrison later that afternoon. He told them that they'd won the battle, but the war wasn't over. There was much work to be done before Englishmen could know that right had prevailed and that King and Parliament were working together. There was still a Royalist army out there, and malignant spies working against the Parliament. No soldier could go home yet. Patrols would be sent out, the town must be repaired, and the Town Line improved in case Prince Maurice returned. Recruits would be brought in and trained. All this must be done by the garrison troops.

At the end, Colonel Blake ordered Tom and his comrades to wait. The men sat on stone steps outside a house with no roof. It had been a stable for the past two weeks, but now the horses were already carrying a detachment westwards, chasing Prince Maurice's army. Gideon looked in at the broken front door and spotted some straw bedding. He nudged Effra and Ifor and they moved back into the room to get more comfortable. Tom stayed outside, watching Bathsua approach. He had made up his mind.

'Tom. I've been thinking. With all the commotion of the siege, there's bound to be damage in Dorchester as well as here. The Royalists have left there, too. So we can go with the Dorchester soldiers and offer to help organise relief to their families. And I'll petition for Quintus's release.'

Tom smiled. 'I've been thinking too, Bathsua. After all this fighting, I want us to be together.'

'I want that too,' Bathsua said. 'But first we've got to get to Dorchester to free Quintus.'

'You have more influence than me. I'm sure with Lady Eleanor's patronage you can make that happen, with or without me.'

'What? Are you envious of me?'

'I'm just sick of this fighting. I can't tell you where I'm to be sent next, or why.'

'Well then, I'll petition for you to come with me.' Bathsua smiled cheekily.

'And then what?' Tom's weariness leaked into his words.

'Then we'll see what plans God has for us. In these times we can only be ready to respond as opportunities arise.'

'But I can only be a baker. And for that I need a bakery.'

'Tom. You can't go back to Poole. Your bakery has gone. What are you thinking?'

'Of course I can. If you can go back to Dorchester, I can go back to Poole. We can go back. Poole needs a bakery. I need to find somewhere safe where we can let the world roll by. Let it tear chunks off itself and blow its own brains out. I want nothing more to do with it.'

'Tom. I know what you're feeling, but your role in all this, this chaos, is to stand up for truth. You can't go inside, shut the door, and leave everyone else to sort things out. It's hard, but you have to face this. After we free Quintus, perhaps we could find a worthy role in Dorchester.' She bit her lip.

Tom grabbed his hair and leant his head against the

damaged street wall of the house. 'I know, but that doesn't stop me aching to make it happen. I'm in this damned army for a year before I can think of wriggling free. Bathsua. You are the only thing I've found since I left Poole that's worth fighting for. I need you. Let's just run away together.'

Bathsua snorted in surprise. 'I can't do that, Tom. My job is to reach out to people. To bring hope. You're asking me to turn my back on that and step with you into a fairytale world where there's only you and me. I can't do it, and you don't mean it. But I thought I could rely on your help when I go to Dorchester.'

'But we could find somewhere else. Maybe London. It can't be war everywhere?'

'You're tired, Tom. Rest now. We can talk later.'

The men were brought into the main room of Colonel Blake's house beside the Guildhall.

'The business with Cooper and Venning was very messy, but it's given Lieutenant de Clare an opportunity to sort out his future. Colonel Fezzard is being held in Poole ready for a court case into his activities in managing de Clare's estates.'

'He's been captured, sir?' Tom asked.

'Aye, so I'm told. Captain Pyne told us you burgled houses for him. That's a serious matter. You've all been ordered to Poole by the magistrate to account for your actions and to tell about Fezzard's crimes. I've written to the court. Your trial will be held there as soon as the lawyers arrive from London.'

'What do you mean, *our* trial, sir?'

'Ignorant boy, you must account for your crimes yourself. Our testimonies will help, but it's not up to us soldiers. You must be tried in Poole.'

Tom looked at Effra.

'That's right, boy,' said Effra. 'I told you to mind your mouth. Now the only thing between us and the rope is a couple of letters written by our absent officers in Lyme.'

'What d'you mean, the rope?'

'The penalty for burglary is death. Simple as that,' said Colonel Blake.

Tom stood dumbstruck as the colonel explained.

'Can you write, Tyler, Bayly? Tyler, then, take down your statements. You must both recount what you know to Lieutenant Rudd and his secretary.'

'And what about us, sir?' asked Gideon, indicating himself and Ifor. 'We did no breaking in for the colonel. We only did our duty.'

'I understand your position, Palmer. But you're also to go back to Poole. It may be you can explain to the court.' The colonel nodded to all four men standing slack-jawed in front of him. 'Hold yourselves ready to move when the order comes to embark. That's all.' He then turned to attend to other matters.

The writing of their story took Tom the rest of the day, with Effra co-operating only grudgingly. His handwriting was a shaky scrawl. He shook and sweated his way through it, until he reached their arrival at Lyme. He could write no more. Gideon and Ifor left them to it.

Tom explained their situation to Bathsua as she was supervising supplies at the town mill.

'I've been planning how we can rescue my brother. Now what?' she stammered. 'How am I to get Quintus out, then?'

'Don't worry, you'll find a way.' Tom watched Bathsua move piles of clothes from one shelf to another, fierce concentration on her face.

She was quiet for a moment before erupting. 'Can I ever rely on you, Tom? You specialise in break-ins, it seems – houses, forts, into my life. You wheedle your way into my affections. You promise to look after Nathan, then you leave him to be killed while you get your dinner. Then. Then you promise to help get Quintus back. But that was just words, wasn't it? You knew you'd be heading back to Poole. So go. I can rescue Quintus alone. I must. Maybe we should go to the other Dorchester, in New England,' she mused. 'You can go. All of you.'

'But what choice do I have?'

'You seemed to be able to make your own choice earlier, when you wanted to run away.' Bathsua walked back into the mill.

Chapter 36

Next morning Bathsua set off for Charmouth without speaking to any of them.

'There's one angry lady. I wouldn't want to cross her today.' Effra poked the fire as he looked at Tom.

'What can we do? Our bodies aren't ours to command. We have to go where Colonel Blake sends us.'

'Aye, who knew we'd be sent back to Poole?'

'Where are you leading us next, Tom Tyler?' Gideon spoke up from behind Effra and Tom. 'When we met, we were callow youths sharing a dead rabbit in a field. Then we get caught up in your criminal gang. Then we spend six weeks in Lyme, where you've been telling us when to poke our heads over the town wall and when to duck down again. Now your crimes are closing in on you, and your spite draws you back to Poole. And we're still tethered to your tail. What next?'

'Find your own squad if you don't like this one, Gideon. I didn't know I was leading you all by the nose. I thought we agreed together what to do, and that I was only corporal until another idiot wanted it.' Tom faced Gideon, nose to nose. 'Well, I lost it some time ago. You can have it. What do I want with a litter of snivelling runts like you? Go and torment someone else.'

'I'd go if I could.' Gideon spat.

Then his head nodded and Tom's nose exploded in blood. As he reeled backwards, his comrade followed and tripped him so that both men fell to the ground.

'Stop that.' Effra's voice cut through the red mist as he threw Gideon to one side and dragged Tom upright by his coat. 'Enough,' he commanded, as he stared each man down. 'We've no choice, none of us. We deal with this together. There's an end to it. The war won't last forever, and we may yet survive. You don't have to marry each other, so stop acting like you do.'

Tom picked up his musket and walked to the jetty to get their orders, leaving the others to gather their meagre belongings and follow.

When he rejoined his squad all he said was, 'We wait.'

They huddled in a loose column with fifty others, close to the quay. They squatted behind a wall, which broke the flow of the salty wind blowing off the bay. Gideon and Ifor chatted and Effra slept. Tom nursed his swollen nose. At least, it didn't feel broken. He looked over Lyme Bay and watched the sea birds wheel in the air. Could he run? Where to? Who to? Since January his comrades had provided the only home, the only security he had. Could he leave them, run away, return to Poole? He was disgraced already. To return as a guilty thief? But he'd only followed Effra. Tom recognised this as a weak excuse.

The tide turned, and the men continued waiting. A boat bumped against the jetty and Captain Drake stepped onto the wooden boards. He strode straight for the church, acknowledging no one.

Another hour passed before he returned and gave the order

for them all to return to their places and fires. There would be no embarkation today. But Tom and his squad were ordered to follow the captain.

Back in the church, they were addressed by Colonel Were. 'You were in Fezzard's regiment. Well, you're needed in Poole, quick as you like. The boat's no longer the fastest route, so you must join a party of horse going that way. My orders are to get you there as soon as possible. The Court Martial of Fezzard started yesterday. Lieutenant de Clare will lead you.' Here, the colonel turned to the tall, thin officer standing next to him.

'Lieutenant. You already know these men. The patrol leaves soon and you travel with it as far as Dorchester, then make arrangements to journey on to Poole. Your horses are outside. Travel quickly. God be with you.' They were dismissed.

'Tyler. Follow me and bring the others,' their new leader ordered.

The four comrades looked at each other.

'At least for this trip we'll be on horseback.' Gideon grimaced.

'My arse still hasn't recovered from my visit to Wimborne in February,' groaned Tom.

'When the army says move, something's gonna hurt,' Ifor chipped in. 'It'll either be our legs from walking or our backsides from riding.'

But at the start of the journey they held their horses and walked up the hill, away from Lyme in a party of thirty horsemen under the command of a captain. They followed an old road winding up the eastern side of the valley leading inland from the town. The signs of the Royalist encampment were everywhere. The fields on both sides of the track were churned up and muddy, and dark grey patches could be seen over the whole hillside where their enemies had lit fires and lain, waiting to crush the defenders. Equipment was strewn in all directions, even though the best of it had been scooped up by the locals days ago.

They shielded their eyes against the glittering sunset in the west and looked across the valley to the hills around Uplyme. Evening shadow obscured details, but their memories of fighting over that ground penetrated the darkness.

It took over two hours to get to the crest of the ridge, where a sheep road from Axminster descended into a valley, then met a grassy down leading to Powerstock.

'These sheep roads are better for horses than our man roads,' the lieutenant explained. 'We can let the horses pick their way without any fuss.'

Progress was slow as their steeds plodded on. They daredn't force the pace, in case of injuring the animals. They descended another hill with a stream tinkling along its bottom, then continued between two bare hills, heading towards the east where the darkness was fading. The land changed from coarse grass to contour ploughing, with a crop of oat stalks showing. They went passed small copses, shadowy in the dawn mist. The moon disappeared, but the light from the new day was held back by a blanket of slate-grey cloud. They were now travelling over broken ground, with only outlines discernible, and they were soon squelching through boggy areas and across open land, searching for a road to take them to Whitchurch Canonicorum.

A wide hedge full of birds practising their songs loomed before them, which they recognised as a holloway. The birdsong cut out as the horsemen negotiated the slope down to the rough clay and cobbled track. The lane exuded a heavy musky smell of wet clay, rotting leaves, fox and badger. They trusted the horses to pick a slow, safe route along the lane, taking them over the hill in single file. When they emerged from the holloway, bright sunlight and long morning shadows lay before them.

'There, sir.' A trooper pointed out a large grey house in the field ahead. It was visible in all its sharp edges and cornices.

Another day had begun. They approached the building. Sleep tugged at Tom, and he welcomed the stop. The party walked the horses into the courtyard of Whitchurch Manor House.

Guards were set and rest taken, and food was offered, resignedly, by the gracious host, Mr Chapman.

De Clare gathered his felonious group around him. 'I know what this journey means for you men. It means a great deal to me, too. I can now confront Fezzard with his crimes against me and my lands.' He couldn't stop a small smile. 'To achieve this, I need you to tell of your involvement in Fezzard's actions.' The officer looked at each of their faces. 'I know you to be honourable men. Your service at Lyme shows loyalty and commitment. For my part, I will present the letters from Colonels Blake and Were, and speak on your behalf. I'm confident you will be acquitted.'

Tom had already turned away.

'What I'm saying is, don't worry. And don't run.'

381

They left in the afternoon, heading out of Whitchurch and, ignoring the road to Bridport, they climbed onto the downs and rode the rolling grassy hills eastwards to Dorchester. The sky was clear blue, with wisps of cloud streaked high up and hanging motionless. A faint breeze blew, but hardly cooled the men, and their progress wasn't fast enough to outrun the flies. They stopped at an elder bush, just coming into flower, and broke off sprigs of leaves to set in their hats and the headbands of the horses to ward them off. As the western light faded, six hours later, they reached the southern gate of the town, tired, sore and bitten.

The guard was surly, but he allowed the lieutenant and his patrol into Dorchester. Lieutenant de Clare left Tom and his comrades with the cavalry sergeant while he and the captain went to report to the officer in charge, and they settled down inside the gate, among rows of cabbages being the grown by the townsfolk.

It didn't take long before a delegation of gardeners arrived. 'You can't camp here. There are huts erected outside the town. Only the garrison are billeted inside,' announced the chief gardener.

'Well, we can't move till we get orders from our commander,' the sergeant replied.

'Your officer obviously doesn't know the rules here, then. There's no discussion. You must move. Now.'

'We've just come from Lyme, where we saved you from an army of marauders. But you should know that better than most. When was it the Royalists left here?' Tom pressed on a sore point.

'We suffer greatly from armies of whatever allegiance. Either we establish control over the troops, or there won't be a town here at all. Lord Essex has said he wants you men to respect our community while protecting us, so you'll have him to answer to if you don't heed my advice.'

'Ah. You are offering us advice,' commented Effra. 'Why didn't you say so? I thought you were ordering us about. If you'd kindly explain the procedure we're to follow, and show your appreciation by providing us with a drop to drink, I'm sure we can sort this out.'

Effra's interruption deflated Tom's rising anger, but all hung on the chief gardener's response. The sergeant smiled, and even the sentries leaned forward to watch the debate. The gardener consulted his colleagues. There were sighs and shrugs, then one turned and headed back into town.

'We, ah, take your point, soldier. Mr Dawson has gone to bring you each a pot of ale. Now you must, in the meantime, decamp and go round to Fordington. Major Underdown is there. He will allocate huts to you.'

'Much obliged,' said Effra. 'But if you don't mind, we'll wait a bit. I wouldn't want to make it difficult for Mr Dawson to find us, with all those ale pots.'

The chief gardener glanced at the sergeant, but he just shrugged. So that's how things stood for half an hour, as the gentle darkness of a summer evening settled on them, and the heat of the day bled away to a coolness needing movement and a cloak for comfort.

Effra squatted down in the cabbages beside his comrades and whispered, 'Shall we run, Tom? Now's our best chance.'

'I've been wondering. If we go north, we could be at Bristol in a few days, surely,' Tom replied. 'Royalist territory.'

'Hmm. I know some folks in Bath. And I need to be heading for London soon.' Effra turned to Ifor. 'Which direction is the gaol, d'you think?'

'It's near the east gate,' Ifor said.

'How about we stroll along to check on Master Quintus?'

'What's in your mind, Effra?' Tom's heart leapt at the thought of keeping his promise to Bathsua.

'Just that we don't know how to help. We need information. Quintus could be sitting on the wall waiting for us, or he could have been sent to London, or he could be dead. Without knowing, how can we help?' Effra shrugged.

'Well, I'm fading fast,' said Ifor. 'Without a good rest I won't be able to keep up tomorrow, so I'm not doing any scouting tonight.'

'You don't need me either,' said Gideon. 'We'll take your stuff and you can find us at the huts when you've done.'

'You expect us back, then?'

'You'll need horses to get anywhere,' Gideon replied. 'So you'll be back for them, at least.'

Tom nodded. 'We'll go while there's still some light to see by.'

'Here comes the ale,' warned Ifor.

'Come on,' nudged Effra.

He and Tom stepped close to an earth bank beneath the wooden town palisade and moved along it to be out of sight when their comrades reached for their drinks.

'Let's see if we can do a bit of good before starting our next career.' Effra spoke over his shoulder as they followed a narrow soil path, passed a smaller gate and arrived at the corner where they had first entered the town all those weeks ago.

Ten minutes later they were leaning against a low, thatched house looking at an imposing building. The outer wall was made of dark bricks, to a height of around eight feet. Further back was the main structure. Pale stones, the ground floor walls, glowed faintly in the dusk, making the bricks of the first and second floors appear to hover above the ground. There were three storeys, with a roof of thatch being circled in the gathering gloom by scores of bats. It had few windows, just a couple on each floor on the southwest side, facing into the town. The north-eastern side was on a slope that dropped down to marshy land beside the river. This was the town gaol. It formed one of the strongest parts of the town wall.

'I don't see any way in,' said Tom.

'That's because you haven't looked carefully enough, boy.'

'What do we do now, then?'

'We ask politely if we can visit our friend's brother. Come on, we've nothing to lose. Let's knock on the front door.' Effra pushed himself away from the corner and strode across the cobbled street.

The two soldiers stood before the single, hob-nailed door, and Tom read the inscription over the gateway.

'Look in yourselves, this is the scope; Sin brings prison, prison the rope.'

Effra knocked on the timber door using the pommel of his dagger. The door remained shut and silent. He knocked again. Still no response. A third knock was followed by faint noises, and then a call. 'Wait, sir. I'm coming, quick as I can.'

The footsteps rose in volume and stopped, to be replaced by the sound of metal scraping and a key turning in a lock. At last, the door swung open on well-oiled hinges.

'Good evening. Can I help?' The man in the doorway was a tall, thin specimen wearing a long dark tunic that reached from his narrow shoulders to his knees. He wore no hat, but his head was covered by a thick mat of straight brown hair reaching to halfway between ear and shoulder. His eyes caught the light from the taper in his hand, which flashed across dark pupils. His mouth stretched in a nervous smile.

'Good evening, sir. We are two soldiers lately arrived to aid the restoration of Parliament's fortunes and we wish to visit a friend of ours we believe is staying here,' said Tom.

'Here? This is the County Gaol, man.'

'We know. The man we seek is a prisoner here.'

'Ah. You mean Master Ironsides? He's in his room. If you step into the porch, I'll tell him you're here. What did you say your names were?'

'We didn't say our names, but...'

'Hold a moment.' Effra reached out a muscly arm to stop Tom walking through the door. 'We've not come for Master Ironside, but I'm surprised he's in control of his visitors, since this is a gaol. You seem a very hospitable gaoler, to me.'

'I'm no gaoler, but you were quite insistent with your knocking. If you aren't here to see him I suggest you find some other place for your soldier jokes. There's no one else here.' With this, the tall dark man swung the door shut, but Tom was partway through the portal.

'Whoa, man. Answer my comrade's question. We're here to visit one who is imprisoned here, and to see how he fares. And you haven't told us who you are.'

Both soldiers were through the door. The gatekeeper was forced back a step, but he barred the way. 'Begone, soldiers. There's nothing to plunder here and no sport to be had. Go, or I'll call the watch.'

'Not till you explain where our friend is. We seek Master

Quintus Hooker.'

At this name, the man took another step backwards and glanced over his shoulder. 'Why do you want him? Who is he to you?'

'We have a message that we'd prefer to deliver ourselves, not through a doorman. So let us in. Is he here, or not? We need to see for ourselves.' Effra's voice had a determined edge.

'You claim friendship, but you force your way in and you give me no tokens that what you say is true.'

'And you've not yet said if Master Hooker is well or not, or even if he's still here,' Effra persisted.

'Show me a token of your friendship and I will pass it to Master Hooker.'

'So, he is here. We only want to speak to him.'

'The token. I must see a token.'

'You're an odd doorman. What's your name, friend?' Effra's tone was belligerent.

Tom was uneasy at their arguing at the edge of the street, the door still open behind them.

'With no token of friendship, how do I know you don't intend harm to Master Hooker?'

'Just a moment.' Tom held up both hands, palms outwards. 'We've come from Lyme Regis. We are friends of Bathsua Hooker, come to speak to her brother.'

'Bathsua? You know my sister?'

'So, you are Quintus?'

387

Chapter 37

Tom and Effra sat on a wooden bench beside a table in the buttery. A single window looked out over the rectangular courtyard and main door. Not much was visible there. The guttering light of two candles was enough to cast everything beyond the window into darkness.

Quintus pointed to the small table, on which were the candles, an open Bible, a loaf of cheese and a beaker. 'I'm sorry. I've not much food or drink to offer you. This cheese and beer is my supper, but you're welcome to share the cheese, if you're hungry.' He sat and broke off a chunk of cheese. 'You were with Bathsua? I had news she was there. How did that happen? Was it to keep Cousin Nathan safe? How is she? Are they safe? What happened there?'

The reminder of Nathan made Tom pause before answering. 'Bathsua is well, or she was last time we saw her. We met her when she was ejected from here. Together, we fled the Royalists, to the west, and found ourselves shut up in Lyme, where we shared the trials of a siege for six weeks, until last week when the enemy left us undefeated.'

'Where is she now?'

'She left us to return to Charmouth. Her plan was to travel here to free you. There wasn't one day in Lyme when she didn't chafe at the delay in coming to your aid.'

Quintus leaned back on his chair and laughed. 'That sounds like my sister. Racing over the countryside looking after cousins, comrades, and all the while planning come here to get me out.'

Effra had been looking around the room. 'So, Quintus. We promised Bathsua we'd rescue you. Yet you seem free and settled and not like any prisoner I've ever met. How come?'

'I suppose the arrangement does look odd. I respect my sister's determination and your valiant aid, but as you see, I don't need rescuing.'

'So what are you doing here?' asked Tom.

'I think it may prove to be a boring story for you. I'd rather hear about my sister's adventures. She and I have travelled much in Dorset and spread the gospel wherever we had the opportunity. Tell me about the siege.'

Tom and Effra exchanged glances, then Tom answered. 'We can do that. But, Master Hooker, you won't find all of it comfortable listening.'

He began the story of the siege, from their entry into the town. Nathan and Bathsua were the focus of his story. Quintus listened with a merry grin on his face as he finished his beer, but he fell silent as Tom recalled the fight in the fog and the death of Nathan. He recovered slightly as Bathsua's part in the defence was explained. He nodded at the mention of Reverend Bush, and shook his head when told of Tom's efforts to stop Bathsua from preaching.

Finally, Tom explained they were keeping their promise to Bathsua, even though they'd parted some days ago.

'My family's no stranger to tragedy, as are none of us.' Quintus spoke slowly after Tom had finished. 'Nathan was a lad of promise. Bathsua and I spoke to him of salvation and his eternal destiny many times, but in that, our most urgent task, we failed, it seems. That makes his loss the more difficult to bear. I'd rather lose Bathsua than Nathan.' Quintus fixed Tom and Effra with fierce, moist eyes. 'And I know that Bathsua thinks the same.'

'Now, sir. We've delivered our news, but it's unclear how we can help you,' Effra said. 'What force keeps you here, when you have the run of the place and the keys are in your pocket?'

'I'm held by cords of honour and integrity, sir. The tightest bonds that can hold a man.' Quintus rose and looked through the small window, onto the courtyard that was now dissolving into night. 'Bathsua and I knew of Dorchester as a beacon of Christian life and practice. Pastor White has made it a city on a hill, a light for other communities to follow. But we heard of practices that are not fully in line with biblical precepts. We came here to find out the truth of it and to speak freedom into people's lives.

'What we discovered was a town abandoned by its leading citizens. The Reverends White and Benn left for London shortly before the Royalists took control last year. Since then the town has tried to keep to their leaders' rule, but we found that 'rule' was oppressive. So we preached Christ. They locked me up and kicked Bathsua out. The people here seem more interested in maintaining one man's mastery over another than in sharing God's gifts equally.

'After a day or so, the town worthies came to terrorise me from speaking out. But I wouldn't budge. They left me here for another two days, then tried a different tack. They sent a message saying they'd no longer detain me. I was free to go. All they required was that in future I present myself to them when visiting, explaining the content of my message. I laughed and reminded them of Saint Paul's experience in Philippi, where he was imprisoned unjustly and wouldn't leave till the magistrates came to apologise for their actions.'

'So why are you still here? Didn't they come to appease you?' Tom asked.

'No, they wouldn't lower themselves. But they want me gone, and they gave me the keys to the place. So I refuse to leave without them acknowledging their injustice towards me.' Quintus leaned back with a smirk on his face.

'What of the other inmate? Is he a prisoner of conscience like you?'

'Master Ironsides has been hit hard by the war. They took his living as rector of Winterbourne Abbas from him, and Parliament sequestered all his lands. He's ordered to pay an outrageous amount of tax, and to stay here till it's all resolved. So you see, neither of us is kept here under lock and key.'

Just then they heard noises in the corridor. Tom immediately jumped to his feet, but Quintus put a hand on his shoulder.

'Don't worry. It's only Master Ironsides. Soon you'll be surrounded by all the prisoners in the County Gaol.'

Scrapings and bangings continued until the door flew open and in stumbled a short, portly man in his fifties. His jacket was open and a mop of white hair was standing proud and untamed on his head.

'Three weeks now,' the man lowed like a bullock. He stumbled over to Quintus without noticing Tom and Effra. 'Three weeks and no word. What could've happened, d'you think, Quintus?'

'Easy, Gilbert. These are troubled times. Who knows what may have hindered your friends' support? But I'm sure they'll come soon. They've not deserted you yet, and those I've met seem very persistent folk.'

'You're right, Quintus. You're adept at keeping my poor boat keel-down and stable. I don't know what comes over me. Is it just that I'm growing old, or is it this ridiculous war? Ah! Who are these fellows? Friends of yours, Quintus, or do we need to watch our pockets?'

'These are comrades of my sister Bathsua.'

'Well then, settle yourselves down. I'll get a bottle and some cheese. I see, Quintus, that your table is, as usual, bare.' The old man rolled back out of the room, and Tom and Effra heard the bangs and scrapes fade into the distance.

'Master Ironsides is an interesting companion. Don't judge him by his entrance. He's a man of worthy parts.'

A few minutes later the party numbered four again, as Master Ironsides settled two bottles of wine and a loaf of cheese on the table and himself on a corner bench.

'This is a more amenable way to spend an evening. I confess, after a sleep I find it difficult to shrug off melancholy, but my spirits have risen already.'

'I find too much of that stuff leads straight back to melancholy.' Effra brought over three beakers from a cupboard.

'Ha. You're right, young man. Applying sack, or any wine, to the ulcers of a day is a delicate business. Too little and the sore is barely scratched and no soothing takes place, too much and the wine merely swells the suppurating wound and spreads the poison.' The old man's mood was lifting. 'Don't think I am advocating intemperance. Master Hooker knows my views, but wine, taken carefully, strengthens and comforts.' He leaned back in his chair.

'I love Herrick's verse about sack –

"Have I divorced thee only to combine

In hot adultery with another wine?"'

'Don't look like that, Quintus. Life's hard and everyone deserves a smile each day. Wine is but one of God's blessings to us.'

'I've never seen anyone reeling drunk on smiles!' Effra said.

'Ha. Good point. That's why temperance in such matters is so important.'

'What say you, young soldiers? How much villainy and ingratitude have you seen founded on a bellyful of wine?'

'I've spent many hours among those using wine to escape a life of grinding toil.' Effra mused. 'It does nothing for their circumstances and often uses up the last pennies of their families. But it deadens pain – for a while. And those moments of relief are essential.'

'You fail to point out the misery inflicted on others while those partakers of the wine release demons inside them. I may disagree with the mayor and councillors of Dorchester, but I honour the work they've done against the damage done to families through strong drink.'

'We agree on so much, Quintus,' said Gilbert. 'Yet we can't stand guard over every man, woman and child and expect them to make choices we'd approve. We must trust to God's mercy.'

'Our only difference, Gilbert, is in the focused application of God's grace as explained in the New Testament. There, the community of believers lived according to clear principles and had the Holy Spirit to empower them to do what they knew God required.'

'But you forget, Quintus. Saint Paul spends most of his letters to the churches expounding on how they should deal with those of their community that were struggling with life, with their faith and with their neighbours.'

Effra caught Tom's eye and nodded towards the door. Both men got up and excused themselves. They went out into the cool night air and sat on a bench in the courtyard.

'What do we do now?' said Tom. 'Quintus isn't in danger.'

'He's having the time of his life, if you ask me,' commented Effra.

'So what do we do?'

'Well, this little excursion is possible only because we've reached Dorchester before Bathsua. Now we know she doesn't need our help to save her brother, we can go back to our own problems.'

'Are you going to run, Effra?'

Effra inhaled the warm summer air and paused before replying. 'I've thought about it. But…'

The door onto the street flew open, forced by a large, booted foot. Tom and Effra stood up and watched a group of men stride menacingly towards them through the darkness. In a few moments they were surrounded and carbines were trained on them.

'Hold fast. Drop your weapons. Who else is here? What's that light?'

Before Tom or Effra could answer, men had taken their swords and burst through the door leading to the kitchen. Soon after, Quintus and Gilbert were deposited into the courtyard.

More men approached and Tom recognised Lieutenant de Clare. Then he saw the small man striding along beside him, and hope fled.

Colonel Fezzard brought his prisoner to the door of the gaol building and was about to issue further orders when he spied Effra, and then Tom. 'I never thought to meet you two again.' Fezzard's laughter was merry, and vicious.

He looked from Tom and Effra to Lieutenant de Clare and back. Tom could see his mind working behind the glittering, piggy eyes.

'Jack, take our friends to the cells, lock 'em in and stay on watch. I want to talk to 'em once the town settles down.'

Jack grabbed the keys from Quintus, and three men pushed the prisoners through the door.

'Leave de Clare with me,' Fezzard barked.

Chapter 38

The bats had left, spreading out on their nocturnal hunts. The gaol was a dark block in the gloom, relieved only by lights in two first-floor windows. Four men in a cell, weakly illuminated by a flickering candle, considered their fate.

'Who was that man?' asked Gilbert.

'That was Sir Lewis Fezzard. The colonel of our regiment and the blackest villain in Dorset, despite all the Irish marauders,' replied Tom.

'And de Clare?' added Quintus.

'He's our officer,' said Effra. 'We're on our way to Poole to speak at the trial of Fezzard, who has ransacked de Clare's lands while he was a ward in his care.'

'So Fezzard must have unpleasant plans for him,' said Quintus.

'Aye, and he'll be right back to speak to us once de Clare's dealt with,' said Tom.

'But what the devil's he doing here?' said Effra.

Each man fell silent as they considered their plight.

Sometime later, Tom and Effra watched as first one, then two, then three women were manhandled along the corridor to the front of their cell. Jack fumbled with the set of keys, found the right one, swung open the door, and pushed the women inside.

'Bathsua?' was all Tom could say, as she and her companions rushed to embrace Quintus.

Effra signalled Tom to be patient. Jack had watched this family reunion, and laughed as he relocked the cell door, before stomping back to his straw mattress.

'Bathsua. I rejoice to see you again, but you've not turned up at the best time.'

'I told you I'd rescue you, Quintus.'

'I think, rather, Bathsua, you've added to our difficulties,' Tom said.

'But how do you come to be here at all?' said Quintus.

'Elizabeth, Daisy and I have walked from Micah's house. When we reached Dorchester, we saw the town in turmoil, with Royalist cavalry sweeping through the streets, and we hid in a church. But I had to find you. So we came on here. My plan was to bluff our way into your cell and somehow help you escape. Gideon and Ifor told us Effra and Tom were here as well.'

'You've seen them?' asked Tom.

'They're at All Saints Church, up the road. They've barricaded themselves in with some townsfolk and plan to defend it. So how did you come to be locked up together?'

'We came here to release Quintus and learnt he didn't need us.'

Bathsua looked at her brother. He said he'd explain later.

'Fezzard burst in on us, locked us up and left with Lieutenant de Clare. But we know we won't be here long. Either Fezzard will return and kill us, or his thugs will,' Tom continued.

'I'm not choosing either of them options,' said Effra.

397

'There is one element in our favour,' said Quintus. 'Show them, Gilbert.'

And Gilbert drew up a set of keys from his trousers. 'We have a set each, Quintus and I. When we were made prisoner they took his keys and never checked for more.'

'Bloody marvellous,' said Effra, taking charge of the conversation. 'Now. How many men are on the landing, Bathsua?'

'We saw five men with swords only. I saw no muskets upstairs, but two are by the door at the bottom of the steps, and two soldiers counting musket balls beside them.'

'What about pistols?'

'I don't know.'

'Hmm. Well, we're now seven and they won't expect an assault.'

'Gentlemen,' said Gilbert, 'I don't think I will be much help to you. Maybe I could protect the women?'

'We aren't here to be a burden.' Bathsua fumed. 'We can crack a man's head well enough.'

'Enough.' Quintus brought order before the argument could carry to their gaolers. 'Effra, you have a plan?'

'Tom and I are the fittest and most prepared for a fight. You follow us, Quintus. The rest of you just stay close and cover our backs. We go in fast and quiet, and we go now.' Effra turned the large black key in the lock and threw the set to Gilbert, who replaced them in his clothes.

The door whined as they pushed it open, but Effra didn't wait to see if anyone heard. He slipped through the gap and padded down the corridor without a backward look.

When he came out into the open area, he was moving fast enough to freeze his enemies for an instant. That was all the time he needed to pick his target.

398

Jack leant against the table with one leg crossed over the other above the knee. He was concentrating on lighting a long Dutch pipe. His eyes focused on the bowl, inches from his nose, and his cheeks sucked and drew air over the smouldering embers.

Someone had just made a joke and the other four men were lolling, either upright or on the straw mattresses. The laughter stopped as Effra shot across the room, grabbed Jack by the neck with one hand and drew his sword from its scabbard with the other. In the time it took for the blade to slide through Jack's body and be withdrawn, Tom had arrived and knocked a man to the ground. He knelt on his back and relieved him of his hand knife, jabbing it into his kidney before he could get hold of his sword.

Quintus bowled into the room and bellowed, 'The army of the Lord is upon you. Flee for your lives!' His coat billowed out around his swaying body and added more drama to this giant-preacher apparition. The guards were overwhelmed. Effra skewered one, and the women fell on another man and together pinned him to the floor. That left only one. He dodged between Quintus and Tom and leapt down the stairs. Effra and Tom followed. The two men outside the door had jumped up at the preacher's shout and were leaning into the corridor as their comrade cannoned into them.

Effra, two steps behind, thumped one on the top of the head as he passed, reaching out for the runner, who was scrambling on his hands and knees, regaining his balance. Tom left his knife in the shoulder of the other guard and was only a couple of feet behind his friend.

The fleeing Royalist sped up as he neared the gate, but he had no spare breath to shout to the guards outside. He was pulling away from Effra, who stooped to grab a cobble from the floor, and let fly at the man's head. The glancing blow slowed him down. He veered to the left and ran sideways into a wall. Tom raced past Effra and made sure the man was unconscious.

'What now?' panted Tom from the courtyard floor.

Effra was still on his feet, but he was bent double, recovering from the exertion. 'Give. Me. A. Moment.' He reached out with his left arm to steady himself against the wall.

Tom looked around and spotted Quintus and the others shepherding the two guards into the gaol. 'Two guards outside the street door. We can deal with them, but what do we do next?'

'We only have two choices, Tom. Either we leg it out of Dorchester or we go after the colonel and rescue our boy before his tiger eats him.'

'Well, that's decided then. We need to deal with Colonel Fezzard. And this is our best chance.'

'What d'you mean? He's somewhere in an armed camp in a big town, on horseback, surrounded by soldiers. Why is this a good time to call on him?'

'Because he's distracted. He didn't plan to catch de Clare here. He left his best men with us and the whole town is in uproar, so we've got a chance to get to him before he knows what's happening,' Tom looked fiercely at Effra.

Effra chuckled. 'You're doing just fine, son. And you've got some good points there. But what d'you think we should do about Bathsua and her bridesmaids?'

'We've made a good team over the last couple of months. I think we can handle it alone, can't we?'

'Right, boy. Call the others, then make the gaol secure.'

Effra bent and rolled the guard over. He was regaining consciousness. Effra dragged him away from the street door before looping a cord of rope round his neck and hooking it through a ring fixed into the wall.

In a few minutes the group had secured their prisoners but found only two muskets, a few cudgels and a couple of swords. They met up again beside the door, ready.

Bathsua stepped up and banged on it. 'Ho,' she called as she opened the door.

One guard pushed to swing it wider. 'Right, mistress. You finished inside, then?'

'Your comrade needs you. He's over by the wall.' She pointed to a dark section of the courtyard, from which they could hear gurgling.

'Quick, he needs help.' Bathsua sounded worried.

The two guards took a few hesitating steps into the courtyard, and that was enough. Their pikes were grabbed, their heads thumped and their legs were kicked from under them. Then they were frogmarched into the gaol, into a cell with the other Royalists.

'It's getting late. Let's go, Effra,' Tom said, when they were back at the street door.

'We need to get to the church. There should be a good number of folk there to defend it now,' Bathsua said.

'We're going to hunt the colonel, Bathsua.' Tom held her shoulders and looked into her eyes.

'No. Tom. This is serious. You're needed at the church. There's not enough men. There's more women on their way, but it will take every one of us to hold it against the Royalists.'

'Hey! You at the gaol! Hold up. We're Dorchester men. Let us in.' This was hissed across from a score of soldiers running

401

up the street. They were soon beside the small group at the door.

'How do you know we aren't Royalists?' said Quintus.

'I just assumed the Royalists would move around in more organised and less argumentative clumps. Am I correct? I see that I am. Open up! We mustn't stay on the street corner, it's dangerous.' The men pushed their way in to the courtyard.

'How many are you? Can you defend this place? Where do you need us?' The officer was looking from one member of the group to another, until he settled on Quintus.

Quintus looked from Tom to Effra, then to Bathsua, before he replied. 'Master Ironsides and I will show you the exits and help you place your men. Bathsua, you take Tom and Effra to your church. We'll meet again once we've beaten off these marauders.'

Effra and Tom, with Bathsua, Elizabeth and Daisy, slipped through the door before the officer could ask further questions.

'This way,' commanded Bathsua as she headed up the high street.

Chapter 39

At All Saints' Church, Bathsua rapped on the barricaded vestry door and the small party was let in.

Tom looked around the nave, which was illuminated with candles, and saw thirty men manning doors and windows, with an equal number of women standing beside them.

Ifor and Gideon spotted them as soon as they entered and hurried over.

As they met they all shared the same news. 'The colonel's here.'

Gideon explained how Lieutenant de Clare was recognised and arrested, while Tom told the story of their meeting with Colonel Fezzard. They all agreed that their only choice was to find him and rescue de Clare.

'Well, if you won't listen to reason, you'd best go now, before we're surrounded,' scolded Bathsua.

As they left the church, armed only with knives and cudgels, Tom turned to Bathsua and said, 'Stay safe.'

'Aye. You too,' she replied. She watched the men scurry away, then signalled to Elizabeth and Daisy and they headed away from the church, heading southwest while the vestry door was re-barricaded.

As Tom, Effra, Gideon and Ifor headed towards the centre

of town, along the back streets they could see Royalists sweep down the High Street towards the church. They paused and heard a roar, answered by lighter shouts and musket shots bouncing across the street from one Portland stone building into another, or thudding into timber frames.

They hurried on and were soon at the junction with South Street, which widened near the High Street into a muddy, uneven space with well-defined ruts in which carts could run between the bumps and puddles. Soldiers were moving in all directions, fanning out from the military camp north of St Peter's Church on the corner. Some headed east to help their fellows subduing All Saints' Church, and others rushed past on South Street. As Tom watched, they turned east at Durngate.

'They'll head round the back of All Saints', I reckon,' said Gideon.

'How are we to find the colonel in this hubbub?' Ifor said.

'Come on, boys,' said Effra, 'We know our man. He's haunted us long enough. We look for the commander, and Fezzard will be beside him. He'll be pointing this way and that, making everyone jump. And he won't be far from a bottle. The best inn in Dorchester is The Henry, over there. Let's go.'

Picking their moment, waiting for a troop of horsemen to pass, they strode across to the other side of the road, where, the house doors all being shut, they hurried towards the next alley that would take them off the street. A dozen yards through the alley, stumbling and cracking shins on a host of obstructions, and they came to a gate leading into a backyard.

'This'll do,' said Effra, as he kicked it off its hinges and walked across a dark, squelchy surface of who-knows-what material and up a short flight of stone steps to a back door.

'No time for niceties,' he said, to no one in particular. The latch resisted his pull, but he shifted his weight back on his right leg and barged his left shoulder into the door. It gave way and Effra stepped from night-time into utter darkness.

The others followed and, like Effra, paused as they entered a thicker layer of black. The group inched its way through the house, towards the main street. One door separated the rear room from the front, and once through it, a shuttered window onto the street allowed some light to penetrate. They now saw they were in some kind of shop, with fabrics and items of clothing in formless piles across the floor. Gideon and Effra felt for the bar, to unlock the wooden shutters.

'Who's there?' came a cry from above.

Tom stepped to the base of the stairs that faced the door leading to the street. 'We're Parliament soldiers, mistress.'

'I don't care if you're the Lord General himself. What d'ye think yer doin' in my premises?' The owner of the voice loomed across a small window at the top of the stairs, lit by a candle on its sill, but Tom could make out no features except a couple of arms waving out from a dark shadow.

'Mistress. We'll be gone soon. We only need to judge the moment to leave you and step outside.'

'Thieves, you are. The lot of you. I don't care if you come in the name of the King or Parliament. All we get is soldiers wearing us down...' The voice was descending the stairs and would have continued in this vein, except for another voice cutting through the bitterness.

'Alice, my love. Shut up! These men have said they want to leave. Your scolding is more like to get them riled than to encourage their departure.'

'Indeed, mistress,' called Gideon. 'We've no quarrel with you, but we need a vantage point. And not for long. We want to see what's going on at The Henry.'

'We can tell you that, sir,' said the male voice. 'We've not yet been disturbed by this Royalist mob, and we want it to stay that way. If you need somewhere to watch and will leave quicker, come upstairs and peek through our upper window. We've been doing that since the Cavaliers arrived at supper time.'

'Horace. What are you doing? We want rid of these vagrants, and you invite them into our chamber?'

Tom could see that the front shadow, now near the bottom of the stairs, had turned to face a smaller dark shape.

'Alice, I'm trying to get us left in peace, without our throats cut, and you seem hell-bent, as usual, on causing aggravation, which is, I think, a surer way to meet our deaths.'

Tom interjected. 'Thank you for your offer. We promise to respect your property while we're here. To see the inn from upstairs would suit us very well.' He ascended the stairs and ushered the couple back to their landing.

The woman objected to hands being laid on her, but her husband pulled her up the last couple of steps. Tom saw then that the woman was not large, but wore a wide cloak to look more threatening.

The four men crouched beside a small window with four glass panels, looking across the High Street to the blazing lights of The Henry inn. The first floor of the shop extended a few feet out over the road, and they could hear clearly men talking at the inn entrance. There was a lot of activity.

A rider clattered up and dismounted. 'Colonel O'Brien?'

he asked of the men forming up on the street. He was directed inside, but then two officers came out.

'I'm O'Brien. Who are you?'

'Captain Cooper, sir. I've news of a large force approaching Dorchester from the east.'

Tom looked across at Gideon. His friend had recognised Samuel's assassin.

'From Poole? I thought we'd have more time than this. How many? How far away?' O'Brien demanded of Cooper.

'I can't be sure, sir, but our scouts met dragoons at Holmebridge. That was over an hour ago.'

The small man beside O'Brien, recognisable to the watchers as Colonel Fezzard despite only being visible in silhouette, then spoke up. 'And where are your men from Sherborne, O'Brien? You said they'd be here by now.'

'Aye. We've still had no word from them. The scouts haven't picked up any signs either.' Colonel O'Brien was slapping his gloves together rhythmically.

'How many are we?' asked Cooper. 'Surely we can hold the town against an attack. They won't attack until daylight.'

'When I want your opinion, Captain, I'll ask for it,' growled O'Brien.

'How stands it?' O'Brien spoke to another officer who had joined them.

'We're mopping up at All Saints' Church and there are pockets of resistance in South Street and at Colliton. We're dealing with that, but the east gate has been taken by the garrison, who have fortified the gaol.'

'What?' exploded Fezzard.

'What men are still in the military camp?' asked O'Brien

'I think we have a hundred and fifty rounding up the

garrison between here and the north gate.'

'Well, get that job done. Tell your men to give no quarter to the soldiers if they refuse to surrender, but to respect the townspeople. There's no plundering on this raid.' When that's done, send as many as you can to the east gate. We must have control there to have any chance of blocking the force from Poole. That may give us time to secure the rest of the town.'

'Good man.' Fezzard slapped O'Brien on the shoulder. 'I'll take my men and clear the rest of South Street, down to the south gate.'

O'Brien looked round, then grabbed Fezzard and moved across the road, away from the subordinate officers. This brought the two commanders beneath the window where Tom and his friends were watching.

''Ware what I told you about de Clare, Fezzard. I don't want murder done this night as well as our normal mischief.'

Fezzard laughed. 'I told you, O'Brien. He was my ward. I bear him no malice, but he's an enemy officer. I just want to keep him close to see if I can show him the error of his ways. Next time we meet, I'm sure we'll be able to share a glass with Mister de Clare in good fellowship.'

'See that you do, Fezzard. I know what you're capable of. This war makes murderers of all of us, but one day it'll be over, and then we must live together again.'

'Not you, O'Brien. You're Irish. You won't live with us. You'll be with your people over the water. Leave the English to live with the English. And I don't want you telling me what I can and can't do in my own land.' Fezzard softened his voice. 'But I tell you, O'Brien, I will look after de Clare as though he were my own brother. So you needn't worry.'

'Right. So. Take your men down the South Street and hold the gate there. I'll send you news of our progress.' O'Brien turned back to The Henry and disappeared through the large oak door.

Fezzard stood for a moment watching his commanding officer disappear, then called Cooper over to him.

Above him in the first-floor room, four men escaped the spell that had held them since the two officers stepped across the road. One raced to the stairs to get to the street. Another, still at the window, hissed a warning and threw an empty tankard at him. The two others sped to second the message of caution. They caught Gideon and dragged him to the ground before he leaped down the stairs.

'Hold! We can't reach him. His men are already joining him. You go out into the street now and you die.' The force of Effra's hissed words brought stillness to the three struggling soldiers.

'What better opportunity will we get?' mumbled Gideon.

'Where's Lieutenant de Clare?' was Effra's answer.

'Of course.' Tom realised that without de Clare their part in the burglaries and thefts would not be excused. Only their aid in helping to expose Fezzard's embezzlement and corruption presented them in a positive light. They needed the lieutenant to help them avoid the gallows. And it was clear that Fezzard would murder him. Soon.

'Where will he be then, Effra?' Tom asked.

'Don't know. Let's just keep him in our sights.'

'Easier said than done,' chipped in Ifor. 'He's disappeared into the inn.'

'But we know where he's headed.' Tom's mind was thinking more clearly now. 'We know he'll be going down

South Street with his men. We can get ahead and see where he stops. Maybe we can free de Clare and escape through the gate.'

'That's assuming he does what he says,' Ifor said.

'Aye. That one's a great liar,' joined in Gideon.

'Well, what are his options?' said Tom.

'He could just ride out with his men and take de Clare with them. That's what I'd do,' Gideon said.

'He would need to ride away from Poole. That's where their enemy is coming from.'

'So, he'd leave by either the northwest gate, at the top o' town or the south gate,' Ifor said.

'There's no reason to think he was lying to O'Brien, and South Street puts him near an exit. So, let's get ahead of him and see what he does.'

They clambered down the stairs to retrace their route into the town.

As he left Effra, spoke to the husband. 'The door. The latch was stiff. I forced it. Here's two pence. Repairs.' He could think of nothing further to say, and the husband gave no response.

'Ah, Effra. I see the influence of Bathsua on you. You've gone soft, you old rogue,' Gideon sneered over his shoulder.

Outside, the group moved parallel with the street, but picked their way through courtyards and back alleys. They recognised a wider yard as the Antelope Inn. There were four men fussing around a two-wheeled tip-cart. On the cobbles beside it was a stack of wooden crates of various sizes. Lights from the inn illuminated the yard as the men struggled with the cart, propped up on one side. Two men adjusted a wheel, while a third soothed the docile horse.

Carter number four held a lantern for his mates.

'There we are,' said Tom. 'Let's borrow the cart and ride down the road.'

'Let's wait till we see if they can fix the damn thing first,' said Effra. 'No sense in making work for ourselves.'

'We've not got long,' said Gideon.

'Right,' said Tom. 'Ifor, you creep down to the junction with South Street and watch for the colonel.'

'That's fine, but don't be long. This is turning into a long night.' And off he loped.

The carters had a lantern raised to light the end of the axletree that was lifted off the ground. One man hit the hub of the wheel held against it with a large wooden mallet, whenever a second man with a small tool told him. The hitting and adjusting continued for what felt to Tom like an hour. Finally, they removed the jacking timbers and lowered the repaired wheel to the ground.

'Load up and let's be off,' said one of the carters.

The lantern was laid on the ground and the three men began loading the boxes.

Gideon moved first. Quietly. He reached the horse-holder and jabbed his knife into the soldier's back, forcing it through a thick woollen jacket while the crook of his left arm throttled any warning call. He twisted the knife and drew it out, releasing a gush of blood and a moan as he lowered the body to the ground, and took over the job of soothing the horse.

Tom and Effra had also reached their targets. The carters turned, just as their assailants sprinted the last few yards to get a strike in quickly. One man went down from a blow to the side of the head. The other two had no time to grab weapons, so they attempted to defend using their arms. Effra crouched with his swing and the club swung low, cracking a leg. Two further strikes brought down his man. Tom's adversary couldn't stop the direct blow to his face, which broke his nose. The second blow knocked him unconscious.

'All done?' called Gideon from the front of the cart.

'All done,' called back Effra.

Tom checked the cargo in the lantern's light. 'Muskets, a dozen of 'em. Matchcord, gunpowder flasks and balls. There's even some bandoliers and a box of grenadoes,' he reported.

Tom and Effra jumped up on the cart and Gideon led the horse out of the courtyard, towards South Street. They stopped as they reached the junction and Ifor joined them, saying the colonel had already gone past.

'I've been thinking,' said Gideon. 'Won't the colonel recognise us?'

'Possibly,' replied Tom. 'But he's only seen Effra and me, so he won't be expecting four of us, and not on a cart.'

'You hope,' added Ifor.

Ifor took the bridle, led the horse into the road and, by the light of a rising moon, settled the wheels into the existing tracks.

They meandered along the road, past Durngate, past houses on both sides, then past a vegetable patch before more houses, while Tom, Effra and Gideon loaded muskets. This they could do in the dark, provided every item was where they were used to finding it, but they couldn't do it bouncing around in a rickety tip-cart. So Effra and Gideon walked behind while Tom, from the cart, handed out wadding and balls as needed. They slipped bandoliers over their shoulders,

412

so they could reach the small tubes of gunpowder to pour down the barrel, and they each had a flask containing the powder needed to pour into the firing pan. Each small patch of wadding required a momentary halt to push it into the top of the barrel. A few musket balls went skidding down the road before they got the hang of the routine. The ramrods were pushed into the barrels by feel, and the balls packed tight. Then the muskets were handed back to Tom, and the routine repeated.

Tom also used the lantern, before they slung it below the front board, to light an end of matchcord. Soon they had eight loaded muskets.

Twice, squads of soldiers hurried past, but no one challenged them.

They clopped along.

'Well, what do we do after this?' said Gideon.

'If we help recapture the colonel, then we'll go to Poole to clear our names.'

'Perhaps, Tom,' said Effra. 'That's a whole pickle of shit to wriggle out from.'

'Our only chance of cutting that gallows noose is for de Clare to represent what we did as just following orders, and to read out what Colonel Blake wrote about us,' said Tom.

'And for that we need the lieutenant alive,' added Ifor.

'What if we bolted, Effra?' Tom was still unsettled. 'Are our chances better if we desert – maybe head for London – or face the risk that de Clare dies, or can't persuade the Poole magistrate?'

Effra wiped his bald pate and sighed. 'Fezzard's a rogue. Rogues don't often get justice, and de Clare's done nothing to deserve murder. There's a risk in this, though. It could all

413

be for nothing, and we'll swing anyway. But outlaws don't live long.'

His comrades nodded agreement, and the horse's steps sounded more urgent on the town cobbles.

South Street was no longer than a mile and they were soon near the town gate; black gaps that during the day were vegetable patches showed the end of a line of houses; more buildings edged the road after the gaps. And not hovels. On the left was a neat terrace of half a dozen houses, with a couple of arches hinting at courtyards within. On the right of the street was an eight-foot wall enclosing a courtyard with two larger, barn-like buildings on the south side. This was the famous brewhouse that produced beer for Dorchester and the surrounding villages.

As the cart drew level with the main gate into the courtyard the four soldiers peered in. There were men fussing around waggons in front of the largest building, a ramp beyond them leading up to the main doors. A fire raged in a metal brazier at one end of the open space, and a line of tethered horses stood by smaller buildings on the north side.

They walked on, hoping to draw no attention. Tom looked through the gate at the horses. He noted how the light from the flames sparkled and reflected off their glossy hindquarters. Then he recognised the white horse, the last one in the line, nearest the wall along South Street. He sat bolt upright and a shiver shot down his neck.

Effra looked behind him. 'What's that, Tom?'

'Fezzard's in the brewhouse. His horse is there. Ifor, pull the cart over to the right.'

The cart drew up beside the brewhouse wall, and the four soldiers huddled together to discuss their next step.

'Oi! You men by that cart. What're ye doing?' an officer of an infantry squad shouted from the opposite side of the street.

Tom and the others swung their muskets up to face this sudden challenge.

'Don't raise your muskets to me, you scum. Fall in at the back of the squad. We've work to do.'

The squad was around twenty-five men strong and a sergeant corralled the reluctant recruits into the rear file. They didn't march far. The hospital was a solid-built rectangular building between the brewhouse and South Gate. The squad of soldiers lined up along a low wall with a gate leading to a timbered facade set ten yards from it. Tom and the others took their place in a line of Royalist soldiers and checked their muskets. Behind them were about two score men ready to storm the building.

'You musketeers,' the officer addressed the line of soldiers standing back from the low, brick wall. 'Fire at the first-floor windows as we charge the ground floor. Ready!'

With that, he turned and gave the order to attack. The storming party surged through the line of musketeers and raced forward.

Tom looked at his comrades. 'You know what to do,' he barked, then lifted his musket and shot the officer in the back.

The others also aimed lower than they were ordered. The four men took two steps back to reload. Then two more.

Tom looked up and down the line to check that no one was paying them attention. 'Right. Let's get to the brewhouse,' he said.

Chapter 40

The brewhouse courtyard was full of horses, carts, waggons, soldiers and barrels. Two large braziers cast lurid shadows over the entire scene. A small tip-cart passed through the entrance and between gates broken by recent fighting. The cart rocked unsteadily, with one man at the front leading a single horse, and a few men walked beside it. They looked stiff and walked awkwardly, as if trying to avoid attracting attention. Rather than heading into the centre of that space, the cart slowly made its way to the far corner.

Ifor led the horse round the perimeter of the yard, past the stables to an area where barrels of many shapes and sizes stood. There were barrels of 36 gallons, standing three feet tall, and small firkins of only 9-gallon size. Many of the casks were larger than barrels, either the common humbertons holding 42 gallons, or hogsheads of 54-gallon capacity. Amongst all this brewing equipment, they drew up the cart and stared at the activity around the braziers and the waggon in the centre of the yard.

Colonel Fezzard appeared on a platform at the top of a ramp.

'What now?' said Gideon.

'We must find de Clare,' said Tom.

'And there's not much time,' added Effra. 'If I can get inside the building, I can scout out the place and find him.'

Tom wasn't sure. 'There's a mob of soldiers milling about. How d'you move unseen through that lot?'

'Well, we've no choice. Either we find out what's happening, quick, or we sit tight and lose the chance to rescue de Clare.' Effra glared at them.

When no one could think of a better plan, he winked at his three friends, passed his musket to Gideon and picked up his club from the cart. 'I'll be off then. I'm heading for that door over on our right. I'll check all the rooms and corners, then get back here and we'll see what's needed next.' And he was gone.

Tom watched his mentor crouch and skip from barrel to barrel, to cart to shadow, and in a moment he faded from view. Still he watched. What would he do if Effra never came back? How could everything that they'd been through come to this, hanging by such a slender thread?

Ifor broke the spell. 'Let's finish reloading the muskets.'

'Hold on. What's going on?' Gideon pointed across to the brewhouse door.

A woman was being manhandled towards the colonel on the ramp above the courtyard.

'That's Bathsua!' gasped Tom.

The three men watched the scene unfold. They only caught snatches of the conversation, but Colonel Fezzard was looking, mystified, at Bathsua.

'Of course. He's never met her. Maybe he won't think she's connected to us.' Gideon sounded unconvinced. Then he recognised the man holding Bathsua by her hair. 'That's Cooper.' Gideon walked forward, and as the three men imagined the tale he was telling the colonel, the blood drained from their faces.

'Gideon!' Tom hissed. 'Come back. We've got to warn Effra. Ifor, keep hold of Gideon and wait here while I find him.'

As Tom moved across to the pile of barrels, he could hear the colonel bellowing to his men to search the buildings and courtyard.

What a bloody mess. How'd we get in a fix like this? Even Effra can't disappear into a shadow and walk around a brewhouse full of half-mad Irish looking for one weedy man being held hostage by a full-mad aristocrat. And now the colonel knows we're here. Tom struggled to control his breathing as he approached the single door at one side of the brewhouse. He paused. Right, Tyler. Pull yourself together and think. No more feeling sorry for yourself. This is it. Just stay sharp and focus.

He lifted the latch on the door and slipped into a dark, narrow passage. The main brewhouse was to his left. To his right were, presumably, storage rooms. There was no light from that direction, whereas on the left, along the passage leading to the main part of the building, was a dull, flickering glow. Surely Effra would have gone that way? Peeping out from the passage he saw he was in the northeast corner of a large open space with, along the south wall, two fires burning underneath tall wooden containers reaching up from ground level for about thirty feet. Against the eastern wall was a stack of full hessian sacks reaching up twenty feet to a raised walkway. The room had the friendly smell of woodsmoke tainted with the burnt aroma of roasting malt.

Stairs led up from the western end of the building to a

wooden first floor level. Effra was near the stairs. There was a pile of firewood close to him; billets of small-diameter wood bundled and tied into faggots. There was a small trolley by the billets, but not much else. A door opened near to the closest wooden cylinder and two men entered the room deep in conversation.

Tom saw Effra throw himself on the floor behind the trolley.

The soldiers, still talking, walked on. Tom watched from his vantage point in the passage, as Effra, beneath the bed of the trolley, raised his head. At that moment, one man turned and spotted the head bob down. 'Hey, John. What's that over there?'

'What? Can't see anything.'

'We'd better check.'

Just then, Effra jumped up and raced towards them.

One turned and shouted. The other stood frozen to the spot as Effra ran past him, swinging his club to crack against the back of his neck while he chased the shouting man. It was too late to prevent the warning. The shouter parried Effra's first attack, but it sent him reeling towards the mountain of sacks. He parried the second thrust, too, but the third swing brought Effra's club down on the top of his head and he collapsed, senseless.

Effra looked round. There was a group of soldiers approaching from the north-eastern corner. He turned to retrace his steps and saw another four men emerge from a door on the southwest side. Three more joined the first group and others came round from the main entrance in the south end of the east wall. Tom calculated the odds. Not good. The smaller group was to the west.

Effra smashed into the smaller group, like a whirling, flashing, giant hornet. In his right hand he wielded the two-foot club, and in his left he had a long knife. The men fell back from this onslaught, but they blocked the way to the passage.

Tom, at the entrance to a different passage, looked for a chance to join the battle and influence the unequal struggle, but hearing the boots of reinforcements coming he ducked down behind a pile of sacks. He shrank back as five more soldiers clattered past to join the brawl, then peeked out to watch.

Effra swung left, over to the trolley, so he wasn't caught between the two groups of men. The men running at him from the other side of the building were on him now, and he used the trolley to keep some at bay, while hammering at those approaching from the opposite direction.

His skill with the weapons was maintaining space for him to deal with each attack separately, but even so, he was using a lot of energy.

More men were called, and Tom foresaw only one outcome if Effra stayed pinned in this corner. Effra feinted to his left with the knife, then launched a scything attack in front. The leading enemy gave ground, and he rushed forward to break through the cordon the group had formed. He raced through his opponents and leapt up the pile of sacks. These split as he landed on them, releasing a cloud of dust and flour into the air.

Tom opened a sack beside him and sniffed, recognising the familiar smell of flour, not barley or malt as he would have expected in a brewery.

Effra was struggling now to keep his lead over his pursuers,

420

sending sacks tumbling backwards and flour spilling into the atmosphere. The whole pile was slipping downwards, and he had to redouble his efforts to grab the walkway that ran along the wall near its summit. He threw his knife and club up to the decking and hauled himself onto it. He had enough time to roll over and slam his fist onto the fingers of his closest pursuer before a further slump in the pile prevented anyone else following him.

Tom, watching this drama, stepped out from his hideout. He stood at the entrance to the room and watched the gang of men pointing and shouting. Then he noticed the cavalrymen standing behind the gang. They were all aiming either carbines or pistols in Effra's direction.

He whispered a prayer as Effra flattened himself on the raised deck.

The first volley missed, but plucked splinters from the undersides of the deck and the adjacent wall.

Effra sprinted for the door at the end of the deck. He yanked it open, then backed along the deck, followed by another attacker with a halberd. Backing along the deck, he parried a thrust. The momentum brought his opponent closer to him, which meant his shorter club and knife were more effective weapons. A quick offensive movement lifted the man off his feet and tipped him onto the sacks below. A cloud of flour exploded round his landing.

Effra now lunged forward again for the door, but it was slammed shut before he reached it. As he turned to look for another escape, Tom heard the cavalry carbines fire and Effra toppled over the deck.

The watching group surged forward to grab their adversary as he lay bleeding on the pile of sacks, while Tom backed, trembling, out of the room, along the passage.

Retracing his steps to the outside door, Tom listened for anyone following him. Instead, the door ahead opened and three more men shouldered into the passage. He reacted instinctively and threw himself sideways into a small dark storeroom. He held his breath and prayed that his thumping heart wasn't as loud as it sounded to him. Sweat formed on his brow and memories of the heated shot and the disembowelled soldier surfaced in his mind. This time, his weakness had meant that Effra had to fight an unequal battle alone.

The men rushed past, heading for the commotion in the large room.

Tom exhaled and struggled to control his quivering body. His breathing slowed, and he clamped his jaw shut, stopping his teeth chattering. He looked around at the details of the storeroom. There were crates stacked against one wall and a stack of shelves jutting into the middle of the room. Behind the shelves he could just make out a shimmering whiteness. He peered for some moments, wondering if this was another manifestation of his fear. Then the whiteness coughed.

'Ho. Who's that?' He whispered.

No answer.

He shifted his weight and shook his head to break free from his terror. When he looked up again, the whiteness had moved from behind the shelves and split into two shapes.

'Tom? Is that you?'

'What? Yes. Who are you?'

'It's Daisy and Elizabeth. We've lost Bathsua.'

The two women came forward, and he stood to meet them. It took all his strength and control.

'Are you wounded, Tom?' asked Daisy.

He swayed against the door. 'No.' His teeth started chattering again.

The women each took an arm and stood beside the young man in the dark room. Tom, even in his struggle, vividly remembered the little courtyard in Lyme and the two women who had showed him such kindness and imparted such strength. He drew strength now from Daisy and Elizabeth.

'I'm sorry. We must get out of here. Fezzard's got Bathsua and Effra now. There's not much time.' Tom regained some composure and, opening the door, gauged when it was safe to move. Then they moved to the corridor, then out into the courtyard. The light from the braziers showed him men milling about everywhere, but there was a general movement towards the main entrance to the brewhouse, to Tom's right. They ran, from dark doorway to the deep shade of the barrels, and then to the tip-cart.

Gideon and Ifor were watching the goings and comings in the courtyard. Much of these focused on the waggon in the centre, and every few minutes soldiers came out of the main entrance, turned to the left and descended to the yard level from the five-foot high ramp. They'd noticed Effra's disturbance as it drew more men into the building.

Tom relayed his version of events and the three friends stared at each other, unsure what to do next.

Daisy and Elizabeth shared their story. 'We were helping the defence of the hospital, down the road, when we saw soldiers arrive here and Bathsua recognised Lieutenant de Clare. She said we needed to get him out quick, before he was killed. We walked in and were looking for him when we were separated.'

423

'How do you "walk in" to an enemy camp and start searching?' Gideon blurted.

'We crept past the horses to get into the building, then grabbed some ale and cups and offered a drink to all the soldiers we met. It was working fine until an officer recognised Bathsua. She was bundled away, and we only avoided capture because we were round a corner and had time to hide.'

A few minutes later they spotted Effra being dragged out through the main doors and down the ramp. Fezzard appeared at the top and shouted at their friend. He pointed at Effra. Tom could see him shaking with the force of his passion.

'Ifor. Lead the horse. We've got to get closer. Rest of us follow the cart.' Tom said.

'Are you conscious, Bayly?' Fezzard's voice boomed over the courtyard. 'Good, because your usefulness is not ended. Yet.' He jumped down from the ramp and stood beside the waggon. 'Come over here, burglar.'

Two soldiers pulled Effra from the ground and dragged him to the waggon.

'Now. You've seen this chest before. It's the one you broke into in April. I've brought it with me as I'm leaving Dorchester soon and need to make sure its contents don't fall into the wrong hands.'

'What... d'you mean?' gasped Effra. 'I took the packet of legal statements and put your false documents in there, just as you ordered.'

424

'And I want you to give them back to me. Now.'

'But... I haven't... got my keys.'

'You don't need them. Here is the key to the chest.' Fezzard held up a squat metal key with a large loop at one end, the bow, and a blunt flag of metal sticking out from the opposite end of the shank.

Effra's reply was inaudible to Tom, but he mouthed the same question. 'If you've got the key, you don't need me.'

'Ah. But we do. I hate to say it, but we can't find the damned keyhole. Who makes a strongbox, then hides the keyhole? You're the only one I know who has that knowledge and until a few minutes ago I'd no idea where you were. I was going to take the whole blasted chest with me, but here you are, so God must really have a sense of humour, don't you think?'

Effra was hauled up onto the waggon, beside the chest by Cooper.

'Now, Carter. I don't want you to get all heroic and play games with me. All I ask is that you show us where the locking mechanism is and open the chest. And in return I will give you a swift and pain-free death.' The colonel stood near the waggon. 'And I'm sure you'll want to cooperate in this, because the alternative is a horrific, painful end that will not be at all swift. Do I make myself clear?' His voice rose to a screech, and Cooper smiled.

At this moment two guards appeared at the main doors, prodding Lieutenant de Clare ahead of them. 'Colonel Fezzard, sir? You asked us to bring out the prisoner.'

'Aah! Yes.' Fezzard's facial features changed from spite to malicious glee as he looked from Effra to de Clare.

Standing near the bottom of the ramp, Fezzard turned to

watch de Clare approach him. He was a slumped, stumbling figure.

'Well, dear ward. How marvellous for us to be meeting for the very last time.' Fezzard grabbed de Clare's chin and held it six inches from his own. 'I've hated you from the moment you came into my care. The wardship was never anything more than an economic device. Unfortunately for you, it tumbled your insignificant life into my hands. And you seemed peculiarly ungrateful for the roof over your head and the food and clothing I provided.'

'You forget, Fezzard, I came to you with wealth and land. It was mine. You were to hold it in trust and deliver it to me, undiminished.'

'Hark at you. Are you a lawyer already, Master de Clare? I have copious debts and it's only reasonable I use the resources available to me to meet them. And that never led to you going without supper, did it?'

'I can bear witness to how many times you failed in your duty, Fezzard. It goes right back to –'

'Enough. Mind your mouth, de Clare. It's a lamentable aspect of our current nasty war that men of the same family find themselves on opposite sides. Fighting and killing each other. And that's how your death will be reported. You died heroically yet tragically, trying to escape from your guards.'

The guards were now pushing de Clare towards the waggon. He fell onto the cobbles.

'Get up! Your destiny awaits. Guards, release him.' The guards cut the cords at his wrists. 'And bring the wench.'

At another signal from the colonel, a line of cavalrymen stepped through the door and stood, carbines at the ready, on the level platform leading to the ramp. Meanwhile, more men formed a wide corridor across the courtyard, while six others blocked the way out through the crippled gates.

'Where's my horse? Bring Silver. Now!' cried Fezzard.

De Clare was on his feet and Bathsua was pushed forward to his side. He picked up the broken knife Cooper threw him and stood beside the waggon, looking round at his enemies. 'And why the chest, Fezzard? Surely you need nothing more to triumph? What secrets are left?'

'Ah. Ignorant boy, that's mere bureaucratic detail. The usefulness of the evidence deposited in Justice Churchill's chest dies with you. Yet the documents he collected are best kept in my possession. The ones Bayly stole are lost to me, but I want to know what others are there before I bury them.'

Tom, Gideon and Ifor spied the extra men and could make out most of Fezzard's speech. His high, reedy voice had an orator's power, though they couldn't hear the other voices.

'What do we do?' said Ifor. The cart was halted thirty yards from Fezzard, behind a line of musketeers.

'I don't know. But we must do something,' said Tom.

'The muskets are double-shotted. We can't be sure to hit the bastard from this distance,' said Gideon.

'We could sting him a bit, though,' said Daisy, as she and Elizabeth helped themselves to loaded muskets.

'No. We need something more definite,' said Tom.

The white horse was led up the ramp to Fezzard, standing now on the level area at its top. Tom's gaze passed over the box of grenadoes, and a final throw of the dice came to mind. But it was a desperate chance that turned his stomach to water. He moved to the back of the cart and uncovered the box of grenadoes. He touched each one with a trembling hand. Every part of him wanted to run away from the bottles

427

of blazing death. An image of his mother and the bakery fire formed in front of him, followed by the blazing floor of de Clare's room in Lyme, then the crumbling furnace where Bathsua rescued Ifor. Lastly, he blushed with shame that he had failed to help Effra in the brewhouse.

'How long d'you think the wick will take to burn?'

'Not long.' Gideon said.

Tom held a spherical metal ball in each hand, while Gideon pushed the wicks against the match of his musket until they caught and fizzed. He hefted the balls to judge their weight and watched how quickly the fuse burned.

'Right.' Tom licked his lips and coughed. 'Cover me. There's only one chance we've got now. It's either this or the gallows.'

With that, Tom forced himself to step out from behind the cart and move towards the ramp. He moved slowly to begin with, but movement broke through the rigid fear he felt in his joints and his pace quickened. The men by the entrance didn't respond. The cavalrymen on the platform by the ramp were unsighted by the colonel climbing onto his horse, and the rest of the men were looking at Effra, de Clare and Bathsua.

Tom barged passed three musketeers, knocking them off balance. He was five paces from the base of the ramp. Fezzard was now astride Silver, and spotted the man running at him.

'Hey,' he called, and looked straight at Tom.

Despite the night, Tom recognised that look from his dream. Why would his father not look at him, but a crazed soldier gaze right into his soul? Tom hurled the first grenado. It flashed past Fezzard's head, bounced over the threshold and into the building. The second followed it.

Tom threw himself to the ground, but the grenadoes just rolled out of sight.

'So, Tyler. You show yourself too. But you've shot your last bolt now. Men, grab him.'

The grenado wicks burned down to ignite the gunpowder within, and the thin metal casing blew apart both spheres to release their pent-up energy. The double detonation swelled outwards into the dust-laden air of the brewery, which multiplied the explosion into a roaring fireball that blew the roof off, knocked the fermenting cylinders over and hurled the walls sideways as a vicious pressure wave pulsed outwards, followed by a sudden downpour of unready beer.

Everything in its path was knocked flat. The courtyard became an empty, silent space, with inert figures and lumps of timber and masonry strewn everywhere. The whole of the superstructure of the brewhouse had burst, and in its place was a giant brazier with an orange, glowing heart and flames licking the night air. Small fires speckled the courtyard, their light flickering in dark, beery puddles. They were the only sign of movement.

Effra regained his senses first. The blast had knocked over the waggon, which protected him from the flying debris. The chest, which was thrown sideways, hadn't landed on him.

He forced himself to look around, and shook his head to clear his brain. There, near to him, lay de Clare, Cooper and Bathsua. The waggon had shielded them, too. There was no movement, though. Effra looked towards the brewhouse and could see Tom lying on the ground.

A few paces from Tom lay Silver. The horse was no longer

a beautiful white charger. He was a loose pile of horsemeat a few yards from the ramp. Most of his white coat had gone, replaced with slick blood and gobbets of raw flesh. Only the head was intact.

Effra's ears slowly recovered from the blast, and sound entered the lurid scene. A scraping nearby brought his attention to the figures on the cobbles. A man rose and staggered as he took in his surroundings. It was Cooper. He noticed de Clare and knelt. Effra thought in his confused mind that the assassin was helping de Clare, but then he stood up, holding a long pistol. Cooper checked that the firing mechanism was working, then aimed it at de Clare's head.

'I hate to leave a job unfinished, de Clare. Goodbye.'

Before he could pull the trigger, a musket was rammed into his ribs.

'You, captain, are the reason my brother's dead. And now you are too. Good riddance.' Gideon fired the musket.

There was a slight pause as the lit match ignited the gunpowder in the firing pan and this fire spread into the barrel to explode the gunpowder nestling beneath the two lead balls, sending them hurtling into the heart of Colonel Fezzard's henchman, who collapsed onto the floor.

But there was still danger. From the opposite side of the dead horse, a black figure dragged itself upright. It shook itself and paused. Effra's senses reeled. Fezzard wasn't dead!

The figure turned towards the brewhouse and saw Tom sprawled in front of the ramp. Fezzard and his horse had been blown right over him. Tom twitched, then rolled onto his side, unaware of the black figure tottering towards him, drawing its sword from its scabbard.

430

'Tyler? You God-damned, interfering idiot.' The sword rose above Fezzard's head, and Tom opened his eyes. As the sword swept down a pistol shot rang out and a lead ball split Fezzard's head open, from right temple to left eye. The sword skittered along the cobbles as Fezzard's body fell sideways.

Bathsua, kneeling, lowered Cooper's pistol.

'Gideon. Over here, man,' Effra called hoarsely.

Ifor walked up behind Gideon and put his arm around his shoulder. Daisy and Elizabeth helped Bathsua to her feet. She pointed to de Clare lying on the ground, and her cousins moved to help him.

Effra hauled himself upright and stepped away from the waggon. He scanned the courtyard. From the wreckage, bodies began moving, but the soldiers of Colonel Fezzard had no stomach for a fight and they scuttled away into the night.

Tom's world was spinning while Ifor helped him to sit. Gradually the speed of the revolutions slowed, and he absorbed more details around him. As his eyes scanned the courtyard he saw figures approaching.

Bathsua stood in front of him, surveying the devastation. 'Fezzard's dead, Tom. And his men have gone,' she said. 'Praise God.'

431

Chapter 41

In the morning light, the people of Dorchester stepped into the streets to discover the source of the great noise that had broken their sleep. Colonel Sydenham and the soldiers from Poole were in charge, and O'Brien and his cavalier horde had retreated northwards, towards Sherborne. The town held its breath to see if there was any more excitement to endure.

When Tom awoke it was the middle of the day. He was in a tent, with five other men lying on the floor beside him. One of them was Effra. He looked pale and shrunken as he lay there. The chirurgeon came in and informed him his friend was doing well. He had removed the ball cleanly from Effra's shoulder, and his pallor was to be expected after that ordeal.

A week later, Effra had recovered enough to face the journey to Poole. Tom had recovered from his concussion, aided by Bathsua. Gideon and Ifor had spent the week visiting taverns and caring for their comrades.

Lieutenant de Clare was cared for by Mr Churchill and his servants. His condition had been critical for a day or two, but he recovered quickly and was keen to report to the commissioners at Poole.

So the group left Dorchester a week after the brewhouse

exploded. And Bathsua and Quintus left too, though they were not permitted to march with their friends. This time, the crowd of townsfolk lining the streets was cheering and wishing them well, rather than jeering. Bathsua treasured up this moment and pondered it in her heart.

At Poole Guildhall, the commissioners from London deliberated over the case of Fezzard's depredations of the Dorset countryside, his ravaging of Lieutenant de Clare's lands and his shocking neglect of duty towards his ward. Their lordships also heard the story of Fezzard's treachery and death. At the end of a short day's hearing, the chief commissioner announced that there was no need to hear any more evidence.

This did, though, leave unresolved the matter of Fezzard's burglars. The commissioners consulted with the Justice of the Peace. There was no getting round the fact that burglary was a felony punishable by death.

The evening shadows had stolen any warmth from the cold stone room where Tom and Effra stood. This was the second day they'd been in the gaol in Fish Street, and the mackerel and cod stench was getting more bearable. Both men prowled up and down the room, seeking relaxation in movement.

Ned Porter turned the key in the lock and stood away from the door to allow the commissioner to enter.

Tom and Effra stood and looked up at the man controlling their fate.

'We have reached a verdict on Lieutenant de Clare's case,

433

and all his estates will be returned to him,' the official began. 'We and the magistrate have also reached a decision about your involvement in the affair.'

Tom gulped.

'The commissioners have heard testimony of your actions during the recent siege of Lyme, and Lieutenant de Clare has spoken of how you saved his life, twice. Colonel Blake himself wrote a letter seeking your pardon.'

Both men strained every nerve to interpret their fate as the commissioner spoke.

'But none of this changes the law of England and, noble as your service has been, it doesn't change the fact that you have committed serious crimes.' The commissioner now stepped down the stairs to face Tom and Effra. 'It seems you are two extraordinary men, and in these troubling times extraordinary men are a danger.' He paused and crinkled his nose. He recovered himself and spoke with more urgency. 'Our decision is that you are to be taken from this place.'

Tom's senses reeled from this standard formula of words; the words used to condemn a man to death. He didn't hear the remaining words of the commissioner, who, once he'd finished speaking, raced up the steps and swept past Ned, leaving Tom and Effra immersed in their own thoughts and the bad odour.

Tom felt paralysed in mind and body. Effra, meanwhile, returned to pacing up and down, a small giggle every so often erupting from his throat.

After some time, Effra's pacing became less strident and he paused. 'Nothing to say, Tom? I thought you'd have said something by now.'

'What is there to say. Our lives are over,' Tom replied.

'What? It seems to me our lives are about to begin, lad,' Effra said.

'Ah. Bathsua's God, you mean? Maybe.' Tom imagined Bathsua attending the hanging.

'Tom! What's amiss? We aren't to hang. Did you not hear the man's verdict? We are pardoned.'

'Are you sure? I didn't catch the whole of what he said. My mind recoiled from the horror.'

'Well, fetch your mind and tell it you ain't gonna die yet. I wondered at your reaction, but you're a strange lad and I left you to your own thoughts.' Effra laughed. 'But God, Tom, think of it. This whole nightmare ended. We lived through it, and we even have some honourable service to perform.'

'What's that?'

Effra laughed again. 'Lieutenant de Clare is a clever fellow and his work as an intelligencer for Parliament is vital. We're to work with him and keep him safe. So we have our lives, and we have a job.'

Tom caught his breath and allowed this news to penetrate his wounded mind. As it did so, the sweetness even over-powered the fish smell.

The ceremonial party of council worthies, lawyers and commissioners walked sedately along the quay. The gold of the councillors' chains glinted in the light reflecting off the sea, and the colour of the merchants' robes contrasted with the drab browns and greys of the townsfolk watching the spectacle.

'This is childish, Tom,' whispered Effra.

435

'I know. But we'll do it, anyway. I can see Merrick and him at the rear of the party.'

'I'm up for giving any of these town governors a kicking. Poxy, stuck-up chuffs.' Gideon was in a foul mood.

The three men skirted the crowd and got behind the dignitaries. As they approached, Effra's gait shifted smoothly into controlled confidence, as Tom knew it would. Effra sidled over to the edge of the quay with Gideon, while Tom angled further in towards the centre of the flagged and stoned space where the ships were unloaded and their wares inspected. He had the bailiff in his sights now, walking behind Sir Balthazar like a big dog waiting for a bone from his master. Tom watched him swinging his cane to keep back the rabble, his head scanning the men in front. Good. That meant he wasn't checking what was going on behind him.

Gideon moved ahead of Effra and pushed his way to the edge of the colourful party in front of their man. Then he slowed down, breaking the bailiff's stride. He lifted his cane and prodded the fellow in the back, at which Gideon turned.

'Oi. Watch what you're doing with that stick, Grandad.' Gideon snarled.

'Don't speak to me like that, pus-face.'

'I speak as I find, and I find you full of shit,' Gideon said, manoeuvring his man towards the quay edge.

The bailiff backed off from this sudden tirade. He was in position, close to the drop into the water; no ships clattering against the upright wooden piles here, which was just as well. Now Gideon stepped aside, and another man walked into his place who looked straight into the official's eyes.

'We meet again, Mr Grist.'

Tom smiled and waited for a fraction of a second to see

436

recognition in the man's eyes. Then he thrust both arms into Grist's chest. The sudden force of the blow swept him off balance towards the quay.

Effra, at this moment, had crouched down behind his knees. To onlookers he was innocently concerned about his shoes, but the position was ideal for tipping the bailiff into the cold seawater ten feet below.

Grist's cry brought proceedings to a sudden halt, and the group of gentry turned about to see the usual crop of bovine faces of labourers and fishermen. A few men at the edge of this crowd of innocence were peeking over the quay and calling down to the unfortunate bailiff, but there was no obvious explanation for why Sir Balthazar's bailiff was in the water.

While the sodden man was helped out of the drink and stood dripping and scowling, Tom positioned himself in front of Sir Balthazar Merrick, who stood beside the Chief Commissioner.

'Pardon me, Your Honour, but I stand before you as one who has suffered a terrible injustice at the hands of Sir Balthazar. Yet, in these parlous times, I seek only an apology, your Honour,' said Tom.

'Do you, now? An apology for what?'

'For the injustice done to me and to my father's memory.'

'You must give me more information, Tyler, if you want me to understand you,' said the commissioner. 'You've been shown mercy by the law. Don't presume on it further.'

'This boy is an impudent rascal who should pay for his insolence,' barked Grist as he regained the quay.

'You're connecting this man to your mishap, Master Bailiff? You require him to pay for an accident?' The commissioner was frowning, but allowed the interruption to continue.

'It was no accident, Your Honour. The boy tipped me into the water.'

'Whatever it was, it certainly livened up a turgid day.'

'He's a vagabond, Your Honour. He was thrown out of Poole six months past. He has no place here.'

'Is this true?' The commissioner addressed Tom.

''Tis true, I was born here. I grew up here and the day I buried my father I was evicted from my home, and they seized my goods and sold me into the army to get rid of me.'

'And who can vouch for this?'

'I remember him, Your Honour,' said Sir Balthazar. 'Tom Tyler. His father was a tenant, and when he died in January, I re-let the premises. The boy attacked me at home that same night and had to cool his heels in the lock-up.'

'And are there any present that can speak for you?'

Lieutenant de Clare pushed his way through the crowd. 'I can, Your Honour. As you know, I owe him my life, and Parliament and this town have benefited from his service.'

'And I say again, Your Honour,' said Tom, 'I ask only a suitable apology from those who drove me from this place.'

The bailiff stepped forward. Tom stepped forward too, and the men looked directly into each other's eyes.

'Look, boy. I've beaten you senseless twice already. Don't make me do it again.'

'That boy is no longer here.'

The bailiff shrugged, 'I've been a man since before you were born... boy. You're no different to the whelp I thrashed last winter.'

Tom laughed and his eyes blazed a challenge.

Sir Balthazar spoke with the commissioner, who then

called over de Clare.

After discussion, the commissioner addressed the crowd. 'Six months is a long time in the affairs of a town like Poole, even without our present upheaval. It's impossible for Master Tyler to reclaim his bakery, but Sir Balthazar has promised to look into the matter and reverse the sentence of vagabondage and also to make some amends for Tyler's loss. Master Tyler has proven to be a worthy soldier, and it's right that his home town recognise that.'

The commissioner looked around and noticed that Tom and Grist were still squaring off, nose-to-nose.

'Master Bailiff. You must smooth your hackles and dry your clothes. You can have no satisfaction from this man today. Maybe tomorrow. And Master Tyler. You'll get no soft reply from me if I find you've sought revenge on the good bailiff. Is that clear?' He waited impatiently until Tom replied and bowed, then nodded and turned away. 'Now then. Didn't someone mention there's fish pie due to be set before me?'

Tom and Grist drew apart, still eyeing each other, as the commissioner and his party disappeared up an alley towards their dinner.

'Tomorrow will come soon enough, puppy.' The bailiff scowled.

'Go, wring yourself out. You look ridiculous in those wet clothes,' Tom scoffed.

Grist squelched along the quay, ducking into the nearest house to get away from the crowd.

'Well, lads, I think now this adventure is behind us. You never know how things will turn out,' Effra said, as he and his comrades walked back into the town.

They had walked with Ifor as far as Longfleet, then said goodbye to the old man, who continued on his way to Blandford with his snapsack on his back, his wide-brimmed hat on his head and a relieved look on his face. He was clearly unfit for military service and had been allowed to return to his home.

By the quay Gideon, took his leave as well. He had to report for duty at the town gate.

'Well, we need to be gone, soon as we can. Mister de Clare said we'd be on the next tide out of Poole,' Effra said.

'Godspeed to you both,' Gideon said. 'You've kept me alive these last months.'

They all thought of Samuel, but didn't speak his name.

'You're a sergeant now, Gideon. Don't let them recruits mess you about. Use Sergeant Smith's scowl to scatter resistance.'

'I'll use your don't-mess-with-me face, Effra. I've never seen anything so terrifying.'

They shook hands, and Effra and Tom headed for the quay. Tom walked beside his friend, thinking of their next task, which was to accompany the newly promoted Captain de Clare to Plymouth.

'You've a good maid in Bathsua, Tom. Don't leave Poole without telling her.'

'No, Effra. I'll not interrupt her preparations for New England. She's no interest in me beyond friendship and she'll be sailing west.'

'Bollocks, boy. She's yours. Go to her. She's waiting for

you. I guarantee.' Effra was hammering his fist on Tom's upper arm.

'But she said...'

'Don't listen to her words. What has she done?'

'Gone to stay with a friend in Hamworthy, just down the road.'

'And?'

'She's preparing to go to Weymouth to prepare for the sea passage.'

'And?'

'She'll be staying there waiting for her brother. I can contact her through Quintus.'

'Who's preaching in Fish Street, Poole.' Effra winked. 'She's yours, boy. The greatest gift you've ever had from God. If she weren't, she'd be in Weymouth already. Go to her. There's just time for you to get to Hamworthy and back before we sail.'

Tom stopped, and his heart swelled as a smile spread from his eyes to his mouth. 'I will.'

end

Book reviews are always welcome. They are important in getting authors and stories noticed, and in providing encouragement and constructive feedback. Please leave a review where you purchased this book to let Steve know what you thought of his first novel. Thank you.

In their next adventure, Tom and Effra seek to uncover a traitor in Plymouth, while Bathsua prepares to leave England altogether and journey across the ocean to New England. Sign up to Steve's email list to be the first to hear news of the next novels in the series, and to also get access to exclusive content, including maps of the main places mentioned in the story.

www.stevecox.co.uk

Author's Note

I have always been interested in the history all around us; it has shaped our world and our perceptions of it. On a visit to Lyme Regis two decades ago I was intrigued and amazed when I read in the Lyme Regis Museum that this small town, set in a valley, with no defences was able to hold off a Royalist army for over six weeks in 1644. I'd never read about this feat and I felt it deserved to be more widely known. That set me on a trail of discovery about the history of Dorset in the Civil Wars of the 1640s. What an amazing bunch of stories there are about this turbulent time.

This novel is a work of fiction, but it is based on real events and includes real people. The defence of Lyme Regis in the story is my dramatic reconstruction of the history set out in Geoffrey Chapman's little book *'The Siege of Lyme Regis'*, Serendip Books, 1982. This book itself is based on diaries and accounts of the people who lived through that time. The situations of Poole and Dorchester in that era are based on maps of those towns researched in the Local History Centres of Poole, Dorchester and Bridport. Tim Goodwin's book *'Dorset in the Civil War'*, Dorset Books, 1995, was very useful, as was David Underdown's *'Fire From Heaven'*, Yale University Press, 1992. In addition to these sources, I have read lots of other fascinating books on the period.

Most of the places mentioned in the books are real, but

the true events don't always match up with the story. For instance, Athelhampton House is a real house. It's still there, near Dorchester. It wasn't destroyed in the wars. Woodsford Castle was a mediaeval fortified house, much decayed by the 1640s, and owned by the Strangways family. It is set in very gently sloped hills and wasn't the focus of an ambush in 1644, as far as I know. Thorncombe is a village in a rural setting. The church can be visited, it was there in the 1640s and had a Royalist vicar. However, the episode about brockling the mortar is entirely made up.

The distances between places is stretched and squashed slightly to fit in with the story, but only a little bit. There really was a brewhouse in Dorchester during the wars, but it was badly damaged at some point during that time and I've not been able to find out how or why.

Colonel Blake is a real historical person, and a great leader. He was able to motivate his men and execute successful strategies on land, defending the besieged towns of Lyme and Taunton, and at sea, as admiral of the Commonwealth Navy, which is impressive. In Lyme, Colonel Ceeley, Eleanor Drake, Captain Drake and Captain Pyne were real leaders. Captain Pyne died during the siege and was greatly mourned. The women of Lyme contributed significantly to the defence in many ways and were praised for their valour in contemporary news sheets.

In Dorchester Pastors John White and William Benn were the spiritual leaders of the town. John Churchill was a Justice of the Peace, an ancestor of John Churchill, Duke of Marlborough, the successful British general of the early 18th Century.

Tom, Effra, Bathsua and their friends and family are

444

fictional. I wanted to tell the story of great events from the perspective of ordinary people. Such folk don't leave many traces in the history books. Much more is said about royalty, nobles and the gentry, which made up about 5% of the population. Yet each of the main characters brings to the story an identity that they stamp on their life and the events that they live through. Just like we do nowadays.

Lightning Source UK Ltd.
Milton Keynes UK
UKHW041948281021
393019UK00002B/169

9 781838 344801